SOME PEOPLE TALK WITH GOD

SOME PEOPLE TALK WITH GOD

A Novel

JOHN ENRIGHT

YUCCA

Yucca Publishing books may be purchased in bulk at special discounts for sales promotion, corporate gifts, fund-raising, or educational purposes. Special editions can also be created to specifications. For details, contact the Special Sales Department, Yucca Publishing, 307 West 36th Street, 11th Floor, New York, NY 10018 or yucca@skyhorsepublishing.com.

Yucca Publishing® is an imprint of Skyhorse Publishing, Inc.®, a Delaware corporation.

Visit our website at www.yuccapub.com.

10 9 8 7 6 5 4 3 2 1

Library of Congress Cataloging-in-Publication Data is available on file.

Jacket design by Slobodan Cedic of KPGS Design
Jacket photo courtesy of BigStock

Print ISBN: 978-1-63158-095-6
Ebook ISBN: 978-1-63158-096-3

Printed in the United States of America

Mine eyes have seen the glory of the coming of the Lord.
He is trampling out the vintage where the grapes of wrath are stored.

SOME PEOPLE TALK WITH GOD

Chapter 1

Most people let their forsythia go wild, a leggy aureate border blaze to welcome spring, but Dominick's mother had trimmed and trained hers so that it was a deep golden globe of late-April blossoms. It was weirdly unnatural, a burning bush in the slanting crystal clear afternoon sunlight of her otherwise still drab garden. Why did he take it so personally?

Dominick was standing at the bay window of his mother's chilly living room, looking out. Behind him sheets covered all the upholstered furniture. The air smelled of undisturbed stillness. Although his mother had lived here in her gated Virginia redoubt for over thirty years, it had never been Dominick's home. No effort had ever been made to make him feel welcome there. On the rare occasions when he had found it necessary to stay over, she had invariably referred to him as a freeloader. It was her house and hers alone. In all its ten rooms there had been room for only her, and her peculiar stark presence was reflected everywhere. Maybe that was what irritated him about the forsythia bush—it was another one of her strange signatures. Even dead she wouldn't go away.

***

The restaurant was too fancy by half, and the food was accordingly mediocre. Dominick ate alone in silence. He might be temporarily sleeping at his mother's house, but he was not living there, much less eating there. He had been eating only in restaurants of late. He always brought something to read and asked for a table with suitable lighting.

Tonight it was an *Audubon* magazine he had picked up out of the pile of mail at his mother's. It was the issue with their annual bird photo awards. He studied the technical info on the cameras, lenses, settings, and film used in each photo. He was pleased to see that not one of the many award-winning photos had been shot digitally. He barely noticed the other diners. At least they all were appropriately dressed. Maybe that was what he was paying for, not this tasteless piece of veal slathered in amateur sauce.

There had been a time when Alexandria was more its genteel self and less like everywhere else. Now he could be almost anywhere in America where the well-off ate. Time, the great homogenizer. He could still be in New York or back on Tavernier Key. Over the years, Dominick's need to be someplace else had been increasingly challenged by places becoming more alike. He had almost given up. He noted the places where the birds had been photographed, places out on the edge—Waimea, Montana, Matagorda, the Yucatan—places he had yet to get to. Maybe people there would be different, different from him. The birds were different. As soon as he could settle his mother's affairs, get her house on the market, and fulfill his only-child obligations, he would be out of here, gone to one of those places or someplace similarly distant. Marjorie, for all her lack of maternal valence, had been the only thing that held him in any inner orbit.

Dominick put off going back to the house as long as he could. It was Friday night, and a band was playing in the bar attached to the restaurant. He stopped in for a nightcap. The music didn't interest him—all music was just noise to Dominick—but he could sit at the bar, sip his Hennessy, and watch the women. It was a different crowd than in the restaurant—young urban professionals gearing up for an expansive weekend. The erratic lighting in the bar made watching more interesting; nothing and no one could hold your attention for long. The women were all surprisingly young and fresh and athletic. The young men, subdued by the female flash, became background. Everyone was at least twenty years younger than Dominick. No one aside from the barman even saw him sitting there at the end of the bar, looking like somebody's father. The Hennessy begged for its companion cigar, and Dominick left to fire up a Romeo y Julieta Churchill in the parking lot.

After that he drove a while, enjoying his cigar, searching for back roads he remembered, which now were all commercial strips interspersed with condominiums. He stopped at a bar in Old Town that was still in the place he remembered it and had a few more drinks beneath the protective glare of multiple flat screen TVs tuned to muted sports channels. Again no one noticed him, so he headed home feeling secure. Not even the familiar wave from the guard at the compound's gate irked him; he would be gone soon.

The house lots inside the compound were large, and the roads curved comfortably among them. America Way led to Chesapeake, then a soft right onto Potomac. There were no other cars. The posted speed limit was twenty-five, but Dominick went even slower. There were always deer out at this time of night. He was in no hurry. All of his mother's lot was hidden from the road behind an extended evergreen hedge, and the long gravel driveway turned among trees so that the house itself was hidden until you came upon it. Two deer—a doe and her fawn—stood in the driveway, frozen in his headlights. He stopped. The mother deer gave him an arrogant stare, as if he were the trespasser. The freeloader. Nonchalantly—acting as if they didn't care that he could annihilate them if he so wished just by moving his right foot from one pedal to another—they strolled off into the darkness.

There was an unknown car parked in the driveway in front of the two-car garage, an old-model Chevy with New York plates. There were lights on in the house. Dominick turned off his headlights as he drifted up beside the dingy Chevrolet. Only once before, while house-sitting a place up in Maine, had he had to deal with burglars. That time it hadn't turned out too well. If he had one of those cell phones now, he could call 911. Then he wondered how this car had gotten past the guard at the gate. Dominick was unarmed—but trying to be a tough guy was what had gotten him in trouble the last time. The front door was locked, so he used his key.

It seemed like all the lights in the house were on. Dominick stood in the foyer, looking from room to room and up the staircase. There wasn't a sound. The house was still cold. He didn't say hello. Then from the kitchen came the noise of a refrigerator door closing. He very quietly shut the front door behind him and moved stealthily, like some burglar himself, down the hallway beside the staircase toward the back of the house and the swinging door to the kitchen. He pulled the door toward him, rather than push it open, and peeked through the crack it made. There was no one at the kitchen table or in the passage to the dining room. He slowly pulled the door further open to view the rest of the room.

There was just one person there, standing with her back to him at the counter beside the sink. The shape inside her tight jeans gave her gender away. The jeans were tucked into chocolate-brown cowboy boots. She was wearing a sheepskin jacket with its raw-wool collar turned up. A mass of hair the color of wet and dry straw was piled haphazardly on the top of her head. Her head was bobbing from side to side, and Dominick could see the thin black wires coming down from her ears.

Dominick looked around the rest of the kitchen, then behind him. There seemed to be no one else, so he pulled the door all the way open and walked in to stand beside the kitchen table. "Ahem," he said, clearing his throat and feeling a bit foolish. There was no response. Then louder, "Hello. I say, what are you doing here?"

When she whirled around, all Dominick saw was the large kitchen knife in her hand. "I am unarmed," he said.

With her free hand she pulled an earbud out of one ear. "What?" she said.

"I said, who are you?" Dominick backed up, looking around for a handy weapon of his own. "And what are you doing here?" From a sideboard he picked up a tall wooden pepper grinder.

"I'm making a salad. Who are you?"

"Why, I . . . I live here." It sounded like a lie even to him.

"Well, there was nothing worth eating in this place. I had to go out and buy stuff, and what do mean you live here?"

"Could you put down that knife, please?" Dominick asked.

She looked at the knife in her hand then at him and the pepper grinder he was holding. She made a motion with her head for him to put that down. They became simultaneously unarmed. "You eaten?" she asked.

***

Her name was Amanda, and Amanda knew who Dominick was. She had figured it out after getting a good look at him. "Marjorie said you were big, balding, and overweight," she said as she set out plates for both of them. "Open that, would you?" She motioned to a bottle of Pinot Grigio on the counter. "And then I could see the resemblance in your eyes."

"My mother described me to you?"

"Only once, really. I don't remember exactly why. She was unhappy about something you had done and was bad-mouthing you."

Purely by house-sitter instinct Dominick opened the drawer where the corkscrew should be, and it was there. He had never used his mother's kitchen, but she would be as predictable as every other American housewife when it came to kitchen-cabinet liturgy. As he opened the bottle of wine, he watched this Amanda. She was roughly his age but well preserved, full-bodied but still toned, no makeup or jewelry except for small silver hoops in her now pod-free ears. Her well-weathered face was late Lauren Bacall with a little more flesh on it. She was tossing a stir-fry in a wok atop the stove.

"Do you know how to turn up the heat in here?" she asked, her back to him.

"Sure, but it won't help. She's out of gas. I've called the fuel people, but they haven't come yet." Dominick opened the cabinet where the wine glasses ought to be and pulled out two. "How long was she in hospital?" he asked.

"How would I know? I was away, and we weren't talking much anyway. You'll eat shrimp, won't you? You're not one of those vegans?" The way she said it made it sound like some Mongol tribe, in off the steppe.

"Actually, I've already eaten, but that does smell good."

"Do you or don't you eat shrimp? I had a West African boyfriend once who thought shrimp was the most disgusting food he had ever seen, and he loved eating tree slugs. No rice. None in the house. Found some egg noodles, though. This could be funky. Yes or no on the grub?"

"Yes, I will try some."

Amanda took off her lambskin jacket and draped it over the back of a chair at the kitchen table. She had stuffed the earbuds into a pocket of the jacket without turning them off, and her disembodied garment now thrummed with a hidden beat. Dominick was pleased by the fullness of Amanda's breasts pressing against her worn work shirt. "Can I be of any further assistance?" he asked, filling their wine glasses.

"Bring the plates," she said. "It's ready. No point in messing up serving dishes." She spooned some noodles onto the plates, then covered them with shrimp, snow peas, and broccoli from the wok. "Do you think you could hunt up some chopsticks?"

Dominick searched but came up with just flatware. He doubted Marjorie ever owned chopsticks. They ate with forks. It was better than Dominick's earlier dinner. "So, Amanda, you live in New York?"

"What? No. Oh, yeah, the car. The Chevy's plates. To me New York means the city, and I don't live there. This could use some soy sauce, don't you think? The noodles need help."

Dominick got up and found a bottle of soy sauce in a cupboard above the stove.

"Where are you living now, Dominick?"

"The past few months I've been down in Florida, the Keys."

"I guess you missed the funeral, too, such as it was."

"I only found out after the fact, from her lawyer."

"That Barnett guy?"

"Yes. Do you know him? He seemed . . . well . . . distant."

"I don't like him."

They ate in silence for a while. The soy sauce helped the noodles. "More shrimp?" she asked.

"No, I'm sated. Thank you. So, where do you live, then?"

"Upstate New York, Hudson Valley."

"And you have a key to this house and a pass through the gate?"

"Why shouldn't I? I've been here more often than you have. Give me that plate. Looks like you liked the shrimp alright."

"Are you staying here tonight?"

Amanda stopped on her way to the sink and turned around. "Where the hell else am I going to stay?" she asked. "I just drove seven hours to get here."

"Well, I guess there are plenty of rooms," Dominick said. How he hated this feeling of control slipping away, like driving on ice. "But I don't understand what you are doing here."

Amanda put their dishes in the sink. It was clear she had no intention of washing them. Then she turned again and looked at Dominick. "I'm here for the same reason you are—Barnett called me."

They were staring at each other. For the first time Dominick noticed that Amanda's eyes were green, a soft almost pastel green, wide-set and with very few lines around them, trustworthy eyes that now started to smile as she tilted her head to one side. "You have not the slightest idea who I am, do you?"

"No. What do you mean? Why should I?" In his metaphor Dominick was now skidding off the edge of a glaciated highway.

"Marjorie never told you about me, never mentioned me?"

"No, never."

"Well, that beats all. That bitch." Amanda had her hands on her hips and was shaking her head, a bemused look on her face. "And I had to know about you all these years—spoiled rotten Dominick, living off his rich daddy's guilt trip, daddy's only charity."

Dominick felt that he should say something, but he didn't know what. This was why you should never talk to strangers.

"She wanted me to hate you. She trained me to."

"Amanda, I haven't the slightest idea what—"

"And yet she never let you know that I even existed. Damn!" She slammed a hand onto the kitchen counter, and the big knife jumped off the counter and onto the floor.

Dominick was on his feet. "Listen, Amanda, I think that . . ." He wasn't sure what he thought.

"I grew up with your phantom, and you were spared me."

"Yes, I was spared you, whatever that means, and I would like to continue that state. I think one of us should leave, now. I'm volunteering unless you would feel better . . ."

7

"No, you're staying. We got some catching up to do, like it or not. Now sit down."

Dominick remained standing. Amanda bent down and picked up the knife. Dominick pushed his chair aside and took several steps backwards. She noticed and laughed and put the knife back on the counter. "Okay, *please* sit down, Dominick, so we can have a little chat and maybe sort this out a bit. Hmm? How about pouring me another glass of wine?

"You aren't Marjorie's only bastard, Dominick. Your Daddy-Warbucks father wasn't her first mistake in that department. She had a practice run a year or two earlier in the minor leagues with my dad. I guess she was more ashamed of me because Dad was just a seaman. I grew up with his family, his sister and his dad mainly, in Vermont. I was almost ten before I figured out that none of the women in my dad's life was my mom. A couple of years later I finally forced my dad to take me to meet her. She was staying at a fancy hotel in Boston. I don't know where you would have been."

"I would have been in boarding school by then," Dominick said.

"After that I got to see her every now and then if she was up in New England. I thought she was cool, kind of an Auntie Mame. It made me different from the other kids, having a mother like that. At Christmas I'd always get something special from her. One year I got a raccoon-collar coat, the only genuine one in school."

"Your dad?"

"He's dead now. He passed on about the same time your father did. I called her when my dad died, and she mentioned that your old man had just croaked too. She took it as some sort of sign. I didn't hear from her much after that, until the last year or so when she started losing it."

"This lawyer, Barnett?" Dominick asked. He didn't really care about Barnett. He just wanted to change the topic. The less he knew about his mother the better. The bottle of Pinot Grigio was empty, and Amanda had taken out a cigarette, which she was now tapping on the kitchen table. "Go ahead and smoke it," he said. "She's not here to stop you."

"No, I can't light up indoors," she said. "It's still her house. You don't give a shit about Barnett. He's got Marjorie's will. I got him to

8

admit that. He's bollixed things up before for her, just to charge more billable hours. I say we fire him ASAP."

"We?" Dominick asked.

"I'd say the fact that he called both of us to be here would indicate we're both in her will. I don't know of any other illegitimate half siblings. Do you?"

"I didn't even know that I had one." Dominick did know where his mother's liquor cabinet was, in the passageway to the dining room, but it was locked. He went back to the kitchen and got a knife to spring the lock. There was Chivas Regal. He brought it back to the kitchen.

Amanda, who had followed him, brought back a fifth of Maker's Mark. "My dad drank bourbon," she said.

"Mine drank Scotch," Dominick said.

Chapter 2

"No, he was gone this morning when I got up. I mean his stuff is still here, but he was gone. Weird dude. And it is freezing here because the furnace isn't working or something." Amanda was sitting at the kitchen table, talking on her cell phone. She was dressed in a flannel nightgown, jeans, boots, and sheepskin jacket. She was drinking instant coffee—all that she could find—into which she had splashed some Maker's Mark to try and make it palatable. The bottle was still on the table, along with the bottle of Scotch and two glasses. Last night's dirty dishes were still in the sink.

There was a screened-in sun porch off the dining room, and Amanda took her mug of coffee out there, still listening on the phone to Morgan. She lit up a Pall Mall, then laughed, then coughed. "No, no. He doesn't look anything like me. He's big and vaguely British. You know, reserved like, doesn't talk much."

Talking on the phone, she had only one hand free for smoking and drinking. She had to find a place to put down her cigarette to take a swig of coffee. There was a pot with a dead fern in it. She laid it there. She laughed again. "No, I'll take that back. I don't think he is gay, just a loner." She took a sip from her mug and listened some more. "Don't count on it." There was the sound of a car pulling up in the gravel driveway. "Listen, Morgan, do what you want about that, get a second bid then. I gotta go. He's back. My best to the rest. Call you later."

Amanda looked down at what she was wearing—her crappy old nightgown. Well, there was no taking it off now as she had nothing else on up top. She stubbed her cigarette out in the dry dirt of the fern pot then dumped what was left in her coffee cup onto it because it was still smoking. She heard Dominick's car door slam and then him coming in the front door. It was strange being around men again. You never knew what they might be thinking.

Back in the kitchen Dominick was laying out pastries on a plate—two large croissants, a sticky bun, and two of what looked to be blueberry muffins. From another white paper sack he took out two large Styrofoam cups of Starbuck's coffee, then shook a small avalanche of various sugar, sweetener, and creamer packets onto the table. "I didn't know how you took yours," he said, not looking at her. "I can't drink instant." As he sat down he pushed one of the cups of coffee toward her. "French roast, nothing fancy."

Dominick was dressed in a dark-blue windbreaker, which he had unzipped. Beneath it was a lighter-blue sweatshirt. He had obviously showered and shaved before going out—he had nicked the side of his chin shaving, and his short-trimmed, thinning black hair was still damp against his skull. Amanda stood for a minute and studied him. She thought he looked older than she, even though he was her junior. He had a large head and large hands, but then he was a large man, well over two hundred pounds she would guess. But he wasn't at all clumsy. He moved with that slow grace big men sometimes have. No rings, no watch, no jewelry. He looked up at her, his eyes inviting her to join him. His eyes were an unremarkable blue, neither friendly nor hostile. She got herself a plate and joined him.

Amanda never referred to herself as Amanda, but she did often privately think of herself in the third person and narrated her life from a place slightly above and behind her actual self. When she did so she invariably thought of herself as younger—sometime in that golden period of twenty to forty when she had never had to worry about how she looked. She pulled her jacket closed to hide her nightgown as she sat down, thinking: *She sits down across from the stranger, who is large—not like a bear, but more like a manatee. She picks up the sticky bun and puts it on her plate. He takes a paper napkin out of a paper sack and hands it to her without looking at her. "Thanks," she says, and he grunts in return. He is eating a croissant, picking it apart with large tapered fingers as if it were a French fortune cookie. He drinks his coffee black. She imagines him a foreigner who doesn't speak English. She is not attracted to him.*

Actually, it had been a very long time since Amanda had felt attraction for any male. It made life a lot simpler. "When I was a girl, I wanted a pony," she'd say, "but I got over it. I went through a similar phase with men." She didn't necessarily dislike men; she just had little use for them. They were like public servants or somebody else's pet. In fact, that was how she identified and remembered men—by the animal species they reminded her of. Women had personal names. Men were Badger or Storky or Snakeface. This dude here would henceforward be Nemo whenever she mentioned him to Morgan and the others, Nemo the Manatee.

"Do you have Barnett's number? We should probably call him and tell him we're here. Get this over with," Nemo said, taking a sip of coffee. He still wasn't looking at her.

Once again Amanda was watching from her observer's post: *She chews her sticky bun, which, like him, she is eating with her fingers. With two different actors sitting there this could be a romantic scene. Even the cold morning sun through the windows is right. Or maybe a Starbuck's ad—the way the big cups with the prominent logos catch the light. She chews and doesn't answer, looking at the top of his balding head as he stares into his coffee cup. The rich boy who never had to work a day in his life, who has no home, no wife, no permanent address. She had lied, earlier. When she recognized him it wasn't by seeing his mother in his eyes. She had recognized him because he so closely resembled his father in the photographs in Marjorie's room—his size, his smoothness, the look that gave her the feeling that a photograph was as close as you would ever get to him.*

"His number's on my cell phone. I'll give him a call," she said.

All the best schools, all the breaks. There was a photo in Marjorie's room of a young Nemo at his Oxford wedding—slimmer, with a full head of black hair—with a bride who seemed half his size. Marjorie was in that photo too, looking fantastic in a rakish purple hat. You saw her first before you saw the bride and groom. Marjorie had celebrated that divorce a few years later. He is picking apart the other croissant now, the one she thought was hers. Now, why had she assumed that? Because if there are two, you share or at least offer? Why did she assume he knew that rule? Or any of her rules, for that matter? The backs of his hands were hairless like a child's.

"I don't know about you, but I would like to get this all settled as quickly as possible," Nemo said.

Why? So you can disappear again? Amanda felt like asking him, but didn't. "I can call him now," she said.

"It's Saturday," Nemo said. "He probably won't be in."

"Cell phone. We'll see," Amanda said, licking her fingers then wiping them on a napkin before getting her phone from her jacket pocket. She got up his number and called. She got his voice mail and left a message.

"I hate those things," Nemo said.

"What?" Amanda said, looking at her innocent cell phone.

"Answering machines, all electronic voices, machines pretending to be human. Isn't it interesting that the more people there are in the world—what is it now, seven billion?—the more dehumanized it gets?" Nemo was still staring into his coffee cup. Then he got up—"You'll excuse me"—and walked out through the swinging door to the hall. She heard the front door close, then his car door, then the sound of his car driving away.

✳✳✳

There wasn't much to Fort Ward. It was billed as the best-preserved Civil War era fortification for the defense of the capital across the river, but time had dissolved its significance. A half dozen painted black field pieces behind a citadel-pointed earthen embankment. It was a park now. Gay couples walked apartment-appropriate dogs. Everything had to be kept on a leash. Fort Ward had never had to face an enemy. Now it looked to be defending itself against the interstate just to the north and the Catholic middle school campus off to the west. Screams from a girls' soccer game blended with the freeway traffic growl through the spring-bare trees. The most symbolic thing about the place was the way the mouths of all the cannons had been sealed shut with cemented-in cannonballs. Of course that was only to keep them from filling up with trash, like the little bags of poodle shit that the leashed humans carried.

Dominick had never been here before. He had only recently discovered his interest in old battlefields and abandoned forts. One of the fine things about such places was that he usually had them pretty much to himself. This was true of Fort Ward on a Saturday morning. There was always a silence in these places that was different from other silences, as if even the birds kept their mouths shut out of respect or fear or shame, as if the place had a memory. In 1861, after the disaster of First Manassas, there had been just sketchy emplacements like this one to halt a Confederate drive on Washington. What if the war had started and ended that way, with a first-move checkmate by the rebels?

Dominick had brought his camera, but there really was nothing to photograph. He was grateful for that. The mood he was in, any photos would have come out bad anyway; and the weather had changed, a low front rolling in and blocking the sun. He debated driving out to Manassas, less than an hour away. But what was the point if it was going to rain? He did not want to return to the feminine den of his mother's house, that occupied territory. Alexandria had been the longest-occupied city in the civil conflict, seized and held by Federal troops from the beginning to the end of the long war, the War of Northern Aggression. By the end of the war, half of the city's population would be freed black slaves. "Contraband" they had been called, as if giving them a made-up name would somehow disguise that they were just property.

What Dominick liked about the past was that you could move around in it, take your time, linger and ponder, even go back to look at things again with second thoughts. Not like the present, where you were always being hurried along lockstep, caught in some involuntary race to keep apace; or the future, populated with the ghosts of what-might-become. You could live in 1861 as long as you chose to. He wanted a camera that could take pictures of the past, sepia-toned photographs of men in rumpled clothes leading wasted horses through a blasted, treeless landscape. A siren passed on the interstate, whooping like some android Indian. Or was it a digitized rebel yell? The past was also soundless. He couldn't remember the sound of his mother's voice. No one ever spoke in his dreams. Only the present came with a soundtrack. He wondered about deaf people's sense of time without that parameter.

"Hey, you, come down from there. You can't walk up there." A black man in some sort of uniform was yelling at him.

Dominick had hiked up to the top of the fortification's earthen embankment, trying to imagine vanished geography.

"That there, is one hundred and fifty years old. You can't walk up there."

"I am descending," Dominick said, then he snapped a photo of the man. A combatant, he thought. Contrabands had built most of these places. It began to rain, big random drops the color and size of bullets.

✻✻✻

The rain brought Nemo home. Amanda heard him come in, but she ignored him, stayed in her room. She had taken Marjorie's room, the master bedroom suite. It had one of those gas fireplaces with imitation logs and a big flat-screen TV. She had lit the fire, and the room was warm; she was watching her afternoon judge shows. After a while there was a knock at her door. She muted the sound and said, "Yes," but not "come in."

"Sorry to bother you," Nemo said from the other side of the door, "but I gather the fuel oil delivery did not happen? I'll give them another call and say it is an emergency. That will cost extra, but it's the weekend, and I'm afraid they won't come until next week otherwise."

Amanda didn't feel like telling him it was toasty warm in her room, especially seeing as he was worried about the cost. He could afford it. Hell, they both could afford it now. "Okay," she said, "and, by the way, Lawyer Barnett stopped by and dropped off some papers. I'll bring them down later."

"Some papers?"

"Her will and some other things for us to look at."

"Oh, that was fast."

"I fired him," Amanda said and clicked the sound back on. The plaintiff in the American-flag tie was getting excited, waving papers around. Judge Joe was not pleased. Nemo could wait, she decided, to hear the good news. She needed more time to think and for Morgan to call her back. It was time for contingency planning, positions and fallback positions. Amanda knew her loner brother did not need money. According to Marjorie, his old man had left him pretty well set up for life. He wasn't avaricious. He had his simple nomadic life and few real expenses. So why had the old lady left half of everything to him? He wasn't expecting anything from her. Was Marjorie just punishing her? Fair play had never been part of Marjorie's MO. Fifty-fifty; half and half was something you put in your coffee, not a guiding principle of sharing. Morgan's guess was that Marjorie was just trying to set up some conflict, stir things up even from the grave. Well, from her urn anyway, wherever that might be. Amanda had forgotten to ask Barnett about that.

Morgan called and they went over the details. Morgan had reviewed Virginia's testate and probate statutes online and figured she could handle the necessary filings, even if she wasn't a member of the Virginia bar. "It ain't straightforward, but it's doable," Morgan said. "You get to handle him. We want to avoid probate if we can. That would really speed things up."

If Barnett's market estimate on the house was right and the balances he had for Marjorie's various accounts were accurate, the estate would be worth about two million dollars after taxes. Amanda went over to Marjorie's walk-in closet and looked at her yards of clothes on hangers, sorted by season and colors. Shoes, toes out, lined the floor beneath them. They were all like costumes ready to wear. There was a rack just of furs. Nothing, of course, would fit Amanda, who was twice the size of her petite mother. She would take all this with her, have it packed and shipped. The girls could see what they could use and sell the rest. Amanda figured a million bucks was more than enough to do the trick, but Morgan thought they should go for it all and that the timing was right, if they could strike quickly.

There was a mirror on the back wall of Marjorie's closet. Amanda saw herself there. Her observer's voice spoke up: *God, she looks terrible. Look at her. She hasn't showered or washed her hair in days, and maybe she could find something different to wear, that outfit's getting pretty old.*

She accompanied herself to the bathroom and watched herself undress and shower and shampoo. She wasn't pleased with what she saw: *That's why you never look at yourself in mirrors any more, you bitch. You're in denial. You are lumpy and pale and lax and unattractive. Put some conditioner in your hair. It didn't used to take so long for you to dry off, did it? I remember when you had beautiful feet.*

An hour or so later she was ready. Her hair was dried and brushed and pulled back with a headband. She was wearing a long denim skirt and her best L. L. Bean shirt with the sleeves rolled up. She had to admit she felt a lot better clean and in fresh clothes. She picked up the file of papers Barnett had left and went out of the room. Seconds later she was back. She had forgotten that the rest of the house was unheated. She put on her down vest and went out again. Then she returned again and found her pack of Pall Malls and lighter in the pocket of her sheepskin jacket. *Get it together, Amanda.* She went out again, closing the door firmly behind her.

Amanda found Nemo reading in the kitchen, sitting at the table in the chair closest to the open oven. He was wearing a chocolate-brown cardigan and smoking a cigar. Beside him on the table was a saucer serving as an ashtray, the bottle of Scotch, and a short glass. He had a pen in his hand and was underlining a passage in the book. The oven had taken the chill off the room, but it was still not warm. Nemo looked somehow right with the cigar; it completed him.

"Marjorie would never have . . ." Amanda said, raising her eyebrows at his cigar.

"Allowed this? No, of course not. I was just making myself at home."

"I thought I'd make some tea." Amanda put the file of papers on the table, taking the teakettle from the stove to the sink to fill it. "The funny thing is she had no sense of smell. She caught some bug once, down in Cancun, that wiped it out for good."

"I didn't know that," Nemo said, sounding distinctly uninterested.

"I think that's how she stayed so thin," Amanda said, turning the burner on under the teakettle. "Nothing tasted good to her after that."

"Pity," Nemo said distantly, still underlining.

Amanda sat down at the table. "You really don't give a shit, do you?"

Nemo gave her a sidelong look. "Not really." He put his pen in the book as a bookmark and set it aside. He took off his reading glasses.

"The mother-son news channel shut down a long time ago. Are those the papers the lawyer brought? What have we got to do?"

Amanda's observer came into the room: *You're looking good, girl. All scrubbed and clean and fresh, not a gray hair showing on your head. Not that he's noticed. Men still do notice you, you know. So, what's with him? Is he as past romance as you are? Maybe it's one of those things that skips generations. The only thing you have in common with him is a mother whose only career, whose only ever paying job, was romancing.*

"There are some documents for us to sign. Are you interested at all in the terms of her will?" she asked.

"Yes, of course."

Nemo rubbed his eyelids before putting his glasses back on. How natural the cigar looked between those big fingers.

"There's the house, of course," he said. "How much debt was she in?"

"Oh, the house was paid off a long time ago. She had even put some cash away. A settlement from your dad's estate?"

"I wouldn't know," Nemo said. "That was all quite clandestine."

"And Barnett seems to think the only money she owes is to him. He's coming by next week with more papers."

"I thought you fired him."

"I did. I told him to bring his bill."

"But won't we need a lawyer for probate and the filings and all?" Nemo pulled the file to him and opened it up. "I don't do courthouses."

"I have a friend who can handle all that, pro bono," Amanda said. The kettle was beginning to steam, and she got up to make her tea. "We should be able to avoid probate."

"How so?"

"Because the house isn't part of her estate." Amanda took her time coming back to the table. Nemo was giving her a questioning look over the tops of his glasses.

He took a puff on his cigar. "It's not?"

"No. A year ago she signed it over to us as cotenants. It's already ours."

"So we can put it on the market right away?"

"Right. Barnett thinks we could get a million and a half for it easy. There's not a vacant house inside this compound."

"The fear of savages," Nemo said, looking back at the papers.

"The fear of what?"

"Of savages, *sauvage* in Middle English, denoting those who lived outside the gates."

Amanda pulled her pack of Pall Malls out of her vest pocket and lit one up. Nemo was right, it was their house now. They could smoke here if they wanted to, in the kitchen anyway, where there weren't any drapes or upholstery to hold the smell and she could air it out before they showed the house.

"A million and a half plus these money market and CD accounts?" Nemo was a quick study.

"Yeah, around two million altogether. It's all pretty clear and compact, all spelled out. Barnett said she knew exactly how she wanted it."

Nemo took another dose of cigar smoke then let it out slowly. "Yes, I can see that. Fifty-fifty, you and me. No one else mentioned. No other gifts, no charities."

"Marjorie was her own only charity."

"Herself, now us. Fifty-fifty. Isn't that strange—giving neither of us a controlling say?"

"Yes, well, I wanted to talk with you about that." Amanda decided her tea was insipid. The bottle of Maker's Mark was still on the sideboard. She got up and clunked some ice cubes into her glass from the night before and covered them with bourbon. She switched outside herself: *You go, girl. He's a cold fish, but feel him out. Remember what Morgan said—just assume your solution is a foregone conclusion. Men have trouble arguing when confronted by a woman's certainty.*

Chapter 3

An interesting aspect of the Civil War was how shifting and porous the boundaries were. There were, after all, families with men fighting on both sides. Dominick knew, for instance, that this part of Virginia had voted against secession until after Lincoln began to assemble an army. Alexandria had once been included in the District of Columbia, the capital of the enemy. It was easier in retrospect to see things as black and white, or blue and gray in this case. An historian's task was to make sense out of chaos by ignoring unimportant things. Bergson's theory of consciousness—the brain as a limiting muscle. Survival relies on our editing out what we don't need to know.

But wasn't it Flaubert who said "God is in the details"? And he didn't mean a Where's Waldo search for a face in the crowd. The details inside the mass, the way a crowd moves or an army retreats one man at a time. Individual deaths, not just numbers of the dead. Personal stories of people with nicknames and secrets. One of Dominick's great-grandfathers had gone AWOL from the Union Army after Gettysburg to walk home for the birth of his daughter. Then he walked back and reenlisted in the same regiment under a different name so as to avoid being shot as a deserter. Those kinds of stories.

There were over 4,000 graves in Alexandria National Cemetery, Union soldiers who had died in one of the many army hospitals that once filled the Old Town. Mostly young men and boys. There was one woman's grave. The place had filled up quickly, with its overflow becoming Arlington National Cemetery just to the north. Two hundred-some US Colored Troops were buried here as well.

Dominick walked down the road between the marshaled white grave markers. Even in death they'd been mustered into formation.

The acres of identical stones, their precise sight lines, their total success at willed anonymity irked Dominick. This was bad history. If there had to be graves, then each should be itself and speak of the person it memorialized. All those lost stories. He had read that among the last interred here were the four men from the Quartermaster Corps who had died in pursuit of John Wilkes Booth. He had come to find them but had soon given up the search. He had noted that the main gate to the burial ground was at the end of Wilkes Street, and somehow that seemed story enough to follow up for one day.

Dominick liked to walk, to reach a certain pace and rhythm that seemed effortless. And there were more birds here—wrens and chickadees and robins, a flash of cardinals and bold blue jays. It would seem that his sister Amanda—if she really was his sister—was more than willing to take on the onus of seeing his mother's estate affairs through to liquidation. She had asked him if he wanted any things from the house, and he'd said no. He didn't even want the memory of them.

He wondered about this Amanda. He knew nothing at all about her. Was she married? She wore no rings. Did she have children? She never mentioned any. What did she do for a living? He found her attractive, in an unlikely way. All the things she lacked—the makeup, the clothes, sophistication—were somehow pluses. He should not trust her, but he probably would. He would ask Barnett about her. If she wanted to deal with all the details, she could have them along with the furniture. As long as it meant he could escape sooner.

Before the war this land now filled with the Union dead had belonged to the family of General Robert E. Lee's wife, a great-granddaughter of Martha Washington. The way of estates, lost in a war, filled with the unremembered. Again he had this place from the past all to himself. He would meet with Barnett, then decide what to do. Why had George and Martha never had children of their own? The only Lees Dominick had ever known were Chinese. He had Barnett's address from his letterhead, a place on King Street. He would stop by there after lunch. He walked back to where he had parked the car, back to the sound of the present, traffic.

The woman at the desk said that Mr. Barnett was with a client, but Dominick could take a seat if he wanted to wait. What were these people called these days? No longer secretary or receptionist. Executive Assistant? Client Services Manager? He thanked her and sat down. He had given his name, but his mother's last name and his were not the same, so he wondered if the woman behind the desk, or Barnett, would know why he was there. This was not a medical waiting room, so there were no magazines arranged on a coffee table, and he hadn't brought a book to read. The only thing to look at was the woman behind the desk, who did not want to be looked at. There wasn't even any art on the walls, as if any aesthetic statement might be too controversial. But it didn't take long. A man came out of the office behind the woman at the desk and spoke to her briefly, and then he looked over at Dominick. He came over.

"Dominick? Frank Barnett."

Dominick stood up and they shook hands.

"This would be about your mother's estate, I gather. You are aware that your sister Amanda has dispensed with this firm's services."

"Yes, she told me that. How about adding one more billable hour so that we can have a little chat?"

"Your timing is good. I just had a cancellation. Come on in." Barnett was built like a box—short, broad chested, square shouldered. His double-breasted silver-on-black pinstriped suit confirmed his intention of looking that way. Dominick followed the expanse of suit into the inner office, which proved to be as sterile as the reception room—no wall of law books or hanging framed diplomas, no family photographs or bric-a-brac about, a blond desktop as barren as a desert. An American flag hung from a pole at one end of a wall of windows; the navy-blue-and-white-medallion flag of Virginia hung at the other end. The view was of the parking lot.

"Your mother was quite a woman," Barnett said as he settled into his high-backed black leather chair behind the desk. Dominick took one of the two cushioned captain's chairs facing him. "Quite a woman, knew her mind, made my job easy. What can I do for you?"

There was something about Frank Barnett, Esq. that made Dominick think gladiator—his thick neck and hardened muscle hands, his steel-gray hair cropped close, a jaw square enough to hold a helmet strap in battle. His suit was like armor. He would look right holding a shield and a short Roman sword, Dominick thought. Barnett was hardly a Spartan name.

"I apologize for my sister's presumption," Dominick said.

"No harm. I was Marjorie's attorney, not yours. Amanda said you already had counsel. It would be best if I could transfer everything directly to him, but—"

"I'm afraid all that is in Amanda's hands. You know, we'd never met before. Amanda and I, I mean."

"No, I didn't know that."

"And I was wondering if there was some proof that she actually is my mother's daughter."

"Yes, there is a birth certificate."

"Fine."

"Not that it would make any difference as far as the will and estate are concerned."

"No, it's not that. I was just wondering. Do you know anything about her that you might tell me? I'm still trying to figure her out."

"Can't help you there. I've only met her twice. Last Saturday when I dropped off the papers at the house and a year or so ago when she came in with Marjorie to change the deed on the property."

"Okay. Can you tell me of any potential problems we might face in liquidating the estate? You know, anything our lawyer should anticipate?"

"Your mother set it up to be as simple as possible. Probate should be pretty straightforward. The only wrinkle I can see is the covenants with the HOA on the sale of the property."

"The HOA?"

"The home owners association of that gated community she lived in. Those groups sometimes act like they are a law unto themselves. But it just takes a little massaging."

There was a soft knock at the door, then the woman from behind the desk out front looked in. "Mrs. Hildebrand is here after all," she said.

"Anything else?" Barnett asked.

"Probably not," Dominick said, getting up. "Thanks for your time." They shook hands. "Martial arts?" Dominick asked.

"Tae kwon do." Barnett said and smiled. It was a cold gladiator's smile.

***

Amanda was hurt. She didn't want to admit it, and she wasn't even sure why. He had said he was tired of being cold, but the fuel oil guy arrived while Nemo was loading his things into his car and he left anyway. He had taken a suite in a hotel downtown. He wasn't deserting her, he said; he was just getting out of her hair. She had asked him for his cell phone number, and he said he didn't have one. A likely lie—driving a Lexus and no cell phone? Right. She had even bought spareribs to make for dinner—all men liked spareribs—and she hadn't gotten a chance to tell him. He had been so agreeable, so non-macho, in letting her take charge of things. She had thought maybe they could get to know each other a bit better. He was her little brother after all, and she really knew nothing about him. There had to be more to him than Marjorie's dismissive anecdotes. Or maybe it was because this hollow feeling she felt inside rhymed with a similar feeling from long before.

Amanda went from room to room turning on the lights. It was taking the house a long time to warm up. It was sort of creepy being here all alone. It felt as if Marjorie had not wholly left the place. There was her distinctive taste in artwork, for instance, unrelentingly nonrepresentational. Every room was servant to one large stark abstract canvas or another. The several pieces of metal sculpture in the hallway looked dangerous, like devices deigned to impale toddlers. The artwork had been there for years. God knew where she got it, which lover. Amanda wondered if the works had appreciated at all over the decades. She would have to have them appraised as well. The faint smell of Nemo's cigar lingered in the kitchen.

She called Morgan's number but got just the voice mail. She needed to talk to someone. Dusk had turned to evening. As long as she could remember she had dreaded nights alone, but tonight's darkness was steeper than usual. She went up to Marjorie's room and turned on the TV, then searched through her backpack for her emergency stash of Xanax. She took two. She would be a big girl about this. No need for her voice to start lecturing her. *Wheel of Fortune* was on. She'd get drunk. But first hide the car keys. A woman contestant bought two vowels. Down to the kitchen. Vodka was needed, Xanax fuel. Don't panic. Everything's under control. Back to the room with the vodka bottle and a tumbler of ice, locking the door behind her. She turned up the volume. She'd be safe and then pass out. It would be like death, but then she'd wake up and it would be morning.

The estate sale lady arrived at eleven. Amanda had been expecting a man. The woman explained that she was just the appraiser. She had a deep Southern accent; otherwise Amanda noticed little about her— she was still in a bit of a fog. There was only instant coffee to drink, and Morgan was not answering the phone or returning messages. The appraiser woman in her charcoal suit toured the house, taking photographs with her phone and making notes. She left an agreement for Amanda to sign. Amanda was glad when the woman left. She sat at the kitchen table, drinking a glass of ginger ale, wondering why it was that ice cubes submersed in ginger ale didn't clink against the sides of her glass the same way they would if the liquid around them was water or whiskey. She moved her glass; the ice cubes didn't clink. There had to be a scientific explanation.

Her mind being empty, her inner other voice returned. Sometimes it seemed like the voice of her mother, putting barbs on the obvious: *You didn't look at yourself in the mirror this morning did you? You don't know anything about looking right. You don't belong here. That woman who just left gave you negative marks. Story of your sorry life. You don't belong around respectable people.* It went on like that until Amanda slipped her earbuds in and turned up some J. J. Cale to drown it out. She didn't hear her cell phone ringing.

***

The Mansion House Suites were alright, but they were just the first step. Dominick had to leave. It was like the same ends of magnets aimed at one another, the opposite of attraction. He had to get out of town. The next day he went back to Frank Barnett's office and retained him as his attorney. He didn't know any other lawyers in town. He thought of this as a tactical maneuver, leaving a centurion as a rear guard when he retreated. He wrote Barnett a retainer check to represent him in the matter of Marjorie's estate. Just a precaution, a chicken's way out.

Barnett seemed to understand. "I'll let Amanda know," he said. "It's still fifty-fifty? Nothing changed? Anything added?"

"Reasonable fees for her handling it all," Dominick said. "Whatever is normal." Dominick had a whole fictive scenario worked out to explain why he had to be elsewhere, but Barnett wasn't interested. He couldn't tell Barnett exactly how he could be reached. "I'll be in touch," he said.

Dominick drove out to Manassas. The rain didn't let up. He stopped at Stony Bridge, where so many boys had died through misdirection. He didn't get out of the car. The very next day he was on the road headed south, for the Keys.

Chapter 4

It came off just as Morgan said it would, and the house was sold. They hadn't got quite what they had hoped for, but it was close enough. Not even that shyster Barnett could find fault with the outcome. He didn't have to know how they had gotten there, and it had taken them less than the six weeks he said would be the absolute minimum amount of time that it would take to close a deal. Amanda had to hand it to Morgan—she had done it again.

At first, the stipulations in the agreement with the HOA seemed designed to inhibit a quick sale. Amanda couldn't list the property as for sale in the MLS. She couldn't put up signs. She couldn't sell the place herself. She had to go through the HOA's own realtor. She couldn't leave the place vacant. It had to be maintained and look lived in. The agreement did not dictate how many rolls of toilet paper had to be in every bathroom, but it could have. It was Morgan, when she got there, who saw a way past all that. She would make a bid to buy the place. "Then we'll see what happens." Morgan was black. She thought that might panic them a bit. It did.

Amanda wasn't there for Morgan's meeting with the realtor and the HOA council member, but Morgan told her all about it when she got back. "At first they called me Mrs. Custis, and I corrected them, saying it's Ms. Custis. The only Mr. Custis was my daddy and he's dead."

They were in Morgan's hotel room in Washington, DC, where Amanda had been staying since the estate sale had cleared the furniture out of Marjorie's house. Morgan was still dressed from her meeting in a vampish black dress with a slit up the side and black stockings. She'd taken off her spike heels. As she spoke she was taking off all the jewelry

27

she had worn—the rings and bracelets and gold necklaces. "I talked down home," she said and laughed. "My Aunt Jemima–Diana Ross impersonation."

"Were they polite?" Amanda asked.

"Oh, they were downright gracious gentlemen. We talked about the price and other fees. The HOA guy, Leonard his name was, talked about the association and its benefits and rules. He gave me a packet of stuff that I left in the cab. I told him I appreciated all that and that I was really in love with the house and that it would be big enough for my family. I asked him about raising chickens there."

"You didn't."

"Shit, he was looking at my legs. I figured I'd ask him about chickens. The bottom line, girl, is that they never got around to quizzing me about how I was going to finance a million-dollar house. They just thanked me for my interest and said that I was a very strong contender to own this wonderful, secure piece of a proper community. A contender? Hell, no one else has bid on the place. You know that. What do you want to eat tonight? I feel like Greek."

A few days later Amanda got a call from the realtor. They had a buyer for the house, a firm offer of almost the asking price. They advised her to take it. The market was tightening up. She agreed. It turned out the buyer was the HOA itself. The money was as good as in the bank.

The bank in this case being a joint estate account that that prick Barnett had made them set up to hold all assets of the estate until the rest cleared probate, at which time it would be split fifty-fifty, minus of course his healthy fee for slowing things up and forcing them into probate at all. It turned out Morgan couldn't turn the trick as estate manager with the circuit court clerk after Barnett objected to her unadmitted status with the Virginia State Bar. So they had to wait.

Amanda saw Nemo's hiring of Barnett as a personal insult and threat. Morgan saw it differently. "Captain Nemo is just looking out for his own interests, that's all. Why should he hang around here waiting for it all to work out? That's what lawyers are paid to do. Besides, I kind of dig the counselor. I like them steely cold and short like that."

Morgan was doing her toenails. She was sitting on her bed, her foot up on the leather-bound hotel directory so as not to drip nail polish on the bedspread. Amanda was stretched out on her own bed watching. The smell of nail polish. In spite of the fact that Morgan was roughly Amanda's age, she still had the petite body of a girl, thin and wiry with smooth long muscles. Her hair was clipped short in a natural Afro, gray unabashedly showing at the temples.

"If you like them like that, why don't you get yourself one?" Amanda asked.

"Way too much trouble," Morgan said, bending over like a kid to blow on her toenails. "They're like pets. You end up spending your time feeding them and cleaning up after them. Much easier just watching them in the wild. Talking about in the wild, when is that brother of yours coming back, anyway? We can't close this all out without him here."

Amanda didn't know the answer. She hadn't heard from her brother since he had left, and the last she had heard from Barnett was that Nemo was out on a boat somewhere. There were all the probate papers and releases for him to sign before Barnett would allow Amanda access to her share of the estate. "What are we going to do about Nemo?" Amanda asked. Morgan had floated the idea of staying in touch with him and his new-found cash.

Morgan was doing the toes on her other foot now. "Don't know. Haven't met the Captain yet. You say he doesn't need the dough, but I've yet to meet a rich man who would turn his back on a million bucks. They can always use another million. It's worth a shot, though. One thing for certain—we get all this done, let him take his half, and get Barnett out of the picture. Get out of Virginia entirely, then see about playing Nemo."

"But how do we stay connected to Nemo? He'll just disappear again."

"I'll think of a way," Morgan said, leaning back to look at her now finished nails. "I don't think I like that color."

***

When Dominick got back to Tavernier Key the condo was just as he had left it. The owner of the condo, an old acquaintance, had died months before, but Dominick had never returned his key, and he just moved in, figuring he would stay until someone told him to leave. It was a pleasure hiding out there where nobody knew him. He called Barnett and told him he was going sailing with a friend and would be unreachable. When the lawyer insisted on having some contact number, Dominick went out and bought the cheapest cell phone he could find, then called Barnett back, telling him this was the number of his friend's cell phone, which would be on the boat with them. Barnett wanted to know where they would be sailing, and Dominick told him into the Bermuda Triangle.

He never went sailing, but after the first few weeks he did wander a bit, down to Key West to visit Fort Zachary Taylor right at the southern tip of the town and of the continental US. The South doesn't get any deeper than this, Dominick thought, but Fort Taylor—and Key West—had remained in Union hands throughout the war. The fort had once been out in the ocean, surrounded by water, but now was surrounded by land and a partial moat. Its guns would now fire out over a state park and crowded beach, their only possible targets passing cruise ships. This fort, like Fort Ward, had never seen any hostile action. Its ten-inch guns had never been fired in anger. The deaths here had all been from yellow fever.

Then one day back at the condo the cell phone started ringing. At first Dominick didn't know what that strange sound was. He was sitting out on the balcony reading. The sound came and went, an irritating jingle. He had left the phone plugged in on the kitchen counter. A far as he knew, it had never rung before. He went in and stared at it and it stopped, but an hour later it went off again and he answered it. It was the lawyer Barnett, insisting that Dominick return to Virginia to close out things on his mother's estate. Dominick claimed he was still on the boat. Barnett told him to then land some place and catch a flight back, the sooner the better. Taking orders from the little device in his hand did not endear it to him, and when he left the condo a few days later Dominick left the cell phone behind, still plugged in and on the kitchen counter.

Florida was one of the first states to secede from the Union. Although the smallest Confederate state in population, it had a high proportion of black slaves. It was also the farthest from the action.

Only one major battle was fought there in the entire war, up near the Georgia border. The Confederates won it. The Battle of Olustee. Who outside of Florida had ever heard of it? But in the ratio of Union casualties to number of troops involved it was the third bloodiest battle of the whole war. At the end of his first day on the road headed north, Dominick stopped at a motel outside of Jacksonville. It would take him at least another two days' drive to get to DC. According to his map, Olustee was just an hour's drive east of where he was. The battlefield was now a state park. It wasn't as if he was in a hurry to get back to Virginia; he'd make a detour.

He checked out of his Jacksonville motel and headed west on Interstate 10, a flat straight slab through filled-in swamp and flatwoods forest, on basically the same general route that General Seymour's federal troops would have taken in February 1864. Dominick found the Olustee Battlefield Historic State Park easily enough, in the middle of Osceola National Forest—a deserted pine barrens hemmed in by swamps and a lake on the north. By all accounts it had been a fierce battle between fairly equal forces. It had lasted all day, with the federal forces finally retreating as dusk approached. There was no one there now on a steamy June morning, just a marker by the road and a monument with a Confederate battle flag lying limply on its pole. But on one single day, three hundred men had died in this space, two thousand were wounded, and another five hundred went missing. Dominick stayed in his car. There was nothing to be gained by walking around in the heat.

Wasn't it strange that at the places built for war—the forts—there were no battles, while simple, innocent places next to nowhere—like here and Manassas—became fed on the dead? In fact, even at Olustee the Confederates had constructed fortifications just a few miles to the west, but the battle never got there. Olustee was now returned to its state of simplicity, but its innocence had been taken away.

Perhaps the only bright spot for the Union in the battle was an uplifting story that made the rounds up North later about the 54th Massachusetts Volunteer Infantry, an all-black regiment that suffered the heaviest casualties. General Seymour had left the 54th Mass along with the 35th US Colored Troops, another all-black group, to defend his rear as his remaining force beat a retreat back toward Jacksonville. Members of the 54th Mass manually pulled a trainload of Union casualties for five miles until horses could be secured.

The fierce rearguard resistance of the black troops was a successful sacrifice. Even after their lines were broken, their presence slowed down the enemy as Southern soldiers dallied on the battlefield to murder the wounded and captured black Union troops, allowing the bulk of the Union force to escape. As he left, Dominick noted that, somehow appropriately, just down the road was a prison.

✳✳✳

Morgan was sound asleep, curled up in her passenger-side seat tilted back as far as it would go. They were somewhere in New Jersey, maybe halfway home. The old Chevy was doing alright, although the front end did start to shimmy when it hit seventy, so on the interstate she had to keep it under that and everyone passed her. Amanda was used to it, but it irritated the shit out of Morgan, which was one of the reasons she went to sleep. That and the fact that the tape she had wanted to listen to was jammed in the tape deck. The car was that old, and so was the tape, Phoebe Snow.

They had to give up the hotel room in Washington when Morgan's credit cards maxed out. "A million in the bank and we can't pay for a hotel room!" Morgan had said, laughing, shaking her head, folding the hotel towels into her luggage. There had been no word from or sign of Nemo. Amanda had signed everything, but Barnett wouldn't allow any release of funds until his client had signed off as well. They had had no choice but to head for home. Home was three hundred miles north, an old house on the Hudson, far enough up the river as to make Manhattan foreign. "Up the river" once meant Sing Sing. Their place was way beyond that.

Diligence, New York, was more real on a map than it was in person. On a road map it was a dot with a name. In actuality it was little more than a crossroads with a past and a borrowed zip code. There once had been a hamlet here with its own dock down on the river. Now at the crossroads there were just old stone foundations hidden in the weed trees. The nearest convenience store was eight miles away, up on Route 9W. Amanda stopped there to buy cigarettes. She got the usual chilly treatment from the clerk.

It had been raining on and off since New Paltz, but now, as sunset approached, the western sky opened up and the remaining clouds took on apologetic colors. Morgan had borrowed Amanda's iPod and was listening to something, staring out the passenger side window. Morgan could get moody when they came back here. Amanda had learned to leave her alone. Otherwise you just gave her someone to pick on, and having someone to pick on did not seem to improve her mood.

You could see the big house from half a mile away, up on its lonely knoll. It was three stories high if you counted the peaked cupola. The late sun lit up the western windows. When Amanda had left, the countryside was just waking up from winter with tentative yellows and greens. Now it was in full-throttle green, tending to blue in the deeper shadows. Winter in the old house had been bleak and hard. Summer would be their reward. That's the way things go—peaks and troughs, highs and lows. Nothing was constantly perfect, but, wow, the place sure needed a coat of paint.

Morgan had taken her earbuds out and was looking up at the house as a view of it flashed between the roadside trees. In a low voice she made the dun-da-dun-dun sound of a horror movie soundtrack. "Home sweet home," she said. "Amanda, honey, when are we going to unload this place?"

"Soon we will have the cash to properly fix the place up. Then we can unload it. Patience, Morgan. It's an investment. It's not about immediate gratification."

"Why don't we just take the money and go to Costa Rica?"

"We could do that, but I despise the tropics."

"Then why don't you stay here, and I'll go to Costa Rica."

"Because it is my money."

Most of the girls were home when they got there, their cars parked as haphazardly as always in the driveway. Amanda and Morgan received a warm welcome. Denise was off at a meeting somewhere, so no one was in charge and the place was a bit of a mess. Morgan put her bad mood to use as she started barking orders. Amanda went to her room. She was worn out from the trip. Seeing as Morgan did not drive, Amanda had driven the whole way herself. Her room was still locked and just as she'd left it almost two months before. She opened the windows. She thought about taking a bath but was too tired. She stretched out on her bed and was almost asleep when a knock on the door brought her back. She thought of ignoring it, but whoever it was would just knock again. "Come in." she said, swinging her legs out of bed and sitting up.

The young woman at the door was a stranger to Amanda. She was thin and hesitant. Her brown hair was parted in the middle and hung straight and lifeless framing a pale face. She was shoeless and dressed in bib overalls and a faded T-shirt. She looked all but ready to disappear. "Morgan said to come up and see if you wanted anything," she said.

"Who are you?" Amanda asked.

"My name is Susan. I just moved in last month."

"Did someone leave?" Amanda rubbed her forehead.

"No. No, I'm rooming with Kathy. Is there anything?" She turned sideways to avoid Amanda's looking at her.

"No, Susan, I don't think so."

"And I wanted to thank you, for letting us stay here and for those nice clothes that you sent. Some of them fit me. They were very expensive, weren't they?"

Amanda tried to imagine this Susan wearing Marjorie's clothes. "You're welcome, Susan, and actually, yes, you could bring me a cup of herbal tea, whatever is down there."

"I have some Sleepytime in my room. I could fix that."

"That would be fine, thanks."

Susan shut the door behind her as she left, and Amanda lay back on the bed. Where did these girls come from? Build it and they will come. She had lost track. They all melded together. Where would they go when the renovations got underway and they had to leave? According to the contractor the whole house would have to be jacked up six feet into the air to replace the foundation, and then the whole place would be gutted and refinished. They all seemed to have come in from the ether; they could return there. That was really Denise's worry.

Susan came back with a hot mug of tea and a small plate of Lorna Doones. "From my private stash," she said. "I only had so many left."

***

God, he was sick of the numbers—the numbers that named groups of men; the numbers that parsed out their lives among the killed, wounded, missing, and captured; the numbered calibers of weapons and the gross tons of horse fodder. What would history be like if numbers were outlawed? Distances, they could stay. Geography mattered—so many days' march. But after a while the numbered rest just numbed. History was not mathematics. Its calculus was conducted without any logical rules or agreed-upon values. All events emerged out of chaos unpredetermined. History was no more a science than interpreting dreams.

As he crossed the track of Sherman's march to the sea, west of Savannah, Dominick wondered if he could have marched three hundred miles in crappy boots with a pack on his back and a Springfield musket on his shoulder. People walked more back then. Things took more time. His cruise control was set at 75 mph. Three hundred miles—Atlanta to Savannah—was a four-hour drive. Of course, he wouldn't be doing any fighting or pillaging along the way. He would leave the pillaging to his half sister. Barnett had told him that Amanda had cleaned out the house and sold it. Quick work. Dominick wondered what she had done with that collection of grotesque modern art the Greek guy had left at the house when he went to jail. Marjorie sure could pick them. He stopped for the night outside of Fayetteville.

The next night he checked back into the Mansion House Suites in Alexandria, and it took only two days to settle things up with Barnett, get all the papers signed and everything. Dominick was surprised that Amanda had decamped. "Where did she go?" he asked Barnett.

"Home, I guess, somewhere up north, in New York. She'll be glad for the release of funds. She seemed sort of desperate for them before she left." They were having drinks in one of those hushed, oak-lined bars lawyers were so fond of. The celebratory drinks were Barnett's idea. "Have you met Amanda's friend Morgan Custis?" he asked.

"No. What about him?"

"Not him, her. Morgan is a woman, Amanda's counsel, interesting woman. I was just wondering if you knew her."

"A Morgan le Fay?" Dominick asked.

"I wouldn't know what that means." Barnett took a sip from his Rob Roy.

"Doesn't matter. Just an old English name, something from prehistory. What about her?"

"Oh, nothing specific. I just found her . . . ah, interesting, as I said, that's all. Well, interesting and attractive in a dangerous way."

Dominick looked around the bar, allowing the clumsy silence between them to linger like second-hand smoke. Ah, hormones, chemical attraction kicking in. Hormones were like dope, bad dope because they made you do stupid things. Other people's private lives, especially their love lives, held zero interest for Dominick. It was the opposite of curiosity, whatever that might be.

"Oh, by the way, she did want you to contact her, either call or e-mail. She left me her card to give you." Barnett pulled a flat leather card case out of his bespoke suit pocket, found the card, and handed it across to Dominick. It was a very simple if embossed business card: just Morgan M. Custis, Esq., Attorney-at-Law, and below that in the right corner a phone number and an e-mail address. He turned it over. There was nothing written on the back. "She implied there was some unfinished business," Barnett said. "It wouldn't hurt to stay in touch. There still may be more wrinkles down the road. I would get your share of the estate account closed out ASAP, by the way, shut down that possible complexity."

"Yes, of course," Dominick said, putting Ms. Custis's card into his pocket. "Where in New York is Amanda living? Did you say?"

"Upstate somewhere. There's an address in those papers I gave you. Say, Dominick, do you think Amanda is gay?"

Dominick glanced at Barnett, this compact, hirsute little man across the table. He probably had to shave twice a day. The question, of course, was not about his sister but about her attorney. "I wouldn't have the slightest idea," Dominick said. "Does that matter somehow?"

"No, of course not. It's just that after I deal with people for a little while I start inventing backstories for them."

"Why is that?"

"I think if I know where they're coming from I can make a better guess as to where they want to go. Being an attorney is all about knowing the answers to questions before they get asked. Just working at my backstory."

"That's rather deific of you, isn't it? Creating other people's pasts for them, their personalisms?"

"Oh, it's all based on what they tell me, plus what little else I can find out elsewhere, of course."

There followed a long stretch of silence, as suited such a hushed bar room. Dominick sipped his single malt. Backstory, backcountry? Men in a bar? Who knew what sparked such memory flashes? But Dominick was reminded of a saloon in the Australian outback filled with blokes and abos getting tanked after work on a payday, the deafening roar of working men joshing and laughing and arguing, smashed glassware and brawls breaking out. The contrast made him smile.

"I don't have a backstory for you, Dominick, if that's what you're thinking," Barnett said. "Marjorie never said zip about you."

Chapter 5

Amanda woke up to the sound of doors closing and people moving about in the house. It was morning, and the girls were up and going off to work. It was good to be home and in her own bed and with nowhere else she had to be. The house full of people was comforting. She burrowed back into her pillows. The day before, she had gotten word from Barnett that Nemo had signed off on everything and that she could now draw down her slightly less than a million dollars from the estate account. So today she should drive into the bank in Catskill and set up the wire transfer of funds, but that could wait. She went back to sleep.

When she got up the house was quiet. All of the cars but hers were gone from the driveway. There was still a mug's worth of overcooked coffee in the bottom of the Mister Coffee pot. The day was already getting warm, and the morning sun filled the back porch. She sat on the steps leading down to the kitchen garden amid the insect hum of a summer's day. She was dressed just in old shorts and a tank top.

Susan surprised her coming around the corner of the porch, dragging a hose. They surprised each other. "Oh, hi," Susan said. She was dressed in her overalls and faded blue T-shirt. "Soak time for the tomatoes."

"Soak away," Amanda said. "Susan, I'm just curious—it really makes no difference—but how did you come to be here?"

Susan laid the end of the hose down in a raised bed of newly staked tomato plants. She had been holding the hose crimped shut; now she released it, and water flowed out. "Oh, Kathy is my sister. She came and got me and brought me here. She said it would be alright."

"Where were you staying before?"

"Oh, I was living in the park. Tompkins Square? In the city?"

"You're from New York?"

"No, Ohio, a little town near Columbus that you never heard of."

"How old are you, Susan?"

"Seventeen, but I'll be eighteen soon, if that's a problem."

"No, no problem, Susan. Are you a runaway?"

Susan turned away and moved the hose farther down the bed. Finally she spoke, in a small but distinct voice, not looking at Amanda. "I don't know what that means. I've been on my own a year now, since last summer. I'm not running away from anything. I'm running to something."

Amanda decided not to ask any more questions. She went back to her room to change into go-to-town clothes. She was checking her e-mail when Morgan burst into her room.

Morgan never knocked, she just entered, talking. "It just occurred to me: don't close out that Virginia bank account completely. Keep a couple of thou in there in case there's anything else that needs to be liquidated to the estate. I just talked to your brother."

"Nemo?"

"The Captain himself. Tell me, does he ever speak in more than monosyllables and three-word sentences?"

"You actually reached him on the phone?"

"No, he reached me. Our buddy Barnett passed on my message for him to call me." Morgan had a handful of papers. "Listen, sis, we have to pay off my credit cards and get them back in the game. We'll put twenty, no, thirty thousand into my account. I'll get a new card if I have to. I have to get down to Manhattan."

"How's that? I need you here. The contractors will be coming."

"Captain Nemo is going to summer up in the Vineyard. He'll be stopping over in New York on the way. He's agreed to meet me there."

"So, you did think of a way to get a hook in him? Good work."

"Well, he caught me by surprise, and all I could come up with was the truth, or a version of it. I'll have to play it by ear when I meet him. He didn't sound very enthusiastic. I think he was just being polite by agreeing to meet me for drinks."

"At least Barnett won't be there."

"Actually, in a way I'd rather deal with shorty than with unknown Nemo. Barnett is a lawyer. I'd have a better clue where he was coming from." Morgan was already dressed to go, in tight jeans, pumps, and a short-sleeve cotton blouse. "I'll go with you to the bank and try to straighten this shit out," she said, holding up her clutch of credit card bills. "I'll take tomorrow morning's train down to the city. Come on. We can eat in town at the inn."

Amanda looked at her laptop screen. She was in the middle of an e-mail and wasn't ready to leave. Her inner voice spoke up, but she didn't. *Okay, once again Morgan calls the shots. Why do you let this black girl order you around? Who died and put her in charge? Some day you will just have to assert yourself. Say no, later, we'll see, anything but yes.*

"Yes," she said. "I'll be right down," and she hit Save Draft and logged off. As she closed the top of her laptop she looked at her hands. Ringless and wrinkled, they looked terribly old, the hands of a stranger.

✳✳✳

Dominick had caught up with his mail back in Tavernier Key. In there had been an open invitation from an old school acquaintance in Martha's Vineyard to come visit during the summer. Dr. Toby was recently widowed and lonesome for companionship in the big old summer house. He could be a bit of a bore, but Edgartown was livable in season. The Keys had become too tropical. It was a lot of driving, but Dominick didn't mind. He liked being on the move. Driving was a form of meditation. Having a destination helped. He could probably stretch out his stay at Toby's as long as he pleased. It was Toby's wife who hadn't liked him.

Alexandria, where he stopped to settle things up with that lawyer Barnett, had been conveniently on the way, and now he had agreed to meet with this Custis woman in New York. He could never go past New York without spending at least a few days there. After all these years it was still the center of his universe, his Mecca Manhattan. He had his favorite little Upper East Side hotel off the park close to the museums, his favorite restaurants. The Custis woman had said that by happy coincidence she would be in the city when he passed through; perhaps they could get together, as she wanted to meet him and had a proposal to share with him. Dominick normally would have said no, but there was something to her voice—a hint of Southern ease—that caught him, and he wondered what kind of woman would stir Barnett's juices. He assumed that, as Amanda's attorney, she would propose something to do with the estate. He had agreed to meet her for drinks. The drive to New York up I-95 was monotonous, but it only took five hours. He didn't stop at any forts or battlefields.

The Reading Room was a bar with just one affectation—its walls were lined with books. It was a locals' bar just off of Lexington Avenue for a clientele with a tweedy predisposition. There was just one TV set behind the bar, and it wasn't tuned to a sports channel. There were no dartboards on the way to the lavatories. Its patrons were mainly serious solo drinkers who, for whatever personal reasons, were not drinking at home that day. Its booths were cushioned and private. Its back bar proudly displayed some thirty-plus brands of Scotch whiskey. It was one of Dominick's old haunts, and he was always surprised to find it still there, a throwback to a time when the city's intellectual life ran on ethanol fuel.

Dominick was early for his meeting with Ms. Custis. He was also pleased with himself. An afternoon spent in used bookstores had delivered two finds—a fairly pristine copy of the forty-year-old *Fortress America: An Illustrated History of U.S. Forts* and a beat-up old copy of *Johnny We Hardly Knew You*, a collection of Confederate Civil War memoirs. He took a booth by the front window, where the light was better for reading, and ordered a pint of Guinness. He polished his reading glasses with a cocktail napkin and looked out the window at the fast-forward passage of Manhattan pedestrians. And what a mix they were of ethnicities and dress and class, all ages and sexes. *E Pluribus Unum*. Did Franklin really lift that phrase from a Roman recipe for salad dressing? He was fairly certain that the waitress who brought him his pint had been here forever. This was Manhattan, after all, a place so accustomed to constant flux that it refused to change.

He neither saw nor heard her come up; he was reading.

"Dominick?" she said, and he looked up from the schematic of Fort Sumter's ordinance lines of fire. She was dressed in a New York attorney's tailored gray suit with beige blouse. "Morgan Custis," she said, and she reached out to shake his hand. "Shall I?" she asked with a slight body gesture toward the seat across from him.

"Yes, please. Please, Ms. Custis, a pleasure to meet you." He half rose. Because Dominick was sensitive about his weight, the first thing that struck him about Morgan Custis was her seeming lack of body fat. She had a handsome, almost pretty face, but she reminded him of one of those Kenyan marathoners who after running twenty-six miles are still not sweating. It was not a body type that appealed to him.

"You got here early; you beat me," she said, following her briefcase into the booth bench across from him. She said it playfully. "I wanted to get here first to see if I could pick you out when you came in. I can see some Amanda in you."

"Did you pick me out right away?" Dominick motioned for the waitress to come over.

"You were the only one in this supposed reading room actually reading."

"Reading and drinking go together. What will you have?"

"A vodka tonic and the *Daily News*," she said, and then to the waitress without looking at her, "Stoli tonic with a twist."

Dominick found Morgan Custis, Esq., to be very easy to talk with. She finished off her vodka tonic and started another before she pulled papers out of her briefcase. Then she let them just sit there while they joked about people who thought themselves important, mainly politicians and other preachers. Dominick enjoyed her put-downs. He ordered another Guinness. It was twenty minutes before she started the pitch for her proposal. It seemed Amanda had decided she would invest her portion of the inheritance into a project she had already begun, and she wanted to offer Dominick the chance to get in on it at the ground floor. It was a real estate development scheme called Diligence Retreat & Spa.

"Diligence is the name of the town where it's located up the Hudson," Morgan explained, "but the name fits because it's to be marketed as a very upscale, self-contained, country-inn-style facility for corporate retreats, think-tank conferences, and the like. Corporations are the only people left with money like that to spend. That's the target market, not the occasional bird-watching tourist or couple up from the city to see the fall colors. There will be a heliport on the grounds, full spa facilities, restaurant, bar, meeting rooms. Someplace the suits can escape to and relax and write it all off."

"Is there a golf course nearby?" Dominick asked.

"No, but that's not the pitch. It's a year-round not a seasonal moneymaker. I mean, you're not a golfer—are you?—and you're a think-tank kind of guy." Morgan motioned to the books beside him on the table. "You are our kind of clientele. You wouldn't mind spending five days in a first-class inn discussing"—she picked up the bigger book and looked at the cover—"historic forts with your peers, would you?"

Actually, the idea repulsed him, but he was enjoying Morgan's company, so without any comment he let her go on. "We've done our market research. It's an unfilled niche, close to New York and Boston and Albany. There are places in the same business making fortunes in places like Vail and Kauai and Taos, all long jet flights away from anybody's home base."

Dominick appreciated the fact that Morgan didn't seem overly insistent about her spiel. She wasn't being a saleswoman. Dominick asked a few more simple questions. She answered them almost flippantly. "Dominick, Amanda asked me to lay out the proposal to you, and that's what I'm here to do."

He didn't know what if anything he was going to do with Marjorie's money, but he was fairly certain it would not be going into some hare-brained executive resort bubble.

"No, counselor. Thank you." Dominick said. "I would be an amateur in that game, and in my experience amateurs always lose to pros. I, of course, wish Amanda—and you—the best success in your venture, but it is not my kind of venture."

"I understand that—if it's such a great idea, how come no one has already done it."

"No, it's not that. It's just that the whole thing is contrary to my nature."

"Well, I brought this prospectus for you to look over at your leisure," she said, pushing a file of papers to him. "If you have any questions or happen to reconsider, you can give me a call. Or stop by for a visit. If you're headed for the Cape, it's only an hour or two out of your way and you get to avoid that terrible stretch of I-95 to New Haven with all the trucks. You can take the Mass Pike back to the Cape, which is a pleasant drive this time of year."

Dominick opened the file. On the front page of the prospectus under the title "Diligence Retreat & Spa" was the photo of a stately three-story antebellum mansion.

"And by the way," Morgan said, getting the waitress's eye and motioning for the check, "Amanda wouldn't mind seeing you. She was hurt, I think, when you left so suddenly, took it personally somehow." Morgan handed the waitress a gold credit card.

"What is this place?" Dominick asked, holding up the photo of the old house.

"Oh, that's the old Van Houten place, the centerpiece of the inn. The rest of the complex will be built out from it. It's all in the plans."

"How old is the house?" Dominick asked.

"It was built in the 1830s, I think. We picked it up basically for back taxes. What we can save of the place will set the tone for the rest. You know—landed gentry, old wealth."

"Is it currently occupied?"

"Right now it's where Amanda lives." The waitress brought the check, and Morgan signed for it. "You're interested in forts. You know there are the ruins of forts all along the Hudson. Have you ever been to West Point? That's on the way to Diligence, fascinating spot, I hear. But then, you probably already know all about such places."

"Does the house have a history?"

"I'm sure it does, but its future is what's important. You know, Dominick, one benefit of becoming Amanda's partner in this is that you could always have a place to stay, a permanent address, what other people call a home."

❋❋❋

It was raining at West Point, and the river in its green velvet canyon was hidden here and there by low clouds. At the Academy gate Dominick went through the routine of getting a visitor's pass, but he declined the guided bus tour. West Point was, after all, just one more fortress that had never known combat, and the rain showed no intention of relenting. He went directly to the museum, whose collection of hand-held weapons, from stone clubs to automatic firearms, was famous. He wanted to see a Springfield musket like the one he would have carried on Sherman's March. He wanted to see a uniform like the one he would have worn. The footwear still bothered him. In the gallery of illustrious alumni were presentations for both Generals Grant and Lee. Again he had this history place all to himself; everyone else off in the present. He spent hours reading the little exhibit cards, until someone came up and told him it was time to leave, the museum was closing. Dominick spent the night at an inn in Cornwall-on-Hudson, still not sure if he was heading on to Diligence or not. Roads were flooding.

***

Amanda couldn't remember if it was supposed to rain like this in June or not. Everyone made such a big thing out of the weather these days, as if none of it had ever happened before. But for three days now it hadn't stopped raining. It was like a tropical rain—constant, insistent, vertical, and warm. The contractors had called and postponed their visit. Morgan had not returned from New York. Denise was still away at her convocation, and the strain of being on their own was beginning to show on the girls. Last night there had been a yelling and door-slamming blowout among several of them that Amanda had to intervene in. She wondered if that phenomenon she had read about—that the hormonal cycles of a group of women living together somehow became synchronized—was happening. The bathroom smelled of menses.

And now this. Nemo was coming. Morgan had called; Nemo had called her from somewhere downriver asking for directions to the house. He had asked Morgan to call Amanda and tell her he was coming to look at the property. Morgan was excited by the news. She had cast the bait out there and he had bitten.

"I think it's called chumming when there's no hook in the bait," Amanda said. "What am I supposed to do when he gets here? Gaff him?"

"Look, sis, I got him there. You keep him there until I get back, maybe late tomorrow. Stall him. Don't say anything about our plans until I get there. Put him up in my room. Is Denise back? No? Shit. Well, maybe the girls will behave with a man in the house. Just remember, low impact. I got the impression your brother shies away from complications."

"But when?" Amanda asked. She would need hours to get ready.

"That's up to him, sis, not me, but I'd say sometime today. By the way, I don't think he is anything like you. Are you sure he's your brother?"

Luckily it was a weekday and all the girls were off at their jobs. Susan would be around somewhere. Amanda had noticed that Susan tended to hide when it was just the two of them in the house. Amanda went and unlocked Morgan's room. It was the room beneath the cupola and really the nicest bedroom in the house, with big bay windows and lots of light. Morgan kept it pretty Spartan. She had come with next to nothing and added little. It was just another room to Morgan. That was one of the reasons why she had no problem with a strange man staying there—there was so little of her there. Amanda found a clean set of sheets and pillowcases on a closet shelf and was stripping the old ones off the bed when Susan strayed into the room.

"I've never been in this room before," Susan said. "Is this Morgan's room?"

"Yes. Give me a hand here, Susan." Making a bed was easier with two people. "Now open up the windows a bit and we'll air the room out." Also on the closet shelf Amanda found the bath towels and wash-cloths Morgan had taken from the Washington hotel, and she folded a set of those onto the foot of the bed.

"Is Morgan coming back?" Susan asked, straightening the pillows.

"No, we have another guest coming," Amanda said, looking around, then added for some reason, "my brother."

"Where does this go?" Susan asked, walking over to the door that led to the enclosed circular stairs to the cupola.

"Up to the cupola, but it's locked, not safe. Susan, what are the plans for dinner tonight?"

"I don't know. After last night nobody wanted to talk to each other, so nobody made any plans. I don't know whose night it is. Nothing's defrosting. Nobody told me to do anything."

"Susan, I have to make a market run. I will have to go all the way to Catskill, so I'll be gone at least an hour and a half. If anyone comes, just let them in and tell them I'll be right back. Okay?"

"Is he your older or younger brother?" Susan asked.

"What difference does that make?"

"I don't know. I've never had a brother. I thought it made a difference who was older."

"In our case it doesn't mean anything."

Chapter 6

The water was deeper than Dominick had expected, but his car made it through alright. When he was halfway into it, too far to turn back, he had seen that it wasn't just that there was water in the roadway but that the stream beside the road had topped its banks and overflowed. He saw more of the bank crumble away as he passed, releasing a further flood. The rain had not let up as he had hoped. If anything it intensified as he drove north. His windshield wipers were on high. He was on back roads now, following Morgan's directions to the Van Houten place. He hadn't seen another car since turning off 9W. He was angry with himself for coming this way and not just driving straight up to Woods Hole. West Point had been hardly worth the visit.

According to Morgan's directions, somewhere along this stretch there would be a break in the woods leaving open fields, and up on a knoll to his right would be the house from the photograph. A bit farther on would be two stone posts marking the entrance to the driveway. Dominick couldn't see much of anything through the downpour, but the forest did end and he slowed down. He never saw the house, but the two tall stone pillars that had once held a gate appeared on his right, and he turned up the driveway between them. *Now pretend you are a multibillionaire CEO arriving for a high-stakes, three-day secret meeting*, he told himself and chuckled once. There were no lights on at the house, which appeared much like it did in the photograph only worse for wear in the storm. The place looked forlorn in the rain, like a Victorian lady of a certain age in all her frumpy finery caught unprepared in a sudden downpour.

Dominick sat in the car and watched the rain. There were no other vehicles in sight. Perhaps no one was home. Maybe Morgan had not gotten his message to Amanda. It was still early. If the rain let up maybe he could find his way back to 9W and find a motel before dark. He had accomplished the purported purpose of this ill-conceived side trip—he would not be investing Marjorie's money in this sad place. Then one of the double front doors of the house opened, and a lanky wisp of a brown-haired girl in faded overalls came out onto the veranda and opened a pink umbrella. She skipped down the steps and came running to his car. He buzzed down his window as she came up.

"Hi," she said, bending down beneath her umbrella. "Nice car. Aren't you going to come in? I'm supposed to make you to home." Everything about her was amazingly plain—her face, her hair, her clothes, her speech. She was like something half made, lacking all finishing touches, a fine start deserted by the craftsman for another piece, a vessel well formed and bisqued but not glazed.

"Yes, of course," Dominick said, "I'll come in. Is Amanda here?"

"Here, take this," the girl said. "I'm already wet."

"Yes, well, wait a second." Dominick buzzed his window back up and turned off the ignition before stepping out of the car. The girl handed him the pink umbrella and ran back to the veranda through the rain. She was barefoot. Dominick followed her.

On the veranda she took the umbrella from him, shaking the water from it as she closed it. "Isn't this rain great? The garden is getting a real good soak. Come on in." Dominick followed her through a vestibule into a hallway paneled in dark wood, past facing closed double oak doors and a graceful staircase with a finely carved balustrade. The wooden floor—of old, uneven if smooth planking—was uncarpeted. She led him back to the kitchen. "I made lemonade. Want some?"

"I was looking for Amanda," Dominick said.

"I know. You're her brother. Here." She handed him a tall glass filled with lemonade. "She went to the store to buy food. She said she'd be back, but that was a while ago. Make yourself at home."

Dominick looked around the room. The kitchen was large and comfy. There was an old stuffed davenport along one wall and a papa-sized stuffed wing chair. There was also a substantial kitchen table that could seat a dozen people. He turned back to see his escort vanish through a side door. If Amanda was expecting him, he probably shouldn't leave. He wondered if there was another road out, beside the one he had taken in. He couldn't go back that way.

The kitchen was on a corner of the house, and there were windows on two walls. Dominick went to one and looked out at the undiminishing rain. The view was of a well-tended vegetable garden with raised beds and beyond that at a distance a barn that had once been painted red. As he watched, the girl in the overalls walked into the garden. She walked as if it wasn't raining, even though her long hair was plastered to her skull by the force of it, water dripped from her nose, and her soaked T-shirt and overalls hung on her like laundry on a line. He wondered if she weighed even a hundred pounds. Her collar bones stood out beneath the wet fabric of her shirt. She didn't notice him watching her; she was busy. The rain had bent and beaten down young tomato plants staked in one of the beds. She was tending to them, lifting them out of the mud and refastening them to their stakes. As he watched her he thought—this is someone's daughter; I wonder if anyone misses her. The lemonade was way too sweet.

Amanda did not return. Dominick had stretched out on the davenport and fallen asleep. He was awoken by the girl shaking his shoulder. "You don't have to sleep here. You have a bed," she said. She was still sopping wet, dripping onto the floor where she squatted beside the couch. Dominick looked up at the windows. The sky was darker, but it was still raining. "I'll show you," she said.

"No Amanda?" Dominick asked.

"No. I don't know what happened, but I'll show you your room."

"Is there another road in here besides the one I took?" Dominick asked, sitting up.

"There's one other way, down toward the river, but it's just a dirt road. Nobody goes that way." Now in the distance there was lightning and thunder. "Please stay until someone else comes."

Dominick looked down at her where she squatted. Was he trapped here? "You're dripping all over the floor," he said. "Aren't you cold?"

"Please stay. You have Morgan's room. It's the best. I'll show you."

There was no escape. "I have things in the trunk I have to get."

The girl jumped up and stuck out her hand for his keys. "I'll get them," she said. "I'm still wet."

Dominick picked out the key that would unlock the trunk and handed it to her. "There are several big bags and one small one. I'll just need the small one. Thank you."

He followed her to the front veranda and watched her. She paused on the way to his car to kick at a frog in a puddle, a playful kick. She came back with his bag and went past him into the house and up the antique stairway. Again Dominick followed. His room was large and mainly empty. There was a queen-size bed, a bureau, and a desk chair at an empty table. An empty space where no one dwelled, a charming room turned into a cell.

"What's your name?" Dominick asked when she put his bag down near the bed.

"Susan," she said. "What's yours?"

"I'm Dominick. Susan, what are we going to do about supper?" Dominick hadn't eaten since breakfast, which seemed like days before. "My guess is that Amanda is having trouble getting back because the roads are flooded."

"I don't know. I don't cook. Someone else always cooks dinner. What's the difference between dinner and supper?"

"None, really. Let's go back to the kitchen and see what we can find to eat. Or rather, I'll go back to the kitchen and see what I can rustle up, while you go get out of those wet clothes and put on something dry for dinner. How's that sound?"

"Okay, I guess. I must look awful."

"Dry your hair too. In fact, why don't you take a nice hot shower while I fix us something?"

Susan's hand went up to feel her lank wet hair, as if she was surprised to find it there. She gave Dominick a strange look then turned around and left.

Dominick found a packet of cheese ravioli in the freezer and a bottle of mushroom-garlic Ragu in a cupboard. There was half a loaf of only slightly stale French bread, butter, and garlic powder. The kitchen was fully equipped, and everything was where it usually was in American kitchens. He set about making supper. Beneath the pink umbrella he made a trip to the car to bring in his other bags so that he could root around in them and find his cigars and a book and the fifth of Glenfiddich. By the time Susan came down, the meal was almost ready and Dominick was seated in the stuffed wing chair with a glass of Scotch, a cigar, and a book.

Susan was wearing an emerald green dress that looked like something his mother might have worn—expensive and showy in an understated way, with a high neck and long tight sleeves. She was wearing no makeup or jewelry, but her hair was clean and pulled back in a ponytail. As if to connect her to the previous Susan, she was still barefoot. Dominick looked at her over the top of his reading glasses. "A very pleasant transformation, Susan. Are you hungry?"

"I think I may be starving," she said.

Dinner was edible. Dominick missed a red wine to accompany it. Susan ate like the teenager she was. There were no leftovers. She insisted on doing the dishes. "That's my job," she said. Dominick returned to his wingback chair and book and an after-dinner Romeo y Julieta. "Funny that Amanda hasn't called," he said. "I mean the power's still on, so the phone lines should still be up too."

"Oh, there's no landline phone here. Denise had it taken out because someone was abusing it. Only cell phones." Susan was drying the dishes.

"And you don't have one?" Dominick asked, wondering who Denise might be.

"Oh, I can't afford one of those," Susan said. "What's that you are drinking?"

"Scotch whiskey. Would you like some?"

"Scotch. I don't remember. It's bitter, isn't it?"

"Yes, it is, very bitter."

"I'll try some." Susan put down her dish towel and brought a glass over to where Dominick was sitting. He poured her a dram. She sniffed it, then went to the sink and added a half cup of hot water to the glass then stirred in some Sweet'N Low before taking a sip. "Why do you call it Scotch?" she asked.

"Because that's where it comes from, from Scotland."

"Like Scotch tape?" Susan asked. "It tastes like smoke. Does that make it good?" She sat on the davenport, tucking her legs up beneath her. "I like it, though. After you get used to the taste you want another sip."

Dominick slipped a page marker into his book and set it aside. He dearly wanted just to read and forget that he was stuck in this place, but there was no way of ignoring this slim incongruous being in green on the charcoal couch.

"Do you think this rain is because of global warming?" she asked, sipping her toddy. "You know, the polar bears dying and all?"

"I don't know," Dominick said. "I've always preferred thinking that the weather and I had nothing to do with one another beyond temporarily coexisting."

"You talk funny. I like that, like one of those British PBS shows. What sort of name is Dominick?"

"A very common name in another century."

"I like the smell of your cigar. Do you like the smell of pot?"

"Susan?"

"When anyone else is here I have to go out to the barn to get high, but now it's just you here and you're smoking in the kitchen and I thought . . . you know, I'd light up too. You seem cool."

"I am cool with it, Susan. I couldn't care less. Fire away." Dominick put his reading glasses back on and picked up his book. Susan put down her glass and whisked off. She returned with a very feminine looking pink-blue-and-white porcelain pipe, but before she sat back down on the davenport she picked up her glass and came over to Dominick. "Please," she said, holding out her glass. "It's not bad." He poured her two fingers more of Scotch, and she fixed herself another toddy.

Of course Susan politely offered the pipe to Dominick as she smoked, and he accepted it for several sweet lungfuls. They chatted about many things. It became a sort of tutorial, as Susan stoned was very curious: "If that's why that happens, then how come . . .?" Dominick wondered, but didn't ask, if she had ever been to school.

In one of the cupboards Dominick had seen a bag of popping corn. He found it and popped a frying pan full of it for them. The Glenfiddich by now was almost gone. They talked a while longer. Susan wanted to know how food stamps worked and why all the frogs were disappearing. At an appropriately long pause Dominick excused himself, said good night, and went off to bed, leaving Susan still sitting on the couch, all dressed up and at the only place she had to go.

The rain hadn't stopped but it had let up. The thunder was now so faint you couldn't compute the distance. He was almost asleep when he heard the door to his room open and close. In the faint light of a far-away lightning flash he saw a female figure in a nightgown carrying a pillow and comforter cross the room. As she rolled herself into her quilt on the floor beside Dominick's bed, Susan said softly, "Don't mind me, okay? I won't bother you. I just can't get to sleep if I'm all alone and it's thundering."

✳✳✳

Amanda spent the night at a Motel 6, sharing a room with Kathy. They had met where the road was washed out. Kathy had texted the other girls to tell them to find other places to stay for the night, seeing as no one would be able to get to the house. Amanda figured Dominick would have been turned back by the washout as well, if he had ever gotten that far. Kathy was worried about her sister being up there all alone, but there was nothing they could do about it. There was no way to call the house. Susan didn't have a cell phone. They were having breakfast at an IHOP when Morgan called. She was taking Amtrak up. Could Amanda pick her up in Hudson? She'd get in a little after noon.

"Is Nemo there yet?" Morgan wanted to know.

"I don't know. I doubt it. I'm not even there." And Amanda explained about the rain and the road washing out. "I'll pick you up in Hudson."

By noon there wasn't a cloud in the sky. It was a perfect sunny June day, except that the temperature was not going to climb out of the sixties. There was no sign of the record rain of the past few days until Amanda drove onto the Rip Van Winkle Bridge to cross over to Hudson. The river was a roiling, rushing, chocolate snake beneath them, carrying trees and what looked like islets of brush and mud downstream. The river hasn't forgotten, she thought. The river remem-bers everything. Someday this bridge will be just a memory, but the river will be unchanged. The Chevy's front end kept pulling to the left so that she couldn't let go of the wheel for long, which made lighting a cigarette something to think about and plan. The dashboard cigar lighter had never worked.

Like a ghost in the back seat her inner voice spoke up: *Ah, addled one, remember your wish list for when you got money in the bank? Number one on the list was not just new tires and an alignment, but a new car altogether, something gutsy, something higher and with more lights. Ah, duh. The money is now in your bank account. Hello. What are you waiting for? For Morgan to pick out the make and model for you? She doesn't even drive.*

And I'll get her her own iPod so she can listen to her music not mine, Amanda thought.

It will still be you driving around Miss Daisy.

A semi truck's horn blared behind her as she remembered at the last minute to merge into the exit lane. She couldn't help it if she wasn't yet used to being rich. What else was on that list of things to buy? She had always wanted to go up in a hot-air balloon. She would get all new expensive underwear. She would fly out to Denver and try to find Ricky. They would finish up the Van Houten place and flip it as quickly as possible. She would finally take that ferryboat ride from Vancouver up to Sitka, getting off at any stop she wanted to and just hanging out. She'd buy some Inuit art.

Morgan's train was right on time at 12:17. They had lunch in Hudson, then drove back across the river. Morgan talked nonstop about the city and the contractors. She never mentioned Nemo or their meeting. Finally, Amanda had to ask. "How did you get my brother to come up here?"

"You know, I'm not sure. I did tell him you were hurt by his just disappearing like that. Maybe he's stopping by to apologize. He did seem almost interested in how old the place is. He was headed up to the Cape anyway. It's only a couple of hours out of his way. Who knows, with a strange dude like that? But when he shows up—if he shows up—let me deal with him. This part is business not family. You know, we might have to incorporate him?"

"Morgan, we really don't need his money. We can finish the job with what we have now."

"Sure, but wouldn't it be nice to have a bigger pile when we start the next project? Look, we got the fish up to the boat. We'll just play him along to see what happens."

"Where did all these fishy images suddenly come from?" Amanda asked.

"Why, my daddy was a fisherman. You knew that. I remember once . . .," and Morgan went off into one of her stories about her Tidewater girlhood and her adored daddy. Pretty soon she had Amanda laughing with her. The Chevy kept drifting to the left.

There was a county crew at where the creek had decided to cross the road, a couple of trucks and a front loader. There were orange traffic cones and yellow cop tape blocking off the road, but the crew wasn't doing much, mainly standing around watching the water flow out of the creek. Two guys with shovels were knee-deep in the mud trying to do something. Amanda had to honk to get someone's attention. An older guy not wearing a hard hat came over and told them it would be a while before the road was passable, "maybe tonight, maybe tomorrow."

"How about the old road by the river?" Amanda asked.

"I wouldn't try it in that," he said, pointing to Amanda's car. "It's trenched out pretty bad here and there. You the ladies staying up at the old Van Houten place? What's that all about? Some sort of convent or something?"

Morgan leaned over across the front seat. "Is there a number we can call to find out when the road will be open?" she asked.

"You can call the Public Works number, ma'am. It's in the book. Someone is usually there twenty-four seven."

"Let's go," Morgan said, adding as Amanda backed-up, "Honkies can't mind their own business."

***

When Dominick woke up, Susan and her comforter and pillow were gone from the floor of his room. At first he forgot where he was. It looked like a barren hospital room. Then he saw the big bay windows and remembered. The room was bright with sunlight. He went to the bathroom down the hall. There wasn't a sound in the house. The

56

downstairs was deserted, too. He walked out onto the back veranda—an empty landscape. He made a pot of coffee. He had the place all to himself and rather liked it. Houses have a feel to them. You didn't have to be a Chinese expert to sense if a place belonged exactly where it was.

I placed a jar in Tennessee,
And round it was, upon a hill.
It made the slovenly wilderness
Surround that hill.

The wilderness rose up to it,
And sprawled around, no longer wild.
The jar was round upon the ground
And tall and of a port in air.

It took dominion everywhere.
The jar was gray and bare.
It did not give of bird or bush,
Like nothing else in Tennessee.

Dominick knew that Wallace Stevens poem by heart. It was a page in his personal hymnal. He also knew houses well enough to feel the confidence that this place expressed. There are people who leave poems behind and people who leave houses. Dominick wondered who it was had built this house, in what—at the time—must have been wilderness. It exuded a familial warmth. It had known a hundred and eighty winters here; it had earned the right to many more. Maybe it was just the tall ceilings and windows, all the welcoming light. Silence suited it. He took his mug of coffee out to the front veranda. No Susan anywhere. The vista there was distant, out toward the valley where the river would be and the forested hills across the river. *It took dominion everywhere.* It took a minute for it to register that the one thing missing from this view was his car, which was no longer parked in the driveway.

Chapter 7

Amanda and Morgan had started out small, flipping row houses in Baltimore on the margins of gentrifying neighborhoods. That was back when property values always increased, and with the right purchase and some hard renovation work you could double your investment in a year or two. They had met, in fact, as competitors for a house they finally went in on together. It was a natural business partnership. Amanda had the sense for what had to be done but hated dealing with contractors. Morgan couldn't care less about aesthetics, but the men they hired to do the work listened to her. Things had gone well for a number of years, then the bottom fell out of the real estate market, and the "correction" that followed closed them out. What they had left, they put into the Van Houten place purchase, picking it up from another speculator who was in even worse shape than they were. It seemed to make sense to go big, as only the top of the market was selling. With the money from Marjorie's estate they just might pull it off, if they could find the right deep-pocket buyer.

Amanda started heading back to the Motel 6 for another night or however long it took for the road to be passable, but Morgan wouldn't hear of it. They checked in instead at the fanciest inn in Catskill, separate rooms. It was a waste of money as far as Amanda was concerned. Morgan got into one of her dismissive funks and went off to her room. Amanda called Kathy and asked her to let the others know that it would be another night at least before they could all get home.

Morgan had her luggage with her, so she had other clothes. Amanda had only her purse and had been in the same clothes for two days. She remembered her wish list for new expensive underwear, but the only place to buy new clothes in Catskill was the Walmart Supercenter just south of town. She picked out a Walmart change of clothes, including an XL T-shirt to wear as a nightshirt. She picked up a toothbrush as well, and some toothpaste and a hairbrush. Then she pushed her shopping cart up and down the aisles, looking at things and trying to remember what she needed for the house, like garbage bags and dish soap. At the checkout counter the man in front of her in line was wearing a shirt that looked like it was made from a Confederate flag. The black girl cashier didn't appreciate it much, Amanda could tell, but she didn't say anything.

Amanda was leaving the store when her cell phone jingled. It was an irate Denise. "What do you mean locking the girls out of the house? Of course Morgan and you would wait till I was gone to evict everyone. There will be a serious price to pay for this."

"No one has been evicted, Denise. What are you talking about?"

"Eviction, lockout, whatever you want to call it. What about their things? What about out agreement? You are just two heartless bitches."

"Denise, there has been no eviction, no lock out. The road to the house got washed out, that's all. No one can get there. Your girls had to find other places to stay for a night or two until the road is fixed. Jesus, Denise."

"Don't you lay that word on me. I heard that all the girls were told was not to come back to the house, and that means just one thing to me—war!"

Amanda tossed her purchases into the Chevy's back seat, still listening to her phone. This was archetypal Denise—injured, bellicose, not listening, defensive, and of the opinion that the best defense was to be offensive.

"Denise, the girls can come back to the house whenever they want, as soon as the road is open."

"You're damn right they can. And don't you and Morgan try any more of your tricks. My work here won't be done for a few more days, but then I will come straight back, not stop in Buffalo as I had planned." There may have been more, but Amanda snapped her phone shut. The arrangement with Denise had been beneficial to all concerned, but it was good that it would soon be coming to an end. If some relationships were made in heaven, this one had come from someplace else and could go back there.

✷✷✷

Nothing else seemed to be missing. Dominick made a quick check of his bags, and everything seemed to be there. His money clip felt a bit thinner, but seeing as he never knew exactly how much cash he had with him, he couldn't say what was missing. His car keys were gone, of course, the only keys he carried. He thought about keys as he toured the now wholly deserted house, because the doors to most of the rooms were locked, and in his experience that was strange.

Dominick had stayed in many homes, and locked interior doors were rare. Some of these bedroom doors even had latches and padlocks. One latch held a cheap gym-locker combination lock. The problem with such latches and locks was that they could be used not only to keep people out but to keep people in. Dominick had vivid recall of the one time he had been locked in a room—a cell, actually, in a small-town Florida jail. It would just be for the night, and he had the cell to himself and there was a cot and he needed to sleep, but he couldn't, not behind a locked door. He had pounded on the door until a deputy came to see what the problem was. After Dominick had explained, the deputy laughed at him and unlocked and opened the cell door. "Now shut the fuck up." At the end of the cell block corridor was a locked gate, but that was alright somehow and Dominick had gone right to sleep.

That had been one of the rare times in his life when there had been no option of escape. Here was another. There was really nothing he could do but occupy the space and time he was trapped in, which was considerably more agreeable than a jail cell. Sooner or later someone would come—Amanda or Morgan or someone, maybe even Susan would return with his car—and meanwhile he had the old house to himself. The only unlocked room other than the one he had slept in he took to be Susan's, which she shared with another woman. The green dress was dropped on one of the beds. The room was an untended mess with clothes strewn everywhere. On one wall were posters for bands with badly spelled names. A teenager's room, lacking only stuffed animals. Now, there was a crime statistic for you—one car and one teenager, and the teenager steals the car.

The first locks were probably just fancy knots, like the Gordian one. When did that impulse give rise to invention? The impulse, the need, to create a locked space? Was it to lock something in, a cage that contained something dangerous or forbidden? Or was it to lock others out to guard what was yours? Was it capture or was it hoarding? A prison or a safe? Whatever, it got pretty complicated—all the different locks on his car, for instance, some mechanical, some electronic. And what good were locks if the key was stolen? Or in the case of the Gordian Knot if someone came up with a sharp enough sword? Ah, the key. If you had the key. The keys to the kingdom, the key to the city. Dominick knew the origins of that. The key that was surrendered would have been not the key to the city's gates but the key to its defensive works, its armory, its parapets—the key to its fortress. Even the doors to what would be the house's front parlor and formal dining room were locked.

Dominick refreshed his coffee and dug out from his luggage the prospectus file that Morgan had given him. Perhaps it could supply more information about the house. There was very little there—built before 1840, designed by the New Haven architect Rodgers Morton, paid for by a Rev. Vestal Van Houten. That was all. As he closed the file a receipt fell out from the back. It was from a Kinko's in midtown Manhattan, dated the morning of the day he had met with Morgan, for the printing of one copy of the 13-page document he held. He really was being offered a singular deal, at least a deal with a singular audience.

Dominick went for a hike around the grounds, through the kitchen garden of immature plants out past the barn to a falling down stone wall. He found a comfortable seat on the wall and lit up a cigar, birdsong off in the woods behind him. The air was chilly, but the sun and the country stones of the wall were warm. From its knoll the place had views in all directions. He wondered how far it was to the river from here. He wondered about the Rev. Van Houten and what caused him to build here. He wondered about lunch. On his way back to the house he noticed a wrought-iron symbol high on its south wall between two second-floor windows. It was a pentagram, much like the ones he had seen on the walls of other New England houses, but this one was slightly different. He couldn't remember another wrought-iron one, and the five-pointed star was enclosed in a circle.

***

The next morning the road was still closed. The backhoe was still there, stuck up to the tops of its treads in the mud where water still flowed over the creek's broken banks, but there was no crew there. Morgan wanted her to try and drive through anyway, but Amanda demurred. The Chevy was not quite an off-road vehicle. "Let's try the back way," she suggested. "Maybe that has dried out enough."

The back way was just a dirt farm road that circled between fields to another farm road that connected to their county road beyond the house—tractor roads, really, that in the winter went unplowed. Diligence was one of those townships whose population had steadily dropped from census to census, where roads led to nowhere outside the past, and parcels of land were named for families long since departed. The Van Houten place's nearest neighbors now were two miles away on another county road. This depopulation was part of the area's appeal for Amanda, along with fact that all the forests were second and third growth after having been once logged to nudity to build the big cities upriver and down. How many places were there these days making such backward progress? As the cities consumed their proximate countryside, hidden pockets of true rural country like this slipped quietly back toward wilderness. The coyotes and black bears were back, with rumors of panthers and wolves. Could the Iroquois be far behind?

Morgan, of course, cared nothing for any of this. Her major concern was that if the county road was not repaired soon, and well, the contractors with their heavy trucks and equipment could not make it to the house. "They ain't coming this way, that's for sure," she said as the Chevy crawled between back road ruts. Having something to bitch about had brought Morgan out of her shell. "I suppose Barnett would know," she said.

"Know what?" Amanda asked, stopping to look at the ruts ahead.

"Where he is."

"Where who is? Barnett? I would hope so."

"No, your brother, Captain Nemo. I mean if we missed his visit because of this rainstorm, how do we get back in touch with him? Go to the right, through the weeds."

"There's a ditch there."

"This side of the ditch. There's room."

"Get out and direct me."

"No way, girl, that's nigger-eating mud out there. These shoes are worth more than this car. When are you going to get a proper vehicle anyway?"

Amanda nudged the Chevy ahead onto the weeds. Her voice spoke up: *There she goes again, worrying about the man connection. First that creep Barnett and now your brother. Doesn't she see that we don't need them? That we can do this without them? Morgan can talk the talk about how useless men are, but when it comes to walking the walk there is still a seductive come-hither sway to her hips and her outlook. Maybe it is time to end all this, not just the deal with Denise and the girls, but Morgan as well. Just end it all, the whole show, house and all. Just take the money and go. That's probably what your mom wanted you to do with it. That was always her position—move right along, buy something new, even time. You can buy time, you know, girl. Time stopped being free a long time ago.*

The lane dipped down into a hollow with willow trees, and suddenly the way was blocked by a car coming at them. Only the car wasn't moving. It was mired up to its bumper in the mud of the slough. It was a black Lexus with a Virginia plate. It was Nemo's car.

"Well, that tops it," Morgan said. "Now, that dude is totally lost."

"That's my brother's car," Amanda said.

"What? That's Captain Nemo's boat? What's it doing here, headed out?" Morgan reached over and gave two long honks of the Chevy's horn.

"What are you doing that for?" Amanda said, irked. "It's not about to get out of the way, and there's nobody in it."

"How do you know? Maybe he's asleep in the back seat or something." But no head popped up inside the car. They sat there in silence for a while. Then Amanda put the Chevy in reverse and turned to look out the back window. "You're not going to check?" Morgan said.

"Check what? There's no one there."

"Maybe he left a note or something."

Amanda crept the Chevy backwards, getting used to mirror steering. "If his car is there, he'll show up. Now we have to get ourselves out of here without having to hike."

They had to back up maybe half a mile before they could find a safe place to do an eight-point turn and head out. It took almost an hour, and Morgan did have to get out and direct her in places.

"I am not doing any pushing," she said, "so do not get stuck." She left her shoes and stockings in the car.

✳✳✳

Dominick had the Van Houten place to himself for another two days and nights. He amused himself by taking photographs, black-and-white shots, searching out shadows with dark straight lines or adjoining grays that contrasted somehow. The house was a treasure of shadows. In one sunset macro shot the peeling paint on a clapboard wall looked like scales on a petrified fish.

He was reduced to eating ramen and canned pork and beans. There was a large selection of teas, but no bread or eggs. He had set up a small space for himself on the back veranda with a comfortable porch chair and an end table out of the hallway. A pork and beans can served as an ashtray. He drank tea, sometimes iced. He read. There was nothing to read in the open rooms of the house, not even cookbooks or magazines; but he had a backlog of books with him, more histories. The days stayed clear and got hotter. By midday on the second day, Dominick thought the raised beds of the kitchen garden might need watering and he found Susan's hose, but when he got there he discovered that the earth was still wet, so he left them alone and went back to his book about naval blockades.

He slept well in the old house. This time of year would have always been its halcyon days—the long amber sunsets lingering late into dusk, all the guest bedrooms filled with summer guests up from the city or down from Albany, children being put to bed, the day's warmth lingering in the rooms, and with darkness the breeze coming up from the river billowing the open-window curtains. Simplicity was the essence of peace, the simplicity of a quiet summer's day to be followed by its sibling.

On Dominick's third morning there—or was it his fourth?—the foreign sound of an engine awoke him, a grumbling like a beast with a chest cold. The sun was already well up in the sky and slanting in his bedroom windows. In the driveway there were the sounds of human voices and car doors closing. The idyll was ending; the simple would soon be slaughtered by the complex. He swung his legs out of bed and put on his pants and shirt from the previous day, feeling like a soldier about to surrender. Just name, rank, and serial number, he reminded himself. Let them—whoever they were—make their own projections and assumptions. In the bathroom down the hall he emptied his bladder and splashed cold water on his unshaven face. Bring it on. There was no choice. He looked at himself in the mirror above the sink, once again a stranger to the face there. He decided against the wrinkled used shirt and went back to his room to change to something fresher.

As empty as the house had just been, it was now full. Voices, women's voices, the sounds of people on the stairs and of doors being unlocked and opened. The toilet down the hall flushed and then a few minutes later flushed again. Footsteps passed in the hallway, a girl's laugh came from somewhere downstairs. Dominick buttoned on a clean shirt. He went to the front window and looked out. There was just one vehicle in the driveway, a big squarish emergency vehicle with a row of lights on top and outsized off-road tires. "First responders," Dominick said. He had a fondness for that term, an action noun with metaphoric possibilities. A winch was attached to the vehicle's front bumper. How appropriate for a first responder to have a winch up front.

The door to the room opened and a woman was standing there, her back turned to Dominick as she called back into the hallway, "No, no. Check to see, but don't let Dave go yet." When she came into the room he could see it was Morgan. She was pulling a wheeled suitcase that resisted coming over the door sill into the room. She cursed at it softly and jerked it in. Then she saw Dominick standing there. She smiled. "So you did find the place after all," she said.

"Yes. Hello, Morgan. So is this your room I have been sleeping in?"

"Morgan, Morgan!" A young woman came to the door.

"What is it, Kathy?"

"I can't find Susan anywhere," then seeing Dominick, "Who's this?"

"This is Amanda's brother. I'm sure Susan will show up now we're back."

"Has he been here all along?"

"I don't know. Have you been here all along, Dominick?" Morgan asked.

"Susan went out a while ago," Dominick said. Name, rank, serial number.

"Went out? What do you mean went out? Went out where? Went out how?" Kathy was getting excited. She came into the room.

"She borrowed my car," Dominick said.

"And you just let her leave?"

"I hope you brought some food," Dominick said. "There's very little left that isn't canned."

"Where is Susan?" Kathy wanted to know.

"He's said he doesn't know, Kathy. We will have to leave it at that for now." Morgan was giving Dominick a curious look. "You can inform the officer downstairs that Susan is missing, if you wish, Kathy. Though I think it may be premature, and you know that Denise does not like having the authorities out here. For a nonmember and a runaway at that." Kathy turned and left, and Morgan closed the door behind her. "What really happened?" she asked.

"Susan stole my car and left a couple of days ago. That's all I know."

"We found your car stuck in the mud on the back road. No sign of Susan."

"Is it still there?"

"Becoming part of the landscape." Amanda pulled her suitcase out of the way. "I wouldn't worry about Susan. She's a teenager. They fly the coop as a matter of nature. She's done it before. I think she runs out of dope and has to go into Catskill to score."

Dominick had noted it at their New York meeting. Morgan had a way of making you feel as if you and she had been friends for a long while and that you were just picking up a conversation interrupted in another place and time.

"Who's here?" Dominick asked.

"Amanda's here and five of the girls. It's Saturday so they're not at work. The road's still blocked, which is why no one came before, but the deputy sheriff gave us a ride around the blockage. Say, you better get a ride in with him if you want to get someone out here to free your car. He was going to head back right away. I'll go down and stop him while you grab what you need for a night. You can leave your other stuff here. It will be safe with me. You're not my size."

Chapter 8

Dominick found the impulse mystifying. To get up every workday and put on a uniform then go out and *enforce*. The job had to satisfy some yearning that Dominick lacked—the need to constantly prevail, perhaps, or to have your already poor opinion of your fellow human beings serially seconded by experience. But then he couldn't understand gamblers either, and for a few that was an addiction. And then there was the attitude, that I'm-right-you're-wrong assumption behind every interaction, an attitude backed up by the unilateral right to use force to prevail. As an enforcer you relied upon the threat of force, and woe to those who dared raise a hand against you. What was it they were called, back in slavery times? Overseers. Only these overseers were nominally our public servants not our private masters. And with the uniform came a certain arbitrariness in how that threat of force or confinement could be employed. Crooks could make great friends—hell, everybody broke the law—but Dominick had never met a cop he liked. Of course that was unfair, because he had always avoided their company. He could not think of another entire class of people he wanted less to do with.

And then there was often a bad haircut, as with Deputy Dave. If Dominick had thought twice about it, he would have followed his bag into the roomy back of the Sheriff Department RV, but instead he climbed into the front beside Deputy Dave, who had been waiting for him with the motor running. He had the air-con on and the windows up even though the morning air was cool and fresh. "Well?" he said.

"Yes?" Dominick asked. Was there something he was missing, like his license to ride?

"Your seatbelt, sir. We can't proceed before you put your seatbelt on."

"Oh, that. Sorry." Dominick found his seatbelt and fumbled trying to get it long enough to click in. He never wore seatbelts. He found them stupid and confining. He had read somewhere that Russians never wore them, that they thought of them as some sort of American joke. What were airbags for? The title Human Control Officer—like Animal Control Officer only more species specific—occurred to him. He finally got the belt clicked. "There we go." And they went on down the driveway and left onto the county road.

"So, you staying up here?" Deputy Dave had to ask. Enforcers get to interrogate for no reason.

"Is the road just out in the one place?" Dominick said. He had long ago learned to answer control officers' questions with questions whenever possible.

"Yeah, just the one place. That your car with Virginia plates stuck up on the Sullivan place?"

"Have you seen it?"

"Yeah, stuck pretty good. You're not good at driving in mud, are you?"

"Is there a towing service available locally?"

"For that job you may have to go over to Hudson. That where you're from, Virginia?"

"And are you from around here?"

They came up to where the creek had decided to escape. There was a full crew working at getting the stream back in its banks and the road open. Part of the pavement had been washed away, and any immediate repairs would be temporary. Deputy Dave stopped his vehicle to let the crew and their front loader get out of the way.

"I'd like to see some identification, sir."

"And why would that be?"

"So that I can make a report on who I transported, sir."

"Is that important?"

"It's required, sir. Your ID, sir."

"And what if I declined to comply with your request?"

"Then I'd have to take you in, sir, and let the authorities deal with it."

"But you are the authorities, aren't you?"

"That would be my superiors, sir."

"But I am your superior. I am a citizen and you are my public servant. I have done nothing wrong. What gives you the right to require anything of me?"

"You a lawyer or something?" Deputy Dave was not pleased, but he was coming alive. A conflict might be brewing, a situation wherein he could allow himself to excel in what he most craved—the sanctioned imposition of his own will. His right hand even moved to the handle of the pistol on his belt.

"Here you are officer, my driver's license," Dominick said, taking the laminated card out of his card case. "Now may I see your ID please? Perhaps we could become pen pals?" The rest of the drive into Catskill went without conversation.

✳✳✳

It was a weird weekend with no cars. As happy as everyone was to get back to their rooms, they felt trapped in the house. When you lived in the country, distances shrank so that the eight mile drive to the nearest store seemed like nothing, and the twenty miles round trip for a burger or pizza or anything more was tolerable. Country roads, no traffic, no cops. But now all their cars were parked along the side of the county road on the other side of the washout. The road crew had said they would let them know when the road was open and send in a vehicle to bring them out, but the road crew wouldn't be working on Sunday, and Amanda thought that the men seemed to be enjoying the women's predicament.

Added to that was the fact that there was very little food in the house, and no one had thought to bring any supplies. Morgan went from room to room commandeering private stashes, which didn't come to much, mainly cookies and crackers and candy bars. There was a sack of rice in the pantry and some bags of dried beans. Morgan fixed big pots of rice and beans. There weren't enough greens in the garden to make more than a single salad. "Diet time, bitches," Morgan announced. On Sunday morning she tried to reach her deputy sheriff to see if she could arrange a shopping trip in his vehicle, but he was off duty.

Denise had been in text or phone contact with all of the girls and had somehow turned all this into Amanda and Morgan's fault. The girls had no problem in showing their hard feelings, and now that they had a shared complaint and common enemies their earlier internal squabbles vanished. Amanda hid in her room with the TV turned up loud.

At Sunday supper Morgan launched a counterattack. "It's called an act of God," she yelled at them, "a fucking act of God. Amanda and I did not cause the skies to open up and the creek to flood. If you want to blame someone, blame God. And in case you haven't noticed, God does not speak through words. God speaks through actions. So maybe God is telling you girls that it's time to toughen up, and maybe lose some weight. I'm telling you to shut up."

It was on Sunday, too, that Susan returned, much to Kathy's relief. Kathy had been obsessing about Nemo and her sister. For some reason every unexplained occurrence and coincidence had to become part of a conspiracy theory. As if any of these poor creatures were worthy of any actual conspirator's attention, Amanda thought. Kathy had let Amanda know that she hadn't liked Nemo's appearance or the way he just slipped away. The fact that he had left in a police car had heavy unknown implications. Kathy even led some of the other girls on a search of the grounds for Susan—presumably for her raped and discarded body. But Sunday after supper, around sunset, Susan showed up to water the kitchen garden. She said she hadn't missed an evening's soaking. She thought the tomato plants were doing well.

The news of Susan's return passed quickly throughout the house, and everyone gathered on the back veranda to hear her story. Amanda sat in a porch chair that Nemo must have moved there because beside it was an end table from the hall with a tin can on it filled with ashes and cigar butts. Susan didn't want to talk, but she was quizzed by her sister and the others. Where had she been? Why had she left? Her story came out haltingly, in pieces, as if she were making up each part of it as she was quizzed. She hadn't felt right sleeping in the house with just a man there. But no, he hadn't done anything weird, though he did drink and asked her a lot of questions. Oh, she had stayed out in the barn. At night she would sneak back to water the garden and get food from the kitchen, canned stuff, crackers and peanut butter. She just wanted to

JOHN ENRIGHT

avoid him, leave him alone. He would sit on the kitchen veranda as if watching for her, so she hid out.

Morgan asked her about the car. Oh, that. It got stuck when she tried to leave to get more supplies. She had slept there because it was warm and secure, no harm. She was afraid the man would get mad at her for getting his car stuck, so she hadn't wanted to talk with him. She had watched him leave in the sheriff's car. Was he under arrest? What had he done? Who had eaten all the greens from the garden?

"Did he rape you? Molest you?" Kathy wanted to know. "Is that why you are hiding, acting this way?"

"Really, Kathy," Amanda said. "She's already said no to that."

"Who is she trying to protect? Your brother? You?"

"I think she is trying to protect herself," Morgan said—she had been standing in the kitchen door listening—"against charges of grand theft auto. Done that before, Susie?"

"There weren't any eggs or bread or cheese or milk in the house. I was just going to the store. It was a nice car to drive."

The ladies on the veranda drifted away to their rooms.

***

When he was younger, Dominick had occasionally fantasized about actually settling in some place he would stop at along the way. If it happened—it hadn't yet—it would be accidental. Some combination of people and circumstances would just keep him from moving on, and after a while he would realize that a life had accumulated around him and that his need to keep moving had lessened. Those things called roots would grow, and he would wake up one morning in a house where he had paid for the washer and dryer, with some pressing home repair job demanding his attention. It was a fantasy never realized. He would cruise a new town, imagining he lived there, pausing in front of houses that appealed to him, wondering what that would be like. But he always moved on. He hadn't met the combination that could stop him. And so it was with Catskill.

Deputy Dave just dropped Dominick and his bag at the curb on Main Street downtown. It was a fine midday Saturday in the middle of the tourist season. Downtown was busy. There was some sort of art thing happening, but Dominick lucked out. On Main Street he found a taxicab, a converted aging Cadillac, whose driver, an equally aging black man, looked like a longtime local. Dominick explained his situation to him. His name was Vernon. Vernon knew of a B & B that might have a room available, and he knew a guy over in Hudson who had a big tow-truck rig and could probably get his car out. Dominick took the room—there had been a cancellation—and before heading over to Hudson he and Vernon had lunch at a cafe downtown. They found Vernon's buddy in Hudson, but he couldn't get to Dominick's car before Monday.

Dominick couldn't tell him where the car was, which raised some suspicion on the tow truck guy's part, and Dominick had to explain that he was just visiting and someone had borrowed his car and got stuck. He said Deputy Sheriff Dave could tell him how to find it.

"Would that be old man Hetzel's kid?" the tow truck guy asked Vernon.

"The same," Vernon said.

"The car ain't stolen, is it?" the tow truck guy asked Dominick.

"No, it's mine. My registration is in the glove compartment."

"It will need some cleaning out if it's that buried. I'll bring it back here and give you a call. Keys?"

"All I can say is that I hope they are in it." Dominick gave him the phone number of the B & B. He had to borrow a phone book to look it up.

The next few days Dominick got to spend not being captivated by Catskill. Oh, it was a nice enough little town, but if he hadn't been stranded there he wouldn't have stayed for more than a meal. Late Monday afternoon the tow truck guy called. He had gotten the car out and brought it back to his garage. The keys had been in the ignition, but the battery was dead. It was packed with mud up to the floorboards. The exhaust pipes were clogged. It would take him a while to clean her up. Say, after lunch tomorrow she'd be ready. Dominick wondered what all this would cost him, but didn't ask. Early Tuesday afternoon he got Vernon to give him a ride back over to Hudson and picked up the car, which had a new smell—part dirt, part chemical. The bill was big, but he paid it without questioning.

There was just one lane now where the road to the Van Houten place had washed out, but it was open. When he got to the house, there were no cars parked in the driveway. On the back seat he had found a blanket and pillow. He took them into the house. As he was about to call out hello, he heard a door slam in the back. Still carrying the blanket and pillow because he didn't know where to put them, he went up the stairs to his old room. The door was open. Morgan was sitting at the desk, a laptop open in front of her. Her back was to him. "That you, Dominick? Welcome back."

"I came to get my things," he said. He felt foolish standing there holding a pillow and blanket like some sort of refugee.

Morgan shut down what she was doing and closed the laptop. "Car okay?" she asked, turning around.

"Four hundred dollars later."

"Ouch. That's an investment. Why not stay another day or two as compensation? Maybe you can even get an apology out of Susan."

"She's back?" Dominick walked over to the bed and dropped the blanket and pillow there.

"Oh yeah, she's back. Probably gone back into hiding now that you're here. Those from your car?"

"Yes."

"She was sleeping there. I think she likes you. How many girls steal a guy's car just so they can sleep in it?"

"I wouldn't know. You ever done it?"

"Honey, I've stolen better things than cars to sleep in. It's always a compliment. No, seriously, stay another day or two. You haven't even said but hello-good-bye to Amanda, and she needs to talk with you. You may not owe her that, but she needs it. She just lost her mother, for God's sake. And I'd like to show you at least some of what we want to do here, just to prove it's not all bullshit."

"That's all very good, Morgan, but . . ." Dominick couldn't come up with an immediate but. He was back in the light-filled room he had felt so comfortable in. He sat down on the bed.

"Where you going to go tonight? Back to some dumpy motel room?" Morgan asked. "And besides, you can help me out. I got a contractor coming out now to scope out the foundation job. He'll act more professional if there's a big white guy like you along for his inspection. You won't have to say anything, just come along."

Dominick noticed that he still had shirts hanging in Morgan's closet. Or had she hung them there? "Where would I stay?" he asked.

"Why, here, of course. I can bunk with Amanda, no problem. You want something to eat? Would you like some good leftover homemade rice and beans? Do you know anything about house foundations? Come on down to the kitchen." Morgan got up and left the room. Dominick followed her. As they headed down the staircase she said, "Drainage seems to be a big deal. I don't know why. The basement here is perfectly dry. You like your beans spicy? I'll add some heat. Those girls."

Dominick followed Morgan into the kitchen. "Yes, about those girls," he said.

"I like having a man in the house," Morgan said, getting things onto the stove. "For me a house is not a home without a man in it. How about a couple of tortillas with that? We finally went grocery shopping yesterday. You didn't leave us much."

The contractor arrived as Dominick was finishing his lunch. Morgan and he were discussing ways to cook catfish. Morgan introduced Dominick as their architect.

"Not from around here, are you?" the contractor said. Dominick had already forgotten his name. He looked like a contractor.

"No, the Washington area," Dominick said.

"Virginia. Saw your plates. Lots of preservation work down there I bet." As they toured the outside foundations of the house, the contractor made several attempts to draw Dominick into shop talk. Dominick just made positive sounds and let him talk.

On their way down the outside cellar stairs to the basement, Dominick held Morgan back to ask for the man's name again. "Bill," she said, "like what we'll get for this consultation." The man was making notes and taking measurements. He had some sort of laser gun that he flashed and consulted every now and then. Dominick wondered how much of that was show, but he said nothing. There were no electric lights in the basement, no windows. Morgan went off to find some flashlights, and Bill went back to his van for his own. Dominick stood on the basement's dirt floor at the edge of the light from the outside door and inhaled. It was an ancient smell, as familiar as it was foreign, the smell of another time. Morgan and Bill returned with lights.

"Dry as a pharaoh's tomb," Bill said. "No problem here. They knew how to build them back then, didn't they, professor?" Bill had decided to call Dominick professor. "I'd take a real close look at each of these beams, though," he said, aiming his flashlight along the ceiling. That's where your real problem's going to be. A hundred and eighty years is a long time for a floor beam."

Morgan had brought Dominick his own flashlight, and he wandered further into the dark cavern. Along one long roughhewn rock wall were lines of narrow plank shelves that once must have held put-up preserves, and there were large empty wood boxes for potatoes or turnips or apples. Further on he was surprised to find raised wooden platforms that looked like they could have been made for sleeping, and a short, crude three-legged stool. Beyond that chamber was another, empty except for a pile of metal barrel hoops lying one on top of another in the dust and dirt as if the barrel they had once held together had vanished from inside them.

"Dominick, we're going back up," Morgan called from somewhere behind him.

"Go ahead. I'll be along in a minute," he said. At the far end of this chamber was what looked to be a low door of unfinished timber set into the wall. There was a simple hammered metal lever latch. When he lifted the latch, the door swung slowly open on a push of warmer, fresher air that smelled more of the present. The beam from his flashlight revealed another long room, empty except for two old trunks, wooden and round-topped with metal hasps, set up on stone ledges along one wall.

"Dominick, are you alright?" Morgan's voice seemed far away.

"Coming," he called, and he closed and latched the door behind him. As he walked back he played his flashlight beam along the floor, where his footprints were all that had disturbed the dirt and dust for as long as it could remember.

Chapter 9

It was Morgan's idea, but Amanda approved. They would go out to dinner, the three of them. There was that Italian place run by Chinese up on 9W. Nemo was resting in Morgan's room. The others were not back from work yet, but would be soon.

"Your brother hasn't been fully exposed to them yet. I'm afraid they might spook him off," Morgan said. "I think this place may be growing on Captain Nemo. After that contractor left today, Nemo had a bunch of questions about the house. He sat out in that chair on the back porch and smoked a cigar and looked, swear to God, like he was to the manor born, surveying his holdings. I'll get him up. We'll go in his car."

Nemo was receptive, and they left just as the first of the girls' cars was pulling up to the house. Nemo drove. Amanda sat in the back. The car had a complicated smell—cigar smoke, leather upholstery, something earthy and strange, and something feminine, the hint of a fragrance like shampoo or lotion. Morgan sat in front and kept up a constant chatter with Nemo. Amanda leaned back and tuned them out.

To the manor born, that's what she said, as if you weren't. As if you are just a sharecropper, a renter, an unlanded house-flipper, itinerant riffraff. Why do you care what she thinks of you? Just look at her up there, sucking up to the master, flashing that . . . What is it but openness? What is it called in chemistry? Valence, yeah, valence. Flashing her valence, that she is a free attachable . . . thing. Look at her slap him on the shoulder as they laugh. That is your brother up there, not hers. Maybe she wants to fuck him. It's been a while since Morgan's last man, at least as far as you know. She would have to be on top. He more than twice outweighs her. Black on white, well, more chocolate on cream. You would like to watch, wouldn't you? Watch her slip his thing into her and ride him. It's been too long, girl. Why did you ever give up on that? Skin on skin, all your muscles aching to get to that one spot.

The meal was unmemorable, pasta in red clam sauce with red wine. Amanda had more than her usual one glass. Morgan and Nemo spent much of the meal telling anecdotes about Washington, a city both of them seemed to know well, and Amanda couldn't compete. They lingered at the table over coffee and aperitifs long after their plates had been removed. The restaurant was almost empty. Morgan was delaying their return to the house as long as possible. Amanda decided to get drunk. She wasn't driving. She ordered the quickest way she knew to get there, a Long Island Iced Tea—vodka, rum, gin, tequila, lemon and Coke—the express train.

It was Amanda who convinced them to stop for a nightcap at The Hill Top. Her inner voice was jabbering away, but she wasn't listening. She had never been inside The Hill Top, though she had passed it many times. It was a local hangout with as many pickup trucks and motorcycles as cars in the gravel parking lot. But, it being a weekday night, the parking lot wasn't crowded. The bar was full, but there was a choice of empty tables and they took one. A younger crowd—jeans and boots and tattoos. A waitress came over and took their order. There was country and western music playing, or maybe it was just bad rock and roll. What was the solvent in alcohol that wiped out years? Amanda felt like dancing. In the soft amber saloon light Morgan and Nemo sitting across from her looked like a much younger couple than they were. Even Amanda's hands looked young.

The Hill Top's decor, while minimal, was unique. It consisted primarily of items of women's underwear stapled to the ceiling above the back bar—many colored, fancy panties and bras like stalactites in a lingerie cave. "Beneath the unmentionables," Nemo called it. Amanda was tapping her foot to the music, sipping her drink—a draft beer now—and watching the young bucks at the bar. It was like a show on the Nature Channel: *"The young adult males, having been turned out from their mother's care, congregate together until rutting season when nature dictates that they compete against each other and the alpha males for procreative rights.*" Summertime garb—work shirts with the sleeves cut off, wifebeater tank tops in either white or black, biceps and attitude. They seemed most relaxed leaning on something.

"The earliest history of bars? Who knows?" Nemo was answering one of Morgan's constant questions. "They go back so far and were such a given that no one really paid them much attention. Fraternal gatherings with libations, no big deal. The archaeologists keep pushing back the date when alcohol became involved. You can buy ales now concocted from recipes derived from the residue found in cups from King Midas's tomb."

"Did they have gold in them?" Amanda asked.

"No, but they were spiced and probably sweet."

A young man had caught Amanda's nature-watching and strolled over from the bar. Maybe he was coming to ask her to dance; she could use that. He wasn't unattractive, though his smile was a little funny. "We don't get many of your type in here," he said. He was carrying a bottle of beer.

"What type is that?" Amanda asked, smiling, expecting some sort of compliment.

"We're not used to mixed company. Know what I mean?"

"No, I don't know what you mean," Amanda said.

"I mean we ain't got nothing against blacks per se, but black and white together is sort of strange to us. Where you from?"

"Diligence," Amanda said. "What's your problem?"

"No, no problem. I was just wondering if the lady'd like to dance," and he turned to Morgan. "Miss? I ain't never danced with a black girl before, and the guys at the bar bet me I wouldn't ask."

Morgan turned to Nemo. "What century is this?" she asked. Then she turned back to the guy still standing there. "Well, lover boy, you asked. Now go back and collect your bet."

"But I asked you to dance. There's another ten in it for me if you do. Come on, I'll buy you a drink."

"I think she already answered your question," Nemo said.

"Nobody's talking to you."

"I'll dance with you," Amanda said. "How's that?"

"No, I want to dance with the dinge, not you, mom. Come on." The guy made a grab for Morgan's arm, and she jerked it away.

"Fuck off," Morgan said.

"I'll buy you a drink."

"I think fuck off means good-bye," Nemo said, standing up.

"Stuff it, old man. What are you doing with this fine piece of ass anyway?"

When Nemo stood up he was much bigger than the young man. "Back off," was all he said. "Back off, please."

As the young man swung the bottle it spewed beer across Amanda and the table. The bottle shattered against Nemo's temple and he fell backwards. He took out an empty table and chairs behind him as he fell. It was a very loud noise. Now Morgan was on her feet, and she took a kick at the man's groin but caught him only on the knee. He was about to take a swipe at her with the broken neck of the bottle still in his hand when someone from the bar grabbed him from behind and pulled him away. Amanda went to her brother, who was sprawled out among the broken pieces of furniture. One half of his face was already painted with blood.

***

Without his reading glasses Dominick had trouble making out the name of the drug on the prescription bottle label, Oxy-something. His eyesight was blurrier than usual. Oxycodone maybe? He knew nothing about drugs, but Morgan said they would help. It was her prescription. There was only a handful of white tablets left in the bottle. He took two then lay back down. Whenever he changed elevations the room spun. He was back in Morgan's room, her bed. He tentatively touched the bandage on his throbbing left temple. He had never been clocked like that before. He vaguely remembered being helped to sit up on the floor of the saloon and the waitress coming with a wet towel to wipe the blood off his face. When she bent over him he could see her tits inside her blouse—nice young tits, no bra, in spite of all the empty bras dangling above the bar.

Morgan and Amanda had helped him to the car, where he talked them out of taking him to an emergency room. They couldn't agree on where the nearest one was anyway. Dominick had a phobia about hospitals. He had never been in one except to visit people dying. Amanda drove, and Dominick stretched out on the back seat, the outside world moving in pre-Copernican orbits around him. He pressed the blood-soaked towel against his forehead. If any of the other girls were up when they got home—all their cars were there—none of them bothered to pop out of their room to say hello. Morgan and Amanda had gotten him cleaned up in the bathroom. He had to sit on the closed toilet to hide his dizziness. Amanda went to find him a clean shirt while Morgan applied a butterfly bandage to his broken skin, then a larger gauze pad on top of that to absorb the blood that still seeped out. Ah, a night out with the girls. Always enjoyable.

Dominick had no idea what time it was. It was dark out. A lamp was lit on the bedside table. He had drifted off after they got him to bed. There was no clock in the room, and he didn't own one or a watch. Not a sound came from inside or outside the house. The table he had fallen on had done something to his back. It was just beginning to cramp up. One bright spot was that at least he hadn't hurt his hands by hitting anyone back. He couldn't even remember what the guy who hit him looked like. Years before, Dominick had learned how to put himself to sleep by slowing and deepening his breathing. The pills, whatever they were, seemed to help. Being exhausted helped as well. He dreamed about getting lost in a city he knew perfectly well and losing his luggage. He dreamt that Vernon showed up to help him.

In the morning he felt old. His back was stiff; his head throbbed. The room was bright, but there was still no sound inside the house. Sitting up brought on a dizzy spell, but it passed quickly. He went to the bathroom to take a piss, dutifully raising then lowering the seat. He ran cold water on his wrists and splashed some onto his old man's face. "Old man," that's what that kid had called him, very prophetic. Or is it properly prophecy when you then make what you prophesied happen? He needed a cup of coffee and some more of Morgan's white pills.

The bottle of pills was on the bedside table, and downstairs there was coffee still hot in the Mr. Coffee pot on the counter. From the thick look and smell of it as he poured himself a mug he judged it to be several hours old. There was also a note from Amanda: "We have to go to Albany on business. Back this afternoon. Go back to bed and stay there."

He took her advice, but after a while the pills kicked in and he felt better, at least the pain seemed less personal. He went back downstairs. Morgan had left the electric torches out on the counter by the kitchen door. He took the biggest one and went down the outside stairs into the cellar. He couldn't get those trunks off his mind. The trunks had looked as old as the house, and if someone had gone to the trouble of furtively hiding them they might hold something worth hiding. He had some trouble finding the room with the low door. The cellar was more of a maze than he had realized, or maybe he was just addled. But he did find it. Behind the door were the two trunks, draped in a gray blanket of undisturbed dust.

The hammered metal clasps on each of the trunks were closed but not locked. The trunks were made of cedar, were the type you saw at the foot of beds in the re-enactments of colonial homes. The first one he opened was half filled with carefully folded fabric, which when he pulled it out proved to be articles of clothing—hand-sewn and roughly tailored jackets and trousers of home-woven wool, unbleached muslin shirts and jerkins. Nothing fancy or fine—warm and worn nineteenth century work clothes. The second trunk was full with much the same contents, only here there were also women's clothes—linsey-woolsey Mother Hubbards and a nicely knitted woolen shawl. They were like costume trunks for a Quacker play, even the smell of them was from another time, camphor and cedar. Also in the second trunk, tucked against one wall, was a long leather case with papers inside and behind it a green-covered ledger. Dominick carefully replaced all the clothes and closed the trunks, latching them as he had found them, but he took the satchel of papers and ledger with him when he left. He couldn't replace the dust to hide his visitation. He relatched the door behind him.

When Dominick got back to Morgan's room his head was pounding again and his back muscles were competing having spasms. He took two more of Morgan's pills. All he had in his stomach was that one cup of coffee, and that couldn't be good, but he was too exhausted to do anything about it. He slipped his purloined finds into an outer zippered pocket of his garment bag and lay back down on the bed. He had bumped his bandaged forehead on the lintel of the low door when he exited, and it was bleeding again. Wasn't that always the way? Blows to bruises, sore spots attracting attacks? He fell asleep before he could find a comfortable position.

***

Denise was back. Her Bronco was parked in the driveway beside Nemo's Lexus when Amanda and Morgan got back from Albany.

"That's not good," Morgan said.

"I'll tell her," Amanda said.

"No, let me. I'll tell it so she will hear it loud and clear."

Morgan went on up to her room. Amanda went out to the kitchen porch with a glass of iced tea to sit in Nemo's chair there. It was such a beautiful day, the end of spring. Little brown birds, house wrens and sparrows, flitted back and forth from the garden to the gutters and eaves of the house, building nests that would have to be cleared out. For Amanda, back to nature meant the expense another season of neglect added onto bringing an old property back to saleable status. Nature was the enemy of real estate. Houses that sold well had been saved from nature and the history of decay. When you flipped a house you were selling the future not the past. Nobody actually lived in the past, especially people with money enough to buy a big house. Their past was what they were trying to escape. All obligations to memory ended when a place passed out of the family. Get real. Denise was history. Morgan and Amanda had agreed on that on the ride back.

Morgan came out to report that Nemo was asleep in her room and Denise's door was closed.

"Asleep or comatose?" Amanda asked.

"He got up to get himself a cup of coffee at some point and he was snoring. I guess unconscious people can snore. I never thought about it before. I found the rental agreement—just thirty days notice not sixty. The sooner the better, I say. We don't need their rent money any more and we don't need the hassle."

"There is the tax thing."

"We'll just keep it until someone figures out to take it away."

"Denise will make a stink," Amanda said. She dreaded confrontations.

"She's a skunk. She always gets her way by raising her tail and threatening to make a stink. Fuck her."

"She's just back from one of her convocations. She'll be filled with her Third Degree gas."

"Let her explode." Morgan came over and picked up the can with Nemo's cigar butts and ashes. "Talk about stinking," she said. She walked out into the garden and emptied the tin into one of the raised tomato beds. "Cuban compost," she called it and she went back inside. It only took a few minutes before one and then another and another of the little brown birds came down and pecked at the cigar butts, flying back to their nests trailing thin strands of tobacco.

✳✳✳

Morgan made the announcement at dinner with everyone there except Nemo. Amanda had taken a plate up to him in Morgan's room. Because serious renovation work on the house was about to begin they would all have to leave within thirty days. The party was over, at least at this address. No more rent was due. Their security deposits would cover the last month, but that didn't mean they could trash the place. It's been fine, but it was time to move on. Denise walked out before Morgan was finished, saying "I don't think so." '

Amanda followed Denise out of the kitchen, caught up with her as she started up the stairs. "Wait up, Denise. You knew this day was coming when you moved in. Well, that day is here. If you want to make it ugly, well, I guess you can, but it won't change the outcome." God, how she had come to dislike this woman. Amanda had always been slow to form dislikes. She prided herself on cutting others lots of slack. It was like food. She was an omnivore. Something had to be really yucky for her not to try it again. She had no allergies. People had to work at becoming unlikable. The list of people and things she disliked was very short. It took too much energy maintaining and feeding a hate list. She looked forward to erasing Denise from her life, moving on.

Denise stopped but didn't turn around. Amanda was at the foot of the stairs, looking up at her wide flat butt in her baggy jeans, her thick ankles and swollen feet stuffed into Crocs, the folds of fat on her back above and below the wide strap of her bra beneath her T-shirt, the back of her helmet haircut of unwashed graying hair.

"You don't get it, do you, you materialist whore?" Denise said without turning around. "There's no way you can win. The powers are aligned against you. This house is ours now, no matter what you think, no matter how many lawyers in fancy cars you bring in. Don't you know that if we did have to leave here I would have to burn the place to the ground, poison the well, and salt all the fields?"

"I'll bring in the sheriff if I have to, Denise."

"Just a charred hole in the ground. It will be our place or no place." Denise continued on up the stairs. The rest of the girls now came streaming out of the kitchen and brushed past Amanda, following Denise up the stairs.

Back in the kitchen Morgan was rinsing and piling dinner dishes in the sink. "They didn't even stay around to do their dishes," Morgan said. "Is today the 21st?"

"Yes. Why?'

"Solstice. Litha Sabbat either tonight or tomorrow. That's why Denise is back."

***

When Amanda brought his dinner up she apologized for not inviting him down to dine with and meet everyone, but they would be having a house meeting and he would just be bored and feel out of place. It was just as well. Dominick didn't feel up to socializing anyway, and if the rest of the girls were like the one he had met—Susan's sister Kathy—their company would not improve his condition. He heard them all come up as a troop after dinner and then there was a spate of doors opening and closing and the toilet flushing. As a professional houseguest Dominick had experienced many strange situations over the years. People who seemed quite normal in the outside world could become weirdly bizarre inside their personal caves. He had taught himself to ignore it as much as possible. Privacy meant a lot to him, too. But this was a new one. A house full of women with locks on their doors. He wondered how many miles of toilet paper they went through in a year.

Amanda had brought him a glass of wine with his plate. The glass and the plate were now empty. He would like a refill of the glass. He opened the door and stuck his head out into the hall. All quiet there; just voices from behind a door at the far end. He took his empty plate and glass and went down to the kitchen. Amanda and Morgan were seated together at the long table. They looked up surprised when he came in. Dominick added his dirty dish to an unwashed pile in the sink then turned to them with his empty glass. "Mas vino, por favor?"

"It walks and it talks," Morgan said.

"It sneaks up on people," Amanda added. "Feeling better, brother?"

"Not so good that another glass of wine wouldn't help."

"In the door," Morgan said, gesturing to the refrigerator, "an open chilled bottle of cheap Pinot Grigio waiting just for you."

Dominick refilled his glass and joined them.

"You know, that and one or two of those oxys I gave you can magically transform pain into pleasure." Morgan tapped his glass with a polished fingernail.

"I try to believe in magic," he said. "If it were true it would help explain so many things so easily."

"Save you a lot of time trying to figure things out for yourself, wouldn't it?" Morgan said.

"All that cause and effect work. Instead, just Shazzam! Look, you guys got a full house here, and, Morgan, I'm sure you'd like your room back. I'll be out of your hair tomorrow."

"Do you think you'll be well enough to drive?" Amanda asked. "You still look a little wobbly to me. You shouldn't fool around with concussions."

"Actually, it probably wouldn't be a bad time to get out of here, at least as far as Catskill or Hudson," Morgan said. "Just lousy timing. I'll tell you why. Not because you're not welcome here—you are—but because our little meeting tonight was to tell the girls that it was time for them to find another place to live, that we were moving ahead with the remodeling and they couldn't stay. Evicting folks is the hardest part of this job, but there's no avoiding it. So, tensions are running a little high tonight, and it could get a little . . . chaotic here. Nothing to do with you or with our proposal, just something that your sister and I have to deal with if we're going to move ahead on this. And we want you in on it. I had new corporation papers drawn up in Albany, with you and your sister as partners, vote determined by amount of investment. You've seen the place now. You can see its potential. All the pre-shovel stuff is done and paid for. We are ready to go. I've got a copy of the incorporation papers for you to look at. I want you to give our proposal your careful consideration, and, to be truthful, this probably won't be the best place for that in the next couple of days. We'll give you a ride into Catskill tomorrow, if you don't feel up to driving. Tonight just rest and stay in the room."

Chapter 10

Dominick was truly clueless. He just stood their like an idiot. His mouth was probably open. It was late. He had been studying the old papers and ledger he had taken from the trunk. The quill-pen writing was generally clear enough, but it was still old style script and slow going. Interesting stuff. He had come downstairs to borrow another glass of wine from the bottle in the fridge. The house seemed quiet. He thought he would sneak out onto the kitchen veranda and have a cigar with his nightcap.

As he came down the stairs to the front hall he noticed that the previously closed and locked sliding oak doors to what must be the front parlor were cracked open a foot, and an unsteady light and a woman's voice came through. Of course he stopped to look. The aroma was burnt sage and sandalwood incense. The wavering light came from candles spaced around the room. There was a ring of young women, a half dozen or so, all dressed in simple white shifts or dresses, seated cross-legged on the floor, facing inward, their heads bowed. They were seated far enough apart so that each with her arms fully extended could hold the hand of the girl on either side. There were three banners on the walls—of an Egyptian looking eye, a Celtic shield knot, and what looked like a disc inside two reversed crescent moons. There was a table with candles and a white and yellow altar cloth draped over it showing a pentagram inside a circle. In front of the table, holding up a binder so that she could read by the candle light from behind her, was a stout older woman in a forest green hooded cape and glasses.

What was it about prayers? They were always said in a false voice not used on any other occasion, the oral equivalent of a fancy italic typeface. She could have been reading Portuguese and he still would have known it was a prayer. But she was reading in English: "I am clothed with the deep cool wonder of the earth and the gold of the fields heavy with grain. By me the tides of the earth are ruled, all things come to fruition according to my season. I am refuge and healing."

Like a fool Dominick pushed the big door just a tad more open so that he could see more of the room. He was still holding his empty wine glass. The movement caught the green-hooded one's attention, and her head jerked down so she could see him through the tops of her bifocals. "Who goes there?" she said in a boldface sans-serif voice. "No one dares break the sacred circle."

The seated girls looked up and then followed her gaze to the door. "That's him," one of them said. The green-hooded one took of her glasses and put her book down on the altar, picking up what looked like a short legionnaire's sword.

"Sorry," Dominick said, "my mistake. Carry on." And he stepped back into the hallway, sliding the door shut. He was quickly back in his room, without his glass of wine or cigar. No one followed him. He locked the door behind him. Who knew how ceremonial that sword was? He felt very foolish. As a boy he had once walked in on his mother as she was being "serviced" by one of her men on the living room couch. The man was on his knees on the floor in front of her, his face buried between her wide-spread legs making muffled noises. Marjorie had just stared at Dominick, neither upset nor embarrassed. She had just raised her hand from the back of the man's head and with a little gesture told him to get lost. He felt a similar way now, a way only women could make him feel. Damn them.

✳✳✳

Amanda stayed in her room in the morning. It was a Friday. Some of the girls had left for their jobs; but there were still a few other cars beside Denise's and Nemo's parked in the driveway. Amanda just wasn't up for the next inevitable skirmish with Denise, back on the same kitchen battlefield. Later, maybe, when she had had time to regroup. She had Morgan bring her up a cup of coffee. Nemo must still be asleep. She had noticed that the lights in his room had stayed on late the night before.

"Let him sleep," Morgan said. "Maybe with a good night's sleep he'll feel recovered enough to drive. Let him go. Right now we got our hands full with the witch goddess. I'll catch up with Nemo later. He doesn't need to see this. It could only turn him off."

"By the way," Amanda said, sipping her coffee, "you didn't mention to me drawing up new articles of incorporation. If Nemo and I are partners, what are you?"

"Secretary/Treasurer and corporate counsel, just your servant, ma'am."

"I'd like to see them, the new articles, I mean. Do you think he'll go for it?"

"I haven't the slightest. He's a strange one alright. He's smart, but he's somewhere else altogether. He's like the original lonely guy, only he doesn't know it. Well, look who's here." Morgan was looking out the window at the driveway. "Deputy Dog."

Amanda came over to the window. There was the Deputy Sheriff getting out of his big square vehicle with the rack of lights on top. There was a big number twelve painted on its roof. As they watched, Denise appeared and hurried out to talk to him. They couldn't hear what was said, but Denise gestured toward the house several times and pointed at Nemo's black car. The officer made a motion with his hand above his head, as if asking about someone's height, then he ducked halfway back into his car and came out with a microphone on a long cord and spoke into it. Then he leaned back in and hung up the mike. He shut the car door, adjusted his belt with his pistol and other cop equipment on it, and followed Denise out of sight toward the front veranda. He wasn't wearing a hat. He was going bald—a tonsure of pale skin showing on top.

"Action central," Morgan said. "The bitch has brought in reinforcements. Stay here. I'll deal with this." Amanda followed Morgan as far as the top of the stairs, so that she could watch and listen. "Hello, Dave. What's up?" Morgan asked as she went down the stairs.

"I'd like to speak to the owner of the black Lexus parked outside, ma'am."

"He's in her room," Denise said.

"What seems to be the problem?" Morgan acted as if Denise wasn't there.

"There has been a complaint, ma'am. I need to talk with him."

"He's resting right now. He suffered a rather nasty blow to his head the other day and is recuperating. Can't I help?"

"Don't trust her," Denise said.

"I don't think so, ma'am. If you'll just wake him up. I'll have to take him in for some questioning."

"Why are you dealing with her? Just go get him." Denise pushed the officer's arm, which, Amanda noted, he did not appreciate. Amanda had always had a soft spot for men in uniform. Not that uniforms were sexy or anything—they weren't—but a sort of sympathy for a man who would put one on and go out into the public. Uniforms and heroes went together. Without his uniform that man down there would be no one at all—just a slight, pale, balding, not quite so young man standing in the hallway. With his uniform he was the polished focal point of all attention and the morning light. It took a certain kind of unironic man to dress up like a hero.

"What's this all about, Dave?" Morgan asked, going down to the bottom stair. "Would you like a cup of coffee? It's a long drive out here."

"No, thank you, ma'am. I've had my coffee for the day. If you would just ask him to come down."

"Dave, do you have a warrant or anything, a reason to be here? I mean, I'm his lawyer, I have to ask."

"No, ma'am, no warrant, but there has been a serious complaint."

"I'll get him," Morgan said and headed back up the stairs.

The officer turned to Denise and asked, "And is the complainant here? She'll have to come in as well."

Morgan stopped and turned around. "And who might the complainant be?"

"Why Susan, of course, that poor traumatized thing," Denise said. "I'll fetch her, officer." Denise came quickly up the stairs, brushing past Morgan and then Amanda at the top.

"And the complaint is?" Morgan asked the officer.

"Rape, ma'am."

Morgan was silent. She nodded her head slowly. "I'll bring him right down, Dave. I'll be going in with you"

"We don't give lifts to lawyers, ma'am."

Amanda followed Denise down the hall. She stopped at one of the bedroom doors with a padlock and went to unlock it. "Don't interfere, Amanda, or I will see that you are charged with harboring a fugitive and obstruction of justice."

"But Susan said nothing like that happened."

"What did you expect her to say? Poor girl, trapped here with him and no way out, no way to call for help. Why do you think she went into hiding?" Denise pulled the padlock off and went into the room, slamming the door behind her.

Morgan was knocking on the door of her room back at the head of the stairs. "That's strange. It's locked," she said.

Then they heard Nemo say, "Hold on. Who is it?"

"Me, Morgan. What's with the lock?"

The door opened. "Forgot I locked it. There was a strange woman with a sword in the house last night. None of my business, of course, but now I know why every door here has a lock. Didn't mean to lock you out of your own room. Sorry."

Morgan followed Nemo into the room. Amanda stayed in the hallway. She was quickly coming to a boil. She rarely got mad, but when she did she had a tendency to lose control. It was like a switch, a red fire alarm that someone had to break the glass to get to and throw, but once thrown it couldn't turn itself off. She watched the door down the hall that Denise had entered. *Obstruction of justice! She will have* **me** *charged? Harboring a fugitive! After the year I've sheltered her and her tribe of misfits that no one else would even think of renting to? That unmitigated bitch. This is it. The last straw, the final insult. Accusing my brother, using my brother!* When the door opened Denise came out leading Susan by the upper arm. With them were Kathy and two of the other girls, a proper squad. They had to go past Amanda to get to the head of the stairs.

"What is going on here?" Amanda demanded, scanning the group. Then she went for Denise, "How dare you drag my brother down to your level." She got her hands onto Denise before the three other girls grabbed her and her arms. Susan broke free of Denise's grasp and stumbled sideways. The girls pushed Amanda back toward the wall, but she managed to get a leg out and trip Denise as she headed for the top of the stairs. She went down with a satisfying thud. Amanda tossed the girl on her right arm aside. The one on the other side was pulling her hair.

"Officer, officer!" Denise was yelling from the floor.

Amanda got in another good kick, catching Denise in the kidneys. Then she was grabbed from behind by her brother—his long arms around her midriff lifting her off her feet—and pulled back into Morgan's room. Morgan slammed the door behind them.

"End of round one," Nemo said, putting her down.

"What was that all about?" Morgan asked.

"I do not believe this. She is accusing my brother, who is nothing to her, of a felony to get at me? If I had a gun I would shoot the bitch. No jury would convict me. I'd be doing the world a favor. God damn it, Dominick, I am so sorry I got you involved in this."

He was still holding her. "Down, big fella."

She hadn't been held in a very, very long time. God, his arms were big. They almost made her feel petite. Somehow he had turned off the switch. She could feel her rage seeping out. "Thanks," she said, and she laid a hand on top of his arm. "I don't know what came over me."

"The Gaelic word for that state translates roughly as warp spasm," Dominick said, and he let her go. "Was your father Irish by any chance?"

"He was," Amanda said. "Everyone called him Mick."

"Wait here," Morgan said. "I'll carry a white flag out there and see what's happening."

***

Well, what could Dominick say? It was a new experience. The charges were so bogus and unprovable that there was no reason to get excited about it. Not that it wasn't a pain in the ass being treated as a felony suspect, but it was different. That sure was one screwed-up household.

The scene at the house had been a burlesque from the get-go. Deputy Dave was out-numbered. He had called for backup, but it took them a while to get there. Susan took off, and her sister and the other girls had to go find her and bring her back. Deputy Dave came up to Morgan's room to check that Dominick and Amanda were there and told them to stay there. He told Amanda to stay away from Denise, who—uninjured—wanted Amanda arrested for assault. He couldn't leave before backup arrived because he had to take both Dominick and Susan in—Dominick to be questioned and Susan to file a formal complaint and be rape-tested. Morgan had to point out that a test would be pretty pointless, seeing as the supposed attack had occurred more than a week before and who knew where Susan had been or what she had been up to since then. Deputy Dave didn't want to take them both in together in his vehicle. That didn't seem right—accuser and accused sharing the back seat of a squad car. Also, seeing as Denise claimed Susan had told her the attack took place in the back seat of Dominick's car, the car would have to be brought in for crime scene tests, so he would need another officer to drive the Lexus. Morgan told Dominick that she could tell Deputy Dave didn't know what he was going to do about Amanda, which probably meant nothing. There were just too many women and too many things going on. And the police radio in his vehicle kept squawking, and he kept running out there to answer it. Pretty soon his nice neat khaki uniform showed large sweat circles in the armpits and down the middle of his back.

Deputy Dave's help finally arrived: a regular squad car with two officers, a man and a woman, dressed in identical uniforms Dominick noted—one style fits all egos. Everyone was parceled out to separate vehicles. Dominick went with Deputy Dave; Susan—recaptured— went with the female officer in the squad car; and the male officer dove Dominick's car. A regular little caravan headed down to the county road, with Morgan and Amanda in her old Chevy taking up the rear and trying to keep up. Deputy Dave and Dominick had nothing to say to one another. Dominick doubted Susan would be saying anything to her escort. The guy driving the Lexus was probably trying to find some AM station he liked. Only in the Chevy would there be a conversation going on.

Having had plenty of time waiting, Dominick was as prepared as possible. He had washed and shaved and put on his most comfortable clothes. Morgan had changed the bandage on his brow, which was now a white patch in the middle of a spreading off-purple bruise. He had filled his pocket cigar case with Romeo y Julietas and slipped it into his windbreaker pocket along with his lighter. He had packed and zippered shut all his luggage, which was now stowed in Amanda's trunk. He had swallowed the last two of Morgan's big white pills. What he had forgotten to do was eat, and his stomach was now grumbling loudly in protest.

"Officer Hezel, are you by any chance hungry, thirsty?"

"What's your problem?" Deputy Dave asked not turning around, which was good because he was speeding and the road here was a series of curves.

"I was just wondering if you were as famished as I am," Dominick said, bracing himself as the van leaned away from another turn.

"Sure. What of it?"

"Well, I recall a drive-thru fast-food place this side of Catskill. How about just pulling in there quickly so we can pick something up before getting to town? I haven't eaten today, haven't even had a cup of coffee. I'm sure you could use something yourself after that scene back there. I'll buy."

Deputy Dave concentrated on his driving for a while. "Well, it is about time for my lunch break. But just the drive-thru. No getting out of the vehicle and no funny stuff."

The drive-thru at the McDonald's was empty when their four-car caravan pulled in. Dominick got a fish fillet sandwich and a coffee. Deputy Dave got something that involved many wrappers and a large beverage with a straw. The three other cars behind them all stopped and ordered things. Then they all parked side by side in the front parking lot. No one got out of their cars. It was a strange sort of all-American picnic—seven people in four vehicles, sitting silently, watching the traffic pass on the highway in front of them, chewing, sipping, swallowing, lost in their own thoughts or lack thereof. The fish sandwich was fine if you ate it fast. The coffee was hot and satisfying. For some reason Dominick wondered what Susan had ordered. Wasn't it strange how her coached accusation had somehow made them a couple? In all seven of their minds somewhere was the picture of Dominick and Susan having sex in the back seat of his car.

Morgan insisted, as his attorney, on sitting in on Dominick's questioning. He didn't mind. She never really said anything, just sat there and scribbled some notes now and then. But Dominick was sure her presence did alter the tenor and content of the detective's questioning. Deputy Dave had turned him over to a plain-clothes detective whose name was Dutch sounding and Dominick immediately forgot. Dominick answered his questions, gave his version of his brief encounter with Susan, denied ever laying a hand on her or even contemplating it. He told about her spending the night on the floor of his room, but neglected to mention her smoking marijuana. Why complicate things? Morgan had reminded him earlier about not volunteering any information or voicing any opinions or speculations. Back to name, rank, and just the facts ma'am. The detective didn't have Susan's formal complaint yet, so he didn't have that many specific questions to ask.

"You say she took your car, but you never reported it stolen." The detective was trying to fill in the time-line. "Why was that?'

"Well, first of all I had no way of reporting it. Secondly, at the time I figured she had just taken it to try and get to the store to buy some supplies. And thirdly, the car wasn't stolen. It was just stuck in the mud somewhere nearby."

"You didn't know where it was stuck in the mud?"

"No, hadn't the slightest."

"You never visited the vehicle while it was stuck in the mud?"

"I didn't even know it was stuck in the mud at the time."

"What were you doing out there in the first place?"

"I was visiting my sister, who owns the property."

"What goes on out there, anyway? Some sort of school or commune sort of thing or what?"

"I wouldn't know," was all Dominick could honestly say. "I was just visiting my sister."

Someone came to the door of the small investigation room where the three of them were seated at a table and motioned to Detective Dutch to come out. When he came back in he said he would like to continue the conversation but after he'd had the chance to review the victim's statement and the forensics from the car. It was Friday afternoon. He couldn't keep Dominick until Tuesday or so when all that would be completed, so he would release him on his own recognizance with his and his counsel's assurance that he would return for additional questioning.

"My car?" Dominick asked.

"Impounded. You are to have no contact with the complainant or other witnesses or parties to the complaint, which means you will have to find a place to reside other than your sister's until this is resolved. I'll need a number where you can be reached."

"But I don't know where I will be," Dominick said.

"A cell phone number will suffice."

"But I don't own one," Dominick said, remembering the one he'd left on the counter in the Tavernier Key condo.

"I'll give you my number," Morgan spoke up. "I'll assure his return."

The detective was giving Dominick a suspicious look. "You do not own a cell phone?"

Dominick shrugged. "I've never needed one before."

"Don't leave the county," was all he said. He made a note on his pad.

In the parking lot outside the sheriff's headquarters it was a fine warm summer afternoon. Dominick felt glad to be alive. He hadn't wanted to admit to himself that he might again have had an anxiety attack of some sort if they had put him in a cell over night. Now he didn't have to concern himself with suppressing that fear. He lit up a cigar. It tasted wonderful. "Where to?" he asked Morgan. "Let's have a drink somewhere, and I could use a proper meal. Where's Amanda?"

"Beats me. Probably already having a drink somewhere herself. Hold on." Morgan pulled her little gizmo out of her purse and touched a few buttons. Dominick walked off a ways; he always felt strange listening to other people's conversations, even if they didn't seem to mind. It was a privacy thing—his privacy. There were appropriate blue birds, well jays anyway, flitting through trees on the street below, a block of age-blackened brick warehouses with boarded-up windows, the geriatric rear end of the town sagging down to the edge of a deserted still waterway. Ah, history.

"Amanda says she went shopping. She'll come back to get us," Morgan said, putting her phone thing back into her purse as she came over. "Well, I guess little Susie blew her interview. Good girl."

"Why do you say that?" Dominick asked, exhaling a thin contrail of smoke followed by a perfect smoke ring.

"Because even county mounties know enough not to let a felony suspect loose if there is anything like a real case against him. I'll bet Susie refused the physical exam and either purposefully forgot or inadvertently screwed-up the script Denise had cooked up for her."

"Oh," Dominick said. "In which case what would be the appropriate present, chocolates or flowers?"

"I think a couple of lottery tickets should do it, or a pack of rolling papers."

"She uses a pipe," Dominick said.

Morgan gave him a funny look. "Now how would you know that?"

Dominick said nothing, just puffed on his cigar and watched the blue jays chasing off gray catbirds from their territory.

Chapter 11

It was still the same, that zone. The end zone she called it, where she could do her little victory dance all alone. It was a forbidden zone, but she had passed over into it again the other night with those Long Island Teas. It had been nineteen months since her last total transgression. Now Amanda sought it out again, the ethanol touchdown. For more than s year and a half she had spent every day consciously not drinking, until that first night at Marjorie's house with Nemo. But since that taste the old desire had come back strong, and now here she was, sitting alone in a Catskill saloon, sipping a Wild Turkey and Coke on the rocks, trying to get to that zone again where nothing else mattered besides being there. The first thought to shed was that it was a mistake going there. She ordered another drink. Another good thing about the zone was that the voice could rarely reach her there.

But a jingle version of "Für Elise" was coming from deep inside her purse, and she dug out her cell phone. It was Morgan. She and Nemo were through with the police and they were wondering where she was. Where was she? Shopping, she said, but she didn't say for what. For a comfy cocoon, for a world of just private thoughts. "I'll come get you," she said. It seemed like a very long sentence. She didn't rush her new drink. She took her time. They could wait a bit longer. She needed more time alone. She was thankful that the bartender and the few other patrons in the bar—all male on a summer afternoon, watching a baseball game—had left her alone. She guessed she was broadcasting that the only companionship she wanted was her glass. But when she went to pay the bartender for her last drink, he said it was already paid for. The gents down the bar had told him put it on their tab.

"Thank them for me, would you?" she said. It was time to go. Amanda liked Catskill. It was a real town. Sure, on its outskirts there was the usual modern American automobile ghetto of neon lights and parking lots, chain stores and fast-food drive-ins; but the riverfront town itself, Main Street and the steep, irregular residential streets above it, had retained a dignified, working-class charm. It was clean; it was neat; it had its pride in tact. It was the county seat. Everyone seemed to know one another. One problem the town did have was no bars. Amanda may have been on the wagon as long as she'd lived here, but that didn't mean she hadn't scoped-out every place she could fall off of it. There really were just the country club—please—and this place, Mickey J's, also on the edge of town.

Amanda had always thought that she was a better driver drunk than sober, up to a certain point of inebriation. Other people agreed that sober she wasn't a very good driver—simultaneously impulsive and absent-minded. But after a few drinks she enjoyed the game of it more and so paid more attention. She thought of it as dancing with the traffic, with the added attention incentive of avoiding the cops. She had never gotten a DUI, and god knew that back in the day she did D while UI. She thought it funny that she was driving to the police station. Maybe she should turn herself in when she got there. Morgan had said it was still possible that she could be charged with assaulting Denise, even if the deputy had chosen to ignore the witch's whining.

The one chunk of downtown Catskill that had been yanked into the late previous century from the one before it was the block-square Greene County government office building on Main St. At least it was brick and simple and not much taller than the other Main Street facades, but its century—the twentieth—was out of sync with all its neighbors. Around the back was the sheriff's office parking lot and entrance, like the emergency room entrance of a hospital. Morgan was there, waiting for her at the curb, but no Nemo. "Where's Nemo?" Amanda asked as she pulled up.

"Yonder," Morgan said, indicating with her eyes the far end of the parking lot, where Nemo stood, cigar in mouth, hands clasped behind his back, looking out at the old buildings along Catskill Creek. "We got to drop him somewhere. I want to get back to the house. I don't trust Denise there alone."

Amanda gave two long honks on her horn to get Nemo's attention.

"What are you doing? Stop that!" Morgan said.

"Just getting him over here so we can leave."

"Laying on the horn in front of the sheriff's office? Shit, woman. Have you been drinking?"

"Just trying to get his attention."

Nemo had turned and waved and was strolling in their direction.

A deputy came out to the sidewalk to see what the honking was about.

"Get out of the driver's seat," Morgan said. "Scoot over."

"What? Why? You can't drive."

"Just move, now."

The deputy came over to the car. "Ladies?"

"Just trying to get our driver's attention, officer. He walked off to smoke a cigar. Here he comes now."

"Smoke a cigar? He can't do that here. This is county property, smoke free."

"I believe that's why he moved away," Morgan said.

"It's still county land," the deputy said.

Nemo walked up to the car. The cigar had somehow disappeared.

"Oh, it's that rapist guy," the deputy said. "You can't park here, Mac."

"We were just leaving, thank you, officer," Morgan said. And as she brushed past Nemo to get in the back seat she said just loud enough for the deputy not to hear, "You drive, don't ask."

Nemo just nodded and went to get in the driver-side door. The deputy stopped him. "Hey, Mac, you know what they do to rapists in the county jail here? The other inmates form a circle with him in the middle and they make him jack-off till he can't do it anymore, then longer. Nobody likes perverts up here."

"Sounds appropriately peer inspired," was all Nemo said as he got in and drove away.

Nemo drove them to the bed and breakfast where he had stayed when his car was being fixed, but they were full for the weekend, a wedding party. Morgan went in and convinced the lady to call around to see what else might be available. The best she could come up with was a hotel room over in Hudson, but all they had left was a smoking room. "I told her he'd take it," Morgan said when she got back to the car where Amanda was listening to an oldies station. Nemo had stayed behind to use the lavatory.

"Do you think we could get your brother to bring charges that Susan had stolen his car?" Morgan asked.

"I doubt it. Not unless he had to for some reason. Why?"

"I just feel like a counterattack is in order."

"But they let him go." Amanda turned down the radio.

"For the time being, thanks to Susan not giving them enough to hold him on."

"Then why get her in trouble?"

"Denise moved Susan out as a pawn. I could toss her back at her."

"Toss whom back at whom?" Nemo asked. Neither of them had seen him come back to the car.

"Susan at the witch," Morgan said, "the truth against a lie. You didn't rape her, but she did steal your car."

"Nix to that," Nemo said. "This will blow over, and the kid's already in enough trouble if they decide to charge her with making a false accusation."

"Never happen," Morgan said, "not on a she-said-he-said sex case. Reeks of blaming the victim. But if you say no, then no it is. I'll think of some other way to get back at Denise."

"Am I still designated driver here?" Nemo asked. He was leaning forward at the driver's side window.

"At least until we get across the bridge and out of the county," Morgan said.

"I am not that drunk," Amanda said. She felt like driving.

"I know where that hotel is," Morgan said. "I'll give you directions."

Actually, Amanda enjoyed the ride. She rarely got to ride shotgun and just watch the scenery go by, look up side roads and into yards, look out at the river as she crossed over it. From the bridge up to Hudson was a ten minute drive through an antique countryside well worn by centuries of human use. The road followed a route established by horses and wagons not automobiles. The hotel was toward the back of the old brick downtown, across a railroad track. They left Nemo and his luggage there and headed right back across the river to Diligence. Morgan was antsy for combat. Amanda was happy to drive. She turned up her oldies station and let Morgan stew.

***

Dominick copied the entire passage out longhand into his notebook:

All those laws which are now in force admitting the right of slavery are therefore before God utterly null and void, being an audacious usurpation of Divine prerogative, a daring infringement on the law of nature, a base overthrow of the very foundations of the social compact . . . and a presumptuous transgression of all the holy commandments.

Nobody wrote like that anymore. The pages and papers that Dominick had taken from the trunk were spiced with such pieces of hyper-rhetoric. This one was a quote written into what Dominick took to be the draft of a sermon, quoting someone named Garrison in a so-called "Declaration of Sentiments." There were newspaper clippings as well, from publications with names like the *Liberator* and *Friend of Man*, all dated from the late 1830s and '40s, that also sounded mainly like scripts for sermons or speeches. Such respect and care those authors took with the language, as if being handed a finely crafted sword to wield. It was the language, mainly, that hooked Dominick's attention—the precision of grammar, the care taken with turning a phrase. If you could filter out the religious hyperbole—that fallacious appeal to authority—these were speakers who loved their native tongue enough to find music in even the most necessary statements. Maybe it had to do with writing with a quill pen and having to think out and rethink out every sentence before committing it to the page. Surely they didn't normally talk this way. Back then there had still been that separation between the spoken and the written word, a low and high language, speech and sacrament, in an age when oratory was still an art form and the best of it sounded like the written word, like scripture. Some of the pages ended with the initials VVH. At first he thought it was WH, then he came upon a letter addressed to the Rev. Vestal Van Houten and realized his mistake.

His room at the St. George Hotel was not a cell—he had the key to the door—but it wasn't much bigger than one. It also reeked of stale cigarette smoke, a smell Dominick found offensive. He had immediately turned off the AC and opened the second-floor window, which looked out on a green dumpster in a brick alley, and lit up a Churchill. He did not like staying in hotels. It was like joining a statistical class with whom he wanted nothing else in common. A house of strangers, and let's keep it that way. So he was glad for the documents from the trunk; they gave him somewhere else to go for the evening.

He did stroll out for dinner. Hudson's main drag, Warren Street, was just a block away, and he found a barbeque joint. He had forgotten how awful he looked with the spreading bruise, now green and yellow around the edges, and the again bloodstained bandage. They gave him a table where no one could see him. The waiter was a swish, one of those gays on parade. "Ouch," he said when he saw Dominick's forehead, "now that's a nasty owie."

"An accident," Dominick said. "I survived." He survived the meal as well.

The green-covered ledger started with pages of cryptic accounting—dates and times of "arv" and "dep" and brief phrases: "Mother & Children," "left for K," "midnight pursuit." It went on for pages and years. The back of the ledger was filled with prose passages in different hands. Dominick set it aside for another day. He slept well, awakened just once by the rumbling rhythm of a railroad train sneaking past as slowly and silently as possible, seemingly just outside his still open hotel window, right through the middle of town in the dead of night. It was a comforting sound.

The next day he lazed in his room reading and copying and he strolled around Hudson. There was some sort of Hudson River School Art Festival going on, and Hudson was crowded with visitors. The shops and eateries here were more upscale than those in Catskill on the other shore, and the tourists were more obnoxious, more of the type who treat a destination as an amusement park rather than as someone else's home. On this side of the river, day visitors could take the train up from New York or down from Albany, a different crowd. Dominick noticed that the once ubiquitous badge of the tourist—the camera around the neck—was a thing of the past. Now folks just held up their cell phones—or something similar and equally small—to snap their photos (were they still called photographs?) of each other or themselves as proof that they were there, somewhere, once. An electronic memory image, nothing actual or substantial. Something virtual—in their term—something that existed not in fact or form but only in essence or effect. Unreal, in other words, as unreal as personal memories, and as fleeting. Substitutes for memory. Speak, digital cloud.

Further out toward the edge of town from his hotel, beyond the reach of tourists, was a local's saloon, the Wunder Bar, a neighborhood joint from anywhere in America, half filled with its regulars. Dominick was the sole outsider. It was late, close to midnight. He had left his room and the hotel when he heard a train approaching and went out to watch it creep past through the park across the street, a string of mixed freight cars, one carrying cattle who looked out at him with, yes, cowed expressions.

In the bar he noticed that all the women wore dangling earrings larger than their ears. He ordered a draft and a shot of Jameson's. At the entrance end of the bar was an anomalous couple sitting alone. They didn't belong together. Not just that she was black and he was white and that she was at least ten years older than the young man, but that Dominick doubted from the way they acted that they even knew each other's names. She was there to eat. The bartender didn't know the guy, but he knew the woman well enough to lean across the bar and give her a kiss. She ordered a glass of white wine; he ordered a coke. They spent most of their time staring at the little bright-screened gizmos in their hands or holding them up against their ears, ignoring one another. She ordered a bowl of chili. There was something about the way the guy acted. Then it struck Dominick—the dude was her latest john and she had conned him into buying her an after-trick meal. The longer the guy sat there, sipping his Coke, the antsier he became to leave; but she was enjoying her chili and her second glass of wine, her time off from work. The young guy was being naively polite, waiting for her to finish the meal he was paying for. When they left they walked off in opposite directions.

By Sunday Dominick was feeling antsy himself. He wasn't used to being carless and trapped. In New York, New York, it was one thing not to have a car, but in Hudson, New York, it was something else. It was a perfect summer day. He wanted to get out, but the town now bored him—another place he didn't belong. He found the scribbled phone number of his Catskill cabbie, Vernon, and called him. Vernon didn't work on Sundays, but for that reason he wasn't busy. He accepted Dominick's offer to pay him as a tour guide for the day.

Vernon showed up in his mature Cadillac after lunch, and they went for a ride into the country. When Vernon asked what Dominick wanted to see, he said, "History. Just show me some history." Vernon nodded and headed south out of town, down the river road. Their first stop was Olana, the bizarre villa built by the painter Francis Church overlooking the valley he had immortalized through gross exaggeration. The parking lot and grounds were packed with art fest tourists. The same was true for the painter Thomas Cole's house, Cedar Grove, across the river in Catskill. "No, no," Dominick said at the sight of the crowds, and Vernon drove on. Back across the river Vernon headed north up toward Kinderhook and Martin Van Buren's family home, Lindenwald. At least here there was next to no one, though the old yellow house of a politician whom historians found faint reason to praise was of little interest to Dominick either.

"He wasn't any friend of black people," Vernon said as they drove away from Van Buren's historic house site. "My people only have negative stories about him and his. They were slave owners, the Van Burens."

"How long have your people been here?" Dominick asked.

"Since before him. Free blacks, too, not runaways. My great-great-granddaddy was a teamster, ran a blacksmith shop over in Valatie. I'll drive you past there. That's where everybody's buried."

Dominick didn't know enough about where he was. He was on terra historica incognita. Church and Cole, the Hudson River School, sure, sidebars to history. But free blacks and slaves existing side by side here on the northern colonial frontier? Clueless. "Vernon, tell me more about your people," he said.

"I'll take you over to Valatie. That's where we're from, not Africa." Vernon said. "We got plenty of time."

The country roads were as always hypnotic. Dominick imagined himself briefly into every passing farm house. On a back road outside the little town of Valatie, Vernon stopped at a pocket cemetery of old gravestones inside a grove of trees. "We're all buried here," Vernon said. "It may not be big-house history, but it's older."

Dominick got out and walked through the graveyard. The grass between the scattered graves was uncut and high, but the place showed signs of periodic care, and there were newer graves back at the edge of the trees—the younger generations encircling their elders, shielding them from the wilderness and the future. It was a serene setting. Rest in peace. If one's image of history was primarily of graveyards, one would be mistaken. The past was no way as peaceful as death. Out of respect Dominick did not stoop to clear and read a single grave marker. At the far end of the cemetery he stopped and lit a cigar. After he had stood silently for a while, the birdsong returned.

Back at the car Vernon was standing in the road, talking on his cell phone. He closed it up and put it in his pocket as Dominick came back. "If you don't mind going on a bit further, I have someone for you to talk to about history," Vernon said.

"Lead on, MacDuff." It was another fifteen or twenty minute drive down empty county roads, most of the way through a dense mixed forest. Dominick finished his cigar. Vernon didn't mind. The windows were open. Life was good. "Vernon, we should stop and get something to eat and a drink. Do you know of some place to do so out here?"

"That's where we'd be headed. You can eat and drink at Jefferson's. That's what they are there for."

"Excellent. And who is it we are to meet there?"

"Someone who knows a lot about what went on and what goes on hereabouts and who wants to meet you." The woods that the two-lane blacktop curved through had become pristine, unbroken, as if the old Cadillac had driven through a lens out of the present into a truer space.

"It's all good, Vernon," Dominick said. "It's all good."

✳✳✳

By Sunday a truce of sorts was being observed at the house. The sides were not speaking with each other, but no fires had been set, no cutlery thrown. As was their custom, Amanda and Morgan made themselves scarce during Sunday, leaving the place to Denise and her congregation for their services. Wiccans came from around the county and across the river to meet and do their thing. This being one of their high holiday weekends, there could be quite a crowd. The house was, after all, legally their church, or house of worship, or whatever. Amanda didn't know what they called it. That was all Morgan's dealing. Somehow she had worked out that as long as the house was a church they didn't have to pay taxes on it, which had meant a lot when they first got the place. In addition, they had been charging Denise and all of her resident coven members rent. So the place made a profit as they waited to fix it up and sell it. The no-men rule was Denise's, not theirs, but it had worked out well, kept the peace. The trip to Albany had been about taking the place back from the church. It was all legal stuff, Morgan's end of the business, where Amanda just acquiesced and signed the papers where she was told to.

This Sunday they drove over to Hudson. The arts festival was happening, and Morgan had gotten them invitations to a reception for sponsors at Olana, the Francis Church estate. Morgan wanted Amanda to work the group of deep-pockets who would be there, looking for possible prospects for their place. Amanda put on her best summer dress and her only pair of heels. Morgan made her promise that she wouldn't drink.

Chapter 12

There were two moose heads above the bar and a militia's worth of antique weapons hanging on the walls, giving a sort of swank Second Amendment feel to a place at a country crossroads. A big room, it was reasonably full with Sunday diners. Vernon and Dominick sat at the bar. Dominick ordered a cheeseburger and a draft IPA. He was famished. Vernon ordered chicken wings. One of the things Dominick liked about being with Vernon was that there was no unnecessary conversation. Vernon obviously didn't think that part of his tour guide gig was entertaining Dominick with small talk. He never said anything about himself or asked a personal question. It was a comfortable silence.

Dominick was finishing his excellent burger when some sort of commotion started up at the restaurant's entrance. Voices were raised. All the heads in the room turned in that direction. A man's voice was saying, "No, no, I have every right to say so. I am the owner. I can refuse service to whomever I choose."

"What grounds do you have to discriminate against me?" a woman's voice asked, calm but purposefully loud.

"You've been told, your paper's been told, that you are no longer welcome here. Why are you causing a scene?" the man answered.

"You got more to hide, Mr. Lubitch? I'm not here as a reporter. I am here as a member of the public to get something to eat. This is a public place, isn't it?"

"Not for you it isn't. Please leave, quietly."

Dominick turned to watch. The standoff was at the maître d's podium just inside the front door. A small balding man in an ill-fitting suit was blocking the way of a large woman in a colorful flowing dashiki. She was smiling. "You're the one causing the scene, Mr. Lubitch. I just came to meet some people."

"You'll excuse me," Vernon said to Dominick as he slowly wiped his mouth and fingers with a napkin, got down from his bar stool, and strolled in the direction everyone was looking. The man in the suit was blocking the exit. Vernon placed a hand on his shoulder pad and said, "Excuse me, sir." The man stepped aside.

"Hi, Daddy," the woman said. "You done eating? I hope they didn't poison you."

Vernon put an arm around her shoulders and said something in her ear that made her laugh, and they headed for the door. Before she followed Vernon out she turned back to the room. "Ta-ta, Mr. Lubitch, and you all can go back to eating. Floor show's over."

There were still some chicken wings left on Vernon's plate, so Dominick had the waitress box them up to take. He finished his ale and paid the bill. Outside in the parking lot, Vernon's Caddy was still there, but no Vernon. Dominick put the plastic bag with the Styrofoam box of left-over wings in the back seat. Across the road from the restaurant was the only other business at the crossroads, a general store. Vernon and the woman in the dashiki came out of the general store with their own plastic bags. She was still smiling. That would seem to be her default expression. She was slightly taller than Vernon and there was nothing linear about her. She was all curves, full-bodied and not ashamed of it. Her brown hair was long and braided and pulled back from her face. Her complexion was café au lait with large darker freckles. Her facial features were also full and softly rounded. Hers was an uncommon comeliness.

"Dominick, this is my daughter Sissy," Vernon said as they came up to the car.

They shook hands. "Pleasure," she said.

"The pleasure is mine," Dominick said.

Vernon got into the driver's seat and Sissy got in the back seat. Dominick retook his front passenger seat.

"It's a perfect day for a picnic, don't you think?" Sissy said. Vernon took one of the roads back into the woods.

"Dominick, you are probably wondering what that scene back at Jefferson's was all about. Well, a couple of months ago I did a piece about Mr. Lubitch employing some undocumented workers, whom he was treating basically as slaves. That got him in some trouble, and I guess that got me on his black list."

"So, you're a reporter then," Dominick said, turning sideways in his seat.

"That's right, for the *Hudson Register Star*." Sissy had found the bag and box with the chicken wings and was finishing them off.

"If she don't get herself fired," Vernon said.

Dominick watched Sissy as she licked and sucked the hot sauce from her fingers. This was becoming a perfect day. They stopped at a park with picnic tables and a pond adjacent to a Little League field where some kids were playing a pickup game. The plastic sacks from the general store held bags of chips and cartoons of dip and bottles of iced green tea. They found an empty picnic table near the pond.

"So, Dominick," Sissy said, opening the chips and dip and handing him a bottle of iced tea, "Daddy says you're interested in our local history. How is that? Are you an historian?"

"No, I'm not an historian. I'm a consumer of history, not a producer. Just curious."

"Not that many people are curious about the past, especially other people's past," she said.

"It's safe. I mean all that stuff has already happened, and to someone else. I just wonder what it was like, that's all. Thanks." Dominick dipped a corn chip into the offered jalapeño bean dip.

"Even though it has nothing to do with you or your people?"

"It's just interesting, that's all."

Vernon got up from the table and stretched out on the grass down the slope toward the pond, out of earshot.

"So you're not a writer?" Sissy was making a lunch of the snacks. "You're not here to write us all up for some magazine?"

"No, nothing like that. I just stopped up here to visit my sister over in Diligence."

"So, you are that Dominick?"

"Which Dominick is that?"

"The one who was picked up over in Greene County two days ago on suspicion of rape."

Dominick said nothing. Was this going to be his new identity? Suspected rapist?

"I'm the local police beat reporter," Sissy said. "It's my job to know this stuff."

"I am neither a writer nor a rapist," Dominick said.

"I figured that, or those trolls in the sheriff's department over there wouldn't have turned you loose. But what's up with being charged with that? I mean, what goes on out at that place? Your sister's place, you say?"

"What's that other dip?" Dominick asked.

"Cheddar cheese," Sissy said, and she laughed as she passed the dip across the picnic table to him. "I like you already, Dominick. My daddy gives you a pass, which means something to me. What do your friends call you? Dom?"

"Just Dominick." He took another swig of sweet green tea. The warmer it got the more insipid—unsippable—it became. What goes on out at that place? Your sister's place. It could be his place. "Sissy, what do you know about the Underground Railroad hereabouts?"

"Pretty much what there is to know. Daddy's people back then were involved in all that. Black folks pretty much ran it hereabouts, even if the white folks took all the credit. Why?"

"Because that is what I would like to talk with you about."

***

Amanda cheated. She grabbed a glass of wine when Morgan wasn't looking. She needed it. Over the years she had gotten pretty good at closing deals, at giving clients what she had made them think they wanted, but she still wasn't good at opening them. *"Hello, total stranger. You look like someone who needs a bigger house. Have I got a deal for you!"* She tried to mix with the crowd at the party, but she didn't know anyone there and everyone else seemed to be old friends. After her second glass of wine she began to wonder what she was doing there. *Is Morgan just playing some game with you, giving you something pointless to do just to keep you busy? She knows you suck at this. And for that matter where is she? Typical of her to stick you with this then vanish somewhere. I swear she is getting more mysterious all the time.*

Amanda wondered what Nemo was doing. Morgan had said forget about him for now, he wasn't going anywhere without his car, and they could catch up with him next week. "He's a natural loner," Morgan said. "Dropping him off at that hotel was like throwing a fish back into the water. But he is more on our side now, don't you think? Common enemies and all?"

But Amanda just felt like a lousy host. He had come there to see her. They had spent next to no time together. And she and Morgan had just shuttled him off to a one-star hotel. All along they had been playing her brother like some sort of patsy: How could they get his share of Marjorie's money? Well, it was different now, wasn't it? In thanks for coming out of his way to visit he'd been stranded, deserted, clocked on the head, had his car stolen, and been accused of a felony. She got out her cell phone and called his room at the St. George. No answer and no one came on the line to take a message. She left the party to have a cigarette. The only place she felt safe doing that was back at the car. Wasn't it funny when something you'd done your whole adult life suddenly became a sort of quasi-crime? It was as if society as a whole had a sustaining need to single out one or another minority segment of its population to demonize for some unshared trait or practice or belief, an innate sense of caste that had to be satisfied somehow. No, it wasn't funny; it was sad.

Sitting in her car, enjoying her Pall Mall, Amanda realized she was not going back to the party. But she couldn't leave without Morgan. She called her cell phone number, but it was busy. Olana wasn't that big a place, but Amanda was damned if she was going to hike back into the crowd in these heels and look for her. She called the front desk of Nemo's hotel and left a message saying that she had called and asking if he wanted to do dinner. Morgan's phone was still busy; when it beeped she had to know it was Amanda calling. The bitch. Amanda lit a second cigarette. She turned the rearview mirror so she could see herself in it. It was that time in a late summer afternoon when the light got golden and everything got prettier, including herself. It was the one light she didn't mind seeing herself in, the one light that made age insignificant. She loosened her hair and shook a strand across her forehead, struck a pose, and exhaled. Yes, that Lauren Bacall look was still there.

"You ready to go, then?" It was Morgan opening the passenger-side door and hopping in. "Any luck with the rich nearly dead?"

Amanda dropped her cigarette out the window and readjusted the rearview mirror. "What have you been up to?"

"Well, that's not exactly my crowd. I was hanging with the colored folk in the kitchen."

"You were not." Amanda started up the Chevy. "You were on your phone."

"Okay, and the catering staff's not black anyway, but Honduran or Hmong or something, non-English speakers, the new underclass. What's it to you? Where to now? It's still early. I'm sure our goddess Denise has got her whole weird flock united against us by now."

"I thought we'd drive up to Hudson and check in on Nemo."

"He's not there," Morgan said. "I just called his room. I'm sure he's out somewhere prowling historic graveyards or something. Leave him alone. He's alright. He's a big boy. But we can definitely head up there to find something to eat, us all dressed up and all. Sometimes they have fresh catfish at that barbeque place. You like catfish. Let's go there."

Amanda headed for Hudson. She really wasn't all that fond of catfish. She had ordered it once out of curiosity—they didn't eat catfish where she came from—and Morgan had made a big deal of it, discovering that Amanda ate catfish. That was a tell-tale trait for some reason. Morgan wouldn't eat catfish herself. "Bottom-suckers my daddy called them. He'd only eat saltwater fish."

Wasn't it strange how you would latch onto something that defined someone else, even if it wasn't true? Her version of Morgan, for instance, had been shaped at their first meeting—of a young (if prematurely gray), uppity black woman playing out of her league. But of course she wasn't that at all. Amanda had taken her for young because her body hadn't seemed to age, and uppity because of her nervous energy. And because she had assumed that Morgan was younger, she had figured she was new to the game, a game in which there were very few black players. Over the years all of that had been disproved and her true age revealed, but Amanda still thought of Morgan as an uppity kid.

Or Nemo, the brother whom she had only known through Marjorie's sarcastic stories. He had always been just the spoiled junior copy of his satanic father, whom Amanda also only knew through her mother's selective presentation. What was Nemo really like? Maybe if she started giving him his real name? No. "Dominick" had been a bad word for too long, a name she'd been taught to hate.

"Will you watch where you're going?" Morgan said.

Amanda had taken the last curve too fast and had to jerk the car off the shoulder back onto the road. "Sorry," she said. "I was thinking."

"Look, I'll do the thinking," Morgan said. "You just drive. What are we thinking about?"

"How we can never really know anyone else."

"Oh, a no-brainer. Why do you think we should know any more than anyone wants us to know?"

"But what if what we think we know is wrong?"

"Then probably you've made that person more interesting than he or she really is. Who are we talking about anyway? Anyone I know?"

"I don't think I'll have catfish tonight. I think I'll have something else," Amanda said, slowing down as they came into the reduced speed zone at the edge of town.

***

"First, I have to ask, what happened to your head?" Sissy said. "Did the police do that?"

"No, that was an earlier accident."

"An accident?"

"My head ran into a beer bottle, someplace called The Hill Top. Know it?"

"Only from police reports. Are local rednecks part of your field research? Do you mind? Your bandage is coming loose." Sissy reached across the picnic table and gently touched his tender temple, massaging adhesive back in place. "Aren't you a little old to be getting in bar brawls?"

"Like I said, it was an accident. Generally I do my best to avoid sociopaths." It felt good to be touched, even briefly, an uncommon sensation.

"Why the Underground Railroad?"

"The period interests me," Dominick said, "and the phenomenon—citizens banding together to break the law."

"A bad law, the Fugitive Slave Act."

"But a law of the land nonetheless, federal law. You said your father's people were involved. Was it pretty active around here?"

"The Hudson was a trunk route toward Canada. Freedom seekers came through here for decades. There were stations all along the river up to Albany, where the route split either west to Buffalo or east into Vermont. Relatively speaking there were a fair number of free black people living in this area then, a couple of thousand between this county and Greene County across the river, so self-emancipators could find help here on their way north. Thousands passed through here. Impossible to say how many. If you're breaking the law it doesn't make sense to keep records, and what records had been kept were destroyed when the stricter law was enacted in 1850. In any event, only the white folks kept count, and they didn't know the half of it."

"So, both blacks and whites were breaking the law?"

"But only the blacks were punished if they got caught. The honkies just got bragging rights at church. You don't mind being called a honkie, do you?"

"That's alright, though I'm not Hungarian," Dominick said.

"What does being Hungarian have to do with it?" Sissy laughed. She laughed easily, effortlessly.

"Origin of the term, originally *hunky*, a derisive Northern black slang term for working-class white guys, Hungarians for some reason. I believe the Black Panthers metastasized the term to refer to any and all of us."

"Good work. Nice to have a single inclusive term."

"Haole, cracker, gringo, gwailo. Take your pick. Tell me, Sissy, where does your name come from? It's unusual. Is it short for something?"

"Actually, my given name is Sister, a long family tradition, but that's too confusing. People think I'm a nun or something. I've been

Sissy since I was a kid. Not even Daddy remembers where it came from. One day I was just Sissy and it stuck."

"Sissy, do you know of any locations, any houses in the area that served as stations on the railroad? You know, places where fugitives were actually hidden until they could be moved on?"

"No, not hereabouts. Like I said, it was kept pretty secret, and of course all the black people's places are long gone. You could always go up to Auburn where there are some historic sites if that's your thing— the Seward House and Harriet Tubman's home, but that's two hundred miles away, not hereabouts."

The Little League diamond was now empty, and Vernon was sound asleep on the grass. Dominick had been putting off his cigar craving since lunch. Now he pulled a Churchill out of his pocket case and prepared to light it.

"Oh, please don't do that," Sissy said. "I despise tobacco. I don't know why it isn't illegal."

Dominick stopped and looked at her. She was actually making a face like a little kid. "Don't you think enough things are against the law already?" he said, but he put the cigar back in his case.

"That's one that should be added. That and alcohol, just vile addictions that don't do anyone any good. If they're going to outlaw any drugs they should start with the big two. Thank you."

This was a conversational topic Dominick had always found it best to avoid. As with any prejudice, giving the holders a chance to hold forth only deepened their prejudicial resolve. "Tell me about Harriet Tubman," he said as he slipped the cigar case back into his pocket.

"I guess she and Frederick Douglass have the honor of representing all the unnamed black people who helped free their brothers and sisters from slavery. She did a lot of fine and brave things in a very long life, starting as a slave. She was a champion manipulator. Up here she made some powerful white friends."

"Wasn't she famously beaten as a slave?"

"When she was just a girl she was hit in the head with a lead weight by her master when another slave tried to escape. Changed her life." Sissy laughed that liquid laugh again. "Made her kind of crazy, I guess, made her the original crazy, angry, powerful black Christian mama."

"How so?"

"Supposedly she had headaches and seizures and attacks and visions the rest of her life, and she'd act on her dreams and visions, which she called revelations from God. I guess no one wanted to stand in the way of someone getting messages from God. She was called Moses, you know."

Vernon sat up on the grass, rubbing the side of his face. "Goddamn mosquitoes," he said.

"Daddy, don't swear. It's Sunday. But they are coming out. We'll head back," Sissy said, gathering the trash from the picnic table. "Dominick, how long are you going to be around? Daddy said you're staying at the St. George."

"I have no idea. That depends upon the Greene County Sheriff's Department, who impounded my car."

"I've got a few books you could look at about what we were talking about. I'll drop them off if you promise not to steal them."

"You live in Hudson?"

"Just outside of town. Come on, Daddy, get up and we'll go."

They dropped Sissy back at her car in the restaurant parking lot. On the drive back to Hudson, Vernon and Dominick didn't talk much. "You and Sissy have a good chat?" Vernon asked.

"Smart girl."

"Don't know where she gets it," Vernon said. "Not from her mother. Sissy's got a college degree, you know, from the campus up in Albany, but it seems to me that smart women always end up sad."

Chapter 13

It was well after dark by the time Amanda and Morgan got back to Diligence. All seemed peaceful at the house as they drove up. There were only the usual cars parked in the driveway. There were just a few lights on inside. The veranda lights were off.

"All quiet on the Wiccan front," Morgan said.

As they crossed the front porch Amanda, who had shed her high heels after they left the restaurant and was walking barefoot, carrying her shoes, stepped in something sticky. "What is this?" she said, stepping backwards.

"Hold on," Morgan said and went inside to turn on the light above the door. There was a broad irregular band of something dark on the veranda floor spread in an arc around the front door. It was a dark reddish brown in the light. Morgan stooped down to look at it, then touched it with a fingertip and tasted it. "Blood," she said. "How melodramatic."

"What in the world?" Amanda just stared at it, then she looked at the sole of her foot. "Of all the nerve." She stepped over the border of blood and joined Morgan in the doorway. "What's next?"

"A little talk with our tenant Denise," Morgan said.

The kitchen was a half-redeemed mess—big black plastic garbage bags of trash stacked against the walls, and on the counter tops pizza boxes with one or two slices still left in them, unwashed serving dishes and utensils, stacks of dirty plastic cups.

"Do you hear a statement being made here?" Morgan asked. "Wait, I'll go get her down here and maybe she can express it in words as well."

Denise, of course, did not come down alone. She brought half of her crew with her. Oh, how Amanda hated these sorts of scenes, these cat fight scenes. With men you could try to use diplomacy and logic and there were parameters; with women there were no rules besides attack. And, it being Denise, Amanda knew she should stay out of it or risk losing it again.

"The girls will finish the clean up," Denise said. "We were just having our meditation hour before we were so rudely interrupted." Denise turned to the girls behind her. "Finish up here," she said. They looked at each other, confused, and then set about bagging the rest of the trash and moving dirty dishes to the sink. "It's been a busy day. What's your problem?"

"What's with the blood on the porch?" Morgan asked.

"As part of Litha we reconsecrated our Covenstead today. It's a ritual."

"It's blood on the porch," Morgan said.

"It is ceremonial blood, an essential aspect of High Priest Lloyd's consecration of the Craftplace."

"High Priest Lloyd?" Amanda asked.

"Yes, he came with his coven from Saugerties to observe Litha with us and to strengthen the spirit of this place."

"Are you going to clean it up?" Morgan asked.

"We can't do that. There is no need. Blood is the essence of nature, as sacred to the Earth Mother as her own menses. Nature herself will cleanse it."

"Not on the porch she won't, not without a little help anyway."

"If you remove it, the Earth Mother's distain will be upon you."

"I'm not washing your mess off the front porch, sweetheart, but I might call the sheriff back here to see where the blood came from."

"It's just ox blood, of course."

"A sacred ox, I hope."

Amanda watched Morgan. How she enjoyed these confrontations. One of the girls had turned and was scowling at Morgan. Morgan turned on her, "What are you looking at, sister?" Then she turned back to Denise and walked over to her. "No more of this shit, Denise, or I will get the law back out here."

"For what?"

"How about harboring an underage runaway car thief?"

The girls behind Amanda all stopped what they were doing and turned toward Denise.

"I did a little background check on your Susan. She's only sixteen and she's wanted back home in Ohio. People there miss her, including the district attorney."

"How dare you! How dare you continue to persecute that poor innocent child!" Denise stood her ground as Morgan advanced.

"Actually, I'd rather leave poor, innocent juvie Susie out of it as well, but you dragged her into this. I'm just saying cut the crap and get out. Time's up. Time to move on and paint some new place with your blood."

"Do you have any idea what that man did to her? Do you? He not only ravaged her but he cast some sort of spell on her, broke her mentally. She was so distraught and confused I've had to send her away for evaluation."

"You did what?" Amanda said.

"She won't be committed or anything, just admitted for observation. With her family's concurrence."

"You mean her sister's," Morgan said.

"Her sister is family. It's for the poor girl's own good. High Priest Lloyd has accepted her into his coven and will take her in for evaluation. He's a psychiatric nurse at a very prestigious clinic. He can get her in as a hardship victim case."

"Had to get her out of the way, did you?" Morgan said, shaking her head. "You're a piece of work, Denise. But that doesn't change anything."

"Except for Susan," Amanda said. "That girl doesn't belong in an institution. You do." There Denise was, using people again. Amanda was still holding her high heel shoes. She threw one at Denise, which missed widely. Denise ducked unnecessarily.

Morgan laughed. "Ladies, ladies, let's not go there. So, Denise, are you thinking that if you get Susan on the right drugs and coached well enough to your script, she will cop to being raped? Or had her presence just become too much a dangerous embarrassment? No matter; your thirty days are ticking."

"I wouldn't count on that," Denise said. "A member of Lloyd's coven is a lawyer, and he said you can't just evict a church. It's prejudicial.

You'll be getting papers soon contesting the eviction. You've got a world of trouble coming. This place will be mine before this is over. Drop that, girls. Come on. Let the help clean up." And Denise turned and left, followed by her obedient crew.

Morgan went and picked up Amanda's shoe where it had landed in the wing chair and brought it back to her. "And I thought I was so clever when I brought that troop in here," she said. "Oh, well, they can't stay once reconstruction begins. How many years have you had these shoes?"

✳✳✳

The offices of the *Hudson Register Star* in Warren Street were only four or five blocks from Dominick's hotel, in the middle of the old brick downtown business district. Sissy had said that she probably wouldn't be there Monday but that she would leave the books for him. She had—two tomes on the history of the Underground Railroad in New York and New England and a folded copy of a paper Sissy had written in college about its activities in Greene and Columbia counties. She had gotten a B+ on the paper. He read her paper first, over lunch. There was nothing fancy about her prose. Her premise was that free blacks had done most of the heavy lifting hereabouts and had been ignored in the historic record. Her prof had faulted her for insufficient library citations—"an over-reliance on anecdote"—when her point was that very little had been previously written about black involvement. There was nothing about Diligence or the Rev. Van Houten in either her paper or the indexes of the books.

Back in his hotel room Dominick called Morgan on her cell phone. There was nothing new on his car. "They'll keep it hostage a couple of days," Morgan said. "Hey, it's their rice bowl. I bet the CI guys over here don't get that many chances to play with their nifty toys. Patience, Nemo. I'll keep checking on it and get back to you as soon as there is any news."

"Who's Nemo?" Dominick asked.

"Did I say Nemo? I meant Dominick. Anyway, I'll keep you informed."

Dominick spent the afternoon with Sissy's books. They were dry if comprehensive, the sort of history that tried harder to seem exhaustive than interesting and pained itself to avoid any appearance of conjecture. As usual he wished for more and better maps. The weather had turned hot, but Dominick didn't want to close the windows. He left them open and turned the air-conditioning to its coldest setting. Hotel rooms were meant to be abused. The edges of the desk were scarred by cigarette burns. The phone didn't ring. Around the time when he started thinking about supper there was a knock at his door. It was Sissy.

"You got the books?" she said when he opened the door. "What are you doing for dinner?" She wasn't wearing a dashiki today, but jeans and a white-on-yellow short-sleeve aloha shirt over a coral tank top. She was smiling. It was one of those smiles that made you want to smile back.

"I thought I would get something to eat," Dominick said, opening the door to invite her in. "Any ideas?"

"Got just the place," Sissy said, but she didn't come in. "Change, and I'll meet you downstairs."

It was true Dominick wasn't dressed to go out. He quickly changed into street clothes and met Sissy in the lobby. The restaurant they strolled to was small and out of the way on a side street off Warren. The menu was one hundred percent vegetarian. The food wasn't bad, but as far as Dominick was concerned tofu and steamed vegetables were only and always tofu and steamed vegetables. They ate with chopsticks. They talked about the Underground Railroad.

At one point Sissy laughed, her private ironic laugh—Dominick had begun to catalog her various laughs—and said, "You know, I have never got to talk about this with anyone else before. My teachers didn't talk with students. Daddy can't understand why anyone would waste their time worrying over things from so long ago. And everyone else is in one kind of denial or another."

"You know a lot of local history," Dominick said.

"Daddy's family has been here for more than two hundred years."

"And your mother's family?"

Sissy put down her chopsticks and took a sip of tea. She was no longer laughing. "You had to ask, didn't you?"

Dominick looked up from his plate. He had innocently asked the wrong question, but there was no taking it back. He said nothing.

"My mother was a prostitute down in the city. Daddy was her pimp. She loved him. She tricked him into knocking her up. Me. They left the city and came up here to Daddy's family to raise me. Daddy traded being a pimp for being a cabbie. My mother died when I was twelve. End of personal history."

"I guess he loved her, too," Dominick said.

"She was an alcoholic."

"Alcoholics can be lovable."

"You really don't care, do you?" Sissy still hadn't picked back up her chopsticks.

"Listen, Sissy, I'm sorry I asked that question, but it really makes no difference to me. You are who you are, not your mother, not your father—you. And I find you engaging and interesting and a bit distracting."

"Distracting?" A half smile returned to her face.

"That's meant as a compliment. What's this?" Dominick poked his chopsticks into a side dish that had just been put on the table.

"Fried okra, my favorite here," Sissy said. "I find it very . . . distracting."

After dinner they sat on a bench in the little park with the railroad tracks across from Dominick's hotel and talked. It was a hot, still night. Sissy was a Christian, one of those unquestioning ones for whom a church was as much a given part of life as family itself or electricity. "Just look at history, religion is everywhere, everybody believes in God," she said. "You can't deny it. It was the churches—Quakers first then the rest—that made the abolition of slavery a political issue in the United States."

"The South was pretty Christian, too," Dominick said. "The Bible has no problem with slavery."

"In case you haven't noticed, we no longer live in Biblical times. Jesus had no slaves."

Sissy, in addition to being a Christian, a prohibitionist, and a vegetarian ("Buffalo wings are my one weakness"), espoused the tenets of feminism and animal rights, gay marriage and pro-choice. Dominick got the feeling that she had few sympathetic local ears for her particular salad of causes. He listened, occasionally making positive sounds. He enjoyed being with her—her youth, her health, her naïve ideology, something. He wanted to reach out and touch her, feel her tight braids or the moist warmth of her skin. It had been a long time since that yearning. He wanted to stretch out the time that they sat there beside one another in the mottled shadows of the distant streetlights. She was laughing again—laugh 4.a: a funny thought from out of nowhere.

"What is it?" he asked.

"I can't tell you," she said, still laughing to herself. "Maybe later, some other time. Look, I have to go. Now. Don't go getting lost on me, Dominick. Good night."

Dominick didn't watch her walk away. Her aroma lingered there without her. He hadn't told Sissy about his discoveries at the Van Houten house, the trunks and the papers. He wondered why he hadn't and if he ever would. Perhaps he should just return them to their hiding place and let whatever secrets they contained resume their aging process. He lit a long-overdue Churchill and waited for the midnight train.

***

The Chevy's front end was getting worse, the shimmy and the pull, and Amanda didn't feel comfortable about driving all the way to Albany and back again. Morgan wanted to go up to see their lawyer. Tuesday morning they'd been served with legal papers. Denise's Wiccan lawyer was seeking a temporary restraining order against the "forcible eviction." Amanda gave Morgan a ride as far as the Hudson train station and promised her on the way that she would look into buying a newer car. But not today; she wasn't in the mood. She stopped at the St. George, but Nemo wasn't in. She left a message that she had stopped by.

When she got back home she was glad to see that Denise's Bronco was gone along with the rest of the cars. So she would have the place to herself for a while. Morgan hadn't seemed worried about the temporary restraining order. "We might as well get it started and done with," she had said. "Don't worry. They haven't got a case."

Amanda had sort of taken over Nemo's place on the back veranda. It was another scorcher day, and she fixed herself a tall iced tea and went out to sit there in the deep shade. Just a couple of days without Susan's attention and the kitchen garden was already drooping and sad. Amanda went and found the hose and started soaking the raised beds the way she'd seen Susan do it. God knows why. Within a few weeks it would all be ground into muck by the contractor's trucks and machinery. The salad greens were recovering. The cherry tomatoes were already setting. *Now don't go getting attached to this place,* she told herself. *It will all be gone soon enough. You already failed once as a farm girl, remember? Reed and you raising goats and giving each of them pet names like Lamb Chop and Rib Roast to remind yourselves what they were bound for. Whatever happened to Reed? I wonder if Ricky knows where her father is.*

She was going off somewhere into the past as she moved the hose from bed to bed. That's what usually happened when she got time alone now, she went backwards. It didn't use to be that way, she thought. There had been a time, she was sure, when she only thought forward and couldn't care less about what had already happened. Now even her dreams were like walking down library aisles of shelved memories. She was somewhere else altogether when the voice brought her back.

"Hey, hi there. There was a car out front, so I figured someone was home, but no one answered the door. Nice garden." She was a large, young, light-skinned black woman, smiling at something.

"You surprised me. I didn't hear you drive up," Amanda said. "Can I help you?"

"Are you Denise?"

"No, I'm not. Denise isn't here right now." Amanda let go of the hose and wiped her hands together.

"Are you a member of the church? I understand this place is a Wiccan church."

"No, I am not a member of any church, and, no, this place is no longer a Wiccan house."

"Still got your pentacle up there," the woman said with a nod toward the side of the house. "Would Susan be around by any chance?"

"No, Susan is gone. She no longer lives here. Look, what is this about? Who are you? If you're police you have to identify yourself."

"Sorry. I'm Sissy." She came over to shake Amanda's hand. "I'm a reporter with the *Register Star*. I'm just following up on the incident report from out here the other day. You know, to get the victim's side of the story."

"There was no victim. Certainly not Susan."

"Oh, but the police report—"

"Was wrong," Amanda said. "Nothing happened. There was no incident, so there is nothing to investigate. And that's enough questions." Amanda walked past the woman to turn off the faucet around the corner of the porch.

"Okay, okay, don't get all hostile." The infernal woman was smiling again. "I just try to get our sisters' stories out there when I can. No Susan, no story." She followed Amanda around the side of the porch. "Would you know where I might find Susan?"

"No, I don't know. And you can leave now. This is my property, and I am asking you to please vacate it."

"Certainly, sister. I'll go. Could I use your ladies room first? It's a ways going back."

"Of course. Inside the kitchen door to your left. You'll find it."

"Thanks," she said. "This is a great old place you got here."

Amanda was embarrassed. Why had she acted so rudely to this woman? She was only doing her job, and Amanda had treated her like an intruder, a threat of some type. It was true that nothing that went on here was any of her business, but if the story was going to get out anyway . . . She followed the woman into the kitchen in time to see her shut the bathroom door behind her down the hall. Amanda washed her hands at the kitchen sink. She had already forgotten the woman's name. She was drying her hands on a tea towel when the woman came back into the kitchen.

"I love these old houses," the woman was saying. "You're lucky to live here. Thanks for the use of your loo."

Amanda couldn't think of anything to say. "I've forgotten your name," she said.

"Sissy," she said, "Sissy Douglas. Yours?"

"Amanda," Amanda said. "Would you like some iced tea before heading back?"

"I'd love some," she said. That smile again. "No more questions."

They were seated on the back veranda—Amanda in Nemo's chair, Sissy on the top step of the stairs to the garden—drinking their iced teas. "You'll have to stake those beans soon," Sissy said.

"Which ones are those?" Amanda asked. "I don't know anything about gardens. This was Susan's job. I was just watering it to keep them alive. I hate to see things die."

"So Susan's not coming back?"

"Question," Amanda said.

"You know, I first got interested in this case after meeting the accused, who also claims that nothing ever happened."

"You've met with him?"

"A couple of times. And I believe him. He is definitely not the rapist type. But you never know."

"No, you never know," Amanda said. What exactly was the rapist type? "But Susan was never raped, never even bothered by the man. She told me so. As a matter of fact, she stole his car, and he chose not to report it." *Now why did you say that?*

"Oh? The alleged-scene-of-the-crime car?"

"There's no reason for you to know that."

"So, she was in his car? The CI guys will probably discover that. They took her fingerprints."

"What difference would that make?"

"If she wasn't in his car to steal it, maybe she was there to be raped." The woman swirled her ice cubes around in the bottom of her drained glass of iced tea.

Amanda didn't like this woman, this Sissy, young and smug, a knowing smirk on her half-caste face. Didn't like what she was trying to do, whatever it was. But if she wanted to find out the truth, that couldn't hurt, could it? Keep her away from Denise, re-direct her somehow. "You should speak with Susan," Amanda said.

"I thought you said Susan no longer lived here."

"She doesn't. They took her away."

"They? Who are they?"

"Denise and someone named Lloyd, a psychiatric nurse. They supposedly took Susan to the clinic where he works."

"Know which one?"

"No. He's from Saugerties is all I know."

"Well, there aren't that many psychiatric clinics this side of Albany. I'll find her. You have anything else you want to tell me?"

"No. Only don't come back here. This is private property, private business. There's no story here."

Chapter 14

Didn't anyone else find it demeaning leaving a message on a machine with a robot voice? "The person with whom you wish to speak deems herself too important to talk with you now at your convenience. Take a knee and whisper your supplication after the rude noise, and we'll see." Dominick refused to leave messages on people's machines. He called Morgan's number twice on Tuesday morning and got just her machine or service or voice mail or whatever they called it. He wanted his car back. He wanted out of the Hotel St. George, out of lovely Hudson, out of the Hudson Valley altogether. Why wasn't he already on the Vineyard?

He called Vernon, who had no answering robots, to come pick him up and take him back to Catskill to see about his car. Morgan had said be patient. His patience had expired. He could be such a passive wuss sometimes. It was time to move on. Vernon came and picked him up, and they headed back to Catskill. At the Greene County Sheriff's Office no one seemed to know where his car was until Dominick found the detective who had questioned him, who told him the lab boys hadn't released it yet. Dominick gave him the telephone number of his hotel.

"That's over in Hudson, isn't it?" the detective said. "I thought I told you not to leave the county. Hudson is in Columbia County."

"There were no rooms available here in Catskill," Dominick said. Was this about to go Kafka on him?

"They found the girl's fingerprints all over the car, including the back seat."

"I told you she took the car."

"They found her hair in the back seat. There were blood stains on the back seat as well. We don't know if she was a virgin or not."

"The blood is mine," Dominick said, pointing to his many-colored brow.

"Did she do that to you defending herself?"

"No, Susan did not do this to me. Look, I just came here to inquire about my car. If you have further questions for me, I'd rather have my lawyer present."

"Well, I still don't have enough to hold you on, but if you flee we'll catch you and that will be another charge." Having authority meant getting to make threats.

Vernon had stayed out in his car. "I was getting a bit nervous there," he said when Dominick rejoined him. "I don't trust those guys. Where to?"

"I have to make some photocopies. Where would be the best place?"

"You mean like Xerox? Probably the library's easiest." The public library was only a few blocks away, a square brick civic building from an earlier age on a quiet side street. Vernon again waited in the car.

There were a dozen or so pages of the papers from the trunk that Dominick wanted copies of, primarily printed clippings and pages from old newspapers plus a couple of pages of sermon drafts. He had decided to return the stash and the ledger to where he had found them. He had no claim to them. He had brought them all with him.

He only wanted copies of the ones he found most curious. He had never known, for instance, that there had been such strongly held sentiments among some Northerners in the 1840s and '50s for the Northern states themselves to secede from the Union because of slavery. Southerners controlled the federal government, which was a slave to slavery. The Constitution itself was despoiled by its immoral acceptance of the despicable practice. No righteous man—or state—should continue allegiance to such a benighted government.

An example, a passage from the fragile page of a newspaper called *Friend of Man* that Dominick placed carefully on the copying machine's glass:

If there be human enactments against our entertaining the stricken strangers—against our opening our door to our poor, guiltless, and unaccused colored brother pursued by bloodthirsty kidnappers—we must, nevertheless, say with the apostle: "We must obey God rather than man."

Nonviolent civil disobedience, all to save your soul. It was clear from the sermons that at least for the Rev. Van Houten it was all about "higher obligations" and assuring your own salvation. Judgment Day was always imminent for these nineteenth-century spirit-heads. There was a strident sense of immediacy in everything they wrote. The world was coming to an end. It seemed best to Dominick to stick it all back in the trunk, back to the past where he had found it and where it belonged. Then he could leave this place. Also, he could retrieve the shirts he had forgotten and left hanging in Morgan's closet when he packed.

Neither Vernon nor Dominick mentioned Sissy—non-topic—as they headed south to Diligence. Along the way they passed The Hill Top bar. "Ever been in that place, Vernon?"

"Nope. Don't go out to bars no more, and if I did I wouldn't go there. The folks that go there are sort of stuck on their own kind. Okay by me. It's their place. I don't need it." There was a long pause as Vernon just drove. "And they call themselves Christians."

Dominick was giving directions and he missed their turn-off. When he finally realized it and had Vernon turn around they had to go back several miles.

After the second turn Vernon said, "Oh, I know where we're going now, the old Van Houten place. Why didn't you say so in the first place?"

"You know the place?" Dominick asked.

"It's been there forever. I had an auntie used to work for the folks who ran the place back when I was a kid. Poor farm land, all ridge top no valleys. They ran sheep on it. That ruined it for good."

When they got to the house only Amanda's old Chevy was parked out front. Dominick had hoped that no one would be there, so that he could just do his business—pick up his shirts and put the papers secretly back where he'd found them—and get out. Now he considered not stopping at all. He had ignored the messages Amanda left for him at the hotel. That had been impolite. Now he would have to apologize. That was society for you—where you had to act insincerely sorry for not doing something you had no interest in doing. But Vernon said he had to use the bathroom, so they parked the old Caddy beside the old Chevy, like a Havana street scene, and got out. Dominick left the papers behind.

"The old place still looks pretty good," Vernon said, "just older."

They both stopped at the top of the steps. There was a wide swatch of what looked like dried blood in front of the door.

"Looks like something ran into an accident here," Vernon said.

"That was no accident." Dominick didn't know what it might mean, but it was a very purposeful declaration of something. "Come on," he said, "we'll go around and in through the kitchen."

"Looks like cow blood to me," Vernon said. "All blood is different."

***

Washing her hair always helped. She didn't know why. It just did. After that woman Sissy left, Amanda went and washed her hair. Sissy's hair had all been in those long tight braids. How often did they get washed? Amanda toweled her hair as dry as she could and then brushed it out. It was such a beautiful day she decided not to blow-dry it as usual but to go sit on the back porch and let it dry in the summer air. She headed to her room to find something to read, something mindless, something distracting, some romance novel she'd already read and half forgotten. She had plenty to choose from. As she passed the top of the stairs she heard something down in the kitchen—a floorboard creaked and a door softly closed. She stopped. She was dressed in just her bathrobe. She tightened its belt around her waist and went down the stairs to check.

For months the girls had been talking about the house being haunted—hearing things and seeing things that weren't quite there, having their personal items go mysteriously missing. Even Morgan had mentioned hearing invisible people going up and down the staircase that lay behind a locked door in her room and led to the cupola above it. Ghosts didn't scare Morgan. She had yelled at them and they went away, she said. Of course, Amanda had heard things, too. Old houses made noises, but usually not in the middle of the day with no wind and no one else around. At the bottom of the stairs she looked down the hallway toward the kitchen. There was no one there. Then she heard the toilet flush in the downstairs bathroom, and its door to the hall opened toward her. She was pretty sure ghosts didn't flush.

When the door closed there was a black man standing there, his back to Amanda as he adjusted the waist of his trousers. He hadn't seen her. Now, what would a black man be doing in this house? He walked to the kitchen, and Amanda followed him.

"Hello?" she said as she came into the kitchen and the man was almost to the back porch door. What was this, African-American visit-your-bathroom day?

The man turned around slowly. He was an older man. He nodded and his eyes smiled. "Hello there, miss." He reached for the doorknob and opened the door.

"What are you . . . who . . .?" Amanda didn't know what to ask. The man walked out onto the porch, carefully closing the door behind him. She was barefoot with a head of wet hair and naked except for the robe. She just stood there and stared at the closed door. Then it opened and Nemo stepped in.

"Hello, Amanda. I've come to get a few things I left behind."

"Who was that?" Amanda asked, pointing toward the porch.

"Vernon gave me a ride out. I still don't have my car. Sorry to bother you. Is Morgan about?" Nemo seemed even further away than ever. The bruise on the side of his head was now yellow and green.

"Did you get my messages?" Amanda asked.

"Oh, yes, thanks. I've been busy. Maybe we can get together for dinner before I leave. Is Morgan . . .?"

"No. She's gone up to Albany, business. You're leaving?"

"Onto Martha's Vineyard as soon as I can get my car back. I'm already two weeks late."

"Oh. Well, I guess it has been kind of hairy around here."

"What's with the blood on the front porch?" Dominick asked.

"Some Wiccan thing. They're supposed to clean it off."

So, just like that he's gone again. Were you expecting him to hang around? For what? But does he have to leave so soon? Who cares about his share of Marjorie's money? He's the only family I have left, and I just found him. Why doesn't he like me?

Will I ever see him again? He's really not such a bad guy after all, but all we have in common is Marjorie and he doesn't want to talk about that.

"Do you have any children?" Amanda asked.

"What?"

"Children, you know, offspring, progeny. I was just wondering if I was an auntie to anyone."

"No, you have neither nieces nor nephews by me."

"Marjorie showed me the photo of your Oxford wedding."

"That was a long time ago and a very short—and childless—marriage. Now I have to go up and get a few things I left in Morgan's closet." Nemo headed for the doorway to the hall.

"It's locked," Amanda said.

"What is locked?" Dominick stopped to ask.

"Her room, and I don't have a key I'm afraid." Of course Amanda did have a key. "I guess you will have to come back, or I could bring whatever it is in to you if I get over to Hudson first. What did you forget?"

"Just a few shirts. Don't worry about it. I can always get new ones."

"They wouldn't fit anyone here. By the way, there was a woman here looking for Susan."

"Oh?" Nemo said. He looked distracted, ready to leave. "And did she find her?"

"No. Susan's not here. Denise had her committed."

"Committed? You mean like to a mental institution?"

"That's right. Denise thinks that in addition to raping her you cast some sort of spell on her or something."

"That's ridiculous."

"Of course it is."

"Where is she?"

"We don't know. Denise wouldn't say, and it's really none of our business."

"But that's not right." Now Nemo seemed perplexed. "The kid is not crazy. She has just been ignored all her life."

"The woman who was here looking for Susan said she had talked to you about the case."

Nemo turned and looked at Amanda. The look was a question.

"She said she was a reporter."

"Name of Sissy?" Nemo asked.

"Yes, that's right. Sissy something. I sent her away. None of her business."

"What did she say about me?"

"Just that she thought you were innocent, that you weren't the rapist type. She seemed more interested in Susan's story."

Nemo stood there silently for a minute, looking off into the distance, nodding his head ever so slightly. Then he said, "You did the right thing sending her off. No need for reporters. Listen, Amanda, Vernon has to get back. I will be in touch. Will you have Morgan call me at the hotel? I have got to get my car released."

As Nemo went to leave, Amanda stopped him, held him by both arms, and on her tiptoes kissed him on the bottom of his jaw, which was as high as she could reach. "In case I never see you again," she said.

❊❊❊

The old Caddy bottomed out a couple times, but Vernon didn't seem too concerned. He was crawling along in low gear. "It seemed a lot shorter when we used to walk it," he said. "Of course, when you're young you're always in a rush. Now I'm too old to be in a hurry."

This side trip had been Vernon's impulse. "When my auntie was working at the Van Houten place my brother and I would come out sometimes, summer days like this, to visit with her and then go fishing. There was a fine spot, out on a point that made a little cove, an old broken-down dock we could get out onto."

"What did you catch?" Dominick asked. He had lit up a Churchill and was enjoying the ride down the two-rut road through a tunnel of trees.

"Shad, sturgeon, and stripers of course. Always had the place to ourselves. Catch a shitload of fish, too much to carry out, throw back the smaller ones."

They were on a small isthmus now. Dominick could see sun sparkling on water through the trees on either side. The road ended at a clearing like a fingernail on the tip of the narrow low slip of land pointing out into the big khaki-colored river.

"I wished I'd known we were coming here. I would have brought some fishing poles," Vernon said. "Hasn't changed, only gotten a little wilder. Dock's all gone." On the cove side of the point there was an uneven line of blackened pier posts sticking up above the water. A cormorant the color of an oil spill took off laboriously from the top of one of them. They got out of the car and strolled down toward the water's edge. The shore of the cove was a chaos of driftwood, including large trees. More birds took wing as the men came into their sight. "Just like it was," Vernon said.

From where they were standing, their view of the wide swatch of river and the far shore was devoid of human imprint except for the white dot of a house on a distant ridgeline.

"How far back do you think that dock goes, Vernon?"

"You mean back in time? I wouldn't know. A ways back, I'd guess. It seemed awfully old when I came here as a boy." Vernon chuckled. "My auntie used to call it Nigger Landing, and she wasn't given to using that word."

They sat down on adjacent boulders above the water. Dominick savored the view and his cigar.

"You got another one of those?" Vernon asked.

"What? Of course. My apologies. I didn't know you smoked or I would have offered earlier." Dominick pulled his cigar case out of his pocket.

"My daughter doesn't like me smoking or drinking, so I let her think I don't; but that cigar smells awfully good. In fact, hold on." Vernon went back to the Cadillac and opened the trunk. He came back with a full pint bottle of Jim Beam. "Might as well double down." Vernon unscrewed the cap from the bourbon and took a drink, then passed the bottle to Dominick in exchange for a Churchill. They sat there in silence for a while, puffing and sipping, passing the bottle back and forth.

"You been in these parts most of your life, Vernon?"

"Except for a stretch in my twenties that I spent downriver in the city."

"Sissy said you were a pimp in New York." Dominick wasn't sure why he said that.

"Oh, that's Sissy's story. I guess she finds it romantic or dramatic or something. I let Sissy keep a lot of her stories. They help her make sense of her life, like she wants to believe that her mother was a whore who found Jesus before she passed on."

"What about Sissy? She married?" Was it the bourbon making Dominick say such inappropriate things?

"Nope. I don't know if she's even come anywhere close to getting hitched. I think she sort of scares the fellas off with all that feminist stuff. Who wants to hear that all the time?"

"You're close though."

"She's all I got left now, and I just let all that stuff slide by. It's like when she was a little girl and she was always wearing costumes, and I'd pretend she was a pirate or a princess or a stranger or whatever disguise she was into, just go along for the ride."

Way out on the river a push boat went by with a litter of barges in front of it. "Did you know, Vernon, that the Indian name for this river, which I don't remember, meant *the river that flows both ways?*"

"Didn't know that."

"So that if you and I built a raft out of some of that driftwood there and pushed off into the current, we wouldn't necessarily go downriver. We might just go back and forth and end up right back here where we started."

"You can go right ahead and test that theory. I'm not getting on any raft." Vernon took another sip of Beam and handed the bottle to Dominick. "I can't swim."

Chapter 15

She couldn't remember a time when she hadn't had an invisible companion. As a small girl it had been her invisible friend Agatha. Then, after Amanda discovered who her mother was, it had become Marjorie and had pretty much continued to be her mother until she died. Since then it was someone unknown, not yet identified; but there still had to be someone there—someone who watched over her, was her constant companion, knew what she knew, saw what she saw. Her secret confidant, her best girlfriend. This wasn't her voice. That was different and usually showed up only to scold her or question her. Her invisible companion was mute and was always not only by her side but on her side. She was the one Amanda spoke to when she thought "Isn't this a beautiful day?" or "Where did I put my keys?" She was the one with whom Amanda shared everything.

Amanda's father's family was Catholic, and growing up she had been exposed to that. All those saints and male gods and the Blessed Virgin Mary she had found just confusing, as made up as the characters in the comic books she wasn't supposed to read. The one thing she had latched onto, that they seemed to have right, was her Guardian Angel. Well, the wings and feathers and all were unnecessary and over the top, but that constant silent sidekick was spot on. She was amazed to think that everybody else might have their own.

At her First Communion Amanda had left a space for her Guardian Angel beside her in the pew, and a nun (one of those witches) had come and told her to move over and close the space. Amanda had told her that was where her Guardian Angel (secretly Agatha) was sitting, and the nun told her that in church all the angels went up to the altar. Amanda moved over as ordered (and Agatha sat on her lap; she didn't want to go up to the altar).

Amanda suspected when she heard someone talk about having God in their life or taking Jesus as their personal savior that they were really just talking about their own insubstantial companion, but one to whom they attributed powers greater than phantom Agatha's or Marjorie's simple empathetic presence. People had different needs, but pretending that your invisible friend was a supernatural god seemed a bit extreme, a pretty weird need.

As far as Amanda could tell, the Wiccans didn't go there. Their gods and goddesses were big and vague, impersonal powers of nature. Wiccans didn't claim that their supreme beings spoke with them (how crazy was that?) or sent them written messages. Amanda liked that. There didn't seem to be any pagan prophets proclaiming that this is the word of god, as if they had found some unshredded document in the deity's office trash or had secretly taped their conversations with the big guy. On the whole it seemed more humble than other religions. Amanda hadn't had a problem when Morgan arranged for Denise and her tribe to occupy the house. They didn't proselytize. They didn't sing hymns. They paid their rent.

But now they were laying claim to some sort of victimhood, as if Amanda was persecuting them for their beliefs when she couldn't care less what made-up stuff they said they believed. Where was that at? Amanda believed they wouldn't want to live in a place undergoing an extreme renovation. She and Morgan would be moving out, too, to someplace nearby so they could see the renovations through to completion. They would have to find a place, too. Were they persecuting themselves? Oh well, Morgan was on the case. They had been through more threatening legal thickets.

Amanda settled into Nemo's chair on the kitchen porch and read her book. It was set in France in the Middle Ages. She vaguely remembered the plot. There was a war going on, and the heroine had been kidnapped and was being held for ransom in a fortresslike nunnery. The hero had to free her even though her father was his sworn enemy. By the time Amanda's hair was dry her eyelids were heavy, and she went up to her room to take a nap, locking the door behind her.

***

His poor car. It was like it was the real victim in all this. It had gotten stolen, stuck in the mud, dragged out, noxiously cleaned, bled on, accused of being a crime scene, arrested, then strip-searched. Its interior had been dusted with white powder and sprayed with strange liquids. The back seat had been removed and put back improperly. There was the residue of something gooey on the steering wheel and gear shift, and there was another whole set of smells. It was not the same car. It was as if it had been raped. But at least Dominick had it back. No thanks to Morgan.

On Wednesday, not having heard back from Morgan, Dominick returned to the Greene County Sheriff's Office, expecting a day of delays and unknown difficulties. He would not answer any questions, but he would not go away either. He had Vernon drop him off and told him not to wait. But once he found his Dutch detective everything went surprisingly quickly. He was told that they had no firm evidence that a rape had occurred and that the girl's story did not "hold up," whatever that meant, and besides she had disappeared without filing formal charges. She was wanted in Ohio. They were deeply disappointed that they couldn't charge Dominick or hold his car. All Dominick had to do to get his car back was sign some papers and wait for one of the lab boys to bring it around. The lab boy turned out to be a woman, who called him a scum bag when she handed him the keys.

Dominick found Vernon in his Cadillac parked in his default location, where Dominick had first found him, on Main Street across from the courthouse. Dominick had already stopped at an ATM and taken out the maximum allowed in a day, $400, which he intended to give Vernon for his services over the past several days. If Vernon wasn't busy, maybe they could have a good-bye lunch. They ate at the same place they had eaten the first time.

Over lunch Dominick complained about the newly trashed interior of his car. He just didn't feel at home there any more. Vernon knew a man in town who did detail work who would clean it for him, return it smelling like a brand new car. After lunch Dominick followed Vernon to an out-of-luck house on a back street at the edge of town, where Vernon's friend looked the car over and gave him a price. Dominick left the car there and got a ride from Vernon back to Hudson and the St. George. It meant one more night in Hudson, but Vernon said he would stop by later and they would go out.

It rained all afternoon, a steady, warm rain. There was no going out. Dominick stayed in his room, but his books didn't interest him. He even turned on the TV at one point, but that was a hopeless distraction. As eager as he was to leave, he could not get Sissy off his mind. Twice he picked up the phone to call her at the newspaper, and twice he put it back down without dialing. He still had her books to return. He could give them to Vernon. He did not necessarily want to say good-bye, but he did want to see her again. He tried to remember the last time he had felt like this. It had been a long time. It was twilight when Vernon returned, an early twilight because of the rain. He said Sissy had invited them out to dinner at her place.

Dominick wanted to bring a bottle of wine, but Vernon pointed out that Sissy didn't allow alcohol in her house, so they stopped for a quart of ice cream instead. Vernon had no idea what Sissy's favorite flavor might be. Dominick was surprised by Sissy's house. It was so . . . well, normal—a two-floor townhouse in a new duplex on a cul-de-sac of identical duplexes. Vernon rang the doorbell when they got there. There was no porch and they were standing there in the rain. They could have been in any suburb standing in the rain.

Sissy was dressed in a dashiki again, a different one, black with gold embroidery, when she answered the door. She was barefoot. She gave her father a hug and a kiss on the cheek as he went in. Then she did the same to Dominick. She took his offered white plastic bag with the ice cream inside and gave him another hug and kiss with her thank you. The second time Dominick hugged and kissed her back. She seemed to like that and gave him a very personal smile, one he had not seen before. She kept her arm around his waist as they walked into the living room. "I'm so glad you could come," she said. Vernon had already settled on a couch in front of a big flat-screen TV and was clicking through channels with the remote control. "Yankee game," he said. Dominick followed Sissy into the galley-like kitchen, where something smelled Thai spicy.

"You're not a baseball fan?" Sissy asked as she put the ice cream in the freezer.

"I'm more of a food fan. It was kind of you to invite me. It's been a while since I've had a home-cooked meal."

"It's nice to have someone to cook for," Sissy said. "It will be a bit longer before dinner is ready. Would you like something to drink? Tonic, juice, tea, coconut water?"

"Coconut water sounds fine," Dominick said. He had never tasted it without rum in it. The kitchen was small, and, being two large people, they pretty much filled it. Sissy poured him a tall glass of coconut water on the rocks. In the living room Vernon had found his baseball game, and the announcers were filling the long empty spaces with their knowing chatter.

Sissy stirred something on the stove and re-covered it. "Daddy said you got your car back. That's good. I guess that means you're free to leave."

"I am overdue where I was headed," Dominick said. He was leaning up against the one kitchen counter and he had to make himself thinner to let Sissy pass. "Sorry, I'm in your way."

"Not at all," she said. "I do not mind brushing past you," and she gave him an extra bump with her hip as she passed. "This place wasn't made for the likes of us."

Their smiles were simultaneous and shared.

"Does the world seem to be getting smaller to you?" Dominick asked.

"No, it's still wide open for me."

Whatever was really behind the look Sissy gave Dominick, he saw it as saying, yeah, I'm a lonesome person, too. He held her gaze for a second before taking a sip of his coconut water without rum. His mouth was dry. He wondered if he was blushing.

She gave him a slap on the arm as she passed by, a familial slap. "Go see if Daddy wants something to drink, would you?"

Vernon said he'd take a tonic, hold the vodka. On his way back to the kitchen Dominick noticed that the dining room table was set for four. "We are four tonight?" He asked as Sissy poured a glass of tonic for Vernon and squeezed a lemon wedge into it.

"She should be down any minute," Sissy said. "Here you go." She handed Dominick Vernon's drink. "Dinner should be ready in about ten."

When Dominick went back into the living room with Vernon's drink there was a second person sitting on the couch watching the ball game with him. It was Susan. "Hello," she said. "I'm sorry."

***

Wednesday, Amanda bought a new car, a Toyota Camry, at a place north of Hudson. They had a champagne-colored one and she took it, wrote a check for it, and left her worthless old Chevy sitting in their parking lot. The Camry still had dealer plates on it as she drove away. She had never owned a new car before. She couldn't believe how quiet it was. When she picked Morgan up at the Hudson Amtrak station when she came in on the 5:35 from Albany she had to get out of the car and wave to get Morgan's attention. Morgan was pleased but found fault with the color, or non-color as she called it. "Just like you to pick something totally neutral," she said.

"It's an earth color," Amanda protested.

"It's anonymous," Morgan said, as if being anonymous were something despicable. Morgan was in one of her moods, looking for a fight, for something to make her feel better.

"Things didn't go well in Albany?" Amanda asked. God, how she enjoyed driving this car. It was like it could read the curves all by itself.

"Why do you say that? Everything's fine. Let's stop to eat. I don't want to go back there yet. Have you heard from Nemo?"

"He stopped by yesterday. I don't know if we're going to see him again. He had that faraway look in his eyes. Oh, and there was a woman reporter snooping around, too, looking for Denise or Susan."

"A newspaper reporter?"

"Yeah. I got rid of her. Doesn't this car ride nice?"

"Yes, they've made some advancements in that department in the twenty years you've been driving that Chevy. Has Nemo gotten his car back? He can't leave without his car."

"He didn't have it yesterday. Is that air-con too cold?"

"Yes. Turn it off. Then he must still be at the St. George."

"He was with some black man. Shall we eat at the French place in Catskill?"

"If we can get a table. A black man?"

"It's still early. Nemo said he left something in your room."

"Some shirts. A black man? There aren't many of those around here."

"I took him to be his driver. How did things go with the lawyers?"

"They're looking into it. We'll fight the temporary restraining order, of course. It's going to cost us something even though it's all bullshit. Wait. Turn off here." Morgan pointed to a parking lot beside a store. They were almost at the turn-off to the bridge to Catskill. "Let me see if Nemo's in. Maybe we could take him out to dinner." Morgan dialed his hotel room, but there was no answer. Amanda pulled back onto the highway and across the bridge to Catskill. They ate at the French place on Main Street famous for its stuffed shrimp. Morgan got to pick a fight with the waiter about the wine. Then she could relax. Amanda didn't care. She was just thrilled about her new car.

✳✳✳

Dinner was strange. Not the food—Sissy's Thai curried eggplant was superb—but the situation. As far as Vernon was concerned Susan was just some new young friend of Sissy's. Susan barely spoke. Sissy played most of the roles—hostess, daughter, observer, friend, control. Dominick didn't especially care; he was just happy to be there, enjoying Sissy's company. They laughed a lot about things that had nothing to do with any of them. At the end of the meal Vernon excused himself to go watch the end of his ball game, and Sissy took dishes back to the kitchen, leaving Susan and Dominick alone at the table.

"I accept your apology, Susan, but for what?" Dominick asked.

Susan was dressed in jeans and a plain white blouse, like the blouse of a schoolgirl's uniform, which made her look even younger than her years. "I . . . you know . . ." She didn't look up. She was pale. "I didn't want you to get in any trouble. I'm sorry if you did."

"Actually, you seem to have managed it pretty well. Denise put you in a tough spot."

"I didn't like that hospital. Sissy got me out. So, are you and . . ." Susan nodded toward the kitchen. "You know—are you two like a couple? You seem sort of . . ."

"No, we've only just met. Why do you ask?"

"Because she asks a lot of questions, and I don't know if I should answer them or not. But if she's your friend then I guess she's alright."

"What sort of questions?"

"Oh, about the house and Denise and what goes on there. I mean, she never asked about you."

"Well, I don't see any reason why you shouldn't answer her questions. That is if you feel like it and know the answers."

For the first time, Susan looked up at Dominick. There was a tiny smile on her face. "It might be fun to make things up."

"It might be fun, but I doubt it would be helpful. Are you staying here then?"

"Sissy has an extra room."

Sissy called from the kitchen, "Susan, come and give me a hand. Ice cream for desert."

After desert Dominick helped Sissy with the dishes in the kitchen. There was no dishwasher. Susan was back in the living room with Vernon, watching TV.

"Susan says she's staying here now," Dominick said, taking a dish from the rack to dry.

"Until I can figure out what to do with her."

"How did you spring her from the hospital?"

"She was a voluntary admission. Given the chance she voluntarily left."

"That simple? She's not eighteen. Her sister must have checked her in. Wouldn't her sister have to check her out?"

"Let's just say Susan went for a ride and didn't go back. That's a pretty disreputable place, not very pleasant. She didn't want to be there."

"She said you were asking her about the Van Houten place."

"Just curious. Not that she's told me anything. All she would say was that she wanted to apologize to you. It was when I mentioned you that she agreed to leave that place. I thought that giving her the chance to meet with you and apologize might loosen her up a bit. She talks to you, I noticed."

"So that's why you invited me over? To loosen up Susan?"

Sissy was putting the last dish into the dish rack. "No, that's not why I invited you over. If anything that was my excuse to myself for inviting you over, because I wanted to see you again and I didn't know how to arrange that and explain it to myself. I'm sorry. I'm not very good at these attraction things. I flunked chemistry." Sissy put a soapy hand on Dominick's arm. "In fact, I wish I had just asked you over without any excuses, so that Daddy and Susan weren't here tonight complicating things."

"I'd like that," Dominick said. Their faces had never been closer. He felt like all the spaces separating them were shrinking. Pheromonal gravitation, he thought. Her eyes were hazel. They smiled.

"You, too?" she said, a personal whisper.

Dominick nodded and smiled back. There was a fresh camaraderie between them, co-victims of a shared disorder.

"Gotta go, lover boy," Vernon said from the dining room door. "Thanks for supper, Sissy, but it's getting on bedtime for me and we have to drive back."

"Scram, Daddy," Sissy said laughing then giving Dominick a playful peck on the cheek. "He's just cute, that's all." Vernon left the doorway. "Can you come back tomorrow night without Daddy? I can lock Susan in her room."

"I should have my car back. I purposefully forgot to bring your books tonight. That was going to be my excuse for coming back. May I return your books tomorrow night?"

"There may be overdue fines."

"I'll gladly pay." The kiss was just a sample, an experiment. Dominick turned to go.

Sissy dried her hands on a dish towel. "What do you think I should do about Susan?"

Dominick stopped at the door to think. "You stole her. She's yours but you can't keep her. She shouldn't or won't go back where you got her. Try contacting her parents, I guess. Meanwhile, if you want her to relax and open up, get her a little weed to smoke. That way you'll be accused not only of kidnapping and harboring a fugitive but of contributing to the delinquency of a minor."

Sissy laughed. Dominick couldn't think of anything he would rather be doing than making Sissy laugh. "Oh, and hide your car keys."

Chapter 16

What defines a person better than the secrets that he does not share? What is more private than selected silence? What is intimacy if not opening those self-locked rooms, those cherished redoubts? Of course, there were always the deeply personal things that no one ever revealed, that often were kept hidden even from one's self. And then there were the foretime episodes so embarrassing or painful or revealing that a palisade had been built around them. Like most fortifications those ramparts had been built to defend against past wars and would never be challenged again. As Sissy spoke, Dominick wondered at the counsel he was keeping to himself, at his continued reticence to interrupt to tell her things he knew and she didn't, to share and not just passively observe.

They were having lunch at Sissy's vegetarian place in Hudson again, and she was talking about writing an article on the Van Houten place. "It would make an interesting story," she said. "There aren't many of those grand old private estates still standing hereabouts." He watched her eat. Lunch was in place of dinner. Sissy's plans had changed as she had to cover a city council meeting that evening. "It's not my usual beat, but they fired the guy who used to do it." She had left a message for him at the St. George, changing their date. He had picked up her note just in time to meet her there.

That morning Vernon had come over to drive Dominick back to Catskill to pick up his car. They stopped at an ATM along the way for Dominick to get more cash. Getting his car cleaned was well worth the sixty bucks Vernon's friend charged. The interior was spotless, and it even smelled like a new car again. Dominick settled accounts with Vernon as well, giving him $500 and thanks. When they parted, Vernon said, "You be good to my daughter now." Dominick wasn't sure how he could be bad to her.

Perhaps by not filling her in on things he knew? For instance, when Sissy said she had been charmed by how original the old place looked, he said, "Oh, you've been there?" although he already knew from Amanda that Sissy had stopped by. And when Sissy said that she would like to take a photographer back there to get some shots but she didn't think that woman Amanda would let her back on the property, Dominick didn't tell her that the woman Amanda was his sister. And when Sissy wondered if Amanda was a Wicca witch—"Isn't that like a witch's name?"—Dominick said nothing. Sissy did not mention that her great-aunt had a connection to the place, so obviously she hadn't learned that either. He kept his secrets of the basement rooms and the trunks and their contents. He let her go on. She seemed so sure of herself, it would be a pity to interrupt.

When Sissy stopped to eat, Dominick asked, "Have you had a chance to talk with Susan?"

"No, she went to her room when you guys left last night, and she wasn't up when I left for work this morning."

"Is this article going to be about the Wicca thing?"

"I guess that could be part of it, like at the end, about recent tenants. I gather it started out as a Methodist minister's house—nice rounded closure there."

"I took some photographs of the place," Dominick said, "but they wouldn't be of any use to you, black-and-white and undeveloped film, not digital like you folks use these days."

"You did? Oh, please let me use them. I'm sure they are great. There's an old guy at the paper, Sid, who still shoots film now and then. He's got his own darkroom. He could develop them."

Dominick was thinking that a feature newspaper article about the old house could only help Amanda and Morgan's real estate efforts, free publicity. He could please Sissy, help his sister out, and get to see his photos all in one—leave town on a triple up note. Sissy was smiling at him again as she chewed, that secret smile. "This Sid knows what he's doing?" Dominick asked.

"An old pro."

"I'll get the film to you this afternoon. See what's on there, if there's anything you can use."

"That means you'll be around a little longer?" Sissy said. "Will I have to keep making up reasons to keep you here?"

Dominick didn't have to answer, as the waitress came to clear their dishes. Out on the sidewalk Sissy gave him a squeeze and a kiss on the cheek before hurrying back to her office. Dominick realized that once again he had forgotten to return her books. Absentmindedly he rubbed his cheek where Sissy had kissed him, then he walked down back streets toward the river, through brick blocks that seemed to go backwards in time as they emptied of people. As far as Dominick could find out, there never had been a fort here.

✳✳✳

Amanda felt pretty dumb. The evening before, when she had picked Morgan up at the station and they had had dinner together, something had seemed different about her, but just *what* hadn't registered. Amanda had been too full of her new car to pay attention. But at breakfast she figured out what was different—Morgan's hair. The streaks of grey at her temples were gone, and she had also had it cut and styled. The difference was subtle but telling. It had taken years off. Without those telltale badges of maturity, there was no reason to question the youthfulness of the rest of her appearance. She seemed altogether younger.

That morning they had both stayed in their rooms until after Denise and all the other girls were gone. There had been another scene with Denise the night before, when they got home, and the truce they struck involved a border established not in space but in time—the combatants would time-share the kitchen. The row with Denise had to do with poor Susan, who it would seem had again escaped. High Priest nurse Lloyd had called Denise to say that Susan had gone missing from his funny farm and to ask if she was back with them. Susan had had a visitor earlier in the day—a Negress, Lloyd had said, and Denise repeated the word. Lloyd had made sure the woman left alone, but later he discovered Susan was gone as well.

When Denise had said Negress, Morgan grinned. "That would be like a tigress or a lioness?" she said. "Amazing how they let them wander free, isn't it?" At that point Susan's sister Kathy had started yelling, demanding her sister back. Facts and logic—that Amanda and Morgan hadn't known where Susan had been taken, that Morgan didn't drive and in fact had been in Albany, that they had no reason or interest in kidnapping Susan—did not prevail. Denise admitted that Lloyd had said "a large Negress," which hardly described Morgan, but then she suggested that it was a conspiracy of some sort.

"Oh, yes, sister, you've found us out," Morgan had said. "Us Negresses have a secret underground cooperation where we kidnap young white girls. We gift them to our menfolk as sex toys."

Denise had backed off then. She had caused her little scene for the benefit of Kathy and the other girls. Amanda figured Denise didn't really care where Susan was anyway. As long as she was gone it didn't matter where. Amanda figured who the large black woman was, but she wasn't about to say so. Wherever Susan was, she was better off there than back here or in that institution. Before Denise and her troop marched off, the agreement to the equal but separate use of the kitchen had been reached.

In the morning it was peaceful. Amanda noted that the girls had even washed and put away all their breakfast dishes. "I don't think they even ate here," Morgan said. "It's not like them not to leave some sort of mess. They didn't even make coffee." It was then, in the morning light, that Amanda noticed Morgan's new look as she was fixing coffee.

"You had your hair done in Albany," Amanda said.

"You just noticed?"

"I just thought to mention it. It's nice. It works."

"Thanks. You should do something with yours, now that you got money to burn. Something to go with your new wheels, say highlights in a complimentary color."

Something had changed with Morgan in addition to her hair. It was as if she were moving to an inner soundtrack, and it was a song that she liked, that she could dance to. What else had Amanda been missing? Morgan's cell phone sounded. She pulled it out of the pocket of her cut-offs as she walked out the back door but didn't answer it until she was out of earshot in the garden. This was new, too. Was it a man? It must be a man. All her trips to Albany. That new jacket she wore on the train. Amanda's recent feeling that Morgan wasn't really here when she was here.

Amanda sat there and listened to the Mr. Coffee hiss and gurgle as it finished up. She was feeling something, but she wasn't sure what to call it. Lonesome didn't quite cover it, and it wasn't something as blunt as jealousy. Morgan had never been hers, so she could hardly lose her. But now Morgan had secrets, and Morgan wasn't supposed to have secrets. Having secrets meant that she was hiding something, that she had things to hide from Amanda. Was there such a thing as a trust rating, like a credit rating? A numerical scale? Amanda didn't want to reduce Morgan's trust rating. It put too many things at risk. But if it was just a man—and say he was married and so on the sly—then it was none of Amanda's business after all. She heard Morgan's laugh from the garden. Maybe it was envy she was feeling, envy that Morgan might actually have something worth keeping private.

Amanda fixed herself a mug of coffee. She wanted to take it out onto the porch to sit in Nemo's chair and drink it, but she was afraid that if she did Morgan would think she was trying to eavesdrop. What a funny word. She sat in the big wing chair instead and watched Morgan out in the garden talking into her palm. This house would be their last joint venture. Things always ran out that way, came to a natural ending, and people went their separate ways. It was a fact of life that nothing lasted. The only thing that did not change was the will to change. Morgan laughed again and made a dancer's gesture toward the sky.

When Morgan came back into the kitchen she said, "Let's get your brother back out here one more time to make our pitch. You call him; insist on seeing him before he goes. He can get his shirts back. It's worth one more try."

✳✳✳

"Why didn't you tell me Amanda was your sister?" Sissy wanted to know. "You just let me go on about her being a witch and all."

"It wasn't important. She's only my half sister, and I knew she wasn't a witch," Dominick said. "I gather you have spoken with Susan then." Dominick was driving. They were in his car, headed for the Rip Van Winkle Bridge again, over the stretch of road that had become so familiar its distance seemed to have shrunk in half.

"Oh, yes. Susan opened up last night after I got home from the council meeting, and I didn't even have to get her stoned. Strange girl. She likes you, for instance, for some reason. She claims she has no past—not that she doesn't remember anything but that there is nothing to remember. When I asked about her parents, she said she didn't have any. And when I said bullshit, everyone's got parents, she said maybe everyone else did but she never had. I have to get her some clothes today. We can stop at Walmart. All she's got is what she was wearing when she went over the fence. There's nothing to that girl. She doesn't weigh a hundred pounds."

"So what did Susan have to say?"

"Oh, that she liked it alright at the house, except for the fact that it was haunted. She liked the garden and the fact that there weren't any men around. I asked her if she had lived in the country before, and she said she didn't know, she doubted it."

"Did she talk about Denise, the Wicca stuff?"

"I gather Susan didn't participate. She called it some sort of church thing that her sister and the other girls did. She seemed scared of Denise. Was Susan like a slave there or something? She didn't have a life."

Dominick had gotten a call that morning from Amanda, inviting him over for a good-bye lunch. He had been about to decline when the idea struck him. "May I bring a guest?" he asked. He didn't say who it was. So now he was headed out to the Van Houten place for one last visit, bringing Sissy along. She had jumped at the chance. For one thing his photos, while artsy and all, were pretty useless for her purposes. There wasn't one proper picture of the house itself, just details and shadows. She wanted Dominick to shoot some more and had brought along the office digital camera. Dominick had stashed his stolen papers and ledger in the trunk of the car. He would try one more time to secretly replace them if he got the chance.

Sissy liked his car—"It smells brand new," she said—but was surprised he had no CDs to play on his fancy sound system. Dominick confessed that he wasn't sure how to use it. He had never even turned on the radio. Along the way he explained that Amanda and her partner had plans to renovate the old place and give it a new life. He would let Amanda explain it; it was their project after all, not his. Sissy asked if he knew anything about the place being haunted, which he didn't, but that gave him the opening to tell her a couple of stories about houses where he had previously been a guest that were supposedly haunted. He got her laughing again, that pleasure.

"You've stayed in a lot of old houses," Sissy said.

"It's a hobby. No, more of a pastime. I have become a sort of professional houseguest to rich people. Rich people tend to live in either very modern or very old, big places. The old places come with stories."

"A professional houseguest to rich people? How does that work?"

"The big houses of the idle rich are chronically empty. I relieve my hosts' anxiety about that by moving in for a while. It's not so much my company they crave as just company. Especially if they have servants, whom the rich feel are always underemployed. I'm clean and I'm quiet; I wear the right clothes to dinner. It's instructive how lonesome people with a lot of money often are."

"You like doing that?"

"I much prefer it to living in hotels, and of course it means I have no bills to pay."

"You have no home address?"

"No," Dominick said. They were on the high bridge over the river now. "No, not any more." His mother's address in Alexandria had always been his fictional official residence. Now he would have to find another. The big bright river, as placid as a lake, spread out on either side of them. Sissy was silent, looking out over the water.

Where it had washed out, the road to the house was still only one temporary lane. At the house there was a brand new tan sedan parked in the driveway, but Amanda's old Chevy wasn't there.

"How are we going to manage this?" Sissy asked.

"Well, you've already met Amanda, so no introductions will be needed. I'll just point out that an article about the place could only help their venture, and we'll take it from there. We will all act like adults and make nice."

"That sounds doable. Wait." Sissy leaned across the front seat and gave Dominick a kiss on the lips. "You can say I'm your girlfriend, if you want to."

"I think I'll let Amanda draw what conclusions she wishes. Oh, and I don't think we should mention Susan at all."

They went up the steps to the front porch, but there was a large swatch of what looked like dried blood between them and the front door that stopped them. Dominick led the way around the side of the house toward the kitchen porch. Sissy went to take his arm, but he shrugged her off. "You behave yourself now," he said, but she just smiled.

That big chair was still on the kitchen porch where he had moved it, and Morgan was sitting in it reading a magazine, her legs tucked up beneath her. Amanda hadn't mentioned Morgan. Dominick hadn't factored her in.

"Hi!" Sissy called out, like family just stopping by.

Morgan looked up, a curious smile on her face. She said "Hello" slowly, a question, then, "Hello, Dominick, how brave of you to come."

"Hello, Morgan. Brave?"

"This place hasn't been exactly good luck for you. Your friend?"

"I'm Sissy," Sissy said, going up to lean forward from the garden path and shake Morgan's hand.

"Well, welcome, Sissy. My name is Morgan, and this here is Amanda." Amanda had come out through the kitchen screen door carrying a tray with glasses and a pitcher of iced tea.

"Actually, we've already met. Hi, Amanda."

"Oh, yes. Sissy, isn't it?" Amanda said. She was not pleased.

"You know each other?" Morgan asked, giving Amanda a queer look.

"My guest," Dominick said. Sissy's smile had a hard edge to it. They made quite a tableau, like something from a Chekhov play, three women like three cats sizing each other up. What had he done? What had he been thinking?

✳✳✳

Amanda couldn't imagine what message Nemo thought he was sending by showing up with that woman. Was he just playing games with them? Mixing things up for his personal entertainment? He claimed he just thought that an article in the local press about the house would improve their real estate prospects. Did that mean he was still considering buying in? He never explained how he and the Sissy woman had come to meet or what their connection was. She acted as if they were more than just casual acquaintances. She laughed at all his lame little jokes. She was young enough to be his daughter, for Pete's sake. She still had that perfect youthful skin. They were of a size together—XL.

Lunch was a disaster. The deviled eggs were way too salty, as if she had salted them twice. She burned the wild rice. A large black bug crawled out of Nemo's salad. Sissy wouldn't eat the salmon. Nemo seemed to withdraw to spectator status. Morgan had morphed into an entirely different social creature, one whom Amanda had never seen before and one who had no use for her. It was Morgan and Sissy's show, as they each called forth and deployed their finest displays of elaborate politesse and insincere deference. Morgan, for instance, whom Amanda knew disdained everything religious, was suddenly solicitous to Sissy's brand of born-again Christianity. Sissy for her part praised Morgan's shady real estate dealings as if they were the height of black female civic entrepreneurship. And, oh, how they loved each other's dirt-poor-roots anecdotes. It was all so blatantly fake it was frightening.

Distracted by disaster, it took a while for Amanda to see where Morgan was heading. In passing, Sissy had asked about the Wiccan thing—the symbol on the side of the house, the rumors about what went on out here—and Morgan had let it pass. Now she circled back there, with a Christian bent.

"Say, you're a local girl, Sissy," Morgan said. "Tell me, are there many pagans hereabouts? You asked before about the witches' coven and all. Those are all local white women. I know that down in Maryland we didn't have witches forming congregations. What's up with that?"

"I was curious about that, too," Sissy said. "You guys aren't . . . ah . . . you know, members?"

"No, no," Morgan said. "We just rented to them, that's all. I'm a firm believer in the First Amendment, freedom of religion, civil rights, etcetera. So, they're not Christians. I figured, so what? They're still Americans, still human. I figured we were doing them a favor, letting them all stay here together, even holding their little meetings here. Those white girls can go through some weird phases, you know? I figured they were harmless."

Amanda noted that when Morgan said "white girls" it was as if Amanda weren't sitting there beside her.

Morgan went on: "But after a while I began to realize that they weren't just not Christian, that they were like the opposite of Christian, anti-Christians. Maybe there was a reason they had been persecuted for so long, why they had to hide out. I guess I am wondering how common that is up here. You know, a lot of strange religious cults came out of this part of New York State. Is it the water or something? More tea?"

"No, actually, we are all pretty much basic Christians up here," Sissy said. "That's what makes the Wicca thing interesting. Who knew there were people like that around here?"

"Oh, so you might be interested in writing about the witches, too, not just the house?" If this was an accusation—and in Amanda's estimation it should have been—Morgan managed to make it sound an awful lot like an invitation. Denise and her troop had nothing to do with the house or its history or their efforts to restore and sell it. If anything, the Wiccan connection would seem to be bad publicity. What was Morgan thinking?

"Now, Sissy, as a Christian woman you must have some feelings about this," Morgan continued. "I mean, they have the right to worship the devil if they so choose, but I could see if it didn't sit well by local norms."

Amanda was beginning to feel all alone. It was like nothing was making any sense, like she was surrounded by strangers jabbering. Nemo was staring off into the distance. As far as Morgan and Sissy were concerned she wasn't even there. Morgan seemed bent on some pointless vendetta. Amanda had told Sissy not to return, and here she was sitting there, poking at her food. They were eating at the kitchen table. Amanda got up and walked out the back door to the porch. No one acknowledged her leaving. Sissy was asking Morgan about Wiccan meetings. How many participants? Amanda's pack of Pall Malls was on the table beside Nemo's chair. She lit one. It tasted terrible.

Nemo followed Amanda out onto the porch, but he didn't stop to talk. He walked right past her toward the path to the front of the house. "Sorry," he said. "We'll be leaving soon." Amanda felt like punching him as he walked by.

Chapter 17

"Morgan, the first time you and I talked about this, down in New York, you said something about my having a permanent place here if I joined in your development scheme. How would that work?" Dominick and Morgan were down toward the foot of the driveway, looking up at the old house. Dominick had walked there to take a long-distance shot of the place for Sissy's article. He was using the newsroom's digital camera that he had gotten from the car. He had never used one of these gizmos before, so he wasn't sure if he had taken a photo or not or how many. He had stopped to light a cigar and enjoy this respite from the verbal jujitsu that lunch had devolved into. To his surprise Morgan had joined him, confessing that she wanted to make one more pitch for his throwing some of Marjorie's money into their Diligence Retreat & Spa project.

Sissy's earlier question about his not having a permanent address had struck a chord in Dominick. What kind of person was it who didn't have an address? A homeless person, someone who lived in his car or under a bridge. For legal reasons he had to have a home address, an official state of residence. It was funny that Morgan had called it Marjorie's money, because he still thought of it that way, as Marjorie's money, not his, and it was her fault that he was now officially homeless, so maybe her money could appropriately solve that.

"We just write it into the agreement," Morgan said. "Basically, your investment would purchase for you a condo unit of your design in the final product, yours to live in, lease, or resell."

"Could I use this address before then? I mean before the place is completed?"

"I don't see why not. You'd be like a partner in the firm. Should I have something like that drawn up for you to look at?"

"Yes, why don't you do that? Do you still have the address of that lawyer Barnett in Alexandria?"

"Oh, yes, Counselor Barnett has stayed in touch."

"Send it to him to look at, the financials and all. I'll consider it."

"Well, hallelujah. I have to admit I didn't expect that. Why the change of heart? Surely not that young thing," Morgan said with a gesture of her head up toward the house. "I wouldn't think evangelical was quite your type."

"No. No, it has nothing to do with Sissy. I need an address, that's all. Why not here? Remote is nice, and I'm assuming I can trust you and Amanda not to rob or defraud me." Dominick was looking at the house now in a different light. It seemed closer, for one thing, more personal; and for the first time he felt an urge to fix things—those sagging gutters, for instance, the uneven sills. He was embarrassed by a rusty air conditioner stuck in an upstairs bedroom window. He hadn't even seen it before. Where would his rooms be? Which exposure? "You will keep as much of the original building as you can?"

"That is the plan," Morgan said. "If you're a partner in the retreat, you'll have a say. I'm excited at the idea of having you aboard. I think you'll provide more than just needed capital."

"The place does kind of grow on you," Dominick said. "Here. I am sure you know how this thing works. Take a picture of the place for me, would you? For Sissy's article."

Morgan took the camera and pushed several buttons. "You already have a couple of fine shots of it here. But, I'll tell you what. Walk up the driveway a bit, and I'll take a picture of you in front of your new future home."

As they walked back up the driveway together, Dominick asked, "What was with the attack on the Wiccans? I never took you to be much of a Christian either."

"Oh, I was just playing with your girlfriend. No harm intended. I just wanted to see how Christian she was. These young people are so sure they know all the answers. It irks me sometimes."

"So how Christian is she?"

"Pretty much your standard max, I'd guess. Gospel Evangelical, the feel good type."

"Trying to turn her against Denise?"

"Just trying to grease her slant. How did you run across her anyways?"

"Sissy is a bit of a local historian. I borrowed some books from her."

"Anything about this place?"

"No, but I wasn't really looking. I will now."

They had reached the front of the house. "Morgan, can you find me a broom?" Dominick asked. Morgan went one way around a corner of the house toward the back porch, and Dominick went the other to where Susan's garden hose was coiled beside its spigot. By the time Morgan returned with a kitchen broom Dominick had already soaked part of the dried blood around the front door. "We can get rid of this, I think," he said. "This Denise's work?"

"You got that right, and I do believe there is some sort of curse attached to what you are doing," Morgan said.

"Just leave the broom. I'll do it. We'll see if it's a unisex curse."

Dominick was making some progress with the dried blood when the front door swung open and Sissy came out. She was half turned, speaking over her shoulder. "I don't know what your problem is, Amanda, or why you want to be that way and go there, but, sure, I'll leave." Sissy wasn't looking where she stepped as she came out the door, and she slipped in the smear of freshly soaked blood. Dominick dropped the broom and caught her before she went down. They stumbled backwards together in a comic tango until Dominick's back scrunched up against a veranda post. Then they both went down, Sissy in Dominick's lap, his hands on her generous breasts.

✳✳✳

After Sissy and Nemo left, Amanda finished cleansing the blood from the porch. She used soap and a scrub brush and all the bleach in the house. Her mood was not especially improved by Morgan's news that Nemo was considering a partnership. "I don't see why we need him or his money or his interference," Amanda said. She was on her knees with the scrub brush.

"That's not very sisterly of you," Morgan said. She was leaning against the front door jam, watching Amanda work. "The poor man has been saddled with this cash from his dead mother that he wants nothing to do with, and you would deny him the chance to transfer it guilt-free to his only sibling? Besides we always need more cash. It means less to borrow, less interest to pay, more freedom to do what we want without loan officers second-guessing everything. Come on, Amanda, this is business, remember? Free money is free money. You know he is incapable of hanging around to interfere. He has no head or heart for this sort of stuff."

"Why did he start doing this? And weren't Denise and her crew supposed to clean up this mess?"

"So, that young woman was the reporter who was here before looking for Susan?"

"You could give me a hand, you know."

"I warned Nemo there was a curse attached to messing with the blood. For all I know it's still attached. I'm saving myself for the next emergency."

Amanda's inner voice had been busy all afternoon. It had had a lot to comment on that Amanda couldn't say out loud, until she did, to Sissy. Now she felt like saying: *Screw you, Morgan. Look at me, down here on my hands and knees like a scrub woman while she stands there like some queen of the estate. Who is in charge here? How does she get off closing a deal with Nemo when he is my brother and it is my mother's money? Always on the outside, aren't you, Amanda my dear? O clueless one. My brother in cahoots with that Sissy woman. Do you think they have sex? And Morgan feeding her that Christian paranoia crap.*

"That woman only wants to write about the sensationalist witches stuff out here, not the house or its history or what we want to do with it," Amanda blurted out. "How could you encourage her like that?"

"You missed a spot," Morgan said. "So, she writes some negative tabloid stuff about Denise and her coven mates? So what? It still puts the place on the map, and it might turn local public opinion against the anti-Christ Wiccans. How can that hurt? Enemy of my enemy and all that."

Amanda got to her feet. She wasn't done scrubbing, but she was finished with it. "You know I don't like having enemies. I never could see the point, the utility of having them."

"You don't choose them. They choose you."

"So, Denise's legal threat about not leaving is serious enough that we have to help incite an actual witch hunt?"

"All's fair in love and war."

"Do you actually believe that?"

"Well, I'm not sure about the love part—it's been too long—but the war part is just good policy. Take what advantage is handed to you. We want them out of our hair; maybe some bad publicity will help the cause. Look, I don't like that Sissy woman anymore than you do—can't stand the type—but your brother brought her in, and now he's going to be part of our team. Let's just see what she does. If I read her right, she is one of those personal relationship with Jesus types. Who knows? Maybe we'll even get Him and His on our side. That would be weird."

"I think you would be allied with the devil if it suited your purposes better."

"What difference would it make? It's all make believe anyway, Narnia stuff. Here, give me that hose. I'll rinse it off. It's still slick as shit. Listen, I'll have to go up to Albany again to get this agreement with Nemo drawn up ASAP, while he's still on the hook, and, yeah, it looks as if Denise has enough of a bogus case about religious discrimination to hold things up if we don't chop her down quick. Can you give me a ride over to Hudson to catch the 4:45? You'll get to drive your new wheels around. I'll get you some CDs for your new deck when I'm up there. Write down whatever you want. We'll have to stop at the bank to move some money around. Look, your knees and shins are all blood colored. Go shower and change. I'll pack."

The Amtrak station in Hudson was down by the river. Amanda got Morgan there in time to catch her train to Albany. Then she sat there in her new car for a while, feeling disconcertedly abandoned for some reason. The thought of going back to the house all alone repulsed her. She hadn't had a chance to talk with Nemo after he and Sissy had gotten themselves up from the floor of the porch and promptly left. She and Nemo hadn't had a chance to talk at all during the toxic lunch. His hotel was up in the back of town. She drove there, having nowhere else to go. Nemo's black Lexus was not in the parking lot. She dialed his room on her cell phone. No answer. She drove around a bit, through the town then out of town to the east into the country, onto back roads, trying to get lost. A slow and gorgeous summer sundown flashed like strobe lights through the roadside trees. She started to cry because there was no one else there to see it. No one anywhere to share. She ended up at dusk back at the St. George Hotel. Nemo's car was still not there. She parked and checked in, a room two floors above his. She found a bar around the corner and up a block, filled with locals. She knew she was going to get drunk, invite oblivion in, and she wanted to be close enough to a room and a bed to stagger back to. The bartender was cute enough. She could watch him as she slipped away, her glance avoiding then lingering on her own face reflected in the back-bar mirror. Reflections are always reversed, she thought, just like thoughts of the past, going backwards. There was chili on the bar menu, and at some point she ordered a bowl. If she had something to eat she could drink longer. The voice in her head had no more to say.

***

The two lowest floating ribs were cracked. Dominick knew it was more than a bruise by the time Sissy and he had made it to the high-way into Catskill. When the pain went from throbbing to stabbing he pulled over to let Sissy drive and got in the back seat to see if he could find some prone or supine position that hurt less. Sissy said the only place to go was the emergency room at Columbia Memorial over in Hudson, and she headed there, back through Catskill and back across the bridge. Every jolt in the road bed registered in his lower back like a spike on the Richter scale. The ER and X-rays only took a few hours. There was nothing they could do for him besides give him a prescription for pain pills.

Dominick's hotel was only a few blocks away from the hospital, but Sissy refused to drop him there. Instead, she left him in the car, took his key, and went up to his room to toss some of his things into a bag. He would stay at her place tonight. He was in too much pain to object. The pain pills they had finally given him in the ER hadn't made much of a dent in how his nerve endings were feeling about all this. He wanted a bed and a pillow to hug.

"*Costae fluitantes*, I think," Dominick said when Sissy came back to the car.

"Cost you what?" she asked.

"No, that term that I just said, I think it's the Latin for those lower ribs. Isn't it strange that I should remember that from anatomy class so many years ago?"

"Yeah, weird. We'll stop at the drugstore, and I'll get you your oxycodone pills. That might help."

"You know, some people have more ribs than others, thirteen pairs instead of twelve. I wonder how many I have."

"According to Genesis you gave me at least one."

"Could I give you these broken ones?"

"And God shaped woman from his broken ribs? I don't think so, not in my Bible."

At Sissy's house Susan was evicted from the spare bedroom and the bed linens were quickly changed. Sissy helped Dominick out of his shoes and socks and shirt and pants. She brought him two white pills and a glass of water, and he eased into bed, trying to find the position that hurt the least. When the pills kicked in he dove into a dream-filled sleep.

When Dominick awoke, Susan was sitting beside his bed, her hand resting on his shoulder. There was still light out the bedroom window, but it was fading toward dusk. Or was it dawn?

"You were moaning pretty loud," she said. She left her hand there. He appreciated that.

"How long?" he asked.

"Were you asleep? Just a few hours, I guess. I was watching TV. You sounded in pain. Does it hurt or was it a bad dream?"

"I tossed you out of your bed. Sorry."

"That's okay. I like the couch. I have the TV. Sissy said you broke your ribs. That sounds bad."

"Sissy?"

"She had to leave, go back to work, I guess. Are you going to die?"

"Not from a few cracked ribs I'm not."

"You want more pills? These are supposed to be really good." Susan was holding the bottle of oxycodone in her other hand.

Dominick really didn't want more pills. It was too soon to take more, and he was suspicious of them. As long as he didn't move, the pain was just an ache. But it didn't seem like a good idea to leave them with Susan. "Yes," he said, putting out his hand for the bottle. "Could you get me a glass of water?"

Funny thing about pain, how it becomes your companion. The two of you sort of work things out, chained together as you are. It is an unequal relationship, as you do all the accommodating. But even pain has to sleep; unconsciousness is its maximum refuge after all. And sleep is now your best friend, too—friend of your friend. Pain is a tutor as well. It teaches simplicity, how meaningless everything else is. It insists on meditation, on inward searching, the perfection of stillness. Pain takes vague, abstract time and messes with it, vividly colors it, can make it crawl and stop and even run backwards. Dominick's fitful slumbers were busy with intense dreams. He dreamed of marching and flying, of being lost in the fog of gunpowder smoke in the battle at Little Round Top as a rifleman in the 20th Maine. He dreamed he was wounded and spent the night dying all alone in an open field, his pain and the stars above him all that he knew, his uniform jacket and shirt yanked aside to confirm the gut shot that would kill him. He dreamed about time as a book with its final pages flipping over all by themselves. He dreamed he was sleeping in that basement room at the Van Houten place, hearing bloodhounds off in the distance, unable to move or escape.

Dominick saw little of Sissy over the next few days. She was busy covering arts festival events, and some scandal was breaking over a local politician. It all meant nothing to Dominick and mattered less. Susan he saw a lot of. She made it possible for him not to have to go down the stairs, so he didn't. She fixed and brought him simple meals—toasted English muffins and instant oatmeal for breakfast, peanut butter and honey sandwiches for lunch, iced tea to drink. He had no appetite anyway. Susan never left the house. She spent her days watching the big TV downstairs, which was always on like another housemate.

Susan also took a lot of showers, several a day. The weather had turned hot, and either Sissy's house had no air-con or it wasn't turned on. Dominick would wake up from a nap and hear the shower going in the bathroom across the hall. He had to wonder what Susan did for so long in the shower. When she would finally emerge from the bathroom a lovely aroma was released into the hallway and through the open door of his room. He would see her pass on the way to the stairs, her long wet hair combed down her back, dressed just in one of the over-large long T-shirts Sissy had brought her from Walmart, barefoot, no underwear. The skin on her thin limbs sticking out of the T-shirt was just a shade pinker than the shirt's pure-white cotton. She was a vision of simplicity, the beauty of plainness. He took to calling her nurse. She liked that.

The second day Dominick was at Sissy's house, Vernon showed up with the rest of his luggage and things from his hotel room. "Sissy said there was no point in you paying for a room you weren't using. So she checked you out. I think I got everything, but I'm not much at packing. You alright here?" Vernon had brought two other things he thought Dominick might need—a cane and a bottle of vodka. "You'll have to keep it hidden from Sissy, of course, but I find a few drinks help the pain pills along considerably, and you won't be operating any heavy equipment in here."

Dominick had lost all track of what day of the week it was, so Sunday came as a minor surprise. Sissy was not up and off to work early but had some time before heading off to church. She came in to chat. With the help of a couple of white pills and Vernon's cane, Dominick had taken a shower and shaved that morning and found fresh clothes. His suspicion of the pain pills had vanished with the pain. He had taken another with the breakfast of toast and orange juice that Susan had brought him. It was from Susan he learned it was Sunday. Following Vernon's advice, he had turned his orange juice into a screwdriver. He was feeling a bit more human and was sitting up in an armchair by the open window of his room reading a book about the Iroquois, which he had found in a hallway bookshelf.

When Sissy came in she gave him a kiss on the cheek. "Look at you," she said. "You don't look like a patient at all, but like a man of leisure."

"My vocation, ma'am. Back on the job."

"You must have thought I'd forgotten you were here, or didn't care. Nothing could be farther from the truth. I've just been very busy, and whenever I got home and looked in, you were asleep."

"My other job."

"Well, you haven't been off my mind for a minute, or your being here, or why the Lord would bring you into my life then keep bringing us closer and closer, until here you are, sharing my house, brightening my life. The Lord put you in my care for a reason, you know."

Dominick had absolutely nothing to say. Sissy was seated on the side of the bed, smiling one of her more beguiling smiles, her head tilted to one side and her full lips slightly parted.

"You know, I have never had a man stay in my house before, and it feels so right because it is you. And to think Daddy introduced us," she said and laughed. "Well, I'm off to church. I'm going to pray to the Lord and ask everyone else to pray to the Lord for us, to let us know what course He wants us to follow." Sissy got up and gave him another kiss on the cheek. "You smell so good," she said. "I'll make us a proper Sunday dinner when I get back."

A while after Sissy left Susan came up to see if he wanted anything, and he asked for another glass of orange juice for a second screwdriver. When she came back with it she asked what he was reading.

"A book about the Iroquois," he said.

"What's that?"

"The Indians who once lived around here," he said, handing her the book.

"Oh, that's okay," Susan said, just glancing at the cover illustration and handing it back. "I don't read."

"You don't read?" Dominick asked. He had never met an adult who couldn't read.

"Maybe I could once, but I don't any more."

"Oh," Dominick said. He took a big sip of orange juice to make room in the glass for the vodka he would add after Susan left. "I don't hear the TV this morning. None of your shows on?"

"It's Sunday," Susan said. "Just guys playing golf and those stupid Christian shows."

"Stupid Christian shows?"

"Just guys stomping around hollering, talking gibberish. Boring. And awful music. You want anything else? I'm going to take a shower."

Looking at the maps in the book, Dominick discovered that the land hereabout had not been Iroquois but Mohican country, as in the last of.

Chapter 18

When Amanda woke up the next morning in her room at the St. George her head ached, her mouth was dry, and her cell phone was dead. She didn't have a toothbrush or a change of clothes, but at least she had undressed before going to bed, and she had gone to bed alone. Look at the bright side. She found two Aleve in her emergency pill stash. As she washed them down with tap water in a plastic cup, she winced, remembering the closing-time pass she had made at the bartender, which he had rebuffed with a laugh and a kiss on her cheek and a "Not tonight, honey." But all in all she wasn't sorry she had taken a night off from her usual boring life. There was a good reason why people drank. She was still horny in that vague morning-after way.

Nemo was not in his room, and his car was not in the parking lot. Amanda checked out of the hotel and had a big greasy breakfast at a café down Warren Street, pretending to read the morning paper as she studied the other customers, all regulars who knew one another and the waitress. She gave them each stories—jobs, families, disappointments. It was as if a night drinking had cleared her head of herself and she could notice things again. An old man with a cane stymied her. She couldn't imagine his life alone. The newspaper she'd picked up was the *Hudson Register Star*. She noted Sissy's by-line on a story about the local arts festival and another about county politics. She didn't read them. She read newspapers the way she had read her textbooks in school—mainly just the headlines and photo captions. Well, Sissy was for real anyway.

On the drive back to Diligence, Amanda buzzed-up the windows, opened the sun roof, and turned on the air-con in her new

Camry. She found the Albany oldies FM station on the radio, cranked the speakers up high, and drove home singing along with the Beach Boys and Rod Stewart. She stopped in a convenience store outside Catskill to buy a pint of orange juice, a pint of cheap vodka, and a cup of ice. She had decided she was going to grant herself a break. She would jump off the wagon, take a vacation, and just drive away somewhere for a while in her beautiful new car. Hell, she could afford it now. She'd buy some new clothes, stay in good hotels, maybe get laid. There was nothing for her to do here besides hold down the fort until things worked out. Morgan, up with her mystery man in Albany. Nemo gone. Denise and her hostile tribe still at the house. She had to dig in her purse to find her cigarettes and then the lighter. This car didn't have a cigarette lighter? No ashtray either, though there was a holder for her cup. She turned up the bass on the sound system. She'd bring her passport, maybe drive up to Montreal. She could shop there, new lingerie. French men. She loved her new car, the way it smelled.

At the place where the creek had washed out the road, there was a barrier across the whole road with a crew of men and machines working behind it. A man in a Day-Glo vest and a hard hat told her the obvious—that the road was closed for repairs. He couldn't say when it would be reopened, maybe tomorrow. She could try the old dirt road around. Not in her new Camry she couldn't. She turned around and drove all the way to the St. George to check back in, along the way buying a toothbrush, toothpaste, and some good shampoo. She would start her vacation anyway.

As Amanda pulled in to the parking lot beside the St. George she saw Sissy coming out of the hotel. She was so unmissable. Sissy didn't see Amanda. She parked off on the side where she could watch. Following Sissy was an old black man, who looked somehow familiar, carrying what looked like Nemo's black leather bags. They spoke for a moment, then Sissy walked off and the man took the luggage to an old taxicab by the entrance and put them in the back seat, then drove off. This scene made no sense to Amanda. When she asked at the desk, she was told just that the gentleman had checked out. "But who are they?" Amanda asked, gesturing toward the outside door.

"I believe they are his servants," the small foreign lady behind the desk said with an accent that made the statement sound matter-of-fact. "He had given them instructions and the key to his room. A nice gentleman, very quiet. All paid up. You are coming back to us? No bags?"

✳✳✳

The cracked ribs were on his right side, so Dominick had to sleep on his left. He seemed to be sleeping a lot. That probably had to do with broken bones and the pain making him tense and the pills and vodka. Besides, there was little else to do but read, and that made him drowsy. After dinner on Sunday—a fine vegetarian lasagna, which lacked only a glass of Chianti to be perfect—he went up to his room for a nap. It was another hot, still summer afternoon. He stripped down to his shorts before getting in bed. A loud sigh escaped him as he stretched out and his tensed-up muscles relaxed. The house was still. He had been taught to think of the rib cage as a fort, a palisade of bone selected by evolution to protect the precious life-giving organs within. Of course, if the enemy—a blow from a war club, the hoof or horn of some prey, the unfortunate fall—broke the defenses strongly enough, the bones themselves would pierce the vitals they were there to protect—defenses destroying what they were meant to defend. He knew from the X-rays that his lung was not hurt, but breathing had become a quite conscious act. He practiced his breathing—long, deep exhalations—pretending he was long-distance swimming. Perhaps that was why his first dream was of sailing.

Dominick never noticed Sissy slipping into bed beside him. He awoke to her soft touch and the warmth of her body pressing against his back. He said nothing. He felt her breath on the back of his neck. She shifted slightly, tucking her knees into the hollows of his and placing a hand gently on his upper arm.

"Dominick?"

"Hmm?"

"Did I wake you?"

"Hmm."

"It's like we never have a chance to be alone together."

"Umm."

"And sometimes I want you all to myself." Her hand slid down his arm in a possessive caress. "I want to get to know you better because everything I do know makes me want to know more."

Her hand came dangerously close to his tender ribs, and he reflexively rolled toward her so that her hand landed on his hip instead. Sissy took this as a positive sign, and her fingers moved on to his inner thigh. "I prayed for direction today, and I had the others pray over me." Her lips touched his shoulder. "Do you know what the Lord told me?"

Dominick didn't answer. He didn't dare for fear he would say the wrong thing and she would stop. He didn't mind any of this. His cock was already unfolding and stretching against his boxer shorts. His nipples wanted to be touched.

"The Lord said that you were a good man, and that I should get to know you better. The Lord, who is love, said that I should follow my heart." Sissy got up on her elbow and leaned over to kiss him. He kissed her back. He had wanted to do that for some time now.

He kissed her again. "Easy," he said as he rolled slowly onto his back with a brief grimace at the shot of pain in his side. She was gentle. She cooed and she laughed as their mouths and bodies got to know one another. There was that smell and that taste to it all that said this was real, that nothing had to be faked or pretended. Beneath her thin chemise Sissy was naked. Her breasts were full and young and beautiful, her nipples like black gumdrops.

With happy sounds she carefully freed him of his boxer shorts. "Oh, oh," she said, as with one hand she grabbed his thickening dick while the other cupped and fondled his balls. The happy sounds continued deep in her throat as she took him into her mouth. Her eyes were closed with pleasure, and her broad bare butt was sticking up in the air. She was very good at what she was doing.

Dominick was not a fan of fellatio, the passiveness of it. In order to keep himself aroused he fondled Sissy's breasts, pinching her nipples taut, then with a gasp of pain at the effort he reached for her pelvis, making her move so that his fingers could find her wet and swollen slit beneath her thick pubic bush. Three fingers inside her, she ground her groin down on his fist and groaned. Now they were that most ancient of impersonal beasts—a couple in reproductive heat. Millions of years of mammalian practice perfected again, a nameless Adam and an anonymous Eve in thrall to what must be done, to the reason why they were alive.

With a final lick to his now rigid dick, Sissy rose up and, stroking his shaft with one hand, swung a leg over Dominick so that she was now straddling him, positioning her dripping and wide-open cunt above her hand holding his cock. A rage of pain invaded Dominick's side. "Sissy, I . . .," he started, gasping for breath. She settled herself down onto him, taking him smoothly inside in one joyous thrust and groan. Dominick's pain was intense, but, god, it felt good inside her, as if the slippery sides of her vagina were milking his erection, trying to pull him further inside her. She pushed backwards, grinding her clit against his shaft, then rose up and thrust back down on him again. "Oh, Jesus," she exclaimed.

This time the pain was so stark and sudden that an involuntary gasp escaped from Dominick. His hands went to Sissy's waist, as he tried to lift her off of him, but he was still firmly inside her, gripped in a spasm of vaginal muscles. Sissy's head was thrown back. She too was gasping as her pelvis pumped above him.

"Stop! Stop! Get off him. You're hurting him." It was Susan's voice from the doorway.

Sissy didn't seem to hear. She fell forward so that she was on her hands and knees above Dominick, just their genitals engaged now, locked together like two dogs as she shivered and shivered and pressed her mouth onto his, her hair around his face. For Dominick there had never been a clearer battle between pleasure and pain, but pain was winning.

"Stop it, stop it," Susan said, now beside the bed. "You're killing him." And with one hand she grabbed Dominick's cock and pulled it out of Sissy's cunt, while with the other she pushed Sissy off of him. At the squeeze of Susan's fingers Dominick came, shooting his spunk onto Sissy's thigh and Susan's arm and hand.

Dominick was not sure of what happened next. He had rolled back onto his side to huddle with his pain, which pretty much blocked out whatever else was happening. No further words were spoken, but Sissy left and someone pulled a sheet up over him, covering his naked ass. It took a while for the pain to subside and his breathing to return to normal. Then Susan was there with a glass of water and two of his pain pills. "Are you going to live?" was all she said.

✳✳✳

With the help of a salesgirl with many piercings and a tattoo on her neck, Amanda bought a new outfit at a boutique on Warren Street. It was not like anything she normally wore, but Amanda had never been good at buying clothes, and the girl—Feather she called herself—was very helpful and found things that fit her. There was a long black skirt and a peasant vest and a couple of revealing blouses to choose between, a pair of sandals and some very feminine panties. Amanda never even looked at the bill; she just signed the credit card receipt.

Back at her room in the St. George, Amanda washed her hair and pampered herself with a long soak in the tub. With her cell phone battery dead, no one could reach her, no one could find out where she was. Was this the thrill escaped convicts felt? She could go anywhere, do anything, be anybody in perfect anonymous freedom, no strings attached. Wearing her new outfit, she had dinner at the fanciest Italian restaurant in town. She was the sole patron eating alone. They gave her a table by the window. She felt mysterious and enjoyed it. Afterwards she went to the bar she had gone to the night before, for a nightcap, and flirted again with the cute bartender. But this night she left early, leaving him an excessive tip.

The next morning Amanda checked out of the St. George again and drove back to Diligence. This time they had one lane completed and open at the washout. She had forgotten it was Saturday. Most of the girls' cars, including Denise's Bronco, were parked in the driveway. Amanda went in the front door and straight up to her room, where she quickly packed a small bag. Before she zipped it up she relented and tossed in her phone charger. She would just bring it; she didn't have to use it. A couple of the girls saw her as she left, but they just stared and she didn't acknowledge them. Back on the highway, she headed north. It was a perfect high summer day. Montreal was less than five hours away on the interstate.

About halfway there Amanda got bored with the thruway monotony, and it was time for a pit stop. She pulled off at an exit marked Ticonderoga Ferry. It wasn't like she had an appointment in Montreal, or even a reservation. An hour before, she had out-distanced her Albany oldies station, and since then she had been driving in silence with just her vagabond thoughts, which were acting as free and wandering as she was. For some reason her thoughts had ended up in her gallery of embarrassing moments, the mortifying memories that made her cringe. There was no suppressing them. There was also nothing to distract her: this exit was one with no services. She drove along through a forest tunnel, reliving scenes that she wished she could redo or at least erase from memory. She drove for ten minutes, past empty lakes and through tiny crossroad hamlets named Severance and Paradox, like comments on her thoughts. She thought of turning back, but now there were no places to turn around, and surely this fine county road went somewhere with a restroom.

Another ten miles of trees brought her to the outskirts of the town of Ticonderoga. She found a restroom, then a restaurant, then a bar and grill. People ignored her. She was a stranger in a town suspicious of strangers. That was alright by her. That suited her fine. From a tourist map she found the old fort down by the water. In the gift shop she bought a postcard that she thought she would send to Nemo, who, according to Morgan, liked old forts. Then she remembered she had no address to send it to, had no idea where he was or where he was headed. Just like all the gone folks in her gallery of botched memories. She found the fort depressing—all stone walls and sharp angles unscathed by battle and not nearly decrepit enough to seem real. At a package store she bought bourbon and ginger ale and cashews and Slim Jims, then she found a motel and checked in. She spent the night behind her triple-locked door watching cable TV, doing her escapist best to avoid listening to the voice in her head. She did not recharge her cell phone's battery. She went to sleep chagrined.

***

"Ready?" Vernon asked. He was standing at the door to Dominick's room.

"Ready for what?" Dominick said. "Probably not." It was Monday morning. Dominick was sure of that because he was reading the Monday morning *Register Star*, sitting up in bed.

"Ready to go," Vernon said.

"I wasn't aware I was going anywhere."

"You mean Sissy didn't tell you I was coming?"

"No, but it's nice to see you, Vernon. Come in and sit down." Dominick gestured to the armchair by the window.

"You're not packed?"

"Am I moving? Where to?"

"My place for now, I guess. Sissy just said come and get you."

"I'm really not ready to travel," Dominick said. Just getting out of bed was a variety of torture. He couldn't imagine a long car ride back to Catskill.

"I put some pillows in the back seat. You dose yourself good. You'll make it."

"Vernon, I—"

"It ain't your say. It's Sissy's. Come on, let's do it."

Susan helped, first by bringing Dominick a tall glass, half-filled with orange juice, that he could fill with vodka to take more pills—three this time—and then by helping Vernon repack what few of Dominick's things had gotten unpacked. Dominick got himself slowly dressed, resting between movements to let the pain subside. He thought of it as a bayonet, something unsterilized. Susan didn't speak when Vernon was in the room, but when he left to carry the bags downstairs she said, "Sissy said you would be leaving. Where are you going?"

"To Vernon's, I guess. Did Sissy say anything else?"

"No."

Dominick grunted getting to his feet from the edge of the bed. He was barefoot. There was no way he was going to bend over to put on socks and shoes. Susan came over to him, bringing his cane. He supported himself on her shoulder instead. She put her hand on his back. "What are you going to do, Susan?" he asked.

"I don't know. Why? Should I do something?" Her hair was still wet from her latest shower.

"Sissy is not throwing you out too?"

"No, I don't think so. She didn't say anything like that. Just that you had to leave. Why?"

"When it is time to go, it is time to go—the houseguest's mantra. Will you stick with me down the stairs?"

"Sure," Susan said with a smile. She hung onto him down the stairs, her thin arm around his hips. At the door Dominick gave her a kiss on the top of her head where her hair was parted, and Susan gave him a little hug.

The trip to Vernon's place was made tolerable by the oxycodone kicking in and a cigar, his first in days. He found an almost comfortable position amidst the pillows in Vernon's back seat. Neither he nor Vernon mentioned Sissy again. Dominick suspected that the opiates were having more than just an analgesic effect. He noted that he didn't feel like talking. In fact, he had very little interest in thinking at all, even though he knew his current situation called for more than spaced-out passivity. He stared out the window.

Vernon seemed to understand. "How many of them pills did you take?" he asked.

The sound Dominick made in response was affirmative but not an answer.

"Okay," Vernon said. "Enjoy the ride."

Vernon's house was off a back road on the other side of Catskill—roads with no road signs and few houses—rocky, canyon country, not farmland. Lots of woods out the thoughtless car window. The gravel driveway followed the contour of the land down into a clearing in a hollow where a low gray-shingled bungalow squatted beneath some tall old trees. Bungalow perhaps was not the right word. It was bigger—longer—than a cottage but just as humble. A weathered brick chimney rose above it. Off to one side was an equally antique shed. The old Caddy scattered chickens in the yard as it pulled up.

Dominick swung his legs out of the back seat and sat there for a minute, catching his breath from the pain that the effort had caused. An arthritic old beagle with a grey muzzle got up from the shade of the shed and came over to him, walking slowly, like two pains visiting.

"That's Mustang," Vernon said. "You got to watch out for him. He's the meanest hound around. Aren't you, Mustang?"

Mustang sniffed Dominick's outstretched hand, took a look behind him into the back seat to see if anyone else was there, then ambled back to his spot in the shade.

"Only he doesn't attack fellow crips." Vernon got Dominick's bags out of the trunk and headed for the house. They were parked at what appeared to be the front door, but Vernon walked off to the left. "Your room is down here," he said as he turned a corner of the house. Dominick followed slowly. There was a small side yard with a honeysuckle bush and the door to another room attached to the end of the house. Inside the room there were a double bed, a dresser, a chair, and two windows looking out at dense greenery speckled with sunlight. A good half of the room was occupied by piles of cardboard boxes. "Used to be Sissy's room," Vernon said. "When she left I started storing stuff in here. You know how that goes."

Dominick did not know how that went, but the bed was freshly made and looked comfortable. He headed for it.

"Sissy fixed that up for you," Vernon said. "I'll get the pillows from the car."

Somewhere between the car and the bed Dominick had picked up a pricker or a sliver or something in the sole of one of his bare feet. His attempt to view the bottom of his foot was called off due to the pain of bending. When Vernon came back with an armful of pillows, Dominick said, "Vernon, I . . ."

"I don't know what you are doing here either, but you are here, so we'll make the best of it. I ain't no nurse, but all you need is bed rest. You'll have to eat my cooking, and I'm gone most of the day, but all that is your problem, not mine."

"No, Vernon, would you mind taking a look at my foot? Something's in there."

Vernon dropped the pillows on the bed and sat down beside Dominick. "Show papa."

Dominick leaned back and put his foot up on his opposite knee. Actually, this pain was a distraction from the rest. The ceiling above the bed was low and there was an old Michael Jackson poster pasted there.

"Yep, a thorn," Vernon said. "Let me get my glasses and a tweezers."

The farther Dominick lay back the more comfortable he became, until he was stretched out on his back, his arms spread wide beside him. His mind was still not dealing in coherent thoughts. What was he doing here in this sharecropper's cabin? Who was this person on the ceiling above him? Both male and female, white and black, a member of Sissy's past pantheon. Who was Sissy?

"Anesthetic," Vernon said, handing Dominick a cold can of Ballantine Ale. It took him but a minute to extract the thorn and the pain went away just like that, so simple. "I got to get to work. Through that door," Vernon pointed to a second door in the room, "is my room then the rest of the house, the bathroom, kitchen, etcetera. Feel free. Keep the outside door closed or the chickens will come in. I'll be back when I get back. You need anything?"

Dominick managed to shake his head. "No, thanks," he thought he said, but he wasn't sure. Vernon left. Dominick heard the Caddy drive off and he got himself properly onto the bed. There was no means of escape. He didn't even know where he was. Did that make him a prisoner? He rolled onto his good side. He felt safe. He fell quickly asleep.

Chapter 19

Amanda did not like Montreal. She did not like being treated like a foreigner, and everything seemed expensive. Her hotel room smelled funny. She did some haphazard, halfhearted shopping, then left after two days. The night before she left she plugged in her battery charger and recharged her cell phone. No messages, not even from Morgan. Usually return trips seem shorter than trips out, but this time the ride south seemed to creep by. She didn't stop until she got to Albany, where she pulled off and gave Morgan's phone a call. No answer, an automated voice-mail box—leave a message at the tone. Amanda had thought she would offer Morgan a ride home, seeing as she was passing through.

There seemed to be an awful lot of traffic headed south out of Albany for an overcast weekday afternoon. Then an ad on the radio clued her in—tomorrow was the Fourth of July, a Thursday holiday. The city dwellers were fleeing their walls for a long country weekend, and Amanda, who was just headed home, had to share the road with them—boxy campers with names like Wilderness Invader, SUVs with canoes lashed to their roofs and dirt bikes on the back, sports cars with their tops down and invariably a white-haired white male behind the wheel.

The Fourth of July, already. What a non-holiday that had always been, an interruption in summer's peace, an inconvenience. Definitely an all male occasion—the village parade with the men in uniform marching almost in step, the marching bands, the antique cars with old guys in old uniforms in the back seat, the old fire trucks, the loud gun salutes, then at dusk the fireworks—all the men toys on full display, not to mention that most patriotic of pursuits, getting drunk with your buddies. Amanda's girlhood memories of the Glorious Fourth was of a workday—she and her aunties and Grandma Win fixing food all day then cleaning up.

One Fourth of July Grandpa Joe had driven them all into Boston. It must have been in '76 for the big celebration, which would have made her eight years old. Of course, they could not afford to stay there. They drove into Boston in the early morning and then drove the three hours back home that night. Amanda remembered just a lot of walking and crowds where all she could see were the backs and butts of adults. Grandpa Joe said she was too big to get up on his shoulders. It was just as well; she had already wet her panties. Someone gave her a cold corn dog to eat. She had hated corn dogs ever since.

Even the traffic on Route 9W out of Catskill was heavy, and she was happy to leave it behind at the Diligence turn-off. The road at the washout was now completed and paved. It was still early enough; perhaps she could beat everyone else home and have the place peacefully to herself for an hour or so before retreating to her room. She looked forward to sleeping in her own bed. As she came out of the last curve before the drive to the Van Houten house she saw the cars parked along the road, almost blocking it. There were four or five of them, clustered around where the gate had once been and would one day soon hopefully return. She slowed to a crawl as she drove up to them. There was a small crowd of people gathered at the driveway entrance, all facing the house at the top of the rise. In front of them was a man dressed in black reading from a book.

Amanda buzzed down her window to ask what was going on just in time to hear everyone in the crowd call out "Amen."

The preacher or priest or whoever he was up front started again, "In the name of the Lord, I—"

Amanda laid on the horn. They could do whatever they wanted to do—at least they knew enough not to go onto her property—but she didn't have to sit there and listen to it. The horn got their attention. "Excuse me," she said. "You are blocking the right of way?"

The people moved aside without a word.

"Thank you," Amanda said.

The preacher dude still stood there in the middle of the driveway, not sure what to do. A minute ago he had been so sure of himself, so in control, another guy in uniform lording it up. Now he had a chance to be a martyr and he stepped aside.

"Carry on," Amanda said as she drove by him.

There was no one at the house, no cars parked there. Amanda let herself in and carried her things into the house, then for some reason she locked the front door behind her and went to check that the kitchen door was locked and latched as well. She didn't know what was going on, but the security felt good, though she didn't like the solitude. From the window of her room she could see the road, where the cars were turning around and driving away. She called Morgan's phone again and left another message: "Where are you? Come home."

***

It was amazing how many Jeopardy questions Vernon got right, on a wide variety of topics. Vernon listened to the TV quiz show as he cooked dinner. Listened rather than watched because the TV set, a nice one, flat-screened and large, was in the living room and Vernon was in the neighboring kitchen with the door open. Vernon would just belt out the answer from the other room. "Madagascar." "Herbert Hoover." "Lost wax method." Occasionally he would miss one he knew: "Oh, that short bitch with the bad haircut, you know."

Vernon did much better than Dominick, who quickly took to yelling out the answers he guessed before any of the three contestants. Dominick was seated in the small, low-ceilinged living room on a tall padded bar stool with a back and arm rests that Vernon had hauled in from somewhere. It had seen a lot of duty as a bar stool, but it was still functional and much more welcoming to Dominick's condition than any of the other available seating—a limo's former back seat that now passed for a couch and two ex-bucket seats.

Vernon's humble abode—as he called it—was not so much a house as a series of rooms that had grown on one another. The two rooms in the middle—the kitchen and living room—were the oldest, the parent rooms, the first homestead, built around the central chimney with its dual fireplaces. Those rooms sloped and slumped with settled age, nary a true right angle remaining. Over the years additional rooms had been added—off the kitchen a small bright room that Vernon called the dining room, and off the living room a later, larger room that was Vernon's. Sissy's room, now Dominick's, had been tacked onto that even later. Another late addition was an indoor bathroom off the living room. What this ensemble of spaces shared was a feeling of usefulness, of having never been abandoned. The people whose tread had worn these pine plank floors smooth had also made sure that the roof was fixed and what was rotted got replaced. There was a wisdom to the old place, the way the windows caught all of the twilight.

Dinner that first night was bacon and eggs and home fries. "I can eat breakfast any time of day," Vernon said. "That's what I felt like tonight." No apologies. Dominick ate, his appetite having returned. It was good. "Fresh eggs," Vernon said. After dinner they watched the end of a baseball game on the big screen, Vernon in one of the bucket seats. Dominick did not care who was playing. It was all the same, which was the same as nothing, to him. He found the repetition satisfying. One batter hit half a dozen pitches foul before drawing a walk. Unlike other sports, but akin to life, the pace of the game was erratic. The action could drag with nothing much happening for innings, then suddenly explode into hits and runs and throws and collisions—like a thunder storm interrupting a summer afternoon—then return to lassitude. They drank ale and smoked Dominick's cigars.

For Vernon there was the added spice of being a fan. He had his cast of heroes and villains. The players had nicknames and personalities. There was history, context—background details and statistics, anecdotes and standings, rivalries and superstitions—and there were his decades of dedicated devotion to his team, whose fate somehow colored his life. Their down years were not worth remembering, but the year that Sissy was born, for instance, they had won the pennant (then lost the Series in six). Every game was personal and real for Vernon in a way it would never be for Dominick, for whom each game was just a passing event to be enjoyed or not and quickly forgotten. Dominick's life was in no way linked to the Yankees or any other team. He was a bystander not a participant, someone who just watched the parade from the back of the crowd but would never dream of marching, of sporting any team's colors.

There was a shot on the screen of two truly fanatic fans in the stands dressed in Yankee pinstripes, one of whom had his bald head and face painted like a baseball.

"It's almost like a religion for some, isn't it?" Dominick said.

"What? Being a half-wit?"

"Being a baseball fan, a sports fan. Going to games like going to church."

"Are folks dressing up like clowns to go to church these days?" Vernon went to the kitchen to get two fresh ales. "I haven't been for a while," he said from the refrigerator, "either to church or a ball game."

"No, I meant that level of allegiance, the identification with an organization."

Vernon came back with their ales. "Well, first off, most religions believe in some god, and there is no god in baseball, unless it's money; and secondly most people think the Yankees are aligned with the devil."

"What do you mean, no gods? What about Ruth, Robinson, Gehrig, DiMaggio? That Vatican over in Cooperstown?"

"Jackie wasn't a Yankee, and those guys were heroes not saints, Ruth especially so. You don't need a church to have heroes."

"But there is belief, that leap of faith—maybe next year."

"Okay, in Chicago maybe it approaches being a cult, but it's not a religion for me. It's a pastime. Did you see that?" An outfielder had run to the wall and leapt just in time to snatch away a home run. "That new kid is good," Vernon said. "He could be another Mays."

They were shown the catch several more times in slow-motion instant replays from different camera angles. The slow-mo sports replay highlight, Dominick thought, the modern equivalent of miracle plays. "Did you ever play ball, Vernon?" he asked.

"Are you kidding me? A poor black kid from the sticks? Not a chance. I'll give you that, though—ball players were mythic figures when I was a kid, like creatures from some Olympus. Only I didn't worship them, I envied them."

***

Denise brought the paper home, Wednesday's *Register Star* with Sissy's article in it. She brought it right up to Amanda's room, as a matter of fact, as soon as she got home. She pounded on Amanda's locked door, and when Amanda opened it Denise shoved the paper, opened to Sissy's feature-page article, into Amanda's face.

"I can only assume you are responsible for this," Denise said, "and that you also pounded this into the middle of the driveway." In her other hand she was holding up a crudely nailed wooden cross on a pointed stake. "You have cooked your Christian goose now!" she said as she turned and stomped off, leaving Amanda holding the newspaper.

Sissy's article was topped by a black-and-white photo of the house taken from down by the road, resembling nothing more than the house on the hill in *Psycho*, and the article was headlined "Historic Reverend's House Now a Church for Witches." Amanda closed and relocked her door. She sat on the bed to read the article. The lead-in made a lame attempt to tie what followed to the Fourth of July. There were several paragraphs of sketchy but not inaccurate history about the house, followed by a lament that so few of the old family estates in the region still remained and that the Van Houten house like other survivors was unprotected by historic preservation provisions. The final third of the article was about the house's current manifestation as a "tax-exempt resident center for the Wicca religion," and for those readers unfamiliar with the term, Wicca was glossed as "the practice of pre-Christian pagan rites overseen by witches and warlocks." At the very end it was mentioned that the current owners of the property—unnamed "outside developers"—planned to renovate the place. It said nothing about the Wiccans being evicted, leaving the impression that it was to be restored as a Wiccan church.

For a while Amanda just sat and stared out the window. It was that hour before sunset when the birds all seemed to wake up before going back to sleep. The window was open. She could hear them exchanging the evening news. She could watch them flitting about or flying off, going somewhere else for the night. She had grown up with these birds, just east of here over in Vermont. She knew all their names—waxwing and nuthatch, catbird and warbler, junco and bobolink. Grandpa Joe had taught her their names and their songs as well. That had seemed such common knowledge that Amanda was surprised later in life to discover that not everyone knew the birds by their calls. They were so distinctive, as simple as naming flowers in a garden. She ignored the knocking at her door as long as she could, then she yelled out "Go away," and it stopped. So simple. Amanda liked things simple. They so seldom were.

***

Vernon said he thought the initials stood for digital video disc. He showed Dominick how to put one in to play and get the video up on the TV screen. There were a lot of different buttons involved. Dominick had him run through it a second time so he could write down the sequence. Vernon said that he could also do it with the remote controls, but Dominick passed. He would just push the buttons on the consoles like Vernon showed him. There was something about even the concept of remote control that he found creepy. The DVDs involved were a boxed set that Dominick had found amongst many others on a shelf beside Vernon's big-screen TV. The title had just jumped out at him—*The Civil War*. There were six discs in the set. Eleven hours, Vernon said. They had been made for TV.

It was lunchtime, Dominick's second day at Vernon's. Vernon had brought home some sub sandwiches for lunch, and Dominick had asked him about the DVDs. He started watching them that afternoon, after Vernon went back to work. Dominick had never watched much TV. He had not known this documentary series existed. He could only sit up and watch it for an hour or so at a time, partly because of his ribs and partly because there was a lot to absorb and think about, an overload of visual images. But it gave him something to do, something to look forward to. By the end of his second day of watching he was beginning to find fault with what was being left out. And wasn't it interesting how history, to be made palatable as entertainment, had to be sentimentalized? There was one Southern commentator who was a master at that. Dominick found the soundtrack music especially cloying. At least there were no commercials.

The third day that Dominick was there—it would have been a Wednesday—Vernon came home with the morning's *Hudson Register Star*. "Sissy did a write-up of your place over there in Diligence," he said, tossing the paper onto the bed where Dominick was curled up on his good side. "Got some barbeque ribs for supper tonight, if that's not too personal," Vernon said as he left.

Sissy's article was not very good—sketchy unsourced history peppered with phrases like "it is believed that" and "reportedly." It was unnecessarily nostalgic for an imagined past. With tabloidesque clumsiness it mentioned witches in its title and ended with a tsk-tsk description of the house's recent manifestation as a home for Wiccan women. There was no input from Morgan or Amanda about their hopes for the restored—and reclaimed from Satan—manse. Of course, Amanda had pretty much thrown Sissy out of the house, but still. All in all, it was not a friendly piece. The writer was unhappy about something but never came out to say what.

Dominick got up from bed and took the paper into the kitchen, but Vernon wasn't there. He was sitting on the bench outside the kitchen door with a can of ale, poking at a charcoal fire he had started in a low hibachi. "Friend of mine in town fixes these ribs—parboils them, bakes them, spices them up and all, but you still have to grill them a bit at the end to get them right," Vernon said.

"I'll pay you for them," Dominick said, lowering himself carefully to the bench beside Vernon.

"Don't worry. They're already on your bill." Vernon nodded to the newspaper Dominick was still holding. "Funny, Sissy didn't say anything about her great-aunt who once lived out there."

"You ever tell Sissy about her?"

"Probably not. Need never arose, I guess."

"Then how would she know? If it's not passed on, it can't be history."

"That true what Sissy says about the witches out there? I didn't see any witches when we stopped by that time, just a nice looking blond-haired lady."

"That was no witch; that was my sister Amanda. But I'm afraid you would be disappointed looking for witches out there. Witches have changed with the times. Now they all look just like your normal working girls. Come to think of it, they probably always did."

"But it's like a regular church and all?" Vernon poked at the coals.

"They have services, rituals, prayers, the normal stuff. What makes a church?"

"That's all harmless enough. Do they do sacrifices and stuff like that too?"

"Vernon, it's a house full of women, only women. I don't think you or I should even try to understand it."

Vernon flattened out the coals with his stick and dropped the grill on above them. "Being pagan and all, I guess they don't go around spouting Bible verses to justify everything. That would be a plus." He stared at the grill. "That's got to get hot. You heard from Sissy?"

"No. How would I?"

"She knows the number here. I haven't heard from her either."

Vernon fetched the ribs from the kitchen and flopped them onto the grill for just three or four minutes a side. They were delicious, with just macaroni salad and some sliced white bread. The Yankees were playing a night game in Detroit. They ate in the living room, watching the game. At one point Vernon said, "Tomorrow's the Fourth, you know, everybody's holiday but not mine. I'll be working overtime through the weekend, driving drunks around. Will you be alright here without your car? It's still parked over in Sissy's driveway, I guess."

"I'll have to be alright without it. I'm not ready to drive yet, Vernon, not unless I get all pain-pilled up, which probably isn't a good idea. I'll just be stuck here. Check in on me every now and then, though."

"Oh, I'll be around. Got to sleep, got to eat. Can't put in them really long hours like I once did, don't see the need."

It was dark now, and in the distance Dominick could hear the soft explosions of fireworks going off.

"Some of my neighbors out here like to get a head start on blowing things up," Vernon said. "They are real patriots."

***

It was good to be back in her own bed, but Amanda still had to get up and take one of her sleeping pills before she could get to sleep. The voice in her head, her mother's voice this time, would not shut up.

It spoke in whatever ear she had pressed to the pillow. It was full of advice, none of which she wanted to hear.

Who knows how long the noise outside had been going on before it woke her up. There was the sound of a car horn honking and people yelling. A male voice, young and cocky and probably drunk, called out, "Hey, witches, come on out." The horn honked again. "Hey, witches, got a young one here for you, says she'd rather be a witch than my bitch." Background laughter and hooting. "Hey, witches, how's about a blow job?"

A voice—Denise's voice—called out from one of the other upstairs windows, "I'll give you a blow job," followed by the explosive blast of what sounded like a shotgun.

"Holy shit, man, they're armed," someone down in the driveway yelled. "Jesse, Jesse, you alright?"

"I'm alright. The bitch missed. Go! Go!"

There was the sound of engines and of tires spewing gravel as at least two cars headed back out the driveway toward the road. A cheer went up from other upstairs rooms. Amanda was wearing just a T-shirt and panties, but she went out into the hallway with everyone else, the girls each dressed in her version of hot weather sleepwear, a few in just robes over nothing at all. They were all high-fiving one another. Denise was in a sarong knotted over her ample breasts, a double-barrel shotgun tucked under one arm.

"My god, Denise, you fired at him," Amanda said, wondering where Denise had suddenly come up with a shotgun.

"I couldn't see him. I shot over his head, just a warning shot." Denise was very pleased with herself. She started giving orders to the girls, stationing them as lookouts around the house. "They'll be back, or more like them. Thanks to that article, we're a target now. This is war. If you see anything move out there, just give a yell, and me and Betsy will be there." The girls all went off in pairs in different directions. "Well, Amanda, it looks like you are in this with us. Unless, of course, you want to leave now, go over to the other side."

"I was not responsible for that newspaper article, Denise. I threw that woman reporter out of the house, twice. I did not put that cross in the driveway. Someone else did after I got home. And this is still my house, not yours, and I am staying. Is that your only gun?"

"Unless you or Morgan has one. Well, war makes for strange bed-fellows," Denise said, breaking the shotgun open to remove the spent shell casing.

"I am not your bedfellow," Amanda said, looking at Denise's cellulite-clotted and varicose-veined lower legs, "but we are in this together until you all move out, which I hope now will be ASAP."

"I'm not defending this sanctuary just to desert it later, sweetheart," Denise said walking away toward her room. "I have no intention of leaving here, unless it is feet first."

Amanda went back to bed and back to sleep, thanks to another pill. In the morning she discovered that the trunk and roof and rear window of her shiny new Camry were stippled with buckshot nicks and craters. None of the other cars seemed to be damaged.

Chapter 20

Dominick's second favorite fact about the Fourth of July was that three of the first five presidents—Jefferson, Adams, and Monroe—all eventually died on that date. His first favorite fact was that the identities of the signers of the Declaration of Independence had been kept secret for more that six months after the signing, as the fifty-six founding patriots hedged their bets about this revolution thing actually working out. Oh, brave founding fathers. The Fourth of July was an anomalous, secular holiday, unattached to any seasonal event or ancient rite of passage whence all the other holidays evolved. What is more secular than politics? A day to commemorate a revolt against paying taxes. God and nature had nothing to do with it.

Dominick watched more of the Civil War documentary. The slaughter and suffering truly had been catastrophic. And really God had nothing to do with that war either. All Christians there. All the martyrs—the supposed souls of those twisted and bloated bodies of boys in the ditches and fields—went to the same English-speaking imaginary heaven. Over 625,000 dead in that misunderstanding, twenty-five times the number of men who had given their lives in the Revolutionary War in order to secure for these kids the inalienable freedom to kill one another. Such a country, capable of jury-rigging a style of temporary greatness out of so many flagrant flaws.

There was nothing uplifting about the Civil War. Dominick took two more pain pills, filled a mug with apple juice, ice, and vodka, and went for a walk. Standing up was more comfortable than sitting down. The old hound dog Mustang decided to come with him. It was a suitably toasty Fourth of July, cloudless and without a breeze. From behind the shed a trail of sorts went into the woods. Mustang led the way. Dominick stopped to light a cigar. The further they walked into the forest shadow the cooler it got. Mustang would wander purposively away then wander back onto the trail. "Where are we going, Mustang old scout?" Dominick said. The pills were kicking in nicely. Mustang didn't answer.

The cabin was old and low and mostly covered in vines, berry bushes, and poison ivy. Its walls were hand-hewn logs. Its door and windows were long gone and its roof was just a few splintered cross-beams. It sat in its own little clearing where the sun filtered down through a break in the forest canopy. Mustang went up and plopped down on the wide flat slab of slate that formed the front door stoop. Dominick found a tree to lean against. "So, what is this, Mustang? The original Uncle Tom's cabin?" Mustang just gave Dominick one of those dog looks that said I am not going to honor that question with a response and went about giving himself a good lick-down.

Aside from the structure itself—its native materials returning to nature—there was nothing man-made there. No glints of shattered window glass or rusting hinges, not a stick of furniture or shard of broken pottery inside. There was a weathered bareness, a purity to the place that demanded to be left in peace. I am a memory, it said, you cannot change me. The now nameless people who made me, warmed me, ate and slept and snored inside me have been gone for hundreds of winters. Do not dare to think you could ever replace them.

"Yes, it was another time entirely," Dominick answered. "I can't even imagine." He suddenly felt very tired. His cigar, his mug, he himself seemed wholly out of place there, caustic intruders, profaners, shameless voyeurs. "I'm heading back, Mustang. You can stay. You look at home here."

And Mustang did stay there, snoozing on the slate slab threshold. The walk back to the house was uphill and seemed much longer. Dominick wished he had brought his cane. When he got back he had to lie down. He was as exhausted as if he had just walked a very great distance into the past and back. Was this what getting old would be like? The aches, the heaviness, the slowness? He found his least painful position with the pillows on Sissy's old bed, and his last thoughts before sleep were of her. He sure missed her smile.

Dinner that night was cold KFC. Vernon apologized, and it was pretty awful, but he had been busy all day. The "Budweiser holiday" he called it. "Cops everywhere in town, having a field day." Vernon did not go out again. "Ain't like the old days," he said. "I don't need the money that bad."

After dark there were again the sounds of distant fireworks. Mixed in among them were distinct sharper reports. "Neighbors got their shooting irons out," Vernon said. They were sitting outside on the bench by the kitchen door. "That's a twenty-two. That one there was a bigger handgun, thirty-eight or forty-five. Whoa, an assault rifle, AK forty-seven or something similar. They got to be liquored up. That ammo is expensive."

Then from down the valley behind them came a different deeper baritone boom. "Now, that is what I like to hear," Vernon said. "That's an old muzzle-loader long gun, flintlock probably. Haven't heard one of them in years. I wonder who has got one of those."

Dominick looked around the yard and noticed that the dog was missing. "Where is old Mustang?" he asked.

"Who knows?" Vernon answered. "Mustang is often gone. This place, me, we're just part of his life. Who knows how many folks out here think of Mustang as being their dog? You got another one of those fancy cigars? Get that grease taste out of my mouth."

✳✳✳

Amanda wanted to call the sheriff, but Denise would have none of it. "Pointless," she said. "They won't come out until after the fact, and besides, this weekend they will be real busy elsewhere." Actually, the day of the Fourth, hot and still, was quiet and uneventful. A few more cars than usual passed by down on the road, slowing as they cruised past; but there were no more intruders.

No one had been tending the kitchen garden since Susan's departure, and it was looking pretty sad. Amanda took it upon herself to water it just to have something to do. While she was doing so a few of the girls sulked in the shade on the back porch. She overheard part of their complaining. Some of the girls wanted to leave—either because they wanted to go home for the long holiday weekend or because they didn't feel safe in the house after the previous night's invasion—but Denise would not let them. She had even confiscated everyone's car keys. She had also scheduled a special command convocation for that evening at sunset. Denise had a little rebellion on her hands. When another girl came out onto the porch, the ones there shut up about their discontents and changed the topic to the weather. Amanda herself had no intention of leaving. She had just done that, for one thing, and it hadn't worked out. She had come right back. She had nowhere else to go.

Denise had her two close cohorts, her lieutenants, who bossed the other girls around. They projected a siege mentality. Denise kept lookouts posted and conducted occasional reconnaissance tours out to the barn and back, carrying her shotgun. Around sunset they all gathered in what Amanda thought of as their altar room downstairs, and she locked herself in her room. One of the plusses about being home was her DVD collection. There were certain ones she used medicinally, like pills, to change her mood—to sooth her, say, or get her spirits up, or just help her achieve an acceptable state of denial—videos that she had played scores of times before but craved again as a safe escape. That dusk she put on *Immortal Beloved*, a film about Beethoven with lots of his music and a scene that always made her cry.

Amanda was lying in bed watching her video and almost there to the desired state of thoughtless absorption when the first rocket screeched overhead. It exploded with a crack-boom somewhere behind them, lighting up the sky outside her window. She was on her feet and at the window by the time the second one was launched down on the road. She saw the flash and heard the whoosh almost simultaneously. For a second it looked like it was aimed right at her window, then it too swooped higher above the roof before it exploded in a flash of red. Whoops of excitement came up from the road, where she could see sets of legs dancing around in a car's headlights. The third rocket swerved erratically to the left and didn't go off, a dud.

Amanda had to find and put on her sandals before rushing to the door. She was not just going to stand there and be fired at. She forgot that she had locked the door and fumbled with the dead bolt. On the stairs she heard the next rocket launch and then crash into the front of the house. Cheers from the road. As she reached the bottom of the stairs the doors to the front parlor altar room were pushed open and Denise in a long lime-green robe emerged, carrying her shotgun. Behind her the girls in their virginal white togas clustered in confusion in the candlelight.

"What? Where?" Denise asked when she saw Amanda on the stairs.

"Fireworks rockets, from the road," Amanda said. "Firing at the house."

"I'll deal with this," Denise said. Then she turned to the girls, still in the room. "You all stay here. Do not let anyone break the sacred circle."

At the front door Denise switched on the outside porch lights before unlocking the door. Amanda turned them off. "They'll see you," she said.

Denise turned the lights back on. "I want them to," she said. "I want them to see what they are dealing with."

Another rocket went off, lighting up the sky above the house as Denise walked out onto the front veranda. She yelled a few foreign words that Amanda did not understand but that sounded like a curse if she had ever heard one. Then Denise raised her shotgun and fired in the direction of the road. She walked to the top of the steps, yelled out the same words and fired again. As she broke the gun to reload, pulling shells out from an inner pocket in her robes, her fire was returned from the road—several guns going off. Amanda could see their muzzle flashes and hear their popping reports, but she had no idea where the bullets went. Denise just laughed and fired both barrels again. There were a few more shots from the road as two cars executed quick three-point turns and drove away.

Remnants of the rocket that had hit the house were still burning in the bushes by the corner of the verandah. Not all the starburst charges had gone off, and some were still exploding in the flames. Amanda ran to get the garden hose. Denise disappeared. That sulfur smell of gunpowder smoke—Amanda remembered it, but it had no association, not even Fourth of July. She wondered if her recently new car down in the driveway had gotten any fresh bullet holes, and for some reason that made her think of dead horses strewn on old black-and-white battlefields like part of the landscape. The rockets' red glare and bombs bursting in air.

After she had hosed them down awhile, all the flames and embers were dark. She was still all alone outside. She carried the hose around to the back of the house, looking for any more hot spots. She didn't find any. The moon was now up above the tree line, stretching out long insecure shadows. They could come back again, she thought, but she figured they wouldn't. They were just boys. They had had their fun for the night, their little battle. It was a long enough ways to the nearest beer joint and back for them not to bother returning. How many rockets could they afford anyway?

Amanda's pack of Pall Malls was still on the table beside Nemo's chair on the kitchen porch. She sat and lit one and realized that her hands and her hair and her clothes all smelled like the smoke from the firecracker fires. She would have to shower and shampoo before going to bed. Inside the house all was still dark and silent as if there was no one home. When she went to go in she discovered that both the kitchen door and the front door were now locked, but she knew of one kitchen window that could not be locked, and she let herself in that way. The front hall smelled of incense, and the sound of Denise's voice reading something cadenced came through the tightly shut parlor doors. In the shower Amanda debated with herself about calling Morgan, but in the end decided not to.

✳✳✳

The next morning Mustang was back, and Dominick was strangely glad to see him. Dominick had never had a dog, never had any kind of pet. His mother would never have tolerated such an unnecessary inconvenience, and there were no pets at the boarding schools he had grown up in. Of course, he had shared houses with other people's pets over the years, but they had always been easy to ignore. Somebody else had taken care of them. The disinterest had always seemed mutual. He could not understand the impulse to have a captive member of another species. All the connotations of that seemed negative to him. He had never trusted people hooked on pets. There was an irrationality there akin to devout religiosity, some sort of arrested adolescent development. But he was glad to see Mustang—who totally ignored him—out at his place in the shade of the shed Friday morning. He was company. Dominick talked to him even though he was beginning to suspect that Mustang was stone deaf. Was this cabin fever setting in? He would have to move on from here soon, but his ribs did not seem to be mending at all. It had been a week now, and he was getting tired of the whole pain and pill routine.

Dominick could not remember having heard the telephone at Vernon's ring before. It was a regular old-fashioned telephone ring, the kind you never heard any more except in old movies. A "land line" it was called these days, a phrase that always made him think of land mines. He was propped up in bed with a pile of old *National Geographic*s he had found in a box in Vernon's "dining room," which was really just a storeroom now where no one could have eaten in many years, it was so packed with stuff. He was reading about Clovis points and a theory of Amerindian migration that had been revised several times over since the article had been written thirty years before. He was charmed by the fact that whenever prehistoric dates were revised they were pushed farther and farther into the past, as if time, like the universe, was expanding at an ever increasing velocity. Not only were you moving forward through time, but the past was accelerating backwards at an even faster rate. He let the phone ring. It was on the wall in the kitchen three rooms away and easy enough to ignore. It was probably a wrong number anyway, as Vernon only used his cell phone—another funny term that Dominick associated with the one call you were allowed after being arrested. Surely that jail pay phone was a *cell phone*. When was the last time he had seen a pay phone, a phone booth? Had all of them been swallowed up by the ever-deepening past?

The second time the phone rang Dominick was in the kitchen, fixing himself a sandwich, and it was harder to ignore, so he answered it. The voice, a man's voice, was vaguely familiar and asked for him. "Speaking," Dominick said.

"Dominick, this is Frank Barnett. I hear you have had an accident. How are you feeling?"

"Why, I am doing alright, Frank. How are you?" Dominick said. What the hell was this all about? The yellow wall telephone had an extra-long spiral cord—that early attempt at a mobile phone—and as Dominick talked on the phone, with the receiver crooked between his shoulder and his ear to free his hands, he walked about the kitchen, putting things back in the refrigerator, opening a can of ale, carrying his plate to the kitchen table and sitting down.

"I'm fine, Dominick, fine. Good to hear your voice. You are probably wondering why I am calling."

"I am wondering how you got this number, Frank. How you knew I would be in this kitchen fixing myself a late lunch." Dominick took a bite of his sandwich.

"Yes, well. I got this number from a woman reporter at the local newspaper, a Ms. Douglas, who told me you were recuperating. From a fall, is it?"

"You could call it that. And how did you find this Ms. Douglas? Just curious."

"Oh, your sister Amanda told Morgan that the last she knew of your whereabouts was this Ms. Douglas checking you out of your hotel."

"A person just can't get themselves properly lost anymore, can they?" Dominick took a sip of ale. "What's up, Frank? Why are you calling?"

"I was in the neighborhood, thought I'd look you up. If you will believe that."

"Not likely. What neighborhood is that?"

"I am staying at a place called the Mount Morris Manor outside of Hudson, nice place. This is a local number. How far away are you?"

"Across the river and into the trees. Is this about the Van Houten place deal? This is uncommon speed."

"Oh, well, Morgan, Ms. Custis, was eager to catch you before you, ah, disappeared again into the Bermuda Triangle or wherever, and I happened to be up in Albany on business, so I thought I would just do my own mini-disappearing act from my life for a few days—you are an inspiration that way, Dominick—and come down here with her and the papers. Beautiful country around here, great view out my room's windows."

"If Morgan is there, say hello to her for me," Dominick said, taking another bite of his sandwich.

"So, Dominick, are you well enough to travel? I would like to get together and discuss this offer and, purely out of curiosity, get out to see the place myself. Could we get together?"

"What's your number there, Frank? And the name of the place again." There was a notepad with a pencil on the wall beside the phone. Dominick went over and wrote down what Barnett told him. "I'll give you a call back. I'll try to get over this afternoon, if I can get a ride." He called Vernon's cell phone and commandeered his cab for the balance of the afternoon. Then he called Barnett back to tell him he would be there. Before shaving and changing into street clothes he took three of the white pain pills, washing them down with another ale. He was floating a bit, enjoying the absence of pain, by the time Vernon arrived.

Passing through town on the way to the bridge, Dominick had Vernon stop at the only store there that sold decent cigars, and he restocked. It felt good to be out of the house. The town and the roads were crowded with holiday weekend visitors.

Vernon knew the place they were headed. "Rich friends," he said.

"A man who wears expensive suits, a lawyer."

"And me unarmed," Vernon said. "I'll keep the motor and the meter running."

✳✳✳

It was silly, childishly silly, but Amanda had trouble getting past it—the fact that Morgan had shown up behind the wheel of a snazzy little red sports car convertible with the top down. It wasn't the car so much—it was just a rental—but the fact that Morgan was driving it.

"All this time I thought you didn't drive, which is why I always had to own the car and be the chauffeur," Amanda said as soon as Morgan showed up.

"Oh, I can drive. I just chose not to, that's all."

"I thought you didn't have a license."

"I don't. I never have."

"They rent cars to someone who doesn't have a driver's license?"

"I had a friend rent it for me. What is your big problem, girl? It's just a car. I saved you a trip. What happened to your new chariot, by the way? It looks like you were caught fleeing a shotgun wedding."

"We have had a few skirmishes out here the past few days. Unfortunately, my car has been the only casualty, friendly fire at that."

"Skirmishes? What do you mean, skirmishes?"

"Local Christians on an anti-Wiccan war path. Nemo's girlfriend ran an article in Wednesday's paper about the place, and we have had unfriendly visitors since, young men mostly."

"Why? What did she say?"

"She just gave the impression that we were establishing some sort of female pagan temple out here, that's all."

"Is Denise here?"

"Everybody is still here. Denise is the one with the shotgun."

"Well, that shit has got to stop," Morgan said. They were in Morgan's room now, and she was standing at the window, looking out. "What happened there?" she asked.

Amanda joined her at the window. Below them were the scorched-black bushes where the rocket that hit the house had burned itself out. "Last night's rocket attack," Amanda said.

"Well, damn. Where is Nemo anyway? Do you know?"

"The last I knew of my brother, Ms. Sissy was checking him out of his hotel over in Hudson. He wasn't there."

Morgan went to the bed and got her cell phone out of her purse. "Well, I think I will have a talk with Ms. Sissy about the serious repercussions of her article. Do you have a copy?"

When Amanda came back from her room with the newspaper, Morgan was just signing off from a phone call: "Follow it up, see, but don't call me. I'll call you. Bye."

Morgan took the newspaper and just glanced at the article's headline and photo. "You haven't spoken with this Ms. Sissy about this, have you?" she asked.

"No. What's to discuss?"

"Well, I am about to track her down and give her an earful. Inciting young men to attack innocent women—that's irresponsible journalism. She owes us big time."

"But what?" Amanda could not see the point of this.

"I'll think of something. The first thing is to get her and her newspaper on the defensive, back on their heels." Morgan flipped to the editorial page, where there was a phone number. As she dialed it she said, "Go on, get out of here. This is my job. Could you bring me up something to eat? Is there any yogurt? That's a dear."

Chapter 21

The Mount Morris Manor inn was exemplary of what Dominick figured Amanda and Morgan envisioned for their Diligence Retreat—an old estate house reborn as a stylish commercial venture. The grounds were extensive and manicured—landscaping would be an additional expense at Diligence—and the manor house itself was only half the age of the Van Houten house and in a later style both more expansive and relaxed. Whereas the Van Houten place had been a well-off minister's homestead, Mount Morris had obviously been designed as an outsider millionaire's summer playhouse, not built for a reverend. It was painted pink for one thing, pink with white trim and a veranda that encircled the whole first floor. All the cars in the car park could have been entered in a "which one costs more" contest.

Frank Barnett was waiting for Dominick and met him on the veranda. He was dressed in creased tan Bermuda shorts and a bottle-blue polo shirt. Neither item looked like it had been worn before. Dominick had brought his cane, more for effect than necessity—an outward sign of his otherwise hidden affliction. Besides, there once had been a time—around the time this house was brand new—when gentlemen routinely carried canes or walking sticks. He leaned on his cane as he lowered himself into a wingback wicker porch chair.

"What exactly did you do to yourself?" Barnett asked as he pulled a chair up beside Dominick's.

"Some broken ribs, and it was done unto me as I was being accidentally gallant. Nice place you have here."

"Think so? I hadn't thought rustic could get so ostentatious. It's almost Southern in its pretension, though, so I can feel at home."

Barnett laughed and gestured down toward the driveway where it curved in front of the veranda. "That helps."

Vernon had pulled his aging Caddy up under the shade of a high tree by the driveway and was out with a chamois cloth dusting off its faded paint job. Dominick was fairly sure this was Vernon's idea of a joke, a comment upon where they were. Dominick had never seen Vernon dust off his cab before. It wasn't dirty.

"So, you and Morgan have gotten together?" Dominick said. Vernon looked up at the veranda, and Dominick gave him a quick knowing smile.

"No point in denying that—fine lady—but only exploratory, private, not public news."

"So, is Morgan staying here, too, or did she just drop you off?"

"No, I am checked in here solo. I could hardly go on with her to Diligence, a house full of women. Good god."

"You got that right," Dominick said.

"Although I do get the feeling that all the other rooms here are occupied either by honeymooners or older couples trying to pretend it's a honeymoon."

The pills were already failing, and Dominick twisted in his chair, trying to find a comfort zone. He had the vial of pills in his pocket. Perhaps if he took a few more he could beat the pain to the departure threshold. He pulled the small orange vial of pills out from his pocket. "Frank, do you think I could get something to wash a few of these down with? Doctor's orders."

"Certainly. I am a sorry plantation host. What would you like? In spite of all the show, this place is just a bed and breakfast, no restaurant or bar, but I can bring something from my room. Water, white wine, Scotch?"

"The first and last of those would be grand, separate, with ice if there is any to be had. Thank you."

Barnett went off. The view from the veranda was south and west, looking down the Hudson Valley. An avenue had been opened in the forest to frame the panorama. The afternoon sun was creeping deeper beneath the porch eaves. Down on the driveway Vernon was not to be seen, probably back in his driver's seat taking a nap. Dominick wondered how the man who built this house had made all his money. His had been an age of exploitative industry, something taken from the land—minerals, coal, grain, or just space itself turned into railroad rights-of-way—after slavery but before Dominick's father's generation of capitalists who just took money from the people whose money they were supposedly managing. A manor from that Gilded Age. Dominick liked the provenance of the house in Diligence better. Barnett returned with a silver tray bearing an ice bucket, glasses, bottled water, and a bottle of aged single-malt Scotch that Dominick had never heard of. The pills went down with the water. The Scotch went down without any ice, an ancient smoky taste. Also on the tray was a file of papers.

Barnett was businesslike, which Dominick appreciated. He said that while he was in no position to offer investment advice, much less about real estate in a market he knew nothing about, he had reviewed the agreement and corporation papers that Morgan had had drawn up, and they seemed in order. He had done that gratis, but if Dominick wanted him to follow through representing him, he would be happy to accommodate and put Dominick back on the hourly clock. Why didn't Dominick take the papers and look them over, then get back to him? Barnett would be there through the weekend. He was sure Ms. Custis would be open to negotiating any changes Dominick might suggest.

The Scotch was mellow. The pills were firing for effect again. The slanting sun had reached his feet. Dominick was enjoying his palatial surroundings and the privileged destination view. He was no longer down in Vernon's little hollow. From his pocket container he extracted a fresh cigar and lit it up. Barnett refused one. Dominick felt like chatting, but he did not know about what. He had noticed before that the pills had a way of inhibiting thinking.

"Did you know about the attack on the house last night?" Barnett asked.

"Attack on the house? What house?"

"Why, your place in Diligence. Some local Fourth of July rowdies, I gather."

"That article," Dominick said.

"I don't know anything about its causes," Barnett said. He poured himself a short shot of Scotch. "Just that Morgan asked me to increase the fire insurance on the place."

"Was the house harmed?"

"Nothing serious, I gather. No need for a police report or a call to the fire department anyway, which would have made the insurance increase more problematic. I do want to get out there. Tomorrow maybe. Will you be free to come along? Or is it too long a ride for your ribs?"

"Attack on the house?" Dominick was having trouble absorbing, picturing such an event.

"What do you think you are doing? Do you know where you are? Who are you anyway?" She looked like a nurse to Dominick—a white dress, a bad haircut, and a pair of black-framed glasses. "Put that out. This is a New Age residence. All tobacco products are strictly forbidden."

Dominick looked at his Romeo y Juliet, which was just warming up, then glanced up and down the veranda. There were only the three of them there. "Frank, do you mind?"

Barnett smiled, "No, I don't mind. Actually, I enjoy the aroma of a good cigar."

"Then, if this offends only you, madam, perhaps you could do yourself the favor of finding something else somewhere else to be offended by."

"Dominick, this is Mrs. Grant, our proprietress," Barnett said.

"In that case," Dominick drained his glass of Scotch and, leaning on his cane, rose from the wingchair, "ta-ta. This cigar, madam, is worth more to me than your approbation." He picked up the file from the silver tray. "Frank, I will get back to you. I will see if I feel up to a trip tomorrow. You know my number if there is any more news on the house. Good day to you."

Vernon was asleep in the car, the driver's seat tilted all the way back and his hat pulled down over his eyes. Dominick had to wake him up.

***

Morgan found Amanda in her room. "I couldn't reach Ms. Sissy in person," Morgan said as she came in without knocking, "but I left a message on her voice mail at the paper. This has got me all worked up—inciting a hate crime. I think I'll go over there in person to talk with one of her bosses. I want to threaten them with a lawsuit, see how they react. At the very least they can publish some sort of correction, don't you think?"

Amanda wasn't sure what she thought any more. She knew she did not like being attacked, but she also did not want to start dragging others into it. She wanted the whole thing to blow over.

"You didn't report this to the sheriff? " Morgan asked.

"No. Denise didn't want to, and after all she fired the first shots, both nights."

"Both nights?"

"Well, the first night, two nights ago, there were just some kids in the drive yelling things at the house, and Denise took a shot at them. Last night, same thing. She just started firing away down at the gate. Look, if we call in the county authorities, it will just bring more attention, make things worse."

"I want this Sissy chick fired," Morgan said.

During their short career together, one thing Amanda had learned about Morgan was that you did not want her for an enemy. In Morgan's world there were the good guys and the other guys. The good guys had proven their loyalty, and you could do whatever you wanted to the other guys; they were like a different species altogether. "Morgan, are we still partners?" Amanda asked. She wanted an answer.

"More than ever, girl. Now we got some real enemies. We re in this together."

"The kids who came out here aren't our enemies. They don't even know us. They just feel free to harass an available target. And the target is not the house or you and me but whatever their idea of the Wiccans is. They've had their little hate fling, made their point. They won't be back. We have to concentrate on getting Denise and her gang out of here, and making them victims only strengthens their hand for staying. Leave it alone."

"This isn't tactics we're talking about here, partner. This is strategy. You cannot just let people attack you and walk away. Sissy attacked us. The thugs—whether they come back or not—are just fallout. She stirred the community up against us for some reason. She fired the first shot, not Denise. Sissy has got to pay. I will not let the bitch get away with it. A cheap shot besides—Christians versus pagans. What century is this?"

From her window Amanda watched Morgan drive away in her little red sports car. It was getting on to late afternoon, but the sun was still high behind the house, casting a stark shadow onto the untended grounds, a silhouette of rooflines with the cupola tower sticking up like a short thick circumcised penis.

What is wrong with you, girl? Why aren't you driving off away from all this instead of Morgan? Because you have nowhere to go and she does? All those trips when you had to drive because she couldn't. What other lies has she been living out with you? A friend rented the car for her? She never mentioned any friend in Albany. Why didn't she ask you to go with her? In the past she would have. Two Amazons are better than one, Morgan used to say when they faced confrontations—good cop, bad cop, yin and yang, sweet and sour, white meat or dark meat. Maybe it is just as well that she is gone. Whatever happens will be simpler without her.

There had been no cars cruising or stopping on the road today—not that Amanda had noticed anyway—no gawkers or prayer groups. All that drama would be over. What Amanda had wanted to hear from Morgan was that Denise and the others had no legal grounds to delay their eviction. Because the sooner the Wiccans were gone the sooner the events of this Diligence Fourth of July would become just forgotten history and the closer Amanda would be to being free.

Don't count on her, the voice in her head, Marjorie's voice, said.

As it turned out, the rest of the daylight and slowly deepening evening passed in rural serenity, the only sounds beside birdsong were the waves of cricket choruses moving up from the river and past them. At some point one of the girls knocked on Amanda's door and invited her down to a communal supper—fried tofu and brown rice and salad. "We are all in this together," Denise said as way of grace before meal. Supper was silent but friendly enough—people passed things to Amanda—and she was thankful for the food. Denise appointed sentinels and watch hours. Any activities down on the road or around the house should be reported immediately to her. Amanda noted that not all the girls seemed honored by their assignments. That night was benign as well.

The next morning, Saturday, Amanda discovered that Morgan had not returned. She knew it was silly to worry about her, but she did anyway. Morgan had not said anything about having another place to stay or about returning to Albany. Could she be arrested for driving without a license in somebody else's rental car? Amanda debated with herself about calling Morgan's cell phone. She did not want to come across as spying. It was none of her business where Morgan spent her nights, and it was not as if they had an appointment or anything. She tried to come up with some excuse for calling, but could not think of a thing that did not sound bogus.

Then, in the early afternoon, cars started pulling into the driveway, a small caravan of them. Amanda ran to find Denise—she did not want her shooting at anyone in broad daylight, she might actually hit someone—but to her surprise she found Denise at the front door not cocking her shotgun but wearing one of her Wiccan gowns, this one the color of marigolds. Denise went out onto the veranda to greet the arrivals, the first of whom was a tall, gaunt man with a funny sort of Chinese beard, dressed in a tan camouflage uniform. They embraced at the top of the veranda steps. As Denise escorted her guest indoors, she stopped to introduce him to Amanda, still standing on the bottom step of the stairway, "Amanda, this is High Priest Lloyd, with members of his Saugerties coven. Lloyd, Amanda."

"Ah, finally," Lloyd said, but he did not extend a hand and barely nodded to her. The downstairs suddenly felt very full as the rest of Lloyd's eight- or nine-person crew—of both sexes—filed in and were greeted by Denise's girls. Denise should have told her. This was like an invasion. Amanda retreated back up the stairs.

Nobody ever tells you anything. Ever wonder why that is? All you can ever do is just react.

Back in her room she decided that at least now she had a bona fide reason to call Morgan—to warn her that the Wiccans were here. In her room the wireless reception was good only by the front window. As she stood there listening to Morgan's phone ring and then the voice-mail message come on, she watched Lloyd's people unload their cars. There were coolers and bags of groceries, sleeping bags and pillows, day packs and long leather zippered cases that could only be holding rifles. The message she left was just, "Call me. It's important."

✳✳✳

Dominick slept late Saturday. The previous day's trip had worn him out. This convalescent stuff was dangerous. It would have to stop. Vernon was gone. As Dominick fixed himself a fresh pot of coffee, he thought about what Barnett had said about the Van Houten place being under attack. Worrying about the fate of a place was new to Dominick, but somebody picking on the old house for any reason sort of pissed him off. It was like an attack on history. That house—he was beginning to think of it as his house—had not done anything to anyone. And what did "being under attack" actually mean? He resisted the temptation—the voice in his head—to get involved. What could he do anyway? A stranded unarmed semi-invalid many miles away. By the time he finally called Barnett at his fancy B&B, the counselor was no longer in. He thought of calling Amanda, but could not find his little leather notebook where he had written down her number. It must still be in the glove compartment of his car, which was still parked over at Sissy's place in Hudson.

This time when the phone on the kitchen wall started ringing, Dominick went to answer it. It was his sister Amanda. "I was just thinking of you," he said. "How did you get this number?"

"The lawyer Barnett gave it to me. He's here, with Morgan. I thought you would be long gone, but he said you were still here, just up in Catskill."

"My exit was interrupted. I couldn't find your number. What's this about the house being under attack?"

"Thanks to your girlfriend's article. That's why I called. I hold you partly to blame for all this, for bringing her out here."

"What is 'all this'? What's going on?"

"Well, right now I have a houseful of armed Wiccans with a siege mentality, and a Christian prayer meeting is setting up down by the gate. Two nights ago it was rockets and gunfire. I don't suppose your girlfriend wants to come out here and tell these folks it's nothing to get excited about, just a piece of tabloid hype?"

"I read the article. She is not my girlfriend. Rockets, gunfire?"

"Fireworks rockets shot at the house and gunfire as in bullets."

"You say Morgan and Barnett are there? Are they staying?"

"Why? What is it to you?"

"I'm coming down there. I'll be there as soon as I can. Do you need anything? Is there anything I could bring?"

"Look, Nemo, that is not why I called."

"Nemo? So I am Nemo. What makes me Nemo?"

"I meant Dominick, and it doesn't matter."

"Did Marjorie call me Nemo? She had other insulting names for me. Was that one I didn't know?" Dominick wondered if Marjorie would have known that Nemo was Latin for No One. She knew things like that. She would surprise you. She had had that kind of education. Nemo was Latin for the Greek *Outis*, the name Odysseus gave himself to fool the Cyclops. Would Marjorie have known that?

"Dominick, what are you talking about? No, I don't need anything. I don't even think I need you here. That is not why I called, and what does our mother have to do with this?"

"Nothing, nothing," Dominick said. Odysseus escaping the Cyclops's cave had always been Dominick's favorite scene. He still sometimes dreamed of it.

"I guess I just wanted to ask you if you could ask your friend if she could write something, I don't know, corrective, neutralizing, maybe an apology."

"I have no control over what Sissy writes."

"If you are coming down, you had better bring whatever you want to eat and drink," Amanda said. There was a long pause. "And bring me a bottle of vodka."

Dominick called Vernon on his cell phone. By the time Vernon got home Dominick had packed his small bag, taken some pain pills, and was ready to go. "We are off to Diligence," Dominick said. "You can just drop me there and get back for your heavy Saturday night business." As Dominick put his bag and his cane and some pillows into the back seat of the Caddy, he was surprised by Mustang climbing in too, then jumping over into the front seat. When Vernon came out of the house and saw Mustang sitting there he laughed. "Old Mustang knows something is up. He rarely rides shotgun anymore." As they drove away, Mustang gave one long look at Dominick in the back seat then turned his gaze forward, sticking his head out the open window, sniffing the wind as it passed. On the way out of town they stopped to shop. Dominick even bought a large cooler to stash everything in, including Amanda's bottle of vodka and a bottle of Scotch for himself.

As they came around the final curve of county road before the Van Houten place, they could see ahead that the road by the missing gate was nearly blocked with vehicles and people. Vernon braked slowly to a stop well before they got there. Someone was speaking or reading something over a poor sound system.

"I'm not driving through there," Vernon said. "Most of those folks will be from Catskill and will know me. Being black in that town is bad enough, I'd rather not add pagan to it." Vernon put the Caddy in reverse and backed the way they had come until he came to a place where he could make a three-point turn. "We'll try another way."

The other way involved dusty and bumpy back farm roads that were murder on Dominick's sore ribs no matter how cautiously Vernon tried to navigate them. After what seemed like miles and a series of right turns they crossed the county road beyond the Van Houten place and bounced along again on two-rut tracks past fields and woods. Mustang was totally alert to everything they passed. Dominick was totally aware of every axle thud and sudden swerve. Vernon seemed to be enjoying the excursion; he was humming something to himself. Finally they stopped, and Mustang scrambled his way out the passenger-side front window and onto the ground with a territory-claiming bark.

"Close as I can safely get you," Vernon said.

Off to their right, in the direction Mustang had headed, past a broken-down fence, was the back of an old wooden barn. Beyond the barn, bright in the slanting late-afternoon sun were the cupola and roofline of the Van Houten house.

"I'll give you a hand getting your stuff up there," Vernon said, "then I got to get back."

Mustang went with them, leading the way actually, his head down, sniffing the trail ahead. Dominick carried his bag, and Vernon dragged the cooler by one handle. All was peaceful at the house. There was no one about. No one saw them come up through the kitchen garden. Vernon lifted the cooler up onto the back porch, and Dominick dropped his bag beside it.

"I am almost out of cash, Vernon. Can I settle with you later?"

"Sure. You're not going anywhere, and I still have most of your stuff hostage at my place. I don't know why you want to get involved in this. It's not like you're from here or anything, but I'll leave you now." Vernon turned to go. Then he stopped by a tomato plant in one of the raised garden beds on which one cherry tomato was red enough to be ripe. He stopped to pick it. "By the way, good women don't deserve to be hurt. Sissy is not just my daughter; she is also a good woman. Come on, Mustang."

Vernon and Mustang walked off together.

Chapter 22

Morgan's return had been typical. Of course, she had not called back, so Amanda had not had the chance to warn her about the Wiccans being there. And by the time she did return that afternoon a crowd had begun to gather down on the road by the driveway entrance. Amanda was watching them from her bedroom window when Morgan's red rental sports car arrived. Its roof was down. There was a man with her. Morgan honked her horn at the back of the crowd and yelled something Amanda could not make out. The crowd slowly parted to let Morgan through, but she stopped in their midst to harangue them. Amanda could only hear random scraps of what she said—"Got nothing better to do?" "Where does Jesus say mess with innocent people?" "Go on, go home and beat up on your dog or your kids."

A few people in the crowd dared to answer her, but not as loudly, so no single voice was distinct to Amanda, just a murmur like a growl. Morgan sped up and turned into the driveway, honking her horn and scattering people. She flashed them the finger as she left them behind. A few rocks and yells followed her—"Already damned." "A Christian community." "Black witch."

By the time Amanda reached the front veranda, Denise and Lloyd were already there—Denise in her marigold gown with her shotgun, Lloyd in his desert camouflage outfit cradling a long hunting rifle with a scope, sort of a late-American Gothic couple. So many cars were parked along the edge of the driveway that there was nowhere for Morgan to park, so she pulled right up to the front steps. She and the man with her were arguing.

"Differently, that's all," the man said, and when he said it, in a slight soft Southern drawl, Amanda recognized him. It was that lawyer Barnett from Virginia.

"What? Should I have thrown money at them?" Morgan said, turning off the car.

"Did you hear what that one boy said?" the man asked, unbuckling his seat belt. "He called me a Nigger-loving Jew."

"That's sweet. So what?" Morgan said.

"I'm not Jewish. I wanted to tell him that, but you just drove away."

"It was not a moment for rationalism. Those were not rational people. What difference does it make if you are Jewish or not?"

"And you almost ran over that woman's dog," Barnett said, extracting himself from the sports car.

"Was that a dog? I thought it was a rat on a leash."

"I don't know why I let you drive," Barnett said.

"Because I knew where we were going."

"And missed the turn-off."

"Stuff it, Frankie," Morgan said as she got out of the car. She looked around at all the vehicles then up at the veranda where Amanda and Denise and Lloyd were standing with a door full of Wiccans behind them. "Popular destination we have here today," she said. "What's with the guns?"

"Self-defense," Lloyd said. "Who are you?"

"That's Morgan," Denise said. "I don't know the male."

"More to the point," Morgan said, coming up the steps, "who are you?"

"This is High Priest Lloyd from Saugerties," Denise said.

"High on what?" Morgan said. "You better point that gun in some other direction, GI Joe. What's going on, Amanda?"

Amanda was staring at lawyer Barnett, who looked ridiculous in shorts and a sports shirt. He was still standing down by the car, taking snaps with his cell phone of them and the house. "What is he doing here?" she asked.

"He's here to land Nemo. Excuse me, what is this?"

"Land Nemo? Nemo is gone," Amanda said, "and this is the pagan defense force. I tried to call and warn you. I left a voice message."

"Wiccan defense force, heh? Listen, your camo highness Floyd—"

"High Priest Lloyd," Denise corrected her.

"Floyd, we won't be needing your defense force now that I and my pass-for-Jewish negotiator Mr. Barnett here have arrived. So you and your clan can peaceably depart ASAP, get back to your very demanding, I'm sure, normal lives. You are excused, and please take all your weapons with you."

High Priest Lloyd laughed. "I do not take orders from women. Much less a colored woman with no respect."

Morgan just smiled and turned to Denise. "Who picks your friends for you, Denise? The same person who picks out your gowns?" Then she looked back to Lloyd and came up the last step to the veranda to face him. "Listen, chief, this colored woman happens to own this property, and as of now she has decided that you and your troop are trespassers and persona non grata—that's ghetto talk for scram. Now."

Lloyd just looked at her.

"Frank, bring my things, would you? That's a dear," Morgan said, still standing in front of Lloyd and returning his stare. Then she turned to the front door, jammed with gawkers. "Excuse me," she said, walking up to them. No one moved. "Get out of my fucking way," she said, and they did. "Amanda," Morgan said over her shoulder as she went in, "can we have a word?"

Amanda followed Morgan up to her room, which Morgan unlocked before going back to find Frank and her luggage. Amanda waited in the room, where the air was stale and hot. She opened the windows. There was something terribly wrong about Barnett being there, but she was not sure what it was. Was he the answer to the quandary of Morgan's behavior, or was he just a new compli-cation? In any event, Morgan now had her cohort in the fight, just as Denise now had hers in Lloyd. Only she, Amanda, was standing alone without a man at her side or her back or wherever. Everything in nature was paired for survival. No other way had worked—it was all male and female, Eden and Darwin and Mendel and family trees. Solo didn't make it in the long run.

Morgan returned, leading Barnett with her luggage. They were laughing.

"He liked it when I saluted him," Barnett was saying as they came into the room.

"But 'nice gun'? Who says something like 'nice gun'?"

"I figured it was something like a pet. If he had been standing there holding a cat, I would have said 'nice cat' just to be polite."

"But he's a psycho," Morgan said, gesturing to where Barnett should put her bags.

"Why acknowledge that? Why remind him he has that excuse?" Barnett put down Morgan's bags. "This room has some real potential. Hello, Amanda. Good to see you again."

Amanda was not sure why she disliked Frank Barnett so much. She just did. It was a given. She had felt that way since the first time they had met in his office with Marjorie. There was like an avoidance phero-mone between them. She was sure it was shared. When he said "Hello, Amanda" he folded his arms across his chest.

In the conversation that followed, Amanda felt ganged up on. It was not that Barnett had much to say—he didn't—but it was as if Morgan with Barnett on her side no longer needed Amanda as a cohort. By just the tone of her questions Morgan seemed to imply that the presence of Lloyd and his crew, the congregation down on the road, and even the newspaper article were all somehow Amanda's fault, or at least her problem.

"I gave that reporter's boss at the paper an earful yesterday," Morgan said.

"Groundless threats," Barnett added.

"We'll see," Morgan said. "He was pretty uncomfortable by the time I left. And Frank met with Nemo, who seems more inclined to sign on than before."

"You met with him?" Amanda asked. "Where?"

"Over in Hudson."

"How did you find him?" Amanda asked.

"I got a phone number from the Sissy woman," Barnett said. "He took the papers with him. Is this the bathroom?" Barnett was at the door to the cupola stairs, holding the doorknob.

"No. That's locked. The john is out and down the hall to your right," Morgan said. She was standing at the window, looking down at the road. As Barnett left the room Morgan said, "Christ, now they have a fucking crucifix erected down there. If they set fire to that sucker, I may just have to borrow Chief Floyd's rifle and shoot someone."

When Barnett came back, Amanda got from him the number where he had reached her brother. She needed some sort of backup, and Nemo was her only option. She left them there, standing at the window watching the scene down on the road. She heard Morgan ask, "If you're not Jewish, Frank, are you a Christian?"

"I'll plead the Fifth on that one," Barnett said.

Amanda called Dominick, and he said he would come out.

✳✳✳

Dominick left his bag and the cooler on the kitchen porch, taking out only Amanda's bottle of vodka. There was no one in the kitchen or in the downstairs hallway. Outside the closed doors to the front parlor/ Wicca chapel was a big pile of shoes, not all of them women's. He could smell the incense and hear someone speaking—a male monotone— behind the closed doors, but he knew better now than to peek in. He went up the stairs and to Amanda's room. He knocked.

"Go away," Amanda said.

"It's me, Nemo," Dominick said. "I brought your vodka."

When Amanda opened the door the first thing she wanted to know was how he had gotten there. "I've been watching the driveway. You didn't come through that crowd."

"There is a back way in," he said, "from behind the barn." He handed her the bottle of vodka. "A siege of Christians?"

"Just citizens exercising their right to be righteous. Thanks for the vodka."

Dominick went to the window to look down at the road, where the crowd had grown and more cars were parked along the shoulder. "Life, liberty, and the pursuit of intolerance," he said to the window pane.

Amanda joined him at the window. "What do you think we should do?" she asked.

"I haven't the slightest idea. We will want to avoid confrontation, obviously, seeing as we are vastly outnumbered, but we can't let them hurt the house."

They stood side by side at the window, watching for a while in silence. Someone, a man, was praying through a bad amplifier and a lousy speaker. They could hear him, but what he said was garbled with feedback and filled with the usual gibberish.

"They seem angry about something. But what?" Amanda asked.

"Beats me," Dominick said. "I guess they are upset by a perceived foreign body in their midst and are gathering together to deal with it somehow. Maybe just pray at it and feel better about themselves."

"But way out here in the country? I'm sure most of those people had to be told how to find the place."

"I guess they're that hungry for an enemy, and some of them are probably just along for the show."

"And why are you here?" Amanda asked.

"Didn't you invite me?"

"No."

"Originally?"

"That was Morgan, not me. She was miffed that you got half of Marjorie's money and wanted us to get all of it."

"She drew up the papers. I thought I might sign them. You said she and Barnett were here. Are they still here?"

"That's her red sports car down there. She is trapped here with her boyfriend for now."

"Fort Diligence Retreat and Spa," Dominick said. "I suppose if we raise a flag it would be a Wiccan banner."

"Dominick, seriously, why are you here?"

Dominick did not know the answer to that question, or at least an answer that he felt like giving to Amanda. It had something to do with Sissy and something to do with the house itself. They were two things he was reluctant to leave behind. He could not remember the last person or place he had been reluctant to leave behind, so it intrigued him.

"If you came back to help me out," Amanda said, "I appreciate it, but I really don't know how you can help."

It had never occurred to Dominick that Amanda might need or appreciate his help or anyone else's. From the first moment he had met her—holding a knife on him in Marjorie's kitchen—he had taken her to be someone whose needs were pretty much self-contained—a woman of a certain age and depth of experience who expected no favors and offered no apologies. He had admired that in an abstract way. Women who could take care of themselves were a plus in his estimation.

"On the phone you mentioned fireworks and bullets and armed Wiccans," Dominick said.

"Denise has brought in reinforcements. Morgan told them to leave, but they haven't yet."

"They are having a prayer meeting downstairs," Dominick said. "How armed?"

"Two or three rifles at least. I don't know what else."

"They have to leave," Dominick said.

"I didn't invite them. They are Denise's guests."

"Let me talk with Morgan and Barnett, our legal brain trust, and see if they have any idea what to do," Dominick said. For some reason he felt as if he was missing something. He glanced down at Amanda beside him—her full head of vaguely controlled wet-and-dry-hay-colored hair, her wide shoulders in a thin white cotton blouse. He had to bend down to see her face. In the second before she noticed him looking he caught the tiredness there, the resignation in her distant blue eyes. Then there was the seed of a smile at the corners of her mouth.

"What?" she said.

She is not Marjorie, Dominick told himself. All women were foreign lands, but not all the same country. He put an arm around Amanda, squeezing her shoulder. "This sort of sucks, doesn't it? And you have been putting up with it for days."

"When a rocket hit the house, I had to put the fire out by myself," she said.

"You didn't tell me that."

"I wanted to leave. I tried to leave, but I couldn't. I came back. I just want to be somewhere else, but I don't know where. Stop looking at me," she said, but as she did so she leaned closer to him, hiding her face against his chest. "Denise shot my new car."

"Well, it seems to me that what has to happen is that everyone else has to leave, and you and I stay here to see this through," Dominick heard himself say. "Both our friends of the Lord down on the road and our disciples of Satan here in the house have got to go. This isn't our battle, and this house is just a focus through happenstance."

"Sounds good, but how?" Amanda said.

"Don't know. Surely both sides have families to go back to. Look, why don't you get some rest, and I will go consult with Morgan and Barnett and see what we can come up with. Are they in her room?"

"Probably. I guess. Are you here to stay?" Amanda pushed herself away at the mention of Morgan's name.

"I brought a bag and a cooler of food. I left them down on the kitchen porch."

"I'll bring them up here. Nothing is safe down there."

"I can do that," Dominick said.

"No, let me. I need something to do. You go strategize."

They left the room together, headed in different directions—Amanda down the stairs, Dominick to Morgan's room, where Frank Barnett answered his knock at the door.

"Well, look who's here, Morgan," Barnett said. "Come on in, Dominick. How the hell did you get here? Drop from the sky?"

"Totally terrestrial, Frank," Dominick said. "Hello, Morgan." Morgan was seated cross-legged on the bed, dressed in a tank top and a pair of short shorts. There was a lot of smooth brown skin showing. She looked different, younger. She had done something with her hair.

"How are you feeling?" Barnett asked.

"Not so hot," Dominick answered. The ride and the hike with his bag had surged the pain in his ribs over his pharmaceutical defenses. "May I?" The only spot he could see to sit down and relieve the pain was the foot of the bed beside Morgan. She scooted herself back as he plopped down. "Back," he said in way of explanation, "ribs." He got the vial of pain pills out of his pants pocket, opened it, and shook three into his palm. "Would you. . .?" he began, but Barnett was ahead of him, was already standing in front of him handing him a plastic bottle of water. Dominick swallowed the pills one at a time. The water was warm but welcome, and from the slightest hint of a cosmetic scent from the mouth of the bottle he knew this was Morgan's bottle of water.

"I suppose whiskey would be contraindicative to those," Barnett said.

"So is flying an airplane, but I will take the whiskey. It seems to speed up the relief." Dominick thought of the pills as his reinforcements being called up. The whiskey would be like the cavalry initiating the counterattack. Barnett brought him a glass with a couple of fingers of his smoky Scotch in it, not corn or rye whiskey like General Grant would have drunk. He drank it down as if it were medicine. Morgan had not said a word, not even hello. His back insisted that he lay down. "Excuse me," he said as he stretched back, still holding the almost drained glass.

"The walking wounded," Morgan said. "Make yourself comfortable. Did Miss Sissy do this to you in bed?"

Dominick chose not to answer her. "What's your plan?" he asked.

"We were considering shooting our way out, but we don't have any weapons," Barnett said.

"We are not staying here," Morgan added.

"How about taking the Wiccans with you?" Dominick asked.

"Do I look like a pagan pied piper to you?" Morgan said.

"Just a wish," Dominick said. "Invite both prayer groups to an all-American ecumenical meal at McDonald's or Pizza Hut. Get them all out of here."

"Why don't you do that?" Morgan asked.

"I thought I'd stay behind to rest my ribs and protect the place. Besides, I just got here and I don't have a car."

"You want to protect the place?" Morgan asked. "Does that mean you also want to come in as a shareholder?"

"I am considering it, Morgan. The place sort of grows on you, and Amanda has nowhere else to go. But I don't have to decide today, do I? I have barely looked at the agreement papers." There was a certain satisfaction in holding Morgan off. She always came across as so damn sure of herself that denying her any immediate gratification seemed a necessary and proper corrective. He sat back up and finished off the Scotch. It or the pills or the stretch-out was working. He was a little lightheaded. This time he thought of the pain as a beggar or blackmailer, whom he just had to pay off to silence for a while. But he had no clear thoughts as he looked around the room. He wondered how many of those pills he had taken today. The vial had seemed worrisomely light. He held out his glass and Barnett poured some more Scotch into it. Dominick took a sip. He hadn't the slightest idea what to say. Surely there was something he should be saying. "I think I will go lay down for a bit, take a rest. Maybe everyone will leave on their own when it gets dark, and you can slip away. I will be in Amanda's room." He took the glass of Scotch with him, but only because he forgot that he was holding it.

Chapter 23

Nemo snored. Amanda did not especially mind the snoring. It was sort of homey actually. She had grown up in a house of snoring men. Every lover she had ever had had snored, some worse than others. Nemo's snoring was polite, almost patrician. It was the other sounds he made as he slept, thrown in here and there amidst the snores—the grunts and growls and gurgles, animal sounds, like something a hibernating bear would make while dreaming about salmon—that got to her.

Amanda had been sitting in her armchair when Nemo came back to the room, a bodice-ripper romance that she had read before open in her lap. She was not even pretending to read it. She was just sitting and listening—listening to but not really hearing the voices drifting up from the road, the whistle and rustle of the breeze in the trees, the sounds of a house full of people. The prayer meeting downstairs must have ended, because there were many voices now and traffic on the stairs and doors opening and closing. Then her door opened without a knock and in came Nemo with a glass of whiskey in his hand, which he put down carefully on the bedside table before dropping onto the bed. "I have to lay down for a bit," was all he said before passing out. Now she had him to listen to as well.

After a while Nemo's noises got to her. They were distracting. Amanda began to feel as if she were eavesdropping on something personal and ought to leave. Besides, she was hungry. It had been many hours since she had grabbed some rice biscuits and peanut butter for breakfast. She headed down to the kitchen.

The kitchen was busy. Most of High Priest Lloyd's troop were as young as Denise's devotees. It struck Amanda how young they all were, barely adults, for whom their childhood memories were still a long way from being historical. Right now they were acting like kids who had just been sprung from church. Some fixing of food was going on, but mainly they were hanging out, milling about in the kitchen and out on the back porch. The addition of Lloyd's young men had made a difference, even if they were outnumbered two to one. There was a new social chemistry in the air. Denise and Lloyd and Denise's lieutenants were somewhere else. No one seemed to notice Amanda's arrival. A simple smorgasbord was being laid out on the table, and Amanda fixed herself a plate. No one seemed to mind. A tall young man with long brown hair and multiply pierced ears asked her if she would like some iced tea. He was pouring himself a glass at the time. He followed her out onto the porch.

"You're Amanda, aren't you?" he asked as he sat down beside her on the edge of the deck. "I think it's great that you have given a home to these sisters. This is such a nice spot."

"What's your name?" Amanda asked, taking a sip of her over-sweet iced tea.

"Brian," he said, smiling.

"Brian, I am only their landlady."

"Are you from around here, originally I mean?" Brian asked, undeterred.

"I grew up nearby," Amanda said, "over in Vermont."

"I've never been there," Brian said. "Is it like this there?"

Where Amanda had grown up was less than a hundred miles away across the river and north. Brian had tattoos on his arms and on his neck and who knew where else. He had a sweet smile and soft eyes. There had been a time when Amanda would have closed on him like a honeybee on a flower. "Brian, why are you here?"

"To show our solidarity, Lloyd said. I'm not sure what that means, but I've always liked coming here. It's so peaceful. What's that bird?" he asked. A mockingbird was complaining about something out beyond the garden. Sometimes what they said sounded like complete incomprehensible sentences.

"That's a Northern Mockingbird," Amanda said. "How long are you staying?"

"I don't know about everybody else, but me and Ashante—that's my ride—got to go back tonight. I got to go to work tomorrow morning."

"On Sunday? What do you do?"

"I work at the country club, at the golf cart shack. Do you play golf? You don't like that tea, do you? They make it too sweet. All that sugar's not good for you. Can I get you some water or something?"

The tea is nowhere near as sweet as you are, Amanda thought. His hands were long and strong and slender, well manicured. "What instrument do you play?" she asked.

"The mandolin mainly, but I am learning the zither. How did you know?"

"Oh, we older women just know such things," she said. She wanted to tell him that he should tell Ashante to go on without him, that she, Amanda, would give him a ride back to Saugerties in the morning in plenty of time to get to work at his golf cart shack. Then she remembered Nemo asleep in her bed and looked at her hands and reminded herself that she was probably as old as Brian's mother. "Yes, Brian, thank you. Could you bring me just a glass of water?"

Amanda scanned the group she could see on the porch and in the kitchen, wondering which of the girls was Ashante, not that it made any difference. Then she noticed Morgan and Barnett at the smorgasbord table with plates, helping themselves and chatting with the kids in there. There was something about this us-versus-them scenario that eclipsed all other differences behind the duality of us in here and them out there. Amanda could not hear what Morgan said, but it was something that made everyone around her laugh.

Amanda put her plate down on the deck beside her glass of iced tea and walked off into the garden, which needed watering. Morgan's routine and hers were now so divergent that she felt compelled to walk away. Earlier Barnett had wanted to talk business with her, Morgan's business, and Amanda had just tuned him out. She could not understand why Morgan herself was not talking it over with her. She wondered what the mockingbird was going on about. She walked to the edge of the garden and into the field beyond. The sounds from the house dispersed behind her. Brian found her out there, halfway to the old barn. He was carrying her glass of water.

"Looking for that bird?" he asked. "What's it look like?" .

"Slate grey, big as a robin, white stripes on its wings. Thanks." Amanda took the glass of water from him. There were ice cubes in it. Brian was a good head taller than she, taller even than Nemo. "What's going on back there?"

"Your friend was talking about a concert going on over in Hudson tonight, part of some arts festival."

"Oh?"

"I guess she and her boyfriend are going to the concert, and she invited everybody else to come along. She said she'd pay for their tickets."

"That's generous of her," Amanda said. There had been a time when she would have been the first person Morgan would have invited along. "Who is playing at the concert?"

"A couple of local groups then Thompson & Tolbert. The girls are all hot for them."

"Of course they are. Ashante?"

"Nah, she doesn't like that country stuff. We'll still be headed back, but we will wait to leave with the others. Safety in numbers like your friend pointed out. Sorry, what is her name?"

"Morgan," Amanda said.

"Yeah, Morgan. She's cool. Hey! What's that?"

Brian had a good foot's height advantage on Amanda's view of the unmowed fields around them.

"Hey, you. What are you doing there?" Brian called out.

And then Amanda saw them—two heads in hoodies popped up amidst the tall grass and headed quickly away, still crouched down. Amanda's first impulse was to grab Brian's arm and then quickly scan the rest of the field for other intruders.

"Just some kids," Brian said. "But let's go back."

Amanda was still holding on to Brian's arm. He did not seem to mind. "Yes, let's," she said, and they turned together, headed back toward the house, its western face ablaze in the sunset. "What country club is it you work at?" she asked. Her hand was on his tattooed forearm, her fingers hiding a green and blue dragon's head.

***

It wasn't easy, but Dominick managed it. He woke up. Someone was shaking his shoulder.

"Sorry, old chap. But we really do have to talk." It was that man Barnett.

Dominick was in a room deep with shadows. His mouth was dry, so he had been snoring. "What's up?" he said to indicate that he was awake. He was not in the least interested in what was up.

"Well, Morgan and I are out of here, for one thing, and I have to head back to DC tomorrow, so I doubt we will have the chance to talk again."

"God speed," Dominick said, again not really meaning what he said. He was still trying to figure out where he was. A strange bed in a strange room in a strange dusk light. Ah, yes, Amanda's room in Diligence, upstate New York. Thoughts began to focus.

"The crowd down on the road has thinned out, so we thought we would head back to Hudson soon," Barnett said.

Dominick had learned a way of getting up that hurt the least. It involved simultaneously throwing his legs out of bed, rolling, and pushing himself upright. It worked again, although he was light-headed for a few seconds. "You and Morgan?" he asked, his place in space and time becoming clearer.

"Me and Morgan and most of the Wiccan kids—a convoy, if you will. Most of those kids don't want to be here any more than we do. It's Saturday night on a holiday weekend, for chrissakes. Nobody wants to either fight or be holed up here. They want to go out and boogie and maybe get laid later if they're lucky. How are you doing? You want a ride out? There's no room in our little sports car, but I could find you a ride with somebody else if you want."

"I believe I just got here." In the room's gloom Dominick saw a glass on the stand beside the table and took a drink, thinking it was water. It was whiskey and burned. He coughed.

"You are supposed to sip single malts," Barnett said.

The Scotch woke Dominick up. "So what are we supposed to talk about?" He coughed some more and put the glass down.

"The corporation papers, your deal on this place."

"Yes?"

"Hold off," Barnett said. "No rush."

"What's changed? I thought you said the papers were alright."

"Oh, the papers are okay. It's just the deal and who you're dealing with."

"Morgan you mean."

"She's a vixen that one," Barnett said. "May I?" Dominick hadn't finished the Scotch in the water glass. Barnett took a sip.

"Aren't you two . . . ?" Dominick could not come up with the proper word.

"She's not my client. You are," Barnett said. "If I gave you a piece of advice now that turned out to be bum later, you might conclude that it was because Morgan and I were . . . What is the word for it? "

"Conjoined," Dominick said, "driving around in the same rental car, spending too much time in the same places. Coupled."

"You do have to admit, Dominick, that she is one fine trim piece of ass."

"Not my type, I guess. But I like Morgan. Is she trying to screw me?"

"I wouldn't say that. She would not mind having the balance of Marjorie's estate to play with, but I am no longer sanguine about what her actual plans are."

"Oh?" Dominick noted the "sanguine." It meant Barnett had practiced this speech. No one, not even lawyers, used a word like that without rehearsing it first. "Why is that?"

"Now that I have seen the place and seen how Morgan feels about the place and tried to talk with your sister about the development plans, the whole thing just doesn't add up right. I don't believe Amanda has even seen what Morgan is proposing to you. My advice to you is to just hold off, delay, disappear for a while—you are good at that—until this blows over and the Wiccans are evicted and the two ladies get their act together."

"Have you shared any of this insight with Morgan?"

"No, of course not, and I would appreciate it if you kept my counsel confidential. I would like to stay friends with Morgan. In fact, I had better go. I don't want to rouse her suspicions."

"You could tell her you were making one last pitch for me to sign."

"I would rather tell her nothing than lie to her." Barnett made a sound Dominick took for a laugh. "In fact, one of the traits Morgan and I seem to share is our reticence to share inconvenient facts." Barnett finished what was left of the Scotch in the glass. "Doing you a favor. You should be careful with this hard stuff and whatever pain pills you are taking. Stay in touch."

It wasn't long after Barnett left the room that Dominick heard activity down in the driveway—voices, laughter, car trunks and doors closing. He watched from Amanda's window as the convoy shaped up for departure. The red sports car convertible with its top down was in front, with Barnett behind the wheel. Morgan was organizing everyone else. It looked like most of the cars were leaving.

Morgan was giving final instructions. "Stay close together and no stopping. No speeding either. If they follow us, we will just have to let them. If we keep it boring maybe they'll just lose interest. Remember, we all stop at the McDonald's on route nine just this side of Catskill to regroup." Then she got in the sports car beside Barnett, and they headed out down the drive in the lingering twilight, the other cars trailing behind them.

The crowd down on the road had thinned out considerably. There were just a half dozen cars and pickups there now. The preacher with his bad sound system was gone, as was the makeshift cross. The dozen or so people still there were sitting in beach chairs or in the backs of pickup trucks. It looked more like a tailgate party than any kind of protest. Only five cars and a pickup with a small Confederate flag on its antenna were still parked in the driveway in front of the house.

Down at the bottom of the driveway Barnett honked well before reaching the people seated in beach chairs blocking the way, a friendly little beep-beep from the sports car's horn. The line of cars crept forward as the people slowly got out of the way. Several people were walking alongside the red sports car, with their hands on the car as if they were either escorting it or trying to stop it. Barnett picked up speed as he turned into the roadway, and more people were now running alongside the car. Voices were raised, but Dominick could not make out what was being said or by whom. Then he heard Morgan call out "Fuck you!" as Barnett shifted into second gear and hit the gas. The other cars followed his lead and picked up speed as a barrage of bottles and cans and rocks pelted them.

So much for not speeding and being boring, Dominick thought, but he noted that none of the people down on the road got in their vehicles and offered pursuit. Instead, they stood as a crowd in the middle of the road and watched the last cars in the convoy race away. A small cheer went up, and it struck Dominick that for the people down there, whoever they were, this encounter might well be considered a victory. They had laid holy siege to the keep of their enemy, and their enemy, or the bulk of them anyway, had summarily decamped, thereby proving the efficacy of something. Of what? Prayer? Solidarity? Virtue?

As Dominick stood watching all this in the dying light, a tall, lanky man dressed in desert camouflage came down from the front veranda and went to the pickup truck still parked out front. He maneuvered it till he had it blocking the driveway directly below the house. Then Denise came out and helped him park the five other remaining cars in close to the house, all pointing out in different directions. It was almost dark by the time they finished.

"You're up," Amanda said as she came into the darkened room. She must have seen his silhouette against the lighter sky out the window.

"Who is the man in camo gear?" Dominick asked, stepping away from the window as she turned on a light.

"That's Lloyd, Denise's counterpart. Pull down the shades, why don't you? Lloyd said lighted windows would just be targets."

"Who else is still here besides Denise and Floyd?"

"No, not Floyd, Lloyd, as in of London. Just Denise's two top girls and two of Lloyd's boys. Morgan enticed the rest of them away to a concert over in Hudson. Are you okay? You didn't look so good when you came in to lie down."

"I'm fine. Sorry about commandeering your bed like that," Dominick said as he pulled down the shade on the other window.

"Well, now that Morgan is gone you can have her room back," Amanda said. "Are you hungry? I brought that cooler you brought up from the porch." It was there in a corner of the room along with his grip bag. "I've eaten and the kitchen is pretty much closed down for the night."

"What did you mean about lighted windows being targets?" Dominick asked.

"Oh, just Lloyd's paramilitary paranoia. He thinks the folks still down there might try to take the place over tonight now that they have seen a mass desertion and have us outnumbered. He and his boys and Denise have worked themselves into some sort of Alamo mindset." Amanda yawned, covering her mouth with the back of her hand. "Sorry," she said. "This day seems to have gone on forever."

"You don't share Lloyd's assessment?" Dominick went over to get his cooler and bag.

"No I don't. Those were kids the other nights. Today's group were just Christians and most of them are gone. They did their thing. They have to be home to get ready for church tomorrow morning. Maybe after church services we will have another visitation. In any event, I've left all the crazed defenses up to Lloyd and Denise."

"I will give you your room back. Thanks for the loan," Dominick said, picking up his stuff.

"Wait," Amanda said. "You'll need the key to Morgan's room." From the desk drawer she pulled out a key chain with a red plastic heart and two keys. "This is the key to her door," she said, holding out one.

"And the other key?" Dominick asked.

"The other is to the stairs up to the cupola. No one else knows you are here, by the way. I didn't mention it."

"Tomorrow is soon enough." Dominick pocketed the key chain and headed for the door.

"Dominick," Amanda said, and the way she said his name called him back. "I'm glad you are here, that you made the effort to come back when things are so . . . so messed up."

Dominick had to smile. There was really little or nothing of Marjorie in Amanda beyond memories. "*De nada*," he said.

She smiled back. "By the way, do you play golf?"

Chapter 24

Dominick had never played golf. While most sports struck him as bizarre, empty rituals, golf had always seemed especially out there toward the edge of dangerous meaninglessness. At least team sports harkened back to the cooperative needs of the hunt, and running and throwing were masculine skills with obvious Darwinian advantages. But the solo wandering and whacking of a rock on the ground with a stick served no survival skill whatsoever save perhaps the de-evolutional pursuit of frustration. An appropriately Presbyterian pastime. Dominick had been surprised to find two sets of golf clubs—hers and his—in Marjorie's Virginia garage. He wondered if Amanda had sold them along with everything else. He could not imagine his mother "out on the links," nor could he see Amanda there.

He let himself into Morgan's room and turned on the lights. The room seemed even sparser than before. The bed was unmade, and her alluring feminine aroma lingered in the still air. He felt a bit of the voyeur. "A fine trim piece of ass," Barnett had called Morgan. Did that explain anything except Barnett's appetite? Morgan was one of those women for whom being unknowable was an asset. He would put off signing the papers.

The ice Dominick had put in the cooler had melted, was now just cold water, but the sealed packets of cold cuts and cheese and the loaf of rye bread were dry, and he made himself a sandwich. He opened a still chilled can of Ballantine Ale. He avoided the bottle of Scotch; besides, he had no glass. This was the room in the house that he unrealistically thought of as one day being his. He turned off the light and pulled the desk chair up to one of the open windows to eat his sandwich. All the rest of the house was dark. In the daylight the view from here was east into the valley of the unseen river and then beyond the rising forested ridgelines of the far shore and the tops of the distant Berkshires. He had not yet seen it in autumn or winter or spring. Tonight there was no moon, and what stars he could see seemed especially distant through the hot summer air. All was quiet down by the road. There were voices in the hallway behind him.

A man's voice: "Is this the room?"

A woman's voice: "Yes, this is it. It's always locked. Amanda may have a key. I'll check."

"Why not just break it down?" the man said.

"Just wait, Lloyd. I'll see if I can get a key," the woman said.

Dominick went over and opened the door. "No need for either. What's up?" Two flashlight beams darted to his face, blinding him.

"Who the . . .? Who is this?" the man said.

"It's what's his name, Amanda's brother," the woman, whom Dominick now assumed to be Denise, said. "What are you doing here?"

"What do you want?" Dominick asked.

"Who let you in?" the man, Lloyd not Floyd, said.

With his left hand, in which he still held the can of ale, Dominick reached over and clicked on the wall switch for the ceiling light. Standing there in front of him in the doorway were Denise in a pair of bulging Capri pants and a hunter's vest, complete with rows of shotgun shells, and the desert camouflage man Lloyd, who sported a stringy and strange sort of Chinese version of John Brown's beard and was carrying a hunting rifle with a scope. In Dominick's other hand he was still holding up what was left of his sandwich. They both were staring at it. "Would you like a sandwich?" he said. "Amanda said the kitchen was closed."

"Turn off that light," Lloyd said. "What are you doing, signaling them?" He reached in to the room to turn the light off.

Dominick turned it back on and kept his hand with the can of ale over the switch. "I was just grabbing a late bite to eat before retiring," he said. "What can I do for you?"

"Stay away from the windows," Lloyd told Denise. Then to Dominick, "Where are the stairs to the tower?"

"I don't think we have met," Dominick said, but Lloyd pushed by him into the room.

"You're alone here?" Lloyd asked.

"Very much so," Dominick said. "I would like to keep it that way."

"No way, Jose. This is war and this here is the high ground. I'm going to station one of my boys up that tower. Where are the stairs? They got to be in this room."

"I was told the cupola was unsafe," Dominick said. "And besides, it is nighttime. What good would it do to have someone up there in the dark?"

"Ever heard of these, baby?" Lloyd said, ripping open the Velcro fastener of a side pocket in his cargo pants and pulling out a bulky pair of binoculars, only they weren't truly binocular because while there were two eyepieces there was only one telescopic lens at the other end. "Night vision goggles. Our eye in the sky." Lloyd spotted the door to the staircase and went right to it. "This it?" he asked and tried the door, which was locked. He raised the butt of his rifle to smash the lock.

"Wait. There is a key," Dominick said. He wondered if breaking down doors was some sort of sacred warlock prerogative that he was interfering with. He still had the keys in his pocket and he unlocked the door. Unlocked and unlatched the door swung out into the room on its own. The first three or four steps were lit by the light from the room, but beyond that was darkness deeper than shadow. "Captain," Dominick said, gesturing up the stairs. Maybe the stairs ended abruptly, or exhausted wood would give out beneath a grown man's weight. The passageway certainly smelled as if no one had ascended it in a very long time. It smelled the way that basement room had smelled when he had entered it, that stifled smell of history.

Lloyd shined his flashlight up the steps. "Denise?" he said.

"No, you go ahead, Lloyd. I'm not going up. I am going back down."

"I'll just check it out," Lloyd said, and he headed up the stairs.

For a minute or so Dominick stood at the open door, listening to Lloyd finding his way upwards. The thought crossed Dominick's mind to close the door and lock it, but that would just give Lloyd permission to exercise his door-breaking rights. There were no crashes or screams. Dominick had put down his sandwich and can of ale to open the door.

He redeemed them now from the desk, but with the room's overhead light now on he chose not to sit at a window. He sat on the bed instead.

There was some activity down at the road. Vehicles were coming and going. A car radio played some sort of jingling music with a thumbing bass, and there was the occasional sound of laughter. Dominick took two more pain pills. Only a half dozen or so were left. From up above, up the stairs, there was the distant but distinct sound of breaking glass. When Lloyd emerged into the room from the staircase door, Dominick asked him about the sound.

"Those windows were filthy and sealed shut. I had to break one to get a good view of the road. They are bringing up reinforcements."

You finally got to break something, Dominick thought. The reinforcements were probably just kids returning from a beer run. "So you just smashed out a window," he said.

"The goggles don't work through dirty glass."

They can see through the night but not dirty glass, Dominick thought. Dirty glass was the past. If you smash it you can see into the future. "What's next?" Dominick asked.

"I'll send up Joshua. He's our best sniper."

"Sniper? To snipe at what?"

"If they try a night attack, you want to protect your periphery from intruders."

"Were you in Nam, Lloyd?"

"No, that was over before I was old enough to get the chance."

"Too bad," Dominick said.

"Yeah, that was a real war, against a real army, with generals and all." Lloyd was headed toward the door to the hall when he stopped. "Say, are you armed?"

"No, I'm afraid not," Dominick said.

"Shame. I really could use Joshua elsewhere." And Lloyd left, closing the hall door behind him.

It was good that Dominick had taken a nap, because the evening was not going to be restful. After Lloyd left he turned off the light and went back to eating his sandwich in the chair by the open window. When he finished he lit a cigar. There was a fresh evening breeze rising up off the river, and off to his left, in what would be the northeast, he could see the white, pink, and green flashes of a fireworks display over Hudson. The flashes seemed all out of sync with the delayed muffled booms of their explosions, a disconcerting disconnect. Bombs bursting in air. That awful song. Through the perilous night.

When Lloyd returned with his sniper, Dominick did not move from his chair. Lloyd did not introduce them. They followed their torch beams up the stairs to the cupola, then Lloyd came back down and was gone. Dominick smoked his cigar. He opened the bottle of Scotch and took a sip, holding it in his mouth to blend with the cigar smoke. It was an old calming exercise, best done with cognac. The distant fireworks ended in a staccato flurry of explosions lighting up a slice of dark horizon sky. Then all was quiet. A wave of cricket chorus passed up from the valley and past them. Was it the pills again? He felt at peace sitting there in the dark, his feet up on his windowsill. He felt he was in the right place. In the morning the sun would come up in these windows, and if he wanted to he could stay. If he wanted to he could probably buy out Morgan and Amanda and make the place totally his, have the house all to himself. He would plant more trees. He would see what it was like in January, snowed in. He would have to fix that window in the cupola.

In the dark Dominick found his grip bag and went through it on the bed. It was not as if he had remembered to pack the penlight torch, but it was in the pocket where he always kept it, and its batteries still worked. He was looking to see what, in his hasty packing, he had brought to read. At the bottom of the bag were the papers and register book he had taken from the trunk in the basement. He had thought he would try again to return them, but now he felt no urgency to do so. If he was staying he could put them back anytime. He also had two of Sissy's local history books that he had borrowed and not returned. If he was staying, he could return them in person as he would be seeing her again, maybe even regularly.

He still had the lights in the room turned off when the door to the hall opened and a flashlight beam searched around hesitantly inside. "Hello," Dominick said.

"Oh, hello," a woman's voice answered. "I was . . . I am . . . looking for Joshua. Is this the right room?"

Dominick aimed his penlight in her direction. It was one of Denise's lieutenants, Susan's sister, whose name Dominick could not recall. "I believe it is Joshua who is upstairs," Dominick said.

"Where is . . . How would I?"

"Over here," Dominick said, and he got up off the bed and led her to the open door at the foot of the stairs. "Up there," he said. "Joshua," he called up the stairs, "you've got company."

"Yo," a voice from above called back.

"There you go," Dominick said, "contact." And he headed back to the bed.

"Josh?" she said, pointing her flashlight up the stairs.

"Come on up," the voice named Joshua said from above. "It's safe."

"It's spooky," she said.

"Okay, wait, and I'll come down to get you."

Dominick could hear her giggling as her savior led her up the stairs. But soon enough they came back down, Susan's sister hanging onto the young man's arm.

"Say, you wouldn't mind spelling me for just a bit, would you?" Joshua asked. "There's nothing happening out there. I left the goggles and the gun. I'll be back in a bit."

"A bit and a half maybe," Susan's sister said. "Come on, Josh."

"No problem. Got you covered," Dominick said. "You kids run off and have some fun. I'm not going anywhere."

"Thanks," Joshua said.

Dominick stripped down to his boxer shorts and stretched out on the bed, resting his ribs. The night was still and hot. The air was heavy. He dozed off.

The next person to come through the door awakening him also did not knock. Dominick wondered if knocking before entering was a custom universally waived during blackouts. It was Lloyd this time. "Do you know this person?" he asked. "She was apprehended sneaking into the house. She says to see you."

Dominick could not see in Lloyd's torchlight whom he was leading by the arm. He showed his penlight on her. It was Sissy. "Yes, Lloyd, I know her," he said. "She's okay. Think of her as part of our reinforcements."

"Okay then, if you say so, but I don't like it. She's not armed. What good is she? You boys do like your dark meat, don't you?" Sissy jerked her arm out of his grasp and came into the room. "All quiet here?" Lloyd asked, gesturing with his torch to the cupola stairs.

"All quiet on the upper front," Dominick said. He kept his penlight pointed at Lloyd's chest. Sissy disappeared into the dark.

"I think the other dude got the better looking of the two," Lloyd said as he left.

From somewhere behind Dominick, Sissy asked, "Who was that?"

"Wiccan homeland security. Lloyd's not much for introducing himself. How are you? How did you get here? Where are you?" Dominick flashed his penlight around the room until he found Sissy standing against the wall at the head of the bed.

"I'm good, I'm good. A little freaked right now. Why are all the lights out?"

"Just part of the game. Why are you here?" Dominick's ribs were complaining. He sat down on the bed. He didn't know where to shine his light.

"Game? What game? Daddy wouldn't come in through the front, but drove way out of the way in the dark to drop me off in the back. He said he had brought you here because there was some sort of trouble."

"Then why did he bring you here?"

"Because I made him. He said that I was the cause of the trouble. That article?"

"That's probably what he meant, but your being here can't undo any of that."

"I had to find out what was going on," Sissy said, and she went to the window to look out. "Daddy said there were people blocking the driveway."

"I guess they're still there," Dominick said. He turned off his penlight, which had been shining into nothing. He could just make out Sissy's silhouette against the night glow of the window. Somehow it seemed right that she was there in this room with him. It felt right that she had come. They had not talked since that interruptus event at her house. He wasn't sure what to say, but the lingering silence felt like his responsibility. "Sissy," he said.

"Yes?" she said, still standing at the window with her back to him. "I'm glad you came. It's good to see you."

"Even in the dark? Is that because the other colored girl is better looking?"

Oh, why do they always go there? Dominick thought. "That wasn't me, Sissy. No, because I missed seeing you, missed your smile and a sort of promise of something I feel when I'm with you." He paused but Sissy said nothing. "And I have a couple of your books to return to you."

Sissy came and sat beside him on the bed. "And that's why I'm here, to get my books back. You're a thief. You took my books. You hijacked my mind." In the silence that followed, her hand found his knee and rested there. "How are you feeling, Dominick? How are your ribs? I couldn't stop wondering about you, worrying about you."

"*Mending* is a good word. I think I will go with mending. So, Vernon brought you in the back way?"

"Yes, Daddy walked me in from the barn to the garden. That man caught me on the porch. He had a gun. I thought he was going to shoot me. I just wanted to see you and see what was going on."

"Well, I am here in the dark and not much is going on."

"Dominick, about that article. That's not the way I wrote it. My editor changed it, the whole thrust of it. He left out the history, just played up the Wiccan thing. 'Nobody cares about history,' he said. 'That shit has already happened. This is a newspaper; we deal with what's new,'" she said in a fake male voice. "I didn't like the way it came out."

"Are you hungry? I can make you a sandwich," Dominick said.

"And about that thing that happened between us at my house? I didn't mean to hurt you. I just . . . I just wanted you, that's all. I lost control." She squeezed his knee. "Those are the two things I came here to tell you. It was easier than I thought it would be, in the dark."

"Well, I guess I am relieved to hear that you weren't just following the Lord's orders."

In the dark beside him Sissy laughed a little purring laugh. She bumped her shoulder into his. "You're not angry with me then?"

"I never was angry, just a bit confused, but that's normal."

"It wasn't God telling me to make love to you. It was me telling me to make love to you. Jesus had nothing to do with it."

"It was on Sunday. You had just come from church."

"So, is this your room?" Sissy asked.

"No, normally it is Morgan's room, but she's gone now so it's mine."

"I could smell your cigar, but then a woman's smell too. Does the fact that you're here mean you may be staying?"

"Why?"

"Because I was selfishly hoping the answer was going to be yes. I want to learn more about you, find out where your secrets are hidden."

"I don't store my secrets. I shred them," Dominick said. His ribs ached. He stretched back on the bed to ease them.

"My father likes you. He doesn't like too many people. Is this like pillow talk, where in the dark you just say whatever comes into your head next?"

Dominick put his hand on Sissy's broad back. She was warm to the touch. "I don't know," he said. "Pass me a pillow to help me out."

Sissy found a pillow at her end of the bed and then hit him with it. "Smells like her," she said.

Dominick put the pillow beneath his head then said, "Let me see what you smell like."

Sissy got her own pillow and stretched out beside him in the dark. "You smell of cigar," she said.

"Not brimstone?"

"I wouldn't know what brimstone smells like," Sissy said, sniffing his ear.

"Sulfur, not nice," he said. "You wouldn't be here." He turned his head to smell her there in the dark "You smell good." This was nice. This was good. He felt at peace.

"Dominick?" Sissy said.

"Hmm?" he answered from the brink of sleep.

"I won't molest you this time. I'll just guard you. Go to sleep."

It seemed to Dominick that the explosion preceded the flash, but he could have been wrong. His eyes were closed and he was somewhere else entirely.

Chapter 25

When it hit the house it rocked her bed. It was the impact not the sound that awoke Amanda. She had been in a deep sleep and woke up confounded by sudden reality, by the nightmare red glow in her room. On warm summer nights like this she liked to sleep in the buff. Now she sat naked on the side of her bed. There was a boom and another red flash outside her windows, followed by gunfire from downstairs—the sound of Denise's shotgun and the crack crack of a high-powered rifle. In the dark she had trouble finding her clothes. She skipped the underwear.

Her first thoughts were of her brother. Morgan's room at the center of the house was much more a target than hers on the corner. She couldn't find her second sandal and switched on her bedside lamp. Almost immediately a bullet took out an upper pane in her front-facing window. She found her sandal and turned off the light. She had latched her door and now in the dark had to find and fumble with the latch. Another flash and boom behind her, more sporadic gunfire.

In the hallway the blackness was complete. Amanda pulled her cigarette lighter from the pocket of her cut-offs and lit it, heading for Morgan's room.

"Who's that? Is that you Dominick?" It was a man's voice from the bottom of the stairway to her right. There was the dim yellow beam of a flashlight with dying batteries down there. "Where's Sissy?" The beam headed up the stairs. At the top of the stairs Amanda and the man almost collided, and Amanda's lighter went out. "You're not Dominick," the man said, then he yelled out, "Dominick! Where are you? Sissy, let's go." And the door to Morgan's room opened.

"Daddy, what are you doing here?" a voice, Sissy's voice, said.

"I wasn't about to leave you here," the man said. He banged his flashlight against the palm of his hand and it brightened up. "We are out of here. This ain't our fight. Let's go. You're done here. Say good-bye."

Then Dominick appeared in the doorway, carrying a small flashlight that cast a thin, bright bluish beam. The other man cast his light first on Sissy, then on Dominick, who was dressed in just a pair of boxer shorts. Amanda stepped farther back into the shadows beyond their lights. It was like she was no longer there. Another flare or rocket or whatever it was went off outside. This one hit the house.

"Vernon, glad you are here," Dominick said. "Can you still get out the back way?"

"Think so. Came in that way. But got to go now. Let's go, Sissy."

"Got to get my shoes," Sissy said.

"You coming?" the man asked.

"No. You go. Take Sissy. I have to check on my sister."

"I heard on the police band that the sheriff is sending a unit out here. Somebody must have complained about something," the man Dominick had called Vernon said. "I'd rather not be here."

"Understood," Dominick said. More shots were exchanged between the house and the outside. Amanda had by now retreated to the door of her room. Sissy reappeared, wearing just a sundress and slippers. Both of the men turned their lights on Sissy. She gave Dominick a kiss and without a word left with her father down the stairs.

Amanda waited at her room for her brother to come and check on her, but he didn't.

✻✻✻

In Morgan's darkened room Dominick searched for, found, and put on his discarded pants and shirt and shoes. He thought about Vernon, who had acquiesced—probably under protest—to bringing his daughter here but then cared enough not to leave her in possible danger. Dominick had been told by people—parents—that there was no understanding parenting until you had done it yourself, that unless you had been a parent you always in some ways remained a child. Something about responsibility, a responsibility Vernon had just reassumed, relieving Dominick of it.

Another red flare was fired from the foot of the driveway. Dominick had decided that was what they were—aerial signal flares like the ones used on boats. This one hit the house just below the windows of his room and shattered into a sprayed display of phosphorescence. It pissed him off. *The idiots. They could set fire to the house.* He would see where they were. With his pocket penlight he found his way up the stairs to the cupola. The night vision goggles were on the floor by the broken-out window facing the road. It took him a minute to adjust to them and scan through the darkness below him before he picked up the green silhouettes of warm bodies. There was a line of them on what must have been the road, then closer a cluster in probably the driveway. Off to both sides individual green ghosts were moving slowly toward the house.

There was another flash, so bright in the goggles that it momentarily blinded him. This flare skittered up onto the front porch below him. *Sons of bitches.* Dominick put down the goggles and rubbed his eyes. Denise and Floyd two floors below answered the rockets with gunfire into the dark. That was answered by shots from outside, which sounded like relatively harmless pistol shots. They were shooting at his house, his sister's house. He could smell the pyrotechnic chemicals burning, eating into ancestral wood. *The fucking sons of bitches, the mindless shithead motherfuckers.*

If there was a safety on the semiautomatic weapon Joshua had left behind, it was turned off. Dominick had to kneel to aim out the broken window, if aim was the right word. Without the goggles he couldn't see where he was firing. He was returning fire as a statement only. He pulled off a burst of five quick shots. The recoil played a little satanic tune on his ribs, and the pain made him sit down with his back against the wall beneath the windows. His fire was returned, and a few more windows in the cupola were shattered. Out the windows now he could see the flickering red glow of a permanent fire.

Dominick pushed himself back up to look out the window in time to see another flare launched. This one lurched erratically over the house, but he could see from where it had been fired, and he pulled off another five rounds at that spot. This was again answered by a barrage of fire. He sat down again below the window. It was July 6th, going on the 7th. The last disastrous engagements at Gettysburg had occurred on July 3rd, 150 years before. By July 6th and 7th Lee was retreating through Maryland, fighting rearguard battles at Williamsport and Boonsboro, nasty encounters to save a retreat from becoming a rout. The next flare smashed through the windows to his left and kept on going through the far windows. Dominick scrambled to the stairs. It was time to retreat from High Priest Lloyd's eye in the sky. He took his weapon with him.

In Morgan's room at the bottom of the stairs the uncertain flickering light from the flames outside had become less uncertain. It lit the room in rust-colored shadows. He headed for the door and Amanda's room. They would have to leave the house to fight the fire from outside with Susan's garden hose. The gunfire had stopped, and off in the distance he could hear a siren.

***

When the next rocket hit the porch and caught fire, Amanda dialed 911. She was back in her room, at a loss about what to do. She just gave the address and said her house was on fire. She didn't know how to report the rest. It would take too long. It wasn't important. She tried to call Morgan, but that call wouldn't go through. Just as well. What could Morgan do? The fire on the porch was not going out and would have to be dealt with. Morgan was safely elsewhere. Time had become erratic—not her sense of time but time itself. It would rush forward at tachycardia speed then abruptly stall into super slow motion. It was in slow motion that she went out into the hall, which was still in solid silent blackness. There was a switch for the hall light at the top of the stairs, if she could find it. She stepped forward, still in slow motion, her hands out in front of her. Then a door to her left opened, and the thin blue light of Dominick's penlight flashed into the hall and pointed directly at her.

"Are you alright?" Dominick asked. "We should go down, don't you think?" He sounded so calm, as if they were just late for dinner or something.

"Fire," she said as they came together. She could sound just as cool as he. They met at the head of the stairs. "There's a light switch," she said, and she took his hand and turned his flashlight away from her toward the wall where she thought the switch ought to be. She flipped the switch, and the overhead lights in the hallway came on.

Dominick was now dressed in more than just his boxer shorts, and in his other hand, the one she wasn't still holding, he was carrying a long rifle. A woman's voice—Denise's—was now calling out from downstairs, "Fire, fire." Another doorway down the hall swung open and Susan's sister and one of Lloyd's young men came out into the light. They looked very frightened and came running toward them. Time now sped up and got chaotic. Denise and now Lloyd were yelling at them from the bottom of the stairs. The two kids were freaking out; the girl was crying hysterically. Outside, the sound of a siren grew louder. Amanda just stepped back and watched. Dominick handed the rifle to the young man and hurried him and the girl down the stairs. Then he gestured to Amanda to wait and went back into Morgan's room. When Dominick came back out he was carrying his black leather grip bag. They went down the stairs together.

The glow of the fire on the porch came in through the windows beside the front door and backlit the entryway at the bottom of the stairs. Denise was there with Lloyd, along with all four of their remaining crew. Denise's two girls were hugging one another, and Lloyd was congratulating the boy on his good shooting. This scene seemed to pass in a second—it didn't concern her—as Amanda headed for the kitchen and the back door. Dominick was right behind her. Lloyd yelled something after them, but they kept going.

The kitchen, removed from the flames, was dark. Dominick switched on his penlight and pointed the way to the outside door. They stopped there. They could see torch beams in the left and right of the field out back.

"I know where I left the hose," Amanda said. "Can you find the spigot to turn it on?"

"Yes, I think so. Off to the left, around the corner," Dominick said. "Shall we? Keep low. You don't know." His hand was on her back.

Say something, say something, tell him, the voice in her head was saying, but "Keep low yourself," was all she could say. She opened the door and they headed out in opposite directions.

***

As Dominick rounded the corner of the house he could see the flashing colored roof lights of a county vehicle down on the road, but it wasn't a fire truck. He found the hose at his feet and picked it up. He followed it to the spigot on the outside basement wall and turned it on. *Now what?* he wondered. There was just the one hose. He stepped away from the house to where he could better see the lights down on the road.

A small voice called out his name as a question. "Dominick? Dominick, is that you?"

He turned on his penlight and flashed it in the direction he thought the voice had come from. This was a mistake. A small-caliber gun barked out in the blackness, then another farther away. He heard one shot whistle past him. He turned out the light and dove head first onto the ground. Within seconds, answering fire—what sounded like Denise's shotgun and a rifle like the one he had fired—issued from the house. More shots came from the direction of the road, then more answering shots from the house. Everyone was firing targetless into blackness. For some reason Dominick thought of the muskets found beside dead boys on Civil War battlefields, guns stuffed with shot but never fired, departed silent pacifists.

An amplified voice came up from the road. "This is the sheriff's office. This is an order. Cease fire. Cease fire. House, cease fire."

This was answered by a rapid burst of shots from Lloyd inside the house and sporadic returned fire from the surrounding fields.

"Cease fire! Cease fire! You have been warned."

In the silence that followed, Dominick headed on his hands and knees back toward where he had come from behind the house.

The small voice was closer this time: "Where is Dominick?"

He was passing the inclined doors that covered the outside stairs to the cellar. He stopped. "Who's there?"

"Dominick? Is that you? Come, this way."

He knew that voice. It was Susan's.

"Come, quickly. They're everywhere," she said, and he heard the sound of the hinges on the old plank door opening. In the now faintly fire-glowing darkness Dominick helped raise the door and found his way onto and down the cellar steps, lowering the door above him.

At the bottom of the stairs Susan switched on an electric torch. "I borrowed this from your glove compartment. I hope you don't mind," she said.

"Susan, what are you doing here?"

"I brought you your car. I thought you might need it," she said. "They didn't shoot you, did they?" She shined the torch over his body.

"They are very bad shots," he said. He felt as if he had been shot in the ribs, but it was just the same old pain. "What do you mean you brought me my car? Where is it?"

"On that road behind the barn. Are you sure you are alright, not shot?"

"But how?"

"I listened in when Sissy talked with her dad tonight. I knew where she had hid your keys. I thought you might want to get away, that's all. It's such a nice car."

"But how did you get here?" and Dominick pointed down to where they were standing.

"Oh, the tunnel," she said. "I knew there was a tunnel from the barn—I used to hide in there—but I didn't know it came all the way to the house. There were people in the field. I didn't want to meet them. So I tried the tunnel. Come on, I'll show you. We can get out that way."

"No. The house is on fire. I have to help Amanda."

"But they'll shoot you."

"I can't just leave her to fight the fire alone."

"Yes, you can."

"No, Susan. I have to go back."

"I'll wait for you then."

✳✳✳

The entire front veranda was in flames. When the fire got so hot that the water from the garden hose turned into steam before it got close to the flames, Amanda dropped the hose and walked away into the night beyond the glare. Nobody stopped her. Her hair had been frizzed by the heat; she could smell it now. The heat at her back was intense and she kept walking away from it through the field. She didn't look back. She would just keep walking.

✳✳✳

Dominick found the end of the hose on the ground, the water running into the earth. No Amanda. He picked up the hose. The flames were now licking around the edges of the veranda ceiling and onto its roof, and the heat hurt his eyes. He dropped the hose and turned away. It was then he saw Amanda's back disappearing into the darkness of the field. He called out her name, but she didn't answer. There was a crash behind him as part of the house fell into the flames in an explosion of sparks. When he looked back at the field, Amanda had vanished into the night.

Susan was waiting for Dominick back at the cellar door. On the way there he had grabbed his grip bag from where he had left it on the kitchen porch. Without a word Susan lit his way down the steps and led him into the cellar toward the back of the house. As he followed her light through the dirt floor rooms he noticed for the first time that she was wearing a long pale skirt that dragged in the dust behind her. Susan seemed to know her way well. They came to the room with the raised wooden platforms and through there to the chamber with the metal barrel hoops on the floor. When Susan raised the latch on the low plank door on the room's back wall, it rushed open toward them. A blast of fresh air, smelling of dirt and field, pushed past them into the cellar like some wild escaped animal leading a stampede. Above them they could hear the house shudder and heave like an old lung gasping for air. They ducked against the stream of air through the low door into the room of the trunks. They left the door open behind them.

Susan continued onward, the air stream fluttering her long skirt behind her.

"Wait," Dominick said. He got his penlight out of his pocket and played its bluish light over the trunks, still up on their stone shelves in the wall. But now both trunks were open and the clothes they had contained were randomly strewn about as if in some teenager's room. Susan had stopped and come back. He played his light on her now. The antique unbleached linsey-woolsey Mother Hubbard had been made for a larger, more mature and muscled woman. It hung on Susan's almost anorexic frame. She looked like a girl dressed up in her grandmother's clothes. A pale, delicate collar bone showed in the rough square neckline.

Dominick said nothing. Susan said nothing. In his grip bag were the long leather case of papers and the green-covered ledger that he had intended to return. Susan stared into Dominick's light and then with a slight twist of her head gestured for him to follow as she turned and headed on into the narrowing darkness.

✳✳✳

The roadblock was where the county road met State Route 9W. They had made it that far without any hassles. Susan had guided Dominick from the dirt farm roads behind the barn back to the county road at a point beyond where all the vehicles were parked at the Van Houten driveway. They had hid for a bit on the side road with the lights turned off as fire trucks and more law enforcement vehicles, with all their lights and sirens on, raced past along the county road.

"They sound like they're in such angry pain," Susan said. She was in the front seat with Dominick, curled up against the passenger-side door.

"Why not? Should they sound happy?" Dominick said. Off to his left he could see the red glow, low on the skyline.

"I could never be an emergency responder," Susan said.

"Why not?"

"I think they enjoy it too much," she said, "night after night, day after day, year after year. They must get off on it, other people's tragedies."

There was a new smell in the car, the smell of the past. It was coming from Susan, from her Mother Hubbard. It was not an unpleasant aroma, just unfamiliar, primordial. After the emergency vehicles passed there was no other traffic, and Dominick pulled cautiously onto the road headed out. When the lights of the state troopers' cars at the roadblock appeared ahead, Susan climbed over the seat into the back and made herself as small as possible in her oversized dress.

"Officer?" Dominick said to the trooper who waved him to a stop. "What's going on?"

"Where are you coming from?" the trooper asked, shining a flashlight into the car.

"Just up the road, a friend's house," Dominick said. "Is there something wrong?"

"Virginia plates?"

"Tourists, here for the festival and to see old friends. What . . .?"

Susan spoke up from the back seat, "Daddy, can't we go? I have to pee."

The trooper had missed Susan in the back seat entirely. He now shown his light on her and then stepped back. "Okay," he said, and he waved them through.

A ways down 9W headed for Catskill, Dominick asked, "Do you really have to pee?"

"No, I'm alright. How are you, Dominick? Are you going to be okay?"

"I am free, I guess," he said, setting the cruise control and leaning back in several types of pain.

Chapter 26

They stopped for the night somewhere in mid-Massachusetts at a roadside motel where the "No" before "Vacancy" was not lit. Susan was sleeping comfortably in the back seat, but Dominick could go no further without some pills. He left Susan sleeping or pretending to sleep when he went in to register. They had stopped at Vernon's place outside Catskill for Dominick to retrieve the rest of his things, but Vernon was not there. Dominick had left him a check and a note on the kitchen table. It seemed best just to keep traveling. Across the bridge in Hudson he had to ask Susan for directions to Sissy's house, but she said no, she was not going back there. "I've left that place," she said. She had already packed all she needed in Dominick's trunk. Like an instant parent Dominick now held responsibility for someone.

He parked the car in front of their room off at the dark end of the motel lot and woke Susan, touching her shoulder. She was happy to stay where she was, she said. "I like your back seat for sleeping. You could bring me a pillow." He brought her two pillows and the blanket from the bed. He opened all the car windows a couple of inches and locked the car.

"Good night, Dominick," Susan said in her small voice, her head already snuggled into a pillow.

"Good night, Susan," he said. "Sweet dreams."

Dominick took two pills, then showered, then took another pill. There were just a few left. Dr. Toby in Edgartown could get him more. Another reason to be Vineyard-bound. He could introduce Susan as his niece. Would Toby care? Maybe. He was New England enough to be a prick about such things in someone else. They would just wing it. Susan would have to lose that dress, though, and return to being her almost invisible self. What would he have to teach her immediately? It was a long time since he had been a houseguest with a female companion, and those were all women who had come from the world they were visiting. He stretched out on the bed in his boxer shorts. The pills were fading in. It was not just pain but cares they took away. They offered distance, safety, a space of his own.

There was a knock at the door, and Dominick got up to answer it. It was Susan. "Got to pee," she said and she walked past him into the room toward the bathroom. She had taken off the Mother Hubbard and was wearing just her panties. From the back Dominick could have counted each of her vertebrae and ribs. She closed the bathroom door behind her. He tried to remember how many vertebrae there were in the human body. He heard the toilet flush, and Susan re-emerged. She stopped at the sink to drink a glass of water from the same plastic cup Dominick had used to wash down his pills.

All the curves of a full woman's body were there, but promised, not pronounced. Her breasts were real but so new as to look fragile, the nipples a tender pink. Her sleep-twisted hair hung down over her slender shoulders.

"Night," Susan said as she walked past him back out the door, stopping to give him an absentminded peck on his lower jaw, as high as she could reach, her sleepy eyes half closed. She walked back to the car and got in the back seat, closing and locking the door behind her. Dominick waited a while and then went out to make sure all the car doors were locked.

The next time Susan knocked at the door and Dominick got up to open it, a blast of morning sunlight greeted him. Susan was dressed again in the Mother Hubbard, which looked even more like something from the grave in the bright sunshine, and she was carrying a small backpack. "Morning," she said as she walked on through to the bathroom. The shower started almost immediately. At the sink outside the bathroom door, Dominick fixed the miniature pot of motel courtesy coffee and got dressed as it dripped. The shower was still going when he poured himself a cup of aromaless brown fluid and stirred in the packets of white powder. The coffee only woke up his stomach to the fact that it was otherwise empty.

"I'm starving," Susan said as she came out of the bathroom, dressed in her Walmart shorts and T-shirt. Her hair was still wet and combed down to frame her face. She was carrying her backpack but not the Mother Hubbard, which was tossed in a corner by the tub with her used towels. "Can we get some breakfast?"

Dominick asked at the office as he checked out, then followed the desk clerk's directions to a diner a couple of miles away on the other side of the highway. They both ate well. The coffee was real. Susan ordered both sausage and ham with her eggs. "No meat at Sissy's," she said. Dominick enjoyed watching her eat. She cleaned her plate then ate what was left of Dominick's toast.

The diner was on the edge of a small town, and on their way back to the highway they had to slow down for traffic exiting a church parking lot. Services had just ended. It was Sunday morning, Dominick realized. Sunday morning in that other world that ran on a calendar and repeated itself with regularity.

Susan was up in the front seat with him now, and she was watching the families leaving the church. "Why were those people attacking your house?" she asked.

"They didn't say," Dominick answered.

"You can guess," Susan said, still looking out the window.

"Then I would guess that they did not like the idea of who was in the house."

"They didn't like the idea? They attacked an idea?"

"Well, they didn't know the people in the house, so I can't say they didn't like the people."

"Maybe they didn't like the house."

"The house had been there a long time. It was a good house. No, I don't think it was the house that they didn't like." Dominick stopped and waved to the cars from the church driveway to cut in front of him. He was in no hurry. He was studying the people in the cars.

"They were trying to shoot you but they didn't know you?"

"We never met," he said. *And he had tried to shoot them.*

"The people down at the road and the people up in the house were all the same. I mean, they were just like these people here."

They were all the same, but they were not like us, Dominick thought. *They belonged some place. They had a place to belong to. Maybe that was what they were fighting about.*

"I think the house burned down," Susan said.

"I think so too."

"It was a creepy old place."

"History also includes what is missing," Dominick said. The last car was pulling out in front of them. In the back seat a boy of ten or twelve went to the trouble of flashing them the finger.

Susan laughed and blew him a kiss in return. "Did you see that?" she said.

"Have you ever gone to church, Susan?" Dominick asked as he fell in at the end of the long line of church cars.

"No. I don't get it. The God thing, I mean. What's that all about? What's the point? Did you go to church?"

"No, never had to," Dominick said. "I never could see the point either."

It was only a few hours' drive before they pulled into Woods Hole and Dominick parked the car at the end of the line for the Vineyard ferry. He got out to go pay the fare in the office. When he came out with his ticket, Susan was standing at the dock railing looking out at the harbor. The ferry was not at the dock or in sight.

"Where are we going?" Susan asked when he joined her.

"Martha's Vineyard," he said. "You'll like it."

"A vineyard?"

"An island."

"Why are we waiting here?"

"We have to wait for the ferry that will take us there."

"A ferry? A boat, not a bridge?"

"It's just a short ride."

"Over water," Susan said, as if proving her point. She turned and headed back toward the car. Dominick followed her. Susan opened the driver's side door and reached in. She hit the trunk release switch and the trunk swung open. She went to the trunk and pulled out her day pack, her only luggage.

Dominick caught up with her. "Susan?"

"It's not my time yet, Dominick. I'm not supposed to cross over water for a while. I'm not sure when, but there is an order, a sequence that has to be followed. It is not yet my time to cross over water."

"But where . . .?"

"Just before we got here I saw a sign for Buzzards Bay. I think I know some people there. I'll look them up. You go on." She slipped her thin arms into her backpack.

"But how . . .?"

"If it's supposed to happen it will, Dominick." She gave him something like a scolding smile.

The ferry's horn sounded behind him. It had rounded the point into the harbor.

"Your boat," Susan said, and she stepped up to give him a kiss on the cheek.

"But wait," Dominick said. He reached into a pocket and pulled out his clasp of folded money. He pulled out all the bills—he had no idea how much, a couple of hundred bucks perhaps—and held it out to her. "You will want to eat," he said.

She took the bills and put them in the pocket of her shorts. "Thanks. I'll eat." The horn sounded again. "And, Dominick, stop looking back. All of that has already happened. It's what about to happen next that matters."

As Susan walked away, Dominick could not help but watch as she hiked between the lines of waiting cars then disappeared behind a truck. A fellow nomad.